SECRETS AT THE COTTAGE BY THE SEA

CAROLINE YOUNG

Storm

To request permissions, contact the publisher at rights@stormpublishing.co

Ebook ISBN: 978-1-80508-532-4
Paperback ISBN: 978-1-80508-533-1

Cover design: Emma Rogers
Cover images: Shutterstock

Published by Storm Publishing.
For further information, visit:
www.stormpublishing.co

ALSO BY CAROLINE YOUNG

Welcome to Anglesey

The Forgotten Farmhouse by the Sea

Secrets at the Cottage by the Sea

To Mum and Dad, Brian and Ruth Heath. Gone, but never forgotten.

*"With her fingers she turns paint into flowers, with her body
flowers into a remembrance of herself."*
R.S. Thomas

ANGLESEY, NORTH WALES

Time seemed to pass more slowly on Anglesey than it did in other places. The blackening clouds took longer to decide to rain, and the sun seemed to spend hours gradually setting. That summer evening, Jude sat and watched it hang as if suspended above the sea for over an hour. When its edges were almost touching the horizon, it began to unroll a glittering strip across the water as if beckoning her to step out onto it. Within minutes, that invitation vanished, and the sun had set.

The air started to chill almost immediately, as the breeze was a cold one. Jude shivered, wrapped her cardigan more tightly around herself, and held her baby a little closer. She breathed in the thick scent of the honeysuckle that scrambled over her garden wall, its sweetness distilling every memory of all the time she had known and loved this place. In the growing darkness, the waves hit the shore with a soft pulse, as they would do throughout the night, while she and her baby slept.

She had come here to hide, to escape, and the island had proved a perfect sanctuary, but she could never have imagined the path her life had taken, a path that had brought her here, to this cottage, to this evening. It had been a long journey, a painful one, but the right one for her to make, without doubt.

When tiny bats began flik-flakking above her head and her baby whimpered, she finally went inside, leaving the door open. She wanted to smell the honeysuckle for a little while longer, and to let the breeze off the ink-dark sea fill the small kitchen. Only when the sky outside was so black that it seemed to press itself against the walls of the cottage did she close the door and shut out the darkness.

The waves and the breeze continued their rhythmic dance on the beach below, muffled but not silenced, and she could still hear the peeping cries of the oystercatchers as they settled for the night down on the rocks below. Like her, they would sleep peacefully and wait for another dawn.

PART 1

TO HIDE AND TO HEAL

ONE

OXFORD

Two years earlier

One morning, three months after her husband, Alex, had died, Jude Fitzgerald decided not to get up. Instead, she lay in bed and listened to the traffic and the radio for almost two hours. By then, she knew every news story, every spokesman's comment, every angle on the key stories of the day word for word. It was only her urgent need for the bathroom that forced her to heave herself out of bed. She went into the kitchen to make tea and was greeted with a small, perfectly coiled cat poo on the floor.

"Oh, come on, Tuna! Use the garden, like every other cat in the street!" she said.

Carrying two large mugs of tea – a habit she was not yet able to break, she picked her way back upstairs, past the scree of abandoned books, single socks, and loose papers, and went into the bathroom for a shower. She had to go to work. Alex would want her to go, everyone told her. As she turned on the water, she remembered the times they had showered together, and how awkward and funny and sexy that had been. Today her shower entailed standing under the hot, running water with her eyes closed for two minutes. And then drinking both cups of tea herself.

When Jude got out and the steam on the mirror cleared, she saw the person she had become. She was thirty-six, but her drawn skin and stringy blonde hair made her look years older. Her face was set in a constant downward turn, and two deep lines now bracketed her mouth.

"I've got her 'upside-down-U face'," Jude said to herself. When her mother, Gloria, had *that* face on, it was always a warning sign. Jude had seen it mostly when her mother told her what a disappointment it was that she wanted to:

"Become an *artist*? After all the sacrifices I've made for you. What good can come of that? Get yourself a proper job, girl, one that pays the rent."

Jude knew that her father, Donald, who had loved poetry and music, would have supported her dream, but he had left them years earlier and returned to the Highlands where he'd been born, to live with a very jolly-looking woman called Brenda. Jude had never blamed him for it, as her childhood home was far from jolly.

She unlocked her front door and bumped her bike down the steps to the pavement before setting off for her detested "proper job". The noise of wet wheels on wet road hit her like a smack in the face. Women were hopping between puddles, their sandalled toes wet and fake-tanned legs splashed with dirty water. She would be very late again, and Helena, the gallery manager and her boss, would be angry again. In fact, Helena had grown increasingly impatient with Jude's lateness, forgetfulness, and the strong likelihood that she would cry at work these days. "These days" being the days since Alex had died: ninety, if you counted the one that had just begun.

Jude worked at a ludicrously expensive art gallery on The

Turl, in the centre of Oxford. Having graduated from Exeter University, she'd come to visit a friend in the city and immediately abandoned her plan of going home to Taunton to work in a café, paint, and be a paid companion for her mother, when she met Alex Fitzgerald. It was a betrayal Gloria had never forgiven her for. Wracked with guilt, Jude had found herself unable to paint since, but loving and living with Alex had amply made up for that sacrifice. He'd been in his final year of law at St Anne's College and unlike anyone she had ever met. Incredibly tall and incredibly thin, he was far from classically handsome. His jeans were always at least an inch too short, exposing an endearing cuff of pale, hairy flesh, and his bottom of the range, wire-rimmed glasses had extra plastic bits to keep them on his bony nose. But Jude had loved him from their first meeting, and he had made her happier than she would have believed possible. Yes, they had been happy, she remembered, and somehow that had made life, and her job, bearable. She had the smiling photos to prove it. Now, neither was the case.

Her friends had supported her (often literally) through the first days and weeks following Alex's death. They'd insisted that she got up, dressed, ate something, and got to the end of each day, so she could go to bed and begin it all again tomorrow. Tom Byers, Alex's best friend from school and his co-partner in the solicitor's practice they had founded, brought her flowers and treats and let her sob in his arms, but Jude dared not tell any of her friends that all these efforts were in vain. Her pain was not "fading a little with each day", as Zoë, her bereavement counsellor, had assured her it would. Quite the opposite, it was intensifying, seeping into every moment of her life like a toxic black ink. She snapped at her friends when she was drunk or tired, but still, they did not abandon her. In her very darkest moments, Jude even wondered if their unswerving loyalty was because they were relieved that, as the unimaginable had happened to her, the odds were stacked against it happening to them. Grief sat like a dark incubus on her heart, an agony she could only compare to a form of medieval torture she'd read about, which involved increasingly heavy weights slowly crushing a person to death. Their suffering only ended the moment their body could bear no more, and their spine snapped. For Jude, that felt very close indeed today.

That evening, her friends came round after work, but Jude wished them gone within half an hour. Jo, Katie, Morag, and Paula (or "The Fearsome Foursome" as Alex had dubbed them) were genuine, kind women, but they had lives and hopes, and she secretly resented that almost as much as she loved them. When they finally tottered off into the orange glow that is the darkness of cities, she knew she was different to them now, set apart, whether she liked it or not. Her father was long dead, she had no siblings, and she had not seen her mother since Alex's funeral, which suited them both perfectly. Alex had been all the family she had needed, but he was gone. A sob rose in her throat at the injustice of her lot, but she swallowed it. Crying changed nothing, she'd learnt.

"It is what it is," she murmured. And it was unbearable.

The babies they'd longed for had never come, and the two she had managed to conceive, she had miscarried. Now, she was on her own in a city full of strangers. Switching off the lamps in the living room, the gloom around her grew until only a tiny circle of light remained around the charity shop standard lamp behind Alex's chair. The book he'd been reading was still there, a legal thriller, alongside his gold-rimmed reading glasses. As she went to turn that final lamp off, Jude was reminded of how Alex had performed what he called the "lights out" ritual every night of their married life before they both went up to bed. Click, click, click: darkness.

She tried to sleep, but memories came into her head unbidden, as they did every night. She saw them on their honeymoon, young and flushed with happiness. Alex had insisted they ride his motorbike, a vintage Harley Davidson, from their wedding in Taunton, up through England and then west into Wales and on to Snowdonia. He'd decorated the bike with plastic flowers, strung empty cans to the back of the seat, and painted *"Chase the dream"* on the petrol tank in looping, gold italics. They had married in February, and Jude had loved it all, every single moment, even the wind chill that had increased exponentially the further north they rode.

"I need to take you to Anglesey next," he had yelled back at her as they sped through the mountains. "You'll love it, I know."

"Why? What's so special about it?" she had shouted back.

"Its wildness, its refusal to compromise and its unconventional beauty. It reminds me of you, my love," he'd replied, smiling at her in the little mirror on his handlebar.

Alex Fitzgerald, her new husband. How proud she had been to call him that. Jude could almost smell the petrol fumes and the warmed leather of his jacket inches from her nose. What she would give to be on the back of that bike and feel that cold mountain wind on her face now.

They'd driven west across Anglesey until they'd run out of road, parked in a forest to avoid having to pay for a ticket and then walked along miles of shingly beach and onto a smooth knoll of land, covered with seagrass and tufts of thrift. At high tide, this became a tiny island, cut off from the mainland. Ahead lay a whitewashed lighthouse overlooking the sea, with a row of tiny cottages huddled behind it. Banks of sand-flecked foam shivered like a fearful animal on the shore, and they'd waded through it, kicking bits into the air and watching them float out over the granite-grey sea and melt. This little tidal island was called Ynys Llanddwyn, and it was linked to centuries of rich folklore and tales of love.

Now, years later, wide-eyed in her dark bedroom, Jude

knew for certain that she had to leave Oxford. She needed to go away to guard her sadness, to bury herself in it until, perhaps, it loosened its grip on her and let her go. She needed to go back to Anglesey. She had promised Alex she would as she had watched him fade, and then vanish forever.

TWO

That night, Jude slept better than she had for many weeks. She'd made the decision to leave, and it still felt right the next morning, as she sat eating dry toast in the living room. Always a good sign, to feel just as sure about a something after a night's sleep, she told herself.

Looking around, she suddenly felt as if she was sitting in an old movie set. Sympathy cards lay where she'd read, closed, and laid them on the mantelpiece many weeks ago, all now thickly coated with dust. Their ancient weeping fig plant was more than tearful now; it was in despair, unwatered since the last days of Alex's illness. The windows were filmed with grime both outside and inside, their sills a graveyard for unfortunate flies. It was time to leave. No loss, no fear could possibly be as bad as Alex dying, Jude told herself. She still lived here, in this house, but it was no longer her home.

Surprisingly, deciding where she needed to go to was far easier than telling other people about it. Jude stood firm amidst her friends' howls of dismay when she invited them round for a "summit meeting", and she held her own as they shot down her reasons for leaving one by one. As her decision to move to

Anglesey was largely irrational, Jude found it easier, less stressful, to parry their attacks by agreeing with them entirely, and then saying she was going anyway. The tension in the room was almost palpable that evening. Tuna the cat even jumped off Jude's knee because it was such an uncomfortable place to be.

"I don't understand why you can't go to Brighton, or Margate, if you're so desperate for the sea," Paula said. "It's a bit, well, *remote*, isn't it, up there?"

Jude wanted to tell her that was exactly what she wanted, but resisted, in case she hurt her friend's feelings. Paula's idea of "roughing it" was her steam iron not working well enough.

"What about work? Helena will freak out if you leave!" Jo said with a grimace. "She knows that you really run that gallery, not her."

"It's time for her to wake up and smell the coffee then, isn't it?" Jude said with a hollow laugh. "I need to go, so I'm going."

"Are you going to sell the house?" Jo said. "Are you sure that's wise, Jude? Couldn't you rent it?"

"Look, Jo, I want to forget this house, not live with its memories," she snapped. "If I sell it, perhaps I can do something really daring. I quite fancy doing my own painting again, rather than selling other people's overpriced crap to fund Helena's Mulberry bag habit."

Her friends quietly nodded their understanding, but Jude saw concern etched on their faces. At times, she felt their overwhelming love for her was just that, overwhelming, though she knew they only wanted the best for her. Right now, what she needed most was to trust herself, even if they didn't. She asked them to leave earlier than usual, saying she had "stuff to do", as she needed to focus on a future she had only just begun to imagine. As she tidied away, moving chairs and plumping cushions, she tried to imagine the glossy guide to her first art exhibition:

"Jude Fitzgerald is an artist, living in a reclaimed barn on

Anglesey with her husband Alex, five children, six cats, and a beach-side studio."

Except it would be just her, no husband, one cat, she hadn't painted anything for years, and there could never be any children. When the doctors told them that her eggs and Alex's sperm might be "genetically incompatible", they'd decided to end the expensive IVF appointments, staged sex, and tearful showdowns. Whether her life would have been any happier now, or any easier, if they'd had a baby together, was a thought Jude quickly dismissed. There was only so much she could bear.

Before putting her house on the market, she had to clean it – a tough, sweaty task that went some considerable way to "preparing her for the rigours of life on the island", she felt sure. Wiping ribbons of greasy dust off the paintings she had done as part of her Fine Art degree, she remembered how Alex had insisted on framing and hanging them in their home.

"These are so good," he'd said. "You're wasted in that bloody gallery."

She hadn't believed him, but now she wondered if she could ever be creative again. All sparks of anything bright and joyous in her had been crushed during those final weeks of his life in that pale green hospice room, where cancer had slowly but mercilessly taken him from her.

She'd not yet sorted out any of her husband's things. The house was still so full of him. His muddy walking boots were by the back door, his splayed toothbrush in the mug in the bathroom, where he had left it after he'd tried to brush his teeth the morning they'd left for the hospice. That terrible day, Jude had known that his leaving it behind was agonisingly significant.

As she sorted, folded, and bagged, she did not cry quietly out of concern that her neighbours Maureen and Dave would hear her; they were away at their daughter's in Slough. Instead, she lay on the floor and screamed, swore and howled, held Alex's sweaters to her face, and tried to breathe her husband in. She wound his old college tie around her fingers, her eyes shut tight. She smoothed his faded T-shirts and made sure the socks she added to the charity shop bags were paired and balled, as he had always liked to find them in his top drawer.

Finally, she put some things into a small box that would, she felt, contain the "essence" of him but be small enough for her to take with her. His *Beers of Munich* key ring went in, then a faded picture of his parents, who'd died in a car crash a year after Alex and Jude's wedding. Next, a silly photo of Alex and Tom taken in a photo booth, along with his Law Society tie pin, his Form Captain badge, the one remaining cufflink of the ancient pair he'd always wore to formal dinners. She remembered exactly when he had lost it, as they'd made giggling, surreptitious love on the riverbank after a May Ball one year. When she found his scratched Timex watch, she put it on her wrist, despite the fact that it had stopped working months ago. Finally, she added his wedding ring made of Welsh gold to her trove of treasures.

"How apt, my love, that I am going to Wales now," she whispered.

But it was when she'd found Alex's blue and white striped woolly hat that grief threatened to overwhelm her. She could see him wearing it so clearly, in the many different, beautiful places they had walked together. It had been far too big for him, but he had loved it, nonetheless.

"You look like some undernourished schoolboy in that daft hat," she'd told him once, as he pushed it up over his ears and away from his mouth so that he could eat a sandwich. They were perched on a rocky outcrop right on the edge of a loch in Scotland. The rain had been so torrential that the tip of his nose was beaded with water.

"It keeps my hair dry, my ears warm, and I love it," he'd said with a grin. "How many things can you say *that* about in life? Not even *you* do all three of them, Mrs Fitzgerald!"

Now, as she folded it carefully and placed it in the box, she promised him she would wear it when she walked along the wind-scoured beaches on Anglesey, and know that a part of him was still with her.

The couple who viewed the house on the day it went on the market, wanted it. They were cash buyers and keen to move in as soon as possible. The agents hadn't even put a "For Sale" board up before a completion date of four weeks hence was agreed on. Jude was shocked and felt a flicker of panic at what she had set in motion, but her determination did not waver.

Tom called round almost every evening in that final month to see how she was "bearing up". As Alex's closest friend, best man at their wedding, and a partner in the same law practice, he'd wept with her in the hospice in the bleak days before his friend's death. Still single despite his rugged, rugby-team good looks and undeniable charm, Tom's constancy was a real comfort. Sometimes, Jude wondered whether he was still attracted to her, as she knew he had been at university. Why else would he listen to her wailing with such patience and forgiveness? No, she told herself, he was just an incredibly kind man who felt his friend's loss as deeply as she did. Anything else was unthinkable. Surely Tom would also consider a relationship between them a betrayal of their memories of Alex? She'd made her choice years ago and never regretted it. Alex made her laugh out loud, and Tom, for all his charisma, didn't.

He'd helped her with the funeral arrangements, the life insurance claim she could not face, and ensured that everyone who needed to know what had happened, knew, with incredible tact and sensitivity, however. He arranged for most of her possessions to be put into a storage unit until she knew whether she would stay on the island, but Jude had already decided to take only what her battered old Fiat Punto could carry. She said that she would have Alex's motorbike shipped to her once she knew where she'd be staying long term. Until then, it would be kept in Tom's shed, as he'd helped Alex restore it and loved it almost as much as he had. With only a week to go before she had to move out, Jude had still not found a home. Rentals were scarce on the island, and her main criterion was that it had a view of the sea. It seemed an impossible ask.

"What about a holiday cottage?" Tom suggested anxiously.

"But that seems so *temporary*," Jude said. "I need to commit to this."

"You need a roof over your head most of all," Tom said. "Let's start with the basics, eh?"

A few minutes of online searching took them to a website called Môn Cottages, which rented holiday homes on the island. Most were big country houses or farmhouses that slept several families and boasted hot tubs and heated terraces, but amongst them were a few, traditional Anglesey cottages with one, or sometimes two, tiny bedrooms. One particular sentence on the site made Jude's heart lift:

Môn Cottages is happy to consider letting many of our smaller and more remote properties for longer periods during the winter months (mid-Sept – Easter). Personal viewing preferred.

"You could start with a month or two, and see whether you like it there," Tom said. "You may not, you know..."

Jude chose to ignore the sadness in his eyes. He would miss her, as they had shared so much in the past year, but he would have to deal with that loss, as she had to deal with hers.

. . .

By 10am the following morning, she was already on the road that threaded up the coast of North Wales, where rows of flimsy pastel caravans in Rhyl and Prestatyn huddled beneath the glowering peaks of Snowdonia. Emerging from one of several tunnels carved through solid rock, she looked to her right and saw Anglesey, crouching low and smooth-backed across the water like a Welsh collie waiting for instructions from a shepherd. The light from a black and white lighthouse offshore winked on and off, warning ships not to come too near the land, and Jude found herself counting the seconds between each reassuring flash as if it was a heartbeat. It was still there, on that beautiful island, waiting for her.

Opening her window, she took some long, deep breaths. She could not have found a place less like the one she was leaving behind, and that was just as she wanted it.

THREE

"Mrs Fitzgerald?" said a woman in smart navy trousers, a white blouse, and a neatly tied red scarf. She was in her early sixties, Jude estimated, but her face was plumply smooth. "I'm Mrs Roberts. Come on in."

"Yes. I've... ah... come about a cottage," Jude said, stepping into Môn Cottages' small office in Menai Bridge.

"Yes, dear. You're in the book. Now – first things first. *Te ta coffi?*"

"Coffee, please," Jude said, thrown, but assuming the Welsh word for "coffee" would sound pretty similar to the English one.

"Now, what sort of place have you got in mind, *cariad*/love? Is it just for yourself, for a couple, or a family?" Mrs Roberts' eyes skimmed Jude's wedding ring. "Working for the university in Bangor, are you? What about the number of bedrooms? For six months, over the winter, is it? Somewhere to work, or relax?"

Jude flinched at the barrage of questions. She felt interrogated, but she would have to get used to people's curiosity, she could see. It was this woman's job to ask these kinds of questions. "It's for just me, actually. All I want is to be able to see the sea."

Two cups of coffee and three custard creams later, the women were on first name terms, and Jude found Mair Roberts' sympathy as unlimited as her kindness. She produced a box of tissues when Jude got sad and became tearful herself when Jude told her how Alex had loved the island and made her promise to return in the last days of his illness.

"*Bechod*/Shame," the older woman said, dabbing her eyes.

When, eventually, they'd stopped talking, Mair put on her reading glasses and pulled folders out of an enormous filing cabinet. She glanced at several, then put them away again with a shake of her head. But after a few minutes, her face lit up.

"Here. I've got just the one for you," she said. "It's a real gem." She showed Jude a photo of a tiny, whitewashed cottage with the sea only yards below it.

"Oh, it's beautiful. But how do you know it's going to be right for me?" Jude asked.

'I just know. Trust me. I'll meet you there at 1pm."

"What, today? But where is it? I don't have GPS, or my phone set up in my car," Jude stuttered. She knew how tiny some of the island's roads were and how easy it would be to get completely lost.

"Just follow the coast road to Rhosneigr for half an hour and you'll see the cottage on your left. Look for it as you come over the hill after *Porth Trecastell*/Cable Bay. Blue door. It's called *Hedd*. You can't miss it, dear. Right, I'd better get on."

With that, Jude was politely ushered out.

The coastal road ran parallel to the mountains on the other side of the Menai Straits. Jude felt like a rally-driver, steaming down steep dips and then urging her little car up the other side of them to be rewarded with yet another spectacular view of the sea and the mountains beyond it. When she first glimpsed the cottage, she gasped. It was even more beautiful than it had looked in the photograph.

The roof was missing quite a few slates and ivy was spooling up the chimney, but this made it seem even more like integral part of the landscape. It nestled amongst a bank of sand dunes just above a tiny shingle cove, and it was at least a mile to the bungalow Jude could see in the distance. There was even a tiny lean-to, which could be a potential new home for Alex's motorbike if she wrapped it up against the elements, but she was not sure she could bear that yet. The Harley had been so much a part of Alex that seeing it, silent and unloved, would make her feel even worse. No, she would come here with the bare minimum, and this would be splendid isolation indeed. Mrs Roberts was waiting for her in her car, her face screwed up with irritation, mobile phone in hand, mouthing "no signal". Jude had never minded less that her phone would no longer summon her with calls and messages, but she knew that her friends would want to keep in touch, and that she might need them to do so. Tom would have plenty to say if she was literally cut off from everyone as well.

"I can get the internet here, can't I, Mair?" she said.

"Broadband is fine, but some mobiles have a few problems at times." She pulled out a large key. "Let's have a little look around, shall we?"

Jude did not need anyone to show her around, or to inspect the softly undulating walls, the original slate flagstones or round-bellied wood-burning stove to know what her decision would be. The older woman talked, but it was only when she heard the words, "So, do you think you'll take it then?" that Jude realised she was expected to say something.

"Oh, yes," she said softly. "Most definitely yes."

"I knew you would. Shall we go back to the office and do the paperwork?" Mair Roberts said. "When do you intend to move in? It's available now, and vacant until just before Easter."

"Is this weekend all right?" Jude replied, with a gulp at how soon that seemed. "I know it's soon, but I..."

"The sooner, the better," Mrs Roberts replied briskly, locking the cottage door. "Needs someone in it, this little place."

"Mair, one more thing. What does '*Hedd*' mean?" Jude asked before they parted.

"It means 'Peace'," the older woman said meaningfully.

"Then it's even more perfect for me than I'd dared to hope," Jude replied.

The day she left Oxford, Jude had never been so glad that the journey to Anglesey took such a long time. She avoided the big motorways, as she wanted to feel as if she was making a calm and reverent journey, a pilgrimage towards her new life. The route she chose took her through the landlocked villages of the Cotswolds, past rows of polytunnels around Evesham, through the lush affluence of Shropshire and on into Wales. Turning off her mobile, she drove in silence so that her thoughts and memories could come and go freely, and they did.

It was late by the time Jude picked up the keys to *Hedd* and completely dark when she nudged her car over the thick tussock grass and into the cottage's parking spot. The sky was astonishingly black, as there was no glow from any nearby town or city; not one star poked through the thick coverlet of darkness. She turned the key in the front door and fumbled inside for the light switch in the kitchen. Nothing happened. If it didn't work, she couldn't sleep here; end of story. Only when the fluorescent strip eventually pinged into life did she exhale and walk in.

"That monstrosity is going to have to go for a start," she said, blinking in its harsh light. "I'll light some candles for now and get some nice lamps soon."

The cottage was obviously damp, as it smelt musty, but somebody had left clean tea towels, some bread and milk, and a tiny bunch of wildflowers in a little glass bottle on the kitchen table. It was not cold, but Jude lit the fire laid in the wood-burning stove, relieved to feel its welcoming tongues of warmth spreading across the room. After a while, Tuna gingerly came out of her cat basket, sniffed around and was asleep in front of the fire within half an hour.

It was past midnight, but Jude wanted to unpack a few things so that this would all feel more real in the morning. The richly coloured rug she and Alex had bought in the bazaar in Istanbul looked fantastic on the flagstones in front of the fireplace. She took down the largest generic "seaside" print from the living room wall and hung one of her own paintings from years ago, a landscape of the endless, stream-ribbed fields of her Somerset childhood. She'd brought her paints, pastel crayons, and some blank canvases, and prayed that inspiration would come. To paint, to create something again, would release some of the heaviness inside her, she hoped. Finally, she hung her two coats (one for wet weather, one for sunshine) behind the front door and added Alex's striped hat to the third lowest hook.

"We're home, love," she said, but no answer came.

Did he really know she was here now? Could he see her, sitting in this little room with their cat, their rug, and his hat? In the first few weeks after his death, she had felt him behind her as she'd washed up or put the bins out. She had almost imagined that she could turn round and touch his sleeve, or hear him laugh at her choosing the ugliest vegetables at the market "because she felt sorry for them". Tonight, only months after she'd lost him, in the quiet of this cottage, she could still feel his presence like a fine net around her, but it was already blurred, his face a little less clear when she shut her eyes. How could she possibly *forget* him so quickly?

"Don't leave me again," she whispered fearfully. "I still need you."

Outside, a breeze had sprung up and icy draughts lifted the

white curtains from the windows like ghosts. Jude sat quite still as the room sighed and settled around her. Both her mobile and her tablet lay useless on the table; no signal at all.

Tonight, the world could not reach her, and she was glad of it. She was cocooned inside these thick walls with their craggy, whitewashed plaster. She felt a strange urge to stroke them, to feel the strength of this little cottage, and the countless winters it had set its face against. She turned the horrible strip light back on and blew out the candles on the table, watching soft wisps of their smoke slowly twist and curl upwards. She'd left her world behind, but here, where her sleep would be lulled by seabirds and waves, she would not allow herself to regret that, whatever lay ahead.

FOUR

Jude had no need of a clock on the island. She did not even plug in the electric alarm clock she'd brought with her, which felt wonderfully rebellious after years of utterly despising 7.10am. The reflected light from the sea filled the cottage with wave-rippled patterns on the walls almost as soon as the sun rose. There was little chance of her staying up until midnight, as she'd done in the city. By about 9pm, she had to drag herself off the sofa and into her bedroom, her eyes heavy with sleep. For the first week in *Hedd*, her whole body ached with tiredness, even though she hadn't done much more than stroll along the beach or unpack a box or two. She had got to the end of another day, which was enough for her to sleep guiltlessly and deeply.

There were no friends to feel obliged to talk to or text, no work to do, no shops to distract her, as they had sometimes done during lonely lunch hours in Oxford. She had taken down the two mirrors in the cottage on her arrival so she would not have to see herself, and she often did not change her clothes for several days. Evenings were spent reading, thinking, or just listening to the crackle of logs in the wood-burner and the distant sighing of the wind and waves. It all seemed so far from

Howard Street, where she had watched the hands inch round the clock each evening until it was time to try and sleep.

Within a fortnight, the skin on Jude's face tautened, as she was spending more and more time outdoors. She slapped on thick dollops of Nivea rather than the expensive creams she'd been buying for years, and she became a dab hand at cooking whatever she had in the cupboard, often straight from the pan. She was soon feeling the benefits of no alcohol and long walks along the beach. It seemed ironic that her body was probably at its most desirable now, when Alex was no longer here to desire it.

Every few days, Jude turned her mobile phone on in a street in Rhosneigr where she knew she would get a signal, and it spewed out missed calls and unread messages. She felt a stab of guilt that, as far as her friends were concerned, she had vanished off the face of the earth, and vowed to stay in touch more. Jo and Katie repeatedly asked if she was "settling in well", Morag said she was "worried about her", and Paula simply texted:

> Hey, I'm six weeks pregnant. Ta da! Georgio
> has ordered a boy!

Jude turned her phone off. She fully understood why Paula had wanted to share such amazing news, and she was truly happy for her, but she was also a little shocked that her friend seemed oblivious of her own doomed yearning for a child. Did the water close over other people's suffering so quickly? And as for her comment about Georgio, her Greek-Cypriot boyfriend, wanting a boy – had Paula really forgotten that both her dead babies would have been sons? She stood still on the pavement as joy, sadness, disappointment, and guilt washed over her, like successive waves. This was hard, very hard, but at the heart of all these feelings was happiness for her dear friend. She responded to all the messages with a blanket text:

Sorry, dodgy signal here. Am fine and hope you
all are. Congrats Paula. Will write soon. J

If she felt drowsy, she lay down for a nap. If she needed
comfort, she filled the bath with steaming hot water and sank
into it. If she was restless, she headed to the beach to see what
the last high tide had washed up. Her friends would probably
have been horrified to see her lank hair and food-stained clothes,
but she did not care. She felt purified, pared down into the
strong, distilled essence of herself.

Sometimes, she strode along the beach, ranting aloud into
the wind that often blew strongly off the sea. She sometimes
shouted her rage at Alex for leaving her and voiced her hidden
jealousy at her friends' tragedy-free lives. Often, she yelled her
fury at Gloria, who'd both condemned her for not being the
dutiful daughter she needed and not been there to comfort her
in her grief, as a mother should. Compassion was something
Gloria never had in her limited repertoire of emotions, and that
hurt Jude now more than ever. Why could her mother not
simply *love* her? It was all she'd longed for as a child, but it was
a wish that had never been granted.

Only once was she caught out ranting aloud at the sky,
when a fisherman was lurking behind some rocks and heard her
in full flow, but he'd simply smiled and nodded as if he
completely understood.

There were days when Jude wept as she had never dared to
in Oxford, with wracking sobs that nobody could ever hear.
Whenever this happened, Tuna silently watched her, her eyes
glass-calm as she kneaded the sofa rhythmically with her claws.
Only when Jude was quiet again would the cat snake over to
her slowly, wind her body around her legs, and purr comfort
from body to body.

As days became weeks, these desperate tears came less
often. She took her watercolour paints and brushes out into the

dunes, to try to capture the colours she saw in the sky and the sea. It felt so unfamiliar that the results rarely pleased her, but if she didn't like what she'd painted, she washed over it with white paint in the evening, ready to use the board again the following day. There was no one here to appraise her work, or push her to do more, or better. There was no Gloria here to tell her to "stop wasting her time" or "do something constructive" (which always meant doing something for her). She was in charge of her own life in every way.

Most of her days were spent in solitude and in silence. Mrs Roberts called in a couple of times on her way to another property, to check that everything was all right, but didn't stay long. Jude drove to the little shop in Brynsiencyn to get food for herself and Tuna, or to a supermarket in Menai Bridge if she was feeling brave, but only when she had to. She watched the autumn weather reflected in the sea, and her moods often changed as quickly as the island's sky, but the heart of her was still and peaceful, and that was a gift in itself. Yes, she was lonely, but whenever she glimpsed the reflection of her face in a window or a rock pool, Jude saw a glimmer of life in it, something she had not seen for many months.

Most days, she walked for miles, wearing Alex's walking hat, as she had promised him she would. Past conversations with her husband played in her head like a soundtrack she couldn't edit or switch off; they "talked" about things they'd done and planned to do. They'd had so many wonderful plans. Sometimes, she wished she could just ride Alex's Harley into the wind and feel her sadness strip away as a snake sheds its skin, but she knew it was being well-cared for in Oxford by Tom and would quickly rust up here in the salty air. On wild days, she wore Alex's favourite fleece, too, sometimes just holding it behind her like a sail to catch the wind blasting off the sea. Fat gulls hung above her, watching, buffeted by each eddy, their feet folded beneath their bodies like the neatest of under-carriages.

In the middle of October, a month after Jude had arrived, Anglesey had the first of its autumn storms. The sea darkened to the colour of wet slate, and huge waves laced the windows of her cottage with a rime of salt. Hanks of seaweed hurtled over the wall into her garden. They looked so sadly marooned that Jude gathered them up in a bucket and took them back down to the beach.

After some of these storms, the beach would be altered in ways that only someone who regularly walked along it would notice. The dunes would be subtly reshaped, whorls of pebbles would magically appear on the sand, and blackened tree trunks, coils of rope, metal food-oil cans, and plastic bottles would be strewn across the beach. One morning, Jude found a dead sheep nestling amidst quivering banks of foam between the rocks, its eyeballs gone, a crow's snack, and its creamy wool threaded with green slime. She decided that it must have been blown off a cliff into the sea, but it looked so peaceful in its soft resting place that she left it there with a light heart.

The shore was a treasure trove to Jude, and *Hedd* was soon littered with bits of driftwood, pebbles, and fragile white sea urchin shells that rarely survived the waves to be found on the beach intact. During the darkening evenings, she spent hours sifting and sorting through her growing collection of sea glass, lining each fragment up along the windowsills of her cottage first in size order, then in gradations of colour. It fascinated her that such viciously sharp edges had been slowly softened by the sand and water into these smooth, misted gems. She studied the lines of tiny pinpricks along each urchin shell, and the black knots in each piece of sea-bleached driftwood. There was such beauty here.

Very gradually, Jude started greeting other regular walkers

with a nod, or a smile, though none of them broke their stride to stop and talk. She'd noticed that, here on the island, people walked for walking's sake – it was simply how they punctuated their day. As autumn advanced and the sunlight grew paler and rarer, Jude lit candles during the day as well as the evenings, to brighten the tiny cottage. The windows were so small that the sun seldom reached into the rooms now. The temperature dropped a little more each week, and keeping warm started to become a concern. Huddled in blankets inside her tiny home, Jude felt as if she had entered a period of stasis, like a chrysalis, breathing lightly to conserve as much body heat and energy as she could.

When she no longer needed to put milk in the fridge as the kitchen was so cold, she finally understood the phrase "in the grip of winter". And for the first time, she began to doubt her decision to come here.

FIVE

The bleak November weather did little to lift her spirits. For the first week, the rain was so relentless that Jude did not get dressed to go out at all, but sat wrapped in blankets on the sofa, reading the Jeffrey Archer and Joanna Trollope novels that had been left in the cottage by past holidaymakers. It was luxurious for a while, spending whole days in her pyjamas, but very soon, loneliness began to seep in around the edges of her brazen defiance of grief. How long would it be before anyone noticed they had not heard from her, or seen her? What was she doing, skulking in this damp cottage in North Wales where nobody except a cat knew, let alone cared, whether she got up in the morning? One drizzly morning, as she was sitting, unwashed and stewing in just her pyjamas and dressing gown, there was a knock on the door.

A caller was so rare that Jude bit her tongue in fright. She opted to do as her mother had done whenever anyone visited (once she had made sure it wasn't the vicar): be completely quiet until whoever it was went away. After a minute or two, the caller knocked again, and a man's face appeared at the living room window and smiled at her. When a hand appeared next to the face and waved, she waved back, before sheepishly opening the door and tugging her grubby dressing gown tighter to cover her breasts. The man stood, still smiling, having parked his huge tractor just beyond Jude's little garden. It looked almost surreal.

"Sorry. I'm not dressed you see, so..." she blustered.

"So I see, but no problem at all. Just thought you might like this," the man said, nodding at the cardboard box he held under one arm. "I've seen you around, and you look like you need some company."

Jude blushed. Was her loneliness so obvious, so palpable that this stranger could see it without ever having spoken to her? She'd come here to avoid people intruding in her life, and she was deeply offended.

"That depends on the company," she replied. "Look, you don't know me, and I don't know you, so don't presume I'm lonely, thanks very much. That's my business, not yours."

The man laughed, a deep, guttural sound that Jude felt in her belly like a soft punch, which completely wrong-footed her. She had missed hearing real laughter so much, she realised. His voice was one that filled the space between them with a rich, warm sound. He was a singer, she was sure, but not a sweet-voiced tenor, as Alex had been. This man was a definite bass, and his deep tones seemed to make the very air around them reverberate.

"*Duw*/God, I'm sorry. I really am. English words make things sound so *sharp* sometimes, when they don't in Welsh," he said. "Please accept my apologies." His phone buzzed. "Sorry, got to get this."

As they stood on the doorstep and he spoke into his mobile, Jude looked at this man closely for the first time. He was incredibly tall, stocky, with wide shoulders and a powerful, compact frame that told of manual work and strength. His face was deeply tanned, and his rich, chestnut brown hair was very lightly streaked with blonde from time spent outdoors, in all weathers, so guessing his age was hard. She estimated late thirties, but he had a careworn air about him as if living life was hard work. Although he was at least a metre away, Jude could smell the land on him, a sweet earthiness that she longed to breathe in more deeply. He was wearing an ancient-looking cap with fishing flies studding the rim, battered jeans and a very faded denim shirt that had moulded itself to the shape of his muscular arms like a second skin. Her overall impression of this man was of definite, but likeable, eccentricity.

As he was speaking in Welsh, Jude had no idea what he was saying, which unnerved her slightly. For a second or two, she worried that he was telling the caller all about the "weird, uptight Englishwoman" he'd just met, but somehow, he didn't look capable of spite. In fact, he had one of the kindest faces she had ever seen.

He ended the call, smiled shyly, and held the cardboard box in front of her expectantly.

"Sorry again about coming across as rude. It's just that he needs a friend too," he said. "I've seen you walking when I'm in the fields, see." He pointed towards the land on the cliff, beyond the cottage. "And you can't walk properly without a dog, can you? Just take a look. He won't bite."

And so Jude looked, and in one corner, no bigger than an aubergine, was a tiny Jack Russell puppy, with white ears, and white fur with milk-chocolate-brown patches covering most of its body.

"Oh, bless," Jude sighed.

"Last of the litter he is, and a bit small. No use as a ratter on the farm, so... I..." He stopped and looked at her hopefully.

"W-w-well, I don't know. I've never had a dog... I..." Jude stumbled, but her hand was now stroking the back of the puppy's head, and his tiny, blood-warm ears. His tail wagged in response to her touch, and his brown eyes blinked up at her, pools of trust. "How old is he? He looks so small."

"Ten weeks. He never got his fair share of food from his mam, so he needs some love, really. Good friend, he'll be for you. Any problems, *Owain Pritchard dw'i*/I'm Owain Pritchard – I'm working at Gethin Hughes' farm up above the beach at the moment."

"I think I've seen you on your tractor, actually. I'm Jude, Jude Fitzgerald by the way. And thank you, for the puppy, but I'm not sure it's right for me. Not sure what my long-term plans are, to be frank," she replied, immediately realising how uptight she did, indeed, sound.

"Well, that makes two of us, Jude, but it shouldn't stop you taking a risk." He paused. "A dog can change your life, honestly. Take him and love him. You won't regret it." He looked at her, eye to eye, and she felt the sincerity in his words. When he placed the box into her arms and turned to walk away, she felt a final, weak protest rise in her throat, then sink down again, unsaid. "Take him and love him". How could she refuse?

"If you need help with anything, I can turn my hand to most things. Just come and find me in the fields, OK? And don't worry about having to get dressed in advance." He winked and walked towards his tractor.

Jude blushed. "Haha. *Diolch yn fawr iawn*/Thank you very much," she said, daring to use one of the few Welsh phrases she'd learnt.

"*Croeso*/You're welcome," Owain said. "I'll keep in touch, see how you're both doing, if I may, that is..."

"You may. I think we'll do just fine," Jude said with a smile at the puppy. "And you were right. I probably do need a friend. I'm not the kind of person to make them easily either."

"Takes one to know one," Owain replied. "*Hwyl*/Cheers."

"Well, you'd better come inside, so that I can take a proper look at you,' Jude said softly, lifting the tiny dog out of the box and cradling him.

His fur was smooth and slightly oily, and his body as warm as freshly baked bread. He responded to her touch by snuggling closer to her, sniffing her rather ripe pyjamas and nuzzling against her breasts. Nothing could have prepared her for the surge of emotion she felt as this puppy pushed against her body, unashamedly sniffing and licking. Is this what mothers feel when they first hold their babies? she wondered. This would probably be the nearest thing she would ever get to that over-whelming love for something so small and dependant. There was no possibility of her not keeping him – none at all.

Jude called the puppy Pip, after his "apple-pip-brown" eyes, and he seemed to grow by the hour. He rejected the expensive wicker basket she bought for him to sleep in at night, but fitted snugly into the small of her back, which she loved. She still missed the familiar warmth of company in bed, and even though this little dog was not Alex, he gave her great comfort.

Pip's need to sniff every pile of seaweed meant Jude had to slow down when she walked along the beach, so she was forced to talk to people when they admired her puppy. She began to look forward to greeting regular walkers, and she always cast a quick glance up to Owain Pritchard's field when she set out, waving if she glimpsed him on his tractor in Gethin Hughes' fields. He always waved back.

One particularly rainy afternoon in December, she spotted an older woman she saw most days coming towards her, head down into the wind. The rain seemed to be coming in sideways across the beach, rather than down from the sky, a phenomenon that Jude had never noticed in Oxford, but regularly occurred here. "Horizontal rain" was how she described it to her friends, which made them laugh. It felt good to be in more regular contact with them now, and to feel able to share light-hearted things again.

"Terrible day!" the woman shrieked, pulling strands of her wet hair out of her mouth.

Jude nodded in agreement, and the two women stood, backs to the wind and rain for a few minutes, watching their dogs play.

"I've seen you here before. You'll have to come over to mine for a coffee sometime," the woman shouted. "I'm Margaret, by the way."

Jude felt a huge lump rise in her throat as if the Welsh woman had told her she loved her. "That would be really nice, Margaret. I'm Jude."

"Maybe not today, though, or I'd have to ask you to strip off first!" Margaret yelled again, squeezing water out of her fringe.

"Now that *would* be a sight for sore eyes," Jude answered.

As each of them ploughed an unsteady course back along the beach, Jude chuckled at the image of herself standing naked in the other woman's house, raindrops dripping from her nipples.

SIX

Tom called her every few days, and Jude began to look forward to his breezy manner and genuine concern for her. It brightened many dull winter days and made her realise that she needed her old friends now, more than ever. He told her that he avoided sending personal emails, associating them with work, so he called her whenever she was able to get a signal and regaled her with vivid descriptions of the unsavoury clients he had to defend in court or the self-important members of the amateur dramatic society he belonged to. She enjoyed their conversations, as it reminded her of a world she'd left behind, but gradually, she detected a need in him that she was reluctant to meet:

"I'd love to pop up for a weekend..."

"Happy to stay in a local hotel..."

"I really feel the need to see where you are..."

"I could ride the Harley up, give her a spin, and take the train back. I think she needs to be with you."

She dithered about how to respond, as she wasn't sure how to. However conflicted she felt about the Harley, it still seemed best to keep it in Tom's dry shed rather than rusting outside her damp cottage. And yes, part of her longed for the reassurance of seeing Alex's old friend again, but his hints at expecting something more worried her. Instead, she told him about her VERY tiny cottage, her VERY hairy puppy (he was badly allergic to dog hair, but loved cats, which had always struck everyone as odd), and her VERY repetitive daily routine, ending by assuring him that she was fine (even if, sometimes, she wasn't). He seemed placated.

Jude dreaded contact from her mother most of all, perhaps because Gloria preferred the formality of letters, which immediately made Jude anxious, expecting complaints and reprimands. She was very rarely wrong in that expectation, so as soon as she saw the creamy envelope and the looping, italic script every month or so, her stomach tightened. Every sentence rang with reproaches for moving so far away; for not getting in touch more; for not caring that she saw nobody for days; for not caring about all her "problems". Jude knew that Gloria wanted to visit at Christmas, to "see where she was living now", as it would help to visualise her daughter in her temporary home, but she could not invite her. The cottage was tiny, and it would be a difficult enough time for her without having a resentful and demanding Gloria to cope with as well.

This year, she was completely oblivious to the approach of Christmas in *Hedd*. Alex was not rehearsing music for the beautiful candlelit carol concerts his choir always put on in Oxford, there were no shops nearby, no till-jingling adverts, and not a fairy light in sight. When she looked out of her windows on any night between 3.30pm and 8.30am, all she saw was thick blackness, except for the occasional passing lights of a fishing boat or yacht. No, Christmas would not be a celebration for her this year.

December on the island was impossible to ignore, however; it was vicious. The cold and damp penetrated into Jude's bones a little more each day, and she sat so near the wood-burning stove that she very nearly singed many of her clothes. As the only source of warmth in *Hedd*, a hissing Tuna fought Pip for the hearthside rug each bitter day, both animals' breath forming a small, dense cloud of hatred. The cold gradually eroded Jude's peace of mind so that, by mid-December, it was almost as all-consuming as grief had been. So, despite her best intentions, she was relieved when her old friends "absolutely insisted" that she came back to Oxford for Christmas. A week in a warm house with sheets that were not cold and clammy was just too powerful to resist.

Unsure whether her old car would make the round trip, Jude booked a hugely expensive ticket to travel by train. Pip would have to come, of course. When she realised that she still didn't know anyone well enough to ask them to feed Tuna, she felt a stab of sadness. This meant that her poor cat would have to come too, an upheaval she would not enjoy at all.

"Jude!" four women's voices bellowed, as she fell into their welcoming arms on the platform at Oxford station. "Welcome home!"

Five minutes later, squashed between their thighs and bottoms in the seven-seater taxi, puppy on her lap and cat basket at her feet, Jude realised that she had not touched, or been touched by, anyone since she had left Oxford more than three months earlier. She'd not even shaken anyone's hand, let alone been hugged, and the fact that she found it so difficult having all these bodies near her now made her isolation feel all the more real. How she'd missed the warmth of real human contact during these long, cold months.

Jude found the lights, traffic, noise, colour, and crowds of Oxford overwhelming after the silence of her life on the island. The five friends went to one of their favourite restaurants on

Little Clarendon Street, but the rumble of conversation, clattering dishes and music made it almost impossible for Jude to feel she could speak to anyone. She began to worry that she really had lost all her social skills and couldn't bear to be with other people anymore. That spelt a very lonely future, for sure.

"I'm quite happy just to stay here, but you carry on," a paralysed Jude told her friends when they suggested more outings, and so they went without her, leaving her to fret alone.

The Christmas Day plan was to eat one course in each house. This was feasible, as they lived very near each other, but Jude felt stressed just listening to the logistics. After months on her own in almost complete silence, her friends' constant chatter and ever-changing plans made her head hurt. On Christmas Eve, it all became too much, and she felt a real need to be on her own for a while. She told her friends that she wanted to go for a walk along the river, following the towpath out to Iffley Lock, and was secretly delighted when nobody offered to accompany her as they were "far too busy". An exhausted Pip stayed snoozing in his bed.

Walking briskly until she reached Christchurch Meadows, she steered well clear of the busy High Street. Blackbirds hopped politely over the perfect lawns, and she could not help but compare such manicured precision with the wildness of her beach on Anglesey, with its storm-born branches and banks of stinking seaweed. Hitting the river again at Folly Bridge, Jude established an easy, walking stride, feeling more relaxed than she had done in days. It was mid-morning, and a crisp, light-skied day, but most other people were obviously doing their last-minute Christmas shopping as the riverbank was quiet. She passed Tom's house with her head down, guilty that she hadn't seen him since she'd arrived back. He wanted to see her, he'd said, ostensibly to sign some financial papers related to some small investments Alex had made years earlier, but she'd not got in touch and felt ashamed about it. He'd probably gone to see his parents in Burford anyway, she told herself, hurrying past, just in case he hadn't.

This was such a familiar walk for her, which added to her sense of ease. Before his diagnosis, she and Alex had often strolled along the river on Sunday afternoons, drowsy after a long lie-in, lovemaking, a huge lunch, and a couple of glasses of wine before he left for choir practice at 6.30pm. She could almost feel his hand in hers now, their strides matching each other, step for step. Then the "ping" of a cycle bell made her jump; she'd forgotten the Oxford protocol of walking to one side on the towpath to let cyclists pass. A young man whooshed past her on his bike, pedalling at incredible speed, the backs of his calves spattered with mud.

"Sorry!" he yelled over his shoulder.

She was now sprayed with mud too, but when she saw that he was coaching a boat out on the river, she understood why he couldn't have slowed down. The crew rowed past, their oars dipping in and out of the water simultaneously, and with a slickness that belied how much effort it took to get that long, heavy boat slicing through the water so fast. As she caught a glimpse of one of the boys in the crew when they stopped to regain their breath, she gasped. His hair, cropped close around his thin face, his metal glasses and the paleness of his hollowed cheeks reminded her of Alex so powerfully that she could hardly breathe.

Her husband had rowed during his college days, and throughout their years in Oxford. Jude had spent many Saturdays idling on the towpath, waiting for his boat to pass. When the boy had recovered his breath and called out to the coxswain, she saw that his eyes did not crinkle at the edges as Alex's had done when he smiled and his voice, echoing over the water, was far less musical than her husband's had been. The knowledge that she would never, ever hear it again hit her like a body blow and she covered her face with her hands.

Passing her old house in Howard Street an hour later proved a bit of an anti-climax. It was half past four by the time she got there, and dark, so all the curtains were drawn. The rowan tree that Alex had planted in the small front garden was black-twigged and bare, with a pile of soggy leaves and a few orange berries rotting at its base. She felt nothing at all as she stood staring at it – it was no longer a part of her life, and she no longer belonged here. At that moment, the only thing she wanted to do was press a button and be walking along her beach on the island or back beside a roaring fire in the woodburner at *Hedd*. And that, she felt sure, was progress.

SEVEN

The uncomfortable fact that it was Jude's first Christmas without Alex was unsaid, but it hovered in the air around all her friends like a magnetic charge. For her, however, it was just another day without him and no worse than many of the others since his death. Gifts were exchanged, and she was genuinely thrilled with the full set of waterproofs her friends had clubbed together to buy her. They, in turn, were delighted with the hand-painted cards she'd made them all, decorated with sea glass and other small trinkets from her beachcombing hauls.

"You said you wanted to start being creative again, up there," Paula said, dangling the shell and driftwood mobile Jude had made for her baby over her rounding belly. "This is a great start."

On Boxing Day, however, things began to unravel. Tuna pooed in the bath, and Paula became very anxious about toxoplasmosis, ("an infection carried in cat poo that could harm an unborn baby", she read from Google). Pip also had an accident on the newly laid laminate floor in Jo and Katie's kitchen, so Jude decided to quit while she was ahead, and altered her train ticket to travel back to Bangor on the 27th. She spent her last afternoon in Oxford trying to dissuade Paula from setting her heart on a water birth with whale music and no drugs; and from telling Georgio's mother what she *really* thought of the hideous baby outfits she kept buying on eBay.

"If it's a boy, he's going to be dressed entirely in frills at this rate," Paula said with a wry grin.

The entire Fearsome Foursome came to see her off at the station, and Jude invited them all to come and visit her on Anglesey if they wanted a break from city life and to breathe some seriously fresh air. They swore to do so, but no dates were mentioned, so it was clear that they had no real intention of venturing anywhere near the wilderness that was North Wales. As the train was announced, Jo asked:

"How much longer do you think you'll stay up there, Jude?"

"Well, my rental contract runs until Easter."

"Do you really want to stay that long?" Katie said tentatively.

"I think so, yes. Well, I don't know how long I want to stay, but I know I don't want to come back yet. I think I do need to get out more, though," Jude replied. "I really think I've forgotten how to be with other people."

The others exchanged looks. They obviously agreed with her.

"So have you made *any* friends yet?" Katie asked. "It must be very lonely..."

Jude hesitated. Owain Pritchard's face popped into her head, and she could almost hear his resonant bass voice implying that he, too, found making friends difficult, but she didn't want to arouse her friends' curiosity by mentioning a man she'd met only once, under very unusual circumstances.

"Yes. I've met Margaret. She's a bit older than me, but she invited me for a coffee... when it's not raining."

"Could be a bloody long wait for that," Paula muttered.

"I promise I'll try to socialise more, before I become even

more of a long-haired hermit," she said, hugging them all in turn.

As the train pulled away and Jude watched her friends smiling and waving, she still envied them their jobs, their partners, and their predictable security more than felt comfortable. No, she was not ready to come back, not yet. She'd not found what she was looking for on the island, or not all of it, and she knew that this was probably because she was not exactly certain what that was.

Hedd smelt very damp indeed when she opened her front door, and there was a pool of water on the floor where the roof had leaked. Jude sighed, put the kettle on, and went outside.

It was pitch black, but the sky was clear and incredibly starry. Small waves hit the shore with the regularity of a metronome; the water was stiller than Jude ever remembered it. Tomorrow morning, she might wake to hear it battering at her windows, a swell menacing at the garden wall. Tonight, however, it was calm as she listened to the dwindling cries of all the seabirds on the beach below.

PART 2

ONE STEP FORWARD, TWO STEPS BACK

EIGHT

True to her resolution to "meet more people", Jude enrolled on a Welsh course as soon as she got back to the island, but when the day of the first lesson arrived, she felt sick with nerves. She'd already downloaded an online course onto her tablet and tried to learn the basics of the language, but perhaps not joining the "complete beginners" class had been a little overambitious.

"Don't say 'no', say 'yes'," she murmured as she parked outside the venue for the very first class.

Despite her best efforts to be positive, her first impressions of her classmates were not good, and none seemed to hold "future friend potential". Everyone looked very serious, with pads and pens or laptops at the ready; an elderly couple even had flasks of tea and a pile of Welsh dictionaries and grammar books. When Jude tried to slide quietly into a chair, the strap of her bag snagged on something, and its contents spewed all over the classroom floor.

"Oh shit!" she hissed, to a suppressed chorus of "tut-tuts".

Scrabbling to pick things up, another woman joined her on the floor and started passing her tampons, receipts, rogue tablets and three freebie IKEA pencils. One glance told Jude that this woman, with her baggy, mock-boho clothes, was also unlikely to hold any friendship potential, which, in turn, triggered a flicker of guilt at how quickly she now judged people. This was not going well.

"Think that's the lot," the woman said, finally handing Jude a hairy lip salve which had lost its top. "God knows what you'd find in the bottom of *my* bag!"

"Thanks," Jude mumbled, adding, in an effort to erase her unspoken unkindness about the woman's slightly "non-mainstream" appearance, "Amazing, the junk we all carry round, isn't it?"

Before the woman could reply, the tutor appeared at the front of the room. She looked pretty scary, her thin lips slashed in unfeasibly bright red lipstick. The class would meet once a week, she told the hushed pupils, and would last from 9.30 until 12.30, with a short coffee break in the middle. During the class, *only Welsh was permitted*, she added, which made everyone gasp.

"*Dim Saesneg o gwbl*/No English at all," the woman said with mock sternness.

The first lesson was mainly spent with everyone introducing themselves, which took a very long time indeed. When it was Jude's turn to speak, she froze until, after a few endless seconds, the tutor repeated the phrase she had used for all the others in the room:

"*Helô Glenys dw'i. Dw'in byw yn Bodedern. Lle dach chi'n byw?*/Hello. I'm Glenys. I live in Bodedern. Where do you live?"

"*Jude dw'i*/I'm Jude," burst out of her with considerable force. "*Dw'in byw yn Porth Nobla*/I live in Nobla Cove."

The words felt like a bulky sock in her mouth, but at least she had said them. She'd never spoken Welsh aloud, apart from the very occasional word or phrase. Glenys smiled at her with genuine appreciation.

"*Da iawn, Jude*/Very good, Jude," she said, before focusing her smile on the colourful woman on her left.

"*Glenys dw'i. Pwy dach chi?*/I'm Glenys. Who are you?" she asked with apparently unwavering interest.

"*Stella dw'i.*/I'm Stella. I..."

Jude squirmed with empathy as Stella's face reddened, and she writhed and struggled to find a phrase, even a word, to add to this nugget. When she failed, Glenys moved on to Dominic, a rather unkempt young man who desperately needed a shave, who said that he'd bought a rundown farmhouse, farmed goats and "needed to improve his Welsh to set up an amazing business here", all in English. Jude and Stella exchanged understanding looks as Glenys frowned at him. During the break, most people huddled around the drinks machine firing questions at each other in loud voices. Jude skirted around them and joined Stella, who'd raced outside as soon as Glenys had uttered the words "*Amser coffi*/Coffee time".

"Bloody hell! Aren't we allowed to speak *any* English in this class at all? I thought that Glenys was going to exterminate Dominic with that glare! And some of that lot are fluent already, or as near-as," Stella gasped. "I'm from *Penarth,* for goodness' sake! This is ridiculous!"

"It's a good idea, though, making us speak Welsh," Jude answered, before adding, "If a real pain in the bum," with a grin that produced a laugh from her companion that made the window behind them rattle.

While Stella checked her phone and puffed on her vape as if it was lifesaving oxygen, Jude looked at her more closely, ashamed that she'd almost dismissed this woman without even speaking to her. She was dressed in a long grey smock, about five strings of beads, and baggy cream harem pants. It was January, but she was wearing flip-flops. Her face was etched with lines and her roots were grey where an old henna rinse was growing out. She must be in her fifties, Jude reckoned, but she had a vibrancy about her that belied any hint of middle-age. When she spoke, she punctuated every comment with a deep suck on the vape, filling the air between them with a mock-strawberry smell. Jude decided that she liked her very much.

As the other pupils began to return to the classroom, Stella hurriedly told Jude that she'd moved here three years ago from High Wycombe after her divorce, that she rarely saw her two grown-up sons (Jake, eighteen, and Liam, twenty), as they blamed her for the disintegration of their family. They now idolised their father, Colin, who was busily climbing corporate ladders while she now worked in a care home near Bangor.

"They said I was selfish for 'abandoning them'," she said. "All I did was go to Majorca for a week on my own. I got so tired with all that *supporting,* all that *encouraging,* all that ferrying to endless activities and after school clubs." A pause. "It was the beginning of the end, mind. My husband said I'd 'got a taste for freedom'. Things were never the same after that." She sucked on her vape and shook her head mournfully.

Jude reciprocated with equal honesty. She'd come here a few months ago; her husband had died (from cancer, which had been terrible), and she had no children. She wasn't working at the moment (having sold a ludicrously overpriced house in Oxford) and wasn't sure how long she would stay in North Wales but knew she needed to be here for now.

"Well, I only came for a fortnight, and that was three years ago," Stella said. "It gets under your skin somehow – know what I mean?"

Jude said that she did.

After the class, they went to "the best fish and chip shop in North Wales", as the newspaper article stuck inside the window proudly told them. They talked non-stop for over two hours. Stella wasn't at all embarrassed when Jude started to cry about Alex and the babies she had lost, and passed her strategic tissues, or serviettes, when they ran out.

"I'm really sorry, Jude. If you wanted a baby, to lose two must have been heartbreaking," she said, her eyes full of tears. "But why did you think coming here would help?"

"It felt as if Alex was telling me to, as he loved this place so much and we'd always meant to come back together," Jude replied. "And so, I promised him I would, towards the end."

"Well, perhaps he knew you could find comfort, a new life. I'm sure you will, but nothing goes as you expect it to up here, I can tell you that much for starters!"

"Right now, I just seem to be wallowing in the past rather than building any kind of future," Jude said. "I even dream in memories."

"Ah, memories, those golden bloody millstones around our necks," Stella said. "You can't get rid of them however hard you try. I still see my Jake as a toddler, needing me. Last time I spoke to him, he sounded so, *hard*, not like my gorgeous little boy at all." She reached out and covered Jude's hand with her own. "Give yourself time, love. Plenty of time."

"But what about you? If you've been here a good while, what made you decide to learn Welsh now?" Jude asked.

"When I started working in the care home a year or so ago, I really wanted to understand what the oldies were telling me," Stella said. "Lots of people just give them another tablet, or wipe their arses, but I wanted to understand what they have to say... before they can't say it anymore, really. And many of them are first language Welsh, so I feel I have *got* to learn it, and it's now or never. They deserve to be heard and listened to."

Jude nodded in admiration, hoping they would not get onto the subject of her own mother, whom she'd not seen for almost six months. Gloria didn't deserve to be heard, as far as Jude was concerned, and she had nothing worthwhile to say when you listened.

"See you here next week?" Stella said, as they parted happily. "I need your moral support!"

"It's a date," Jude answered. "We can be bottom of the class together!"

NINE

The relentlessly grey skies of February pressed down on Jude's cottage with a heavy, viscous gloom and the rain seemed never-ending. The first anniversary of Alex's death, February 8th, was a day she had dreaded for so long that she was almost beside herself when it actually arrived. Leaving all the sympathetic messages from friends unread, she trudged along the beach, head low, or paced around the cottage howling like a desperate, caged animal, as that terrible day inched past. By 3pm, the exact time he'd died, she was too exhausted to weep any more, and went to bed in her clothes. When she woke up in darkness several hours later, she felt as if a terrible fever had peaked and left her.

"First anniversary done," she said to Pip, who snuggled into her more closely.

The days between Welsh lessons stretched endlessly. Although her main reason for coming here had been to be alone, Jude realised that seeing Stella was now the highlight of her week. Owain had obviously moved on from working at the Hughes' farm above her beach, as she never saw him in the fields anymore, and Margaret had looked terribly tired the last few times she had seen her, and had never repeated her offer to come round for coffee. It was impossible to guess what was going on in other people's lives, but Jude wondered whether, in North Wales, "You must come for coffee" was on a par with "See you around", or "We must meet up" in towns and cities. It meant nothing at all. She tried to paint but couldn't find a way of expressing herself that felt right, and the canvases she did make a start on were all furiously painted over in the evening.

"I can't even do *this*," she said after a whole morning spent fruitlessly trying to create something that she could, perhaps, build on. "Who am I, if I can't even paint any more? Is there any part of my life that isn't a complete and utter failure?"

Luckily, her pets were unable to answer her.

She knew that Alex would tell her to "stop being so passive" and "*do* something" about how low she was feeling. She had to try to get to know the people in her community better, he would say. She'd driven to supermarkets elsewhere on the island, as they either offered more choice or sold delicious treats like smoked houmous or stuffed peppers that reminded her of her former life, but the local shop in Llanfaelog that she had only been to once or twice did seem to be a hub for people who lived in the area. The sign above the shop door said that "Mrs Menna Jones & Mrs Anwen Williams" ran it, and she reckoned that the woman usually behind the counter seemed about her age. They had never gone beyond "Just those, please" and "£10.50, thanks" in their previous dealings, but today, it was time to push the boundaries a little. She walked in with a fixed smile and a pounding heart.

"Hi. Are you Mrs Menna Jones or Mrs Anwen Williams?" she asked breezily. In the silence that followed, she wished she hadn't.

"Menna Jones. Anwen is my sister, but she's not here," the

woman said eventually, without looking up from the figures she was checking. Jude noticed that she was dressed completely in black – black T-shirt, black cardigan, black trousers, black shoes. The thought that perhaps she, like her, had been bereaved flashed across her mind, but she resisted asking if Anwen had recently died, which would explain why she wasn't here.

"Right, I see. I'm Jude. I live in the little cottage on the shore – *Hedd*, it's called."

"Oh yes," Menna Jones answered, her eyes flicking up for a second before returning to her figures. "I know it. Another holiday let."

"I'm here for the whole of the winter, actually," Jude replied. "I love it here, I really do."

There was another silence, broken only by the low burr of a radio somewhere in the distance. Jude swallowed hard.

"Bit chilly today. Such a cold wind," she said.

Menna looked up again, and her painted-on eyebrows arched, like drawn bows. Her face said that she had no time for trivia: she had figures to check. "Yes. It's February weather."

"Yes, of course. Right, er, I'm looking for some fresh basil," Jude continued. This was clearly going nowhere. The elderly couple on the other side of the shop had stopped talking and were now staring at her. Was she really such a freak? She had put on clean clothes and brushed her hair for the occasion, for goodness' sake.

"Fresh basil," Menna repeated, her local accent adding a sharpness to each consonant. "Sorry, we don't have any of that."

"Right, yes, OK, good," Jude gabbled. "A jar of pesto will be fine. Do you... I mean if you...?'

She heard tongues touching palates as the elderly couple tut-tutted in unison, or rather "tsk-tsk-tsked" in unison. Jude had spoken to so few people that week that her voice barely sounded like her own any more. Her words seemed to hang in the air like an unwelcome smell.

"We don't keep pesto either," Menna answered. Her eyes were not unkind, but they were not kind either. Jude noticed that her baggy black T-shirt had "I am woman. I am tired" printed on it, in faded grey lettering. "The posh supermarket in Menai Bridge will have some, though."

"Great. Fine," Jude said. "I thought I'd just ask here first." She squeezed a chocolate bar next to the till absent-mindedly, and Menna's eyebrows arched even more sharply. "Sorry, sorry. I didn't mean to..."

Backing up like a startled dog, she knocked a pyramid of soup tins flying. Now thoroughly panicked, she scrabbled after them as they rolled across the floor, wanting desperately to be anywhere on earth except in this stupid little shop. Tears were coming soon, she knew, and by the time she felt a hand on her arm, she was shaking violently.

"Leave them. I can put them back, you know." Those brows were still arched, and Menna Jones' face still looked stern, but the voice was comforting, and she had deep brown eyes, kind eyes, Jude saw. The elderly couple were bending over, picking things up from the floor next to her and putting them onto the counter.

"*Diolch*/Thank you," Jude whispered. She was still shaking and could feel hot tears rolling down her cheeks. Nobody spoke, and she felt as if the air was creaking, as it did in *Lord of the Rings* just before the trees began to walk.

"Don't worry about it," Menna added. "It's just soup, doll."

"We heard about your husband, *cariad*/love. Terrible for you," the old lady said, the English words almost unrecognisable in her Welsh accent.

"Cruel thing, cancer," added her husband, pressing a rogue can of leek and potato soup into her hand. "You'll be all right up here. Best place for you."

Menna guided Jude to a chair and popped open a can of Fanta for her ("for the sugar"). She drank gratefully and tried not to allow herself to feel embarrassed that everyone seemed to know all about her, and that her private tragedy had been prised open like a reluctant mussel. Mair Roberts had told everyone, probably, and she would only have meant it kindly, but this was so different to how people behaved in Oxford. As Jude wiped away her tears with the back of her hand, the old man placed a hand on her shoulder.

"There, there," he murmured. *"Popeth yn iawn rwan*/Everything's OK now."

But there was an expression on Menna's face like a gathering of clouds.

"My dad died six months ago, of throat cancer. Awful to watch him go downhill it was, day by day," she said slowly.

"Oh – I'm so sorry to hear that," Jude said. "And yes, it is awful, I know."

"*Duw*/God, yes. Bloody cancer." Her brown eyes were of tears now. "The worst time of my life."

When the elderly couple had paid for their few items, they "tsk-tsked" again as they shuffled towards the door, and Jude realised that this was the sound of sympathy, not the tutting of disapproval she'd assumed it to be.

"Menna will sort you out. Heart of gold, she has. Just looks bloody fierce," the old man said, closing the shop door behind him with a wink.

The two women stood in silence for a few moments, listening to the freezers hum.

"I could get some pesto in, if you like," Menna said. "Save you making the trip to Menai Bridge," she said.

"That would be great, but I don't want to put you to any trouble," Jude answered, suddenly feeling that something momentous had just happened. How could pesto unleash such strong emotions?

Menna smiled, which utterly transformed her face and made her look years younger. It was a smile worth waiting for.

. . .

Just over a week later, as Jude was debating whether to brave the drizzle and walk Pip or hope against hope that it stopped before it got dark, she heard a soft knock at the door. When she opened it, Menna was standing there, holding two jars of pesto.

"It's come in. I ordered some green and some red, in case you prefer one to the other," she said. Her expression made it clear that anyone who cared really needed to get a life.

"Oh, thank you *so* much," Jude answered. "Will you come in, for a... *panad*," she asked, hesitating as the Welsh word for "cuppa" slipped out unbidden. Menna glanced up at the sky in response.

"Later, perhaps. Bet your little dog could do with a walk first, though," she glanced at Pip, and smiled. "It's a nice day."

Jude also looked at the sky. True, it wasn't raining as torrentially as it had been earlier, so, yes, perhaps it was "nice" for Anglesey in February. She put on her waterproof mac, trousers, and wellies, however, just in case it got any "nicer".

TEN

For weeks, if Jude was not wrapped up in blankets and sitting in her living room in front of the fire, it was where she longed to be. Pip spent the day on her lap, or at her feet, nestled under the bottom of the sleeping bag she'd taken to wearing as an extra layer, which suited them both perfectly. Her bed was icy cold when she climbed into it at night, buckets collected the drips from the now numerous leaks in the roof when it rained and the days were short and relentlessly gloomy. But meeting Menna, who lived so near her, had changed everything, and there was nowhere Jude would rather have been.

Every lunchtime, her new friend knocked on her door to walk with her. Sometimes, they didn't say much, except for commenting on things they noticed on the beach, or laughing about their squelchy, sodden socks. Menna was more at ease with silence than anyone Jude had ever known, except Alex, and being with her made her feel calm, and sure that good things could happen again. She listened as Menna told her about her father, and how they'd run the shop together for years whilst Anwen, her sister, had "done bugger all in the shop until Dad was dying", and how bitter she felt that Anwen had inherited more than she deserved to after his death. In return, Jude told her how she had always wished for a sibling, and that she hoped the sisters would find a way to mend the rift between them one day. For both women, this quiet hour simply made these cold, dark winter days pass more easily, and they were thankful for it.

"I hear it was Owain Pritchard that gave you Pip," Menna said one day.

Jude felt a tiny flip in her stomach and was glad that they were side by side so that Menna wouldn't see the blush she felt burning her cheeks. This reaction both surprised and embarrassed her. How could meeting that unusual Welshman once have had such a strong effect on her equilibrium?

"He did, yes. Not that I asked him to. He just called one day and presented Pip to me in a cardboard box," she said as gaily as she could.

"Typical," Menna replied. "Impulsive, but kind, that man. Need to watch your step with him, though. He seems like a real joker, and he can be, but he comes with some *serious* baggage."

"Don't we all, but I don't think we'll see each other again," Jude said, more brusquely than she'd intended. "I think he just knew I needed a friend."

Menna hesitated for a moment, and then took her arm. "Of course! And now you have two – me *and* Pip!"

"Well, *three*, actually. I've got one in my Welsh class, called Stella, and perhaps a fourth, a very enthusiastic goat farmer called Dominic."

"*Da iawn*/Good," Menna said with a measured smile. "There'll be no stopping you now – you mark my words."

And Jude felt warm, despite the icy wind they were striding into, to hear her friend say so.

· · ·

Stella was also quickly becoming a close friend, and she was unlike anyone Jude had ever met; being with her was both exhilarating and exhausting. Her loud voice and strong South Welsh accent, coupled with her bizarrely multi-layered outfits, meant that she more than filled any room and often left Jude feeling as if she needed to come up for air. Conversations jumped from topic to topic randomly and were so difficult to pilot through that Jude was reminded of one of Alex's old nicknames for her: "Mrs Non-Sequitur". However, in reality, big, brash Stella was hugely lacking in self-confidence, and could easily be reduced to tears by a brusque barman or a sad memory, which was painfully like Jude. They met for chips and an offload after every Welsh class, and it was one of the highlights of both their weeks. Both women were living a life in isolation from everyone they had ever loved, and this formed the strongest of bonds between them, despite their age difference, a factor which crossed neither of their minds.

"How can you bear it, not seeing your boys?" Jude asked her one day.

"What choice do I have?" her friend answered. "They opted out of my life. I can't really talk to them now. I used to wear smart clothes and designer shoes and drive a Range Rover in High Wycombe, Jude, if you can believe that. I tried so hard to be a "yummy mummy". They don't really know me, as I am now."

"Perhaps they would like to, though," Jude replied. "Why don't you invite them both up for a few days? Show them the town."

Then both women laughed out loud at the daftness of that idea. The boarded-up shops and overall air of deprivation and decay in Bangor were both overwhelmingly sad and a world away from the consumer capital that was High Wycombe, where Stella's family still lived.

"Liam told me to 'get lost' the last time I asked him to visit.

Said I was to stay out of his life, had no right to be involved in what he did any more," Stella said, sniffing back tears. "I think he told Jake to have nothing to do with me either. He'll be starting at university soon..."

Jude felt a flush of guilt. She remembered her last conversation with her own mother, when she had been equally keen to shut her out of her life. Perhaps she'd been as callous to Gloria as Liam had been to Stella? In so many ways, her always distant, always frosty mother deserved it, but her lovely friend did not. Nevertheless, the feelings stirred up were uncomfortable ones, as kindness was usually Jude's default behaviour.

"Jake probably needs you more than ever now. He just can't tell you," she said. "Leaving home is a huge milestone."

"I tried, but I'm not going to brood about it," Stella said. "No point."

Jude reached out and covered Stella's hand with one of hers.

"Hey, let's do something totally bonkers to cheer ourselves up," Stella suddenly said. "Shall we sprint to the end of the pier? Hug random strangers? Eat an ice cream from the bottom up?"

In the end, they marched to the nearest salon, where Stella had her eyelashes dyed blue, and she persuaded Jude to have her long hair cut into a choppy bob. As the hairdresser snipped and primped, Jude was forced to look at herself in a mirror, to watch herself chat, move, and smile. Since she'd removed all the mirrors in *Hedd*, this was a very disorientating experience. She looked older, and her face was not the face she'd known before Alex had died, but she looked well, she decided, better than she'd ever done, in some ways. Stella clapped and cheered when the hairdresser had finished.

"You look fantastic, Jude. You really do. It's time to get out there and knock some poor bloke dead. Dominic's rather dishy, don't you think?"

Jude had rolled her eyes, as Dominic was also decidedly whiffy at times, but on the bus home, she allowed a vignette to play out in her head: the scene of a man, any man, finding her attractive, and she him.

"No. That can never happen," she murmured. "I'm on my own now."

She was glad that the elderly lady sitting next to her was dozing, and did not ask why tears were rolling down her cheeks.

Just as there were signs of winter ending and the first, bright white lambs had appeared in the fields, Mrs Roberts gave Jude a month's notice to leave *Hedd*. Her six months' tenancy would be over around mid-March, and the first of the season's holiday-makers had booked the cottage for Easter.

Although she'd known this would happen, the thought of someone else opening the curtains each morning to see her beach, and her sky, upset Jude enormously. Staying on the island for longer would be hard, and being here was sometimes incredibly lonely, but going back to Oxford was unthinkable. She knew every nook of this tiny cottage, with all its flaws; she had run her hands over its uneven walls so often that it was a part of her, a steady centre, holding her together. After two sleepless nights, she drove to Menai Bridge and asked to speak to Mrs Roberts. The older woman made her a coffee, compli-mented her new hairstyle, but seemed a little on edge.

"I really want to stay in *Hedd*, Mair," she said. "I have the money. I'll pay the summer rental prices."

"Ah. I knew you were going to say that, but you can't, Jude," Mrs Roberts answered with a sigh. "The cottage is fully booked from Easter onwards I'm afraid. That was always the deal."

Jude put down her biscuit. It was time to play dirty.

"Look, the roof leaks, badly, so it needs a new one. It also needs central heating, and it stinks of damp. Everything goes mouldy in the cupboards and the windows don't fit properly. You may find that people might not be happy to pay top whack to stay there this year, Mair, honestly. It had been empty for a while before I rented it, hadn't it? Well, it shows."

Mrs Roberts put down her cup and saucer and folded her hands in her lap. Jude had struck a nerve.

"There are lots of other cottages for holidaymakers on Anglesey, but *Hedd*, well, I just can't imagine leaving it yet, and it really isn't fit to let in the state it's in."

Mrs Roberts said nothing, but looked at the paperwork on her desk and aligned her pens. "I will have a think, and see what can be done, Jude. *Hedd* is very popular because of its location, but the owners are aware there are things that need... sorting. They are not very – what's the English word for it – *amenable*, when it comes to spending money on the place, shall we say." Her brow furrowed; this was difficult for her. "I'm sorry it's unpleasant for you there, I really am."

"Oh, I can live with it, but perhaps not if I was paying hundreds of pounds a week for the privilege," Jude said.

Mrs Roberts squirmed in her chair. "I'd have to move all the people booked in to other properties and inform the owners why." She tapped her pen on her front teeth, as her mind worked. "What about the work being done with you there, over the summer? Would you consider that, if I negotiated a lower rent for the inconvenience? That's only fair."

"I'd consider anything that lets me stay there," Jude replied immediately. "And thank you for trying. I really appreciate you sticking your neck out for me."

The puzzled look on Mair's face told Jude that she had not understood this idiom at all.

"You'll hear from me within a few days. I will see what I can do, but I really can't make any promises. And they won't want to spend much."

Holding the door open, she added, "Are you sure you want

to stay there, dear? I've got some other nice ones, especially if you're able to pay summer season prices." There was a look of real concern on her face. She was almost old enough to be Jude's mother, and now, she was behaving as if she was – but a far more considerate version.

"I'm quite sure, Mair," she replied.

In fact, she'd never been so sure of anything in her entire life, except when Alex had asked her to marry him on a punt in Oxford, his borrowed Panama hat tilted rakishly to the left. *Hedd* was her home now.

ELEVEN

It was a very long week until Jude got her answer, and her heart somersaulted every time she heard a car slow down on the road that ran past the cottage. She longed to ring Mair Roberts several times a day but knew better than to try. She simply had to wait and hope.

The cottage now smelt very strongly of mildew all the time, so Jude was forced to open its tiny windows wide, which made it even chillier, but when Mrs Roberts was due to call, she closed them so that the stink of damp and rot was almost overwhelming. It was pouring so hard when she arrived that Jude had not even heard her car pull up. The older woman wrinkled her nose as the ghastly smell reached her. After a moment or two, Jude scanned her expression, as she had learnt to do when she'd talked to one of Alex's consultants, and she saw hope in it.

"Well, my dear, it wasn't easy, and re-booking everyone in other cottages will be a nightmare, but you can have the cottage for a flat fee of £2,000, plus bills, until the middle of September if you want it. The owners want to send surveyors over to estimate what needs doing but is this acceptable to you as a way forward?" Mrs Roberts said in one breath. "I laid it on pretty thick, about all the problems here, *cariad*/love. It needs sorting, I can see."

Jude hugged her so hard that she heard a tiny bone click in her back. "Thank you, thank you very much." When she released her, both women had tears in their eyes.

"I think you are meant to be here as long as you need to be," Mrs Roberts said, emotion snagging her voice. "I hope you don't mind, but I did tell them how much you loved the place, and, well, why you had come here. I just thought that, if they knew that, well, you know..." She glanced at her anxiously, and Jude realised that the older woman was worried that, this time, she had gone too far in telling others her personal business.

She laid her hand on Mrs Roberts' arm. "It's fine, Mair. You got them to agree to let me stay, and that's all that matters. Do you know who'll be coming to estimate for the job?"

"Well, there are a couple of local firms who take on casual labourers, and so charge less, so one of them will probably quote; them, and a bigger company as well, I expect, to make the owners feel better about accepting the cheap one," Mrs Roberts replied.

Jude nodded. "I see. Same old, same old, but at least I can stay here, whoever's doing the repairs. Let's celebrate with a *panad*/cuppa – or would you prefer a glass of wine?"

When Mrs Roberts left half an hour later, Jude clambered back into her sleeping bag as she was already chilled. After much thought, she wrote a long email to each of the Fearsome Foursome, explaining that she was staying on the island all summer and why. She described the people she'd met, her routine of Welsh and walks, and tried to help them visualise Menna and Stella, but her words could not bring them into focus, and they sounded like silly stereotypes. No, she could not find the right words to describe them, as both women were wonderfully idiosyncratic, so she simply said "my new friends". She struggled even harder to try and help her Oxford friends understand how she loved the harsh, flat Anglesey landscape, her freezing cottage, even tatty, gum-strewn Bangor High Street, but she tried, as hard as she could, to do so.

Their replies popped into her inbox within an hour. They varied from:

Jude, wtf? You'll go bonkers. I need you here!

from a very-pregnant Paula to...

So, can we come and visit you, if it's actually not raining all summer as well as all winter?

from Jo and Katie, to...

A summer by the sea sounds good to me,

from Morag.

She emailed Tom, too, as he had been in touch with her most often, asking her when she was coming back and whether she wanted him to courier the Harley up to her yet. His reply did not surprise her at all:

I don't understand your decision, but I respect it. Please consider my house always available to you if and when you decide to return. I have more than enough room, as you know. I miss you. P.S. The Harley sends love too.

The postcard to her mother took her a long time to write. She threw three cards away before she was happy with the tone and wording. In the end, it sounded even more stark than she'd intended it to, but space was limited, and her absolute priority was not to open any real avenue of communication with Gloria:

Dear Mum,

*I hope you're well, and that your arthritis is better than it was.
I'm sure the new tablets will help. I have decided to stay in
Wales for a while longer. The rent is cheap, and I have made
some friends. I've got a little dog, a Jack Russell called Pip. Sorry
not been in touch more, but you've got my email address and
mobile number if you need to contact me quickly. Most people
use them to get in touch these days, Mum. I am doing well, and
hope you are too.*

*Love from,
Judith*

She did not expect a reply after their last, acrimonious,
conversation before she had left Oxford (when Gloria had told
her that she was "making another stupid mistake") but she felt a
little better, having "checked in" with her mother. If she could
keep her a few hundred miles distant for a little longer, all the
better, for both of them.

TWELVE

Like the flick of a switch, April marked the beginning of spring on the island, and the weather seemed to change several times a day. Bursts of sunshine lit up the fields and hedgerows with a brilliance that defied any artist's palette, and the landscape was a vivid mix of greens, whites, blues, and the mottled grey of the seashore rocks. There were still many dull days, but on fine ones, the sky above Porth Nobla was clear and sunny, broken only with thin skeins of egg-white cloud, and the sea changed colour as you watched it. It was as if the island opened up like a long-sealed treasure box, finally exposing its glories for all to see.

Stella had been to *Hedd* several times, but she had not yet invited Jude to her cottage in Tregarth. Jude knew that her friends were women who'd all moved here from England, as they both had, and she became almost fixated on meeting them. They were bound to have lots in common, she told herself and she needed to "connect" with more people; that was where happiness lay, or so everyone told her.

"I'm just not sure you'll like them," Stella said, whenever Jude suggested a coffee or a lunch with her friends yet again. "I'm not sure *I* do, but beggars can't be choosers up here. Until I met you, I thought I'd never have a real friend again, someone I could be myself with."

"That's lovely to hear, and don't get me wrong, I'm grateful for your friendship, and for Menna's, but I think I need to feel I'm part of something, not just a satellite orbiting around groups of friends but always basically on my own."

"Jeez, girl, your overactive imagination amazes me," Stella replied. "OK, I'll arrange for you to meet the Tregarth ladies, but don't get your expectations up."

"I won't," Jude replied, but she felt a flutter of excitement as she set off after Welsh class to follow Stella to Tregarth the following week. Stella's cottage was at the top of a narrow track, with moss-softened stone walls on either side and a stream running past the front door. The cottage was completely covered with Welsh slate – the roof, the walls, even the porch. Today, the air was damp, and the dark grey slates had a reptilian sheen. The cottage looked anything but welcoming even though the front door was wide open and a gust of laughter billowed out of it.

"They'll have let themselves in, I expect. I never lock the door," Stella said over her shoulder to Jude when they arrived. As she lifted her flounced skirt and petticoat clear of all the brambles, it struck Jude for the first time that her friend often looked faintly ridiculous, but in the most brilliant of ways. Both women manoeuvred past several rusted bikes and the skeleton of a lawnmower as they neared the front door. Jude could just about tell where the path to it had once been and tried to stay on it.

"Is all this stuff yours?" she asked, snagging her cardigan on an old rake.

"It's 'rewilding', Jude, or returning to nature. I like it that way, actually," Stella snapped. She was clearly nervous.

It took a few moments to get used to the gloom inside the hallway. Jude could hear Stella moving ahead of her, but all she could see were dark, furniture-shaped shadows looming in from both sides, which made the space she had to walk in extremely limited. The darkness smelt of damp, smoke, and something sweetly perfumed. Suddenly, she heard a "whoop" from somewhere ahead of her:

"Stella! We're in here, darling! One bottle down already!"

"They've all walked, as they live in the village, so it could be a boozy one," Stella whispered.

Suddenly, the door to the kitchen at the back of the hallway opened, and Jude blinked and rubbed her eyes as she shuffled forward, feeling her way through the doorframe. The air had a faint tang of cigarette smoke, but the dominant smell was of patchouli, which filled the room with a swirling fog from burning joss sticks. In an instant, Jude was back at an 18th birthday party in Taunton Rugby Club.

"Hello. You must be Judith," a voice said from somewhere to the right of her.

"No, not *Judith*. It's JUDE, remember?" another voice added.

"Like the Beatles song."

A hand grasped hers, and Jude smiled in the right direction, but visibility was on par with driving through Snowdonia in heavy rain. Other hands fluttered towards her, bangles jangled and smiles exposed flashes of white teeth, but these were soon extinguished by the yellowy fug of joss-stick smoke. When Jude could finally focus, she saw that everyone was wearing several layers of very plain, very baggy, clearly very expensive clothes, and the overall effect was like being in a roomful of tents. This was obviously the look Stella was aiming for too, but not quite getting right. She was so nervous when Stella introduced her to the others that their names slipped out of her memory like water through a colander. She prayed she would remember them when she needed to. Each woman summed themselves up with admirable succinctness:

"Moved from Milton Keynes four years ago. And we thought that place was bad!"

"Came from Cheltenham for my other half's 'dream job' three years ago. Bloody nightmare ever since."

"Been here for six years and still working on my escape plan once the eldest leaves home."

Jude nodded but felt a ripple of alarm run through her body. This did not feel good at all. She should not have come here.

Stella distributed bowls, plates, and cutlery around the table, and refilled glasses before they were even near empty, to "get the party started" as she put it. Jude noticed that the faint smell of smoke was coming through an open window behind her, where a brimming ashtray bore witness to many cigarettes smoked outside before she had arrived. She had never liked her Oxford friends smoking years ago, when they were younger, but here in Wales, where the air had a gem-like clarity, she disliked it even more.

For the next half hour, Jude hardly spoke, but just smiled, nodded, or looked interested when she hoped it was appropriate. There was no pause in the general hubbub, or any sense of anyone even listening to what anyone else said. Stella, sweating, stirred pots, cut more bread, and dressed salads over near the sink with her back to everyone, but took almost no part in the conversation. She looked ill at ease, even from behind, Jude decided. How could she call these awful women "friends"? They were her contemporaries, sure, as they were clearly in their late fifties, but they had nothing in common with Stella at all.

Having said that, she knew that she had met lots of people just like them in Oxford. Alex had always called them the "back-to-the-studio-for-some-more-news-about-me" brigade. They'd usually worn pricey brands, had children called Tilly, Millie, and Ollie at expensive private schools, and were always having building work done on their houses. She had told Stella about these people, and her friend had laughed in knowing recognition, and yet here were more of them, sitting around her table in Wales, wearing a slightly baggier, blander uniform.

The conversation ranged from marriage, the menopause, and men's middle-age paunches to the dire state of Bangor High Street and the amount of bad buskers until, after several bottles of wine, it veered off into areas that Jude felt were far too personal to tell someone they had never met before, and induced embarrassed blushes she was glad nobody could see. The Fearsome Foursome would never have overshared, or behaved like this, to a woman they barely knew, experts in Prosecco consumption as they indubitably were.

"I've decided to take up spinning," said one woman Jude had managed to recall was "Bex".

"Ah, spinning. Exercise bike, or wool?" added one called Maddie, looking around to see who thought she was funny. Everyone seemed to, except Jude, who had not been listening.

"I found a gorgeous old spinning wheel in one of our outhouses, and Mike says he can make it work again," Bex shouted above the returning murmur of conversation. She *really* wanted everyone to listen to her.

"Well, I remember when David restored the kids' bikes from ones we'd found at the tip," chipped in Isabel. She had five children and had moved here from Bristol, but Jude had completely forgotten why, if she'd ever been told. "Result!"

"Yes, you've become a real native, Issie. Do you eat meat pies and shop in Poundland now too?" Bex replied, with a sour look on her face.

There was a brief silence during which Stella coughed very near the salad bowl and the others flinched in disapproval. Jude could feel her friend's embarrassment from across the room, and she shared it; this was excruciating in every way. Isabel moved the conversation on to the weather in North Wales (always raining), the locals (monosyllabic, in either Welsh or English), and the schools (a bear-pit). Finally, she got onto her allotment, and expounded on how much her children had enjoyed growing things and how hard it had been to find an allotment up here.

"In Bristol, it's easy. Everyone has one."

"Surprise, surprise," Maddie said. "Everything was easier back in the civilised world."

Focusing on the tiles above Stella's oven, Jude breathed in very deeply in an attempt to zone out. Never had "beaming-up" seemed like a more attractive prospect. Spouses' jobs or not, she wondered why these women were all still here if they hated it so much. They had done nothing but complain about everything the area had to offer, and if they'd done so from the start, and openly, she was quite sure it had not helped them settle or be accepted here. She decided to focus on eating something quickly and then making a swift exit, but after a few minutes, she sensed a new atmosphere: it was very quiet, and everyone was looking at her.

"Sorry?" she blurted. "Did you say something to me?"

"We did indeed. Time to tell us a bit about *you*, Jude," said Bex with a smile she probably intended to be kindly. "We've done all the talking so far."

"Oh. Right. Nothing much to tell, really," Jude said, aware of how rude she sounded. Bottoms rustled and shifted on chairs.

"She only meant why you came *here*, of all places?" Maddie said, blinking stupidly. She had drunk the most wine and was still going. "Stella tells us that you moved from Oxford. Now why on earth would a young woman like you do a thing like that?"

Cackles of laughter from around the table. Jude found herself wondering if she would be like these women in twenty years' time. It was not a pleasant possibility.

"Stella talks of nothing else but 'my brilliant friend Jude' these days," added Bex, mimicking Stella's broad Porthcawl accent with a smile. "We hardly see anything of her." Her dark eyes glittered, and Jude had a sudden memory of the insects in *James and the Giant Peach*.

"You know all about us," added Meg, leaning forward onto one elbow, expectantly. "We need to get to know *you* a little."

Jude gulped. Yes, she did know a lot about these women, all of which she wished she didn't. She knew that Maddie had an enlarged vulva, which caused her to be in a permanent state of arousal. She knew that Bex and her husband had hardly spoken for two months after he had had a fling with their daughter's riding instructor. She had heard all about Isabel's unbearable-sounding children and their endless achievements, and how her eldest daughter was anorexic.

"Jude came here for some peace and quiet, as a change from Oxford after, well, after..." Stella said, her eyes wide with panic. She looked like a goldfish in a bowl... a terrified one.

"You came for a new start?" Maddie said, draining her glass. "We wish."

"It must be soooooo hard, on your own, though," Bex added. "We were all so sad to hear about your loss."

A low murmuring around the table told Jude that the women were now expressing sympathy.

"Having a husband and kids aren't always the easy option you know," Bex added bitterly. "I should know."

More cackling. Jude now visualised a coven of witches, in tents.

"Perhaps you need to meet someone new," Maddie said.

"Slim pickings up here on the relationship front," Isabel said. "It's a good thing you haven't got kids, though; they make it even harder, believe me."

Jude felt sick to her stomach as she realised that Stella had obviously discussed her life, her "losses", in detail, and that she'd become "a topic of conversation". What exactly did they know about her? Did they know about her fertility problems or her longing for a child? Had her friend gossiped about what she only now realised was her greatest fear, that she would never love or be loved again? That sent a shot of horror through her, acid-sharp. For Jude, trusting Stella had not been easy, and now she felt that her trust had been betrayed in the cruellest of ways, and that her unbearable struggles were just a tasty snippet of gossip. She stood up and put both palms flat on the table. Her voice, when she spoke, was so low and calm and strong that she hardly recognised it as her own.

"Let me confirm the juiciest details for you, ladies. I came here because my husband died of cancer last year, as you clearly already know. We weren't actually able to have children, as you probably also know, as our genes were deemed 'incompatible'. Yes, I'm completely on my own, but I don't want to meet someone new. I don't need a man to be happy. I don't need anyone." Jude hoped they had not heard her voice quaver as she said these last four words.

"We all need to be loved, Jude," Stella said softly.

Jude stared at her, aghast. "Stella, I really, really loved my husband. He was kind, interesting, and we were faithful to each other in every way, even until death." She paused. Tears were very near now. "And I think it's unbearably cruel that he's dead when idiots like you are still alive."

She surveyed the circle of open mouths around her.

"Thanks for lunch, Stella. I'll see you at Welsh."

"I'm so sorry, Jude..." she mumbled. "It wasn't... I did warn you... shall we...?"

Jude left the house without a backward glance.

THIRTEEN

She slept very little that night. The shock of Stella's betrayal, coupled with disappointment that the Tregarth women had proved so toxic, so far from her sensitive, kind Oxford friends, hit her very hard. Jude felt a familiar stab of guilt at how she had ghosted them all when she'd first come to the island, and how worried they must have been about her. The feeling that she could no longer see Stella as any kind of soulmate was acutely painful, but it was the realisation that they'd struck a raw nerve in saying she needed to "meet someone new" that had stung her most of all. Were they right? Is that why she was still so unhappy, a year after Alex's death? Doubting all her bereavement counsellor had told her about the passage of time and the healing force of nature, she strode alone along the beach once more, railing at the sky.

"How dare they tell me what I need, what I want?"
"What do they know about grief or loss?"
"Their kid failing a violin exam is their idea of a tragedy!"
"I refuse to be judged by The Tented Coven!"

. . .

Stella called at *Hedd* the next afternoon, after her shift at the care home. If there had been anywhere for Jude to hide when she saw her car pull up, she would have done so. She was so deeply hurt by what had happened that she could see no way their friendship could survive it.

"I came to explain, Jude. So that at least you know my side of things."

She looked ashen. Her orange hair was scraped off her face into a scrawny ponytail, exposing at least an inch of white roots. She was wearing old jeans, black boots, and a baggy black jumper full of holes. Jude had no intention of asking her inside, and so they stood on the doorstep in an awkward face-off.

"I don't think there's much you can say, Stella," Jude said. "You made me into gossip fodder. How could you do that? I'd never even met those awful women before yesterday, but they knew about Alex, about... *my personal affairs*." She paused. Stella looked as if she was about to cry, and Jude, too, could feel the prick of tears. "I trusted you when I told you those things. I thought you were my friend."

"I am your friend! And I knew you would hate those women, but you *insisted* on meeting them," Stella said. "I'm really sorry I told them anything, but believe me when I tell you that all I ever said was that your husband had died a year ago, that you had no kids, and that I thought you should get out more, perhaps even meet someone else. And I *do* think that, Jude!" She paused, but when no response came, gabbled on. "For instance, Dominic's really nice, you know. Anyone who loves goats as much as he does has got to be a gentle and kind..."

"Will you shut up about bloody Dominic! I didn't come here for a man, Stella, let alone a smelly, badly dressed one who keeps goats! You know that. I came here to be left alone, so please leave me ALONE!"

Stella winced. "I know that you think that, but you will always be alone if you don't at least try to rejoin the world, Jude.

Welsh class with a load of pensioners and me really doesn't count as living life!" She grabbed one of Jude's hands, but she yanked it away.

"Stop telling me what I want!" Jude shouted. "I don't want a man! I had the best one ever, and he left me, forever. He was everything to me, but he *died.*" She was sobbing now, head in her hands.

Stella came closer and wrapped her arms around her.

"I know. And it's truly terrible, but it's more than a year since he died now, and your life has to go on."

Jude snapped her head up and glared at her. "A year is nothing. *Nothing*, do you hear me? Three hundred and sixty-five endless, terrible days, that's all this year has been for me."

"I know it probably feels like that, but it's as if you've, well, set your course, Jude – made up your mind to be alone forever, never to love anyone else, even though so much of you wants to, I know." She paused again, and then went on, her voice softer, gentler. "And I also know that's why you were so upset with me and those awful women, because there was truth in what they said to you. Everyone needs to love and be loved."

"You said that, because you're kind, but they didn't say anything kindly, did they? They were so... *probing.*"

Stella sighed. "I agree. But they are as they are for many reasons. We met when we were all fairly new up here, out of context, adrift in confusion and regret, and we sort of bonded out of lack of choice and clung to each other like some kind of life raft. Now, we've moved apart and have nothing in common except the past. They're snobs, they look down on me, and they're pretty insensitive, but they're *human*, Jude. We all have faults and regrets."

Jude wiped her face roughly with the back on one hand. "They had plenty of both, that's for sure."

"Forget about them. I care about *you*," Stella replied. "You're cutting yourself off from new possibilities by being like this, and life is short. If the oldies in that bloody home have taught me anything, it's that."

Jude felt her anger ebb a little and she looked at her friend directly for the first time.

"But I'm scared, Stella," she whispered. "I don't even know who to *be* anymore. It's so hard, to feel as if you're always on your own, even when you're with other people."

"Oh, I know it is. I deleted myself from my own life, remember? I do understand and I do know that feeling of isolation even in a crowd."

"I know you do, and I am truly sorry for that, but my life was deleted for me in a few, awful weeks. At least you had a bit of a chance to prepare yourself, and to know that what you were leaving behind hadn't made you happy," Jude said. "All I'm trying to say is that it felt as if those women were sniffing for meat to put on the bones of bare gossip, and it was, well, *traumatising*."

"I know, and I'm more sorry than I can ever say for what happened, Jude. But they're scared and unhappy, too, you know, under all that talk and bravado. And remember – their biggest dread is that you'll be happier here than they are."

A long silence, until Jude said, "That doesn't excuse their behaviour."

"It doesn't, you're right. But perhaps it *explains* it a bit."

Jude sighed. "Yes," she said, and paused. "I don't know what to do, Stella. That's the problem. I can't go back, I know that, however much I miss my friends, but I sometimes feel that I can't stay here either."

"You can, but you might need to change the channel, if you see what I mean," Stella said, sitting down nervously on the bench outside the cottage door and waiting while Jude did the same. "Look, Welsh lessons and our weekly chinwags are a start, but perhaps we could invite Dominic along too, as our friend, to expand things a little for us both, help us make more connections. He's a sweet man, and I think he's a bit lost even if you can't bring yourself to fancy him." She winked at Jude, who shook her head. "Walking with Menna is good, but I do feel that you need to, well, dip your toe in the water a bit more. 'Life is out there' and all that tosh."

"I'd hoped to dip my toe in new friendships yesterday – and look how that turned out!"

"Very badly, yes, but really you're still hiding, aren't you, closed-in with your grief and lashing out at anyone who pokes at the bars of your cage?" Stella said. "Including me."

Both women said nothing for several minutes, and the only sound was the soft splashing of the gentle waves on the shore below them.

"Coffee?" Jude said, eventually, with a weak but genuinely warm smile.

"Only if I know you understand – a bit, at least."

"I think I do, and I'm sorry for lashing out at you," Jude answered. "But I will only fully forgive you if you a) stop trying to matchmake me and Dominic and b) permanently upgrade to a better class of friend as of today. Like *moi*."

Stella nodded her unhesitating agreement.

FOURTEEN

One glorious Thursday afternoon at the end of May, as Jude was filling an old sink she'd found behind the cottage with bedding plants to add some colour to the little garden, a large lorry pulled up on the road beside *Hedd*. Two men climbed out of it and grunted a greeting in Welsh. She returned it with a strained smile. It looked like the building work was beginning today.

"So much for 'liaising about a start date'," she muttered.

"Hi. We'll just get on, if that's OK," one of the men said, clearly intending to even if it *wasn't*. "You'd better stay inside until we're finished."

Within hours, *Hedd* was completely covered with a web of metal poles and wooden planks, and every room was dark, as the scaffolding cut out more and more light. Radio music blasted through the open doorway so loudly that Jude had to shut it, and she began to feel like a prisoner in her own home. Going out risked getting in their way, or getting clobbered by a metal pole, and staying in was claustrophobically horrible.

But she stayed inside all day. When, at 5pm, one of the men knocked on her door and told her that they were leaving, Jude saw that her garden was littered with scaffolding brackets, discarded poles and muddy skids where they had been dragged across the grass. Her sink full of flowers was buried under a big oilcloth banner with *Seren Scaffolding* on it.

"Bit of a mess. Sorry about that," the man muttered, pulling the banner off the sink roughly and tying it, crookedly, to the scaffolding poles.

"Could you try to keep it tidy? And do you think you could manage without the radio on tomorrow, or at least have it on a bit quieter?" she said, her voice shaking. This place was her sanctuary, and she felt as threatened as any vixen protecting her den.

"Oh, we're not doing the roof, love. We just do scaffolding. The builders will be here next week." He raised his hand, walked towards the lorry, and drove away. Imagining their conversation about "that English cow" all too vividly, she burst into helpless tears. Her instinctive, immediate reaction was to drive to Rhosneigr, where she could call Tom.

"Tom, sorry to bother you at work, but I agreed to let them do the roof while I'm here over the summer, but I think it's going to be awful, and I don't know if I can..." Her sobs overtook her.

"Hey, sssssssh, I can't understand you, Jude," he said, battling against a cacophony of voices in the office. "It's busy here today. Call you back in five mins, OK? I'll find somewhere quiet."

His voice was calm and steady, as it had been through the final, ghastly days and nights at the hospice. Then he had gently tended to her as if she were a child as she wept and railed against what was happening to Alex. When he rang her back, she didn't hesitate.

"Tom, can you come up this weekend?" she blurted. "I know I keep telling you I'm fine, but I had a horrible experience with some nasty women last week, and a friend has let me down, and now this, and the roofing work is going to start on Monday... I just feel... I can't take any more!" Again, she broke down.

"I'll be there late tonight, and I can talk to the roofing people on Monday. I'll let you know when I set off, and when I should reach you." He paused. "Jude, would it be OK with you if I ride the Harley up? She really needs a good run..."

Jude froze. Could she actually bear to see another man on Alex's beloved bike, even it was Tom Byers? How would it feel to hear that engine's low roar, to smell those familiar fumes in the air once more? After a few seconds, she knew she had to accept it, however. Tom was right, the Harley needed to be ridden. "Sure," she said.

"Great. Look, we'll sort this out, we've been through far worse than this together, haven't we?"

His words washed over her like a warm bath, and she felt her body begin to relax muscle by muscle.

"Yes, we have. Thanks, Tom," she said softly. "I feel so alone sometimes."

"You won't be for much longer. I'll go home now, pack, and set off. It will be wonderful to see you, and spend some time together, just like old days," he replied.

Any niggling reservations Jude had had about relying too much on Tom, and what he might want from her, evaporated. He was a dear, dear friend, and she told herself firmly that he knew that. She was overthinking things, as she so often did. Right now, she needed comfort, trust, and someone with a clear head, and he offered all of them.

Several hours later, Jude was considerably less relaxed. It was almost 8pm by the time Jude heard Tom arrive on the Harley. Her eyes immediately filled with tears at the sound of it. As she listened to him turn off the engine, lock the bike, and remove his luggage from the top box, she had had time to a) calm down, b) have another momentary panic about seeing Alex's beloved bike again, and c) get very nervous indeed about how it was all going to work with Tom here all weekend. She'd cooked a chilli for supper, but she still had a niggling concern that the cottage only had one bedroom and a very small and uncomfortable sofa bed. As they both knew how things stood, however, she was sure everything would be absolutely fine.

Heart pounding, she waited inside in silence, until she heard Tom crunch up the shingle path and rap on the door. It crossed her mind for a second or two that she could adopt Gloria's "ignore it" technique and he might go away, but that possibility popped like a bubble when she heard him say, with his familiar almost-boyish shyness:

"Jude? Am I in the right place? Are you in there?"

She opened the door, smiling, and was confronted with a bunch of gorgeous, if slightly squashed, flowers. Above them was a grinning Tom, his blonde hair flopping over one side of his face just as she imagined it had done when he was in the cricket team at school.

"Sorry, probably not the most sensible gift to bring on the back of a bike," he said, placing the flowers very carefully on the ground. When Jude felt herself being wrapped in his arms and she inhaled the musky, familiar smell of him, a tide of sheer relief washed over her, and she felt safer than she had done in a very long time. She invited him in quickly, catching only a passing glimpse of the Harley; it looked absolutely immaculate.

Once Tom had carried his bags, the flowers, and two bottles of wine inside, he seemed restless, even a little nervous. They'd known each other for many years, but had rarely been alone together for very long, let alone just the two of them for a whole weekend. He paced around the tiny cottage as if checking an inventory, and as it was so small, that didn't take long, which left him even more restless. Pip yipped and scampered around his feet, and he tried to disguise his irritation: Tom was not a dog-person, in any way, and she could see him guiltily sniffing within ten minutes of arriving, as his allergy took hold. Trying to be upbeat, nonetheless, he told Jude that he'd loved being responsible for the Harley, and that she'd run like a dream all the way here. He also said he'd eaten en route, which meant that the reassuringly everyday event of eating her chilli was off the agenda. She hadn't got a TV, and her eclectic music choice was very far from his, she'd discovered years ago, and the silence soon began to feel awkward. What on earth should they do now? Jude wondered.

"Shall we go for a swim in the sea?" Tom said, just as she was considering broaching the subject of sleeping arrange-ments. Perhaps that was at the root of his anxiety, as it was defi-nitely the main source of hers.

She hesitated. "What, now? It's getting dark, and I, well, haven't actually been in the water here at all yet," she replied, immediately aware of how weedy that sounded. "It's been too cold; it's been winter, you see."

"Oh, OK then. Just thought it might be a fun thing to do," Tom said, his face a picture of boyish disappointment. "I thought 'wild swimming' was all the rage these days."

Jude stood up suddenly and stamped her foot on the floor. "It is, and you're right. It would be fun. So let's do it!"

Tom laughed, an easy, honeyed sound that filled the room and made her realise how much she had missed a man's company. He was not Alex, but his presence was so very comforting.

"Great," he said. "But let's drink a toast to 'The New Jude', to give ourselves a bit of courage before braving those Welsh waves, eh?"

And so, half a bottle of Prosecco later, they raced down onto the beach like excitable children and ran, unhesitatingly, into the water. It was freezing cold, but surrendering to the sea felt wonderful, and as darkness slowly fell and the surface of the sea became a wide, black slick around them, Jude knew that she had not felt this happy, this alive, since her husband had died.

FIFTEEN

The very last thing Jude had intended to do was sleep with Tom, but looking back, it had been inevitable. They'd run out of the sea and up to *Hedd* like pink-skinned chipolatas, and scrubbed themselves dry before the glow of the booze was conquered by the chill of the water. They were ravenous now, so they gobbled the chilli Jude had cooked, and tore off hunks of the fresh bread from her favourite Oxford bakery that Tom has brought with him, to mop up the sauce. Another bottle of wine was opened, and soon drunk. It felt so good to really relax, Jude thought, looking over at her old friend who seemed just as happy as she felt.

"You remembered I loved that bakery," she murmured. "That's so kind of you."

"Yup. I even picked up some of their croissants, as I knew they were your favourite weekend breakfast," Tom replied, adding, "Yours and Alex's of course," in a quieter voice.

Jude took a large gulp of wine, and he topped up her glass immediately.

"I miss him desperately," she said. "But somehow, having you here, it feels as if he's here with us again, doesn't it?"

Tom nodded. "Yes. He would like us to be... together like this, I think."

"Would he? Do you really think so?" Jude replied, hearing the doubt in her own voice. "I don't know what I think, really, whether he would..."

Tom laid a hand gently over one of hers. "For now, let's just enjoy each other's company and take comfort in that."

But later, Tom came to sit next to her on the sofa, where she had retreated with Pip to try and sober up a little and think clearly. He handed her a coffee, and then turned to face her. He was flushed, nervous, and Jude knew, without a flicker of doubt, what was coming next.

"Jude, you know I have always... *cared* about you, don't you? You know that when you chose Alex, I accepted it – of course I did – but my feelings for you never changed because you married him. Like me, they waited for this time, this moment in both our lives," he said.

Jude said nothing but felt the silence press on her temples like huge, strong hands. Breathing deeply, she could not risk replying as she had no idea what she would say. She would stay quiet and wait for all this to pass instead, as surely it would if she did not react or respond?

"I know how much you miss him. I miss him too, every single day, but for us, there's a second chance," Tom whispered, stroking her cheek. "I am so very fond of you, and I want to be with you, Jude. I can take care of you, and make sure you never feel lonely again."

As she felt his arm snake around her shoulders, Jude focused on putting her coffee cup safely on the floor. When she looked up again, Tom's face was inches away, and then his lips were touching hers. She closed her eyes and let him kiss her, long and slow, and she felt a familiar tingling beginning between her legs. This man smelt so familiar, sounded so familiar, and reminded her of such happy times that she did not stop him peeling off her clothes and lying her down on the sofa. As he entered her, she kept her eyes closed and imagined another time, another face rising and falling above her, gently making love to her as he had done so many times.

"Alex," she said into his hair, a soft whisper. "My darling."

But Tom did not hear her. Afterwards, they lay in silence, until she heard the rhythm of his breathing change and become slower, more relaxed. Covering him with a blanket, she went off to sleep in her bed.

The next morning, Jude was awake before dawn, her head pounding both with regret and the amount of wine she'd drunk after months without any alcohol. Slowly and deliberately, she laid the breakfast things out on the little dining table in her kitchen, placing plates, cups, and knives for this second person in her cottage, this man. How she wished it had been her husband, but if last night had confirmed anything, it was that Alex was gone and she would never, ever make love with him again. Tom, this kind, loving friend she had known for as long as she had known her husband, was here however, saying that he wanted her and would care for her as Alex would have done. So why did she want him to leave without saying a word about what had happened last night?

The rest of that weekend passed slowly and painfully, as Tom realised that Jude could never return his feelings for her. He slept on the sofa bed. They walked miles of the coastal path, picnicked in secluded coves, and talked for hours about the past, and the future, as she made it as clear as she could that she could never love him. It was almost impossible to get him to believe it.

"I needed some comfort, and you gave it. Maybe, just

maybe, you needed some too," she said, as she saw his face fall. "I know that's not enough for you, but that's all I can offer. We can never have a relationship, Tom, and I think I can never love you as you want me to," she found herself saying eventually, when subtlety seemed to have no effect. "I'm truly sorry."

"Well, then comfort will have to do. I can't make you love me right now, Jude, but I hope you will one day," Tom told her as they sat outside her cottage watching the sun set on their final evening together. "I know you chose Alex back then, but I always felt I came a pretty close second."

An awkward silence fell where he clearly hoped some reassurance would be. Jude remembered the terrible conversation in the pub, where she had told Tom, all those years ago, that she wanted to marry Alex, not him. He'd cried like a child, and his suffering had almost broken her heart.

"I know you think that, and I remember how... *fraught* it all got between the three of us back then, but right now, what I need most is your help in a more practical way," she said as kindly as she could. "I'm a bit swamped, Tom, I really am, and I could do with some advice from an old friend on how to cope with these bloody builders."

"Ah yes, the builders," he replied, with a sigh. "Of course."

"I know they're replacing the roof, and it will be a bit chaotic, but the scaffolders didn't show any respect for the fact that I live here, and that's what got me into such a state last week," she said. "How do I establish some boundaries? It's going to be a long project and, I mean, I'm living here on my own and..."

Tom shook his head. "Look, Jude, I have to say this. Are you absolutely sure you want to stay here over the summer whilst they rip this place apart around you? It will be noisy and messy and probably hard to live with. You could come back to Oxford with me and..."

"I can't go back yet, Tom. I can't. I need to stay here," Jude replied without hesitation.

Another painful silence. Jude hated hurting him, as she knew she was doing, but she couldn't force herself to love him. She needed his help and his friendship now more than ever.

"I see. Right, then we'll have to draw up some 'rules of engagement' for the builders, but I do need to set off really early tomorrow. I can't hang on until they arrive. I'll get the train and leave the Harley here with you. I'm sure you can find somewhere safe to keep her, and she belongs here with you now, I think."

Jude noted that he had changed his mind about staying to speak to them in person, but she understood. He was deeply hurt, and she wished with all her heart that she could rewind time back to Friday afternoon and do things differently. She said nothing about the Harley, or her concerns that it would quickly rust in the sea air, as he clearly wanted to leave it here. It marked a kind of ending between them.

"OK. I understand why you need to go, but I want you to know, Tom, that your advice will be always invaluable to me," she said. "And your friendship."

PART 3

EXPECT THE UNEXPECTED

SIXTEEN

Tom was true to his word and helped Jude write a list setting out some pointers for the builders in the morning, before they started work, based on what she'd told him mattered to her:

- Please respect my privacy
- Please keep noise to a minimum
- Please clear up at the end of each day
- Please don't squash my flowers

It all sounded simple enough, but she felt better waving goodbye to him at 5.30am armed with his suggestions. By 8am, there was still no sign of anyone starting any work, so she set off through the dunes with Pip, ranting about "bloody unreliable builders".

About an hour later, as she walked through the dunes to *Hedd*, she saw a red van parked outside and a man clambering across the roof. To the left of the cottage, another lorry was lowering a skip onto the grass. She quickened her pace, she had to tell them how she wanted things to be before they turned their music up to maximum.

When she opened the garden gate, she saw line upon line of new slates propped against her wall like a neat little army. The scaffolding poles and brackets had been picked up, too, and laid down on one side of her lawn. Some hands were tying a yellow plastic chute to the top layer of scaffolding, but she could not see who they belonged to. Edging closer, Jude saw a man's head appear behind the chute, a piece of orange string between his teeth. He had a very ruddy complexion and a mop of sun-streaked curls. It was Owain Pritchard, and he was smiling at her.

"Oh – *helô*/hello. *Sut dach chi?*/How are you?" He looked at Pip and smiled. "He looks well. It's good to see that," he said.

Jude struggled to respond. Of all the things she had antici-pated, she had not expected Owain Pritchard to be repairing her roof. Wasn't he a *farmer*?

"Pip, oh yes, he's been a godsend, honestly. I can't thank you enough for bringing him to me," she said, feeling more than a little flustered.

"One good deed deserves another, Mrs Fitzgerald. I'd kill for a *panad*/cuppa. I'll just finish tying this, and then I'll come down."

"A *panad*? Sure, yes. It's good to see you again, Owain, but, well, I assume you've done this kind of work before?" Jude stut-tered. "Oh, and do call me Jude."

Owain looked at her quizzically. Because he was so tall and had to look down at her, Jude suddenly felt as if she was somehow under observation, exposed beneath the microscope of his piercing gaze. "I do any kind of work that pays me, but, since you ask, yes, I've done a few slate roofs, so I do know what I'm doing, yes," he said.

"Great, fine. I just feel that we do need to sort a few ground rules out before you start," she said, knowing how pompous this all sounded as soon as she'd said it.

"You mean whether you need to be dressed when I arrive

each day?" he replied with a wink. "*Does dim ots gen i*/It doesn't matter to me."

"No, I mean…"

"Will I do my best to do a good job and make this as quick and painless an experience for you as possible? Yes, I will," he said.

"Good. So, how long do you think the job will take?" she asked, trying to hold on to some semblance of the poise and control she had intended to convey.

"About a week, give or take, but there's internal repairs to do as well once the roof's fixed," was his reply. "Two weeks max. That suit you?"

Realising that the bullet pointed list from Tom was now a) silly and b) obsolete, Jude nodded meekly and went inside to put the kettle on.

Although it was strange to hear someone spidering across her roof and tossing old slates to the ground with a crash, Jude soon found Owain's presence strangely comforting. When Tom texted her mid-morning:

How's it going? I miss you already.

All fine, thanks again for all your help. I really appreciate it

She knew with absolute certainty that she had made the right decision to turn him down. If she was to love again, it had to be the right man, at the right time. Tom, right now, was neither.

At lunchtime, Owain let a beautiful Welsh collie out of his van, and she shot out and headed straight for the sea. Pip followed, bouncing up and snapping at her ears and tail. Jude came out of the cottage, and they both watched their dogs play on the beach below like proud parents.

"Make a good pair, don't they?" the man said. "*Mawr a bach*/Little and large."

"They do indeed," Jude replied, realising as she looked up at this huge man that the epithet could apply to them too. Owain really did tower over her, just as Alex had done. It crossed her mind that perhaps she had a weird "thing" for men over six feet because she certainly found him very attractive, as she had her husband. She pushed the thought away before give-away blushes overcame her. "What's her name – your dog?"

"Meg," he replied. "And she's my best friend in the world. Well, my only friend, in fact."

When Jude heard his words, and the hollow laugh that followed, she sensed a sadness beneath them. Hadn't Menna said that this man came with plenty of baggage? For the first time, she allowed herself to wonder what that might be.

"That's a beautiful Harley over there," Owain said. "She needs to be kept out of the salty air, though, or she'll rust in no time. I've got a good, strong cover I can bring over tomorrow if you like. My younger brother had a motorbike once."

Jude noticed that this man, like Alex and Tom, fondly called the Harley "she", which pleased her. She also noted a more subdued tone in his voice when he mentioned his brother, but knew better than to ask personal questions, having been the recipient of so many herself of late.

When Menna called later for their daily walk, Jude felt the need to introduce her to Owain, in case she knew of him (and had thus felt free to expound upon his character, as everyone did up here), but had never actually met him (which was not a necessary criterion for expressing a view on someone). Her courtesy was totally unnecessary.

"Oh, I know this one all right," Menna said, grinning. "We

go way back. *Sut wyt ti, Owain? Go lew*?/How are you, Owen? Not too bad?"

For the next couple of minutes, they talked so loudly, and so fast, that Jude was unsure whether they were speaking Welsh or English; they wove the words of both languages so closely together. She hardly understood any of it.

"We went to school together," Menna summarised.

"*You* went to school, Menna..." Owain added sheepishly. "I was probably up to no good somewhere else."

He released a burst of real laughter now, which made Jude smile.

"Have you heard any of Jude's Welsh yet, Owain?" Menna asked. "She's learning, going to classes in Bangor."

"Is she now? *Wel, wel*/Well, well. No. Not had that privilege yet. Don't think she knows quite what to make of me at the moment." He winked at her.

There was a slight frisson in the air, and Jude felt Owain watching her closely, as if judging how she was going to react. He was right, there was something about this unpredictable man that completely disarmed her.

"I'll need my Welsh to improve pretty fast to understand you two!" she said with a nervous laugh. "Shall we go, Menna?"

The two dogs raced up the beach, and Owain shut Meg back in his van in case she followed them.

As they set off, Menna took Jude's arm and murmured, "Be careful with him. I know I told you that before, but remember that he may be a big boy, but he's very easily hurt."

"What do you mean?"

"I just mean he has a difficult life, and all that winking and laughing is a front to hide it. That's all I'm saying. You have been warned."

Jude wanted nothing more than to fire questions at Menna about Owain and his "difficult life", but she bit her tongue. If she was meant to know more, she would, in good time. He fascinated her already.

SEVENTEEN

Owain Pritchard and his red van arrived at 8am exactly every morning. As the island slid slowly into the heat of summer, the sun shone with a brilliance Jude found hard to believe when she remembered the relentless gloom and unending rain of the winter. By the end of his first week, she was standing on the doorstep as he pulled up each day, pointing to Alex's – now-repaired – watch on her wrist, and saying, "*Eto, ar y dot*/Again, on the dot."

She was no longer, technically, alone all day, and that simple fact lifted her spirits enormously. She smiled when she heard him scrabbling across the roof, and *Hedd* now seemed too quiet during the long, light evenings after he'd left. She made him a drink when she was doing so for herself, and, on hot days, they took turns to buy each other a whippy ice cream from the van in the beach car park. They laughed when they realised a) that they both loved lashings of additive-rich raspberry sauce on their cornets, and b) decided this was probably because they had never been allowed any such "unnecessary" treats in childhood. After a few days, as Jude became more used to Owain's strong accent and slightly "off-the-wall" humour, they spoke to each other using an easy mix of both their mother tongues. Jude had heard local people blend their Welsh with English words and marvelled at the ease with which they did so. This man was particularly skilled at weaving them together, so much so that she soon stopped noticing which language he was using.

"Isn't it called 'Wenglish', when people use English words in the middle of a Welsh sentence?" she asked him one day.

"I think it's just the language expanding and evolving, as it needs to do," Owain replied. "It has to be a living thing, a language, I believe – not a monument set in stone. Do you agree?"

She agreed. It was brilliant to be able to speak the limited Welsh she had learnt, freely and without fear of her tutor's piercing glare when she made a mistake.

"It'll look lovely, with these beauties on the roof," Owain said to her one morning, pointing at the neat rows of new slates that had been delivered a few days earlier. "It deserves the best, this little place. Welsh slates are more expensive than Spanish ones but much better."

"*Mae'n wir iawn*/That's true indeed," Jude answered. "I'm glad you're using local slates. I love looking at the seams of colour in each one, with all their blobs and blotches."

"Yes, they tell a story, I always think. A story of millennia spent under the ground, waiting for their moment to shine. We all wait for that, don't we? That time when we can be our true selves and proud of it."

A pause, as she recognised that he had chosen his words with care.

"Don't you think the name of this place suits it? I used to come here as a boy, on my bike. *Hedd* was always a place of such peace."

"It's a very special place, for sure," she replied.

Owain, happy with her answer, started sweeping up, and as she watched him, Jude realised that she felt completely at ease in this man's company and could be "her true self" with him. He reminded her of Alex with his caustic wit and in his willingness to *listen* as well as to talk – a rare quality indeed. Somehow, having this tall, kind man around all day every day felt like slipping back into a comfortable domestic routine she had all but forgotten. She found herself hoping that the job took as many days as possible.

After her initiation into wild swimming with Tom, Jude swam in the sea almost every day. In fact, she wondered why she had wasted so many months not doing so. She became proud of her toned, slim body and tried as hard as she could to love it again, despite what it had failed to give her. The sea around the island changed colour and mood, it seemed, every single time she went into it, and the feeling of abandoning herself to its constant movement was the nearest she could come to bliss. The little cove below her cottage was rarely susceptible to the powerful riptides that harrowed a path along some of the coastline. Sometimes, in the semi-darkness of a summer night, she swam naked, feeling the water caress every part of her without guilt or shame, under a wide, velvety sky just prickling with stars.

One Saturday morning, with a whole empty weekend stretching ahead, she decided to go to Aberffraw for a swim. A glorious sandy bay fringed with grassy dunes, this was one of the most beautiful beaches on the island and one of the least crowded as it was a long walk from the car park if you were laden with blow-up boats, windbreakers, paddleboards, and picnic clobber. Only the most dedicated of beach-lovers bothered.

It was a startlingly sunny day, and the sand sparkled, reflecting the light from a cloudless sky. Pip scampered ahead as Jude searched along the tideline for perfect shells or bleached-white driftwood. There were a few people on the beach but not many. When she reached the rocks on the far side of the bay, clouds had begun to gather overhead and a brisk breeze began to blow sending the top layer of dry sand careening down the beach and into Pip's eyes, so she walked back to the more sheltered side of the bay where a wide channel ran between the rocks and the open sea. The tide was on the turn now, and the suck and drag of the water left scores of hermit crabs scrabbling for a foothold in the sand.

Changing into her bathing suit quickly, she walked towards the sea with the confident, easy stride she'd adopted to help her suppress any doubt whatsoever that she really was going into the always-bracing water. As the cold reached her thighs, she felt the power of it on her skin, swirling around her as the outgoing tide fought for dominance over the incoming one that had preceded it. The waves grew higher, deeper, and once they had crashed over her, the water rolled back with such force that she almost lost her footing once or twice. Whorls of seaweed eddied past her as she swam a few strokes before feeling herself being sucked out into deeper and deeper water with each incoming belt of waves. This was different, Jude realised, struggling to make headway. Today, the sea did not feel like her friend at all.

She tried to steady herself, to plant her feet and wade back into shallower water but could not. Instead, she was carried further out, deeper than she had ever been before and too deep for her to touch the seabed. The current was incredibly powerful now, and the surface of the water around her had a strange, oily sheen as it swirled around her flailing body. This was a riptide. The moment she became aware that she was in danger was not a split second, but protracted, as if in slow motion, as she watched the beach retreat a little further from her very gradually, until she could hardly make out Pip barking frantically at the water's edge. Finally, instinct kicked in.

"Help!" she shouted. "Help me!"

In the distance, she could see a man walking a dog. It was starting to drizzle now, and he was pulling up his hood, which meant he was not looking out to sea, or seeing her.

"HELP!" she screeched, her voice edged with panic as she struggled to swim nearer to the shore, but felt herself being carried inexorably away from it. Gasping as she trod water frantically, she saw Pip race over to the man's dog and start playing with it. A flash of white fur, a black tail... the dog was Meg, which could only mean that the man must be...

"OWAIN! HELP ME!!" she screamed. "I can't..." but the next wave broke over her head, swallowing her words as she sank beneath the surface.

It seemed like a lifetime until she felt a very strong arm pull her above the surface of the water, though it could only have been a minute or so. Next, she felt another arm wrap tightly around her chest and heard a man's voice, a familiar voice, through the crash of the waves.

"Let me do the work. Keep your head up, try to relax and don't fight against me."

"I... I'm sorry, so sorry," she said, as she felt his body pull hers through the water with long, steady strokes.

"Don't talk, just let me get you somewhere safe, OK?" Owain said. "Let your body go limp as if you're floating."

And so she did. When they reached the beach and he hauled her upright onto her trembling legs, she collapsed into his arms and sobbed.

"Tell me you'll never do that again – go swimming here on your own, I mean," he said, wrapping her towel around her. "The sea around this island is never predictable. You have to expect the unexpected and respect its wildness." He was trying to pull his trousers back on, hopping on one leg as he tried to aim one foot into the correct hole. Jude tried not to stare at his taut, muscled calves as he did so.

"I'm truly sorry. You must think I'm a complete idiot. Well, I guess I was," she said. "Thank goodness you were here."

"You're not the first to get into trouble on this beach, and you won't be the last. I live in that house, and I've seen it all, believe me."

Jude looked at the house he was pointing to, a large bungalow overlooking the edge of the beach. The thought that it was a family home, not that of a single man, came into her head immediately.

"Have you and your family always lived at Aberffraw?" she asked, rubbing her hair vigorously with a towel. It had stopped raining, but she felt chilled and desperate to be somewhere warm. Would he invite her back to his house for a coffee, perhaps? They had shared so many companionable coffees at *Hedd*, after all. She soon had her answer.

"Just me and my wife," he replied. "On that note, she'll be wondering where I am, so I'd better get back. Saturday's our shopping day. I hate it." Indeed, his face was a picture of misery. "You sure you're OK now?"

Jude nodded wordlessly. So he was married. He was going home to his wife, to do their weekly shop together, leaving her shivering here before going back to her roofless rented house alone. Tears pricked, and she turned away quickly. "Yep. All fine now. *Diolch*/Thanks. You saved my life."

But as he walked away across the beach, she felt that she'd lost something precious that morning: hope.

EIGHTEEN

Things were different with Owain after that day. Before it, Jude had known nothing about him. After it, she knew that he was married, which was still little enough, but changed everything. In many ways, he seemed even more relaxed with her because she now knew the truth. He still made endless wisecracks, but also seemed to want to talk to her at any opportunity about all sorts of things. To Jude, it felt as if he'd now given himself permission to be fully himself with her, because she knew he could never be more than a friend. Each day, he suggested different conversational topics, as she had seen fishermen cast flies out onto the water, to see which one she would "bite". They discussed the hypnotic fascination of sheepdog trials, the alleged corruption of the local council, and the best spots to see porpoises off the northern coast of the island. They talked about singing, and Owain confirmed her suspicion that he sang in a church choir. He told her that he had wanted to be an architect, but that "life had intervened". She told him about Alex, his life, his passion for music, his illness, his death, in the hope that he would share more personal information with her, but he did not. Instead, he returned again and again to one subject that was particularly close to his heart and that he had obviously had to keep largely secret in his daily life of manual labour: his love of poetry.

"My father Donald loved poetry too. He used to read it to me, and I loved hearing it even though I hardly ever knew what the words meant."

"R.S. Thomas is my favourite," he told her as they sat on the dunes and watched Meg and Pip play together on the beach below one gloriously sunny evening. "Not comfortable poems, though – there's plenty of rage in there. A lot of Welshmen still feel that rage, I think, and I see myself in the men he describes, toiling through life without hope."

"I confess to never having read any of his poems, but I think my dad loved them too, as I know he always loved Wales," Jude said. "I remember him talking about the 'deep soul' of the people here. Now, I know what he meant."

She was deeply touched when, a few days later, Owain handed her a thin leather-bound book, its cover and all the pages softened and stained with age. It was R.S. Thomas' *Collected Poems 1945-1990*.

"I think you will like them. I hope you will," he said. "Just to borrow, mind. First edition, that is. I'll be in big trouble if my wife ever finds out how much it cost."

Jude was speechless as she began leafing silently through the pages. "Oh listen to this!" she exclaimed. "This sounds just like you, when I first saw you!"

That bare hill with the man ploughing,
Corrugating that brown roof
Under a hard sky.

"Yes, that sounds like me," Owain said. "Grubbing a living on the land, when I had so many dreams, once…" He moved towards the door.

Jude did not feel she could ask him what those dreams were, but she could feel his disappointment like slivers of ice in the warm air.

That evening, Jude sat in her garden reading the poems in Owain's book as the bees hummed and dipped in and out of the honeysuckle 'trumpets' around her.

Alone, far from friends or family on this North Welsh island, Thomas' words arose from the page like a song, and Jude felt she really understood them. For the first time, she got a sense of how her father had felt, trapped and miserable, and why he'd escaped into these poems and, in the end, known that he had to leave her and live a different life. In many ways, she'd eclipsed their marriage, as they had fought bitterly about how to bring her up. Gloria had favoured the Methodist strictness she had grown up with, whereas Donald had wanted their girl to experience everything, to spread her wings. She had become *"the tool for hurting one another",* as Thomas put it, a weapon that had destroyed their love. Gloria blamed her for that, and for her husband leaving them for Brenda, and starting life again up in the Highlands, where his ancestors had been crofters.

"Poor Dad," she murmured. "You lived without hope until you couldn't bear it anymore, and then you left us. And Mum didn't let me see you again until you didn't even know me."

She thought of her father and mourned what she had lost, but it was Owain's voice that rang in her head as she read these soulful poems. Perhaps he was trying to tell her something by lending her this treasured book, something that he could not say to her in any other way? She heard the lilt of his accent, the rhythm of his speech, and she could see him in the quiet, strong Welshmen of Thomas' poems:

Remember him, then, for he, too, is a winner of wars,

Enduring like a tree under the curious stars.

But what was Owain enduring? She knew he was unhappy, but he had never even told her his wife's name, or whether they had any children. Why would he be spending so much time with her if his family life was good? Doubts and questions rose to the surface of her thoughts, a constant ebb and flow of wondering.

One scorching Friday afternoon, as Owain was nearing the end of the work on the cottage roof, things changed between them once more, like a subtle change of gear. Jude sat in a deckchair in the shade, fanning herself with the prize-winning South American novel she'd been vowing to read for a month, and wondering how to fill yet another lonely weekend. She'd just drifted into a doze when the sun was blocked, and she opened her eyes to see Owain standing in front of her, hands on hips. Her first thought was dread that she had been snoring and he had been watching her.

"*Reit 'ta*/Right then," he said, twirling a very faded baseball cap round and round in his left hand. "I've finished for the day. Bit early, I know, but it's Friday, so I won't start the flashing now." He paused as if he knew that what he had to say next was difficult. "Next Tuesday should see the job finished and me gone."

"Oh, OK," Jude answered. She started to get up, and Owain immediately took a step back as if he was terrified of touching her.

For a few moments, they both stood awkwardly and in silence. Just as Jude was wondering whether she should say something, and if so, what, Owain blurted, "*Gawnnifyn-damdro,osdachch'isio*/Wecouldgoforawalk,ifyoulike."

Jude's brain took several seconds to translate and separate

this slur of words. As she did so, Owain moved from foot to foot and clasped both hands behind his back as if unsure what to do with his limbs. Jude found this incredibly endearing.

Keeping her voice as casual as she could manage, she replied, "*Wrth gwrs*/Of course. I'll get Pip's lead. The dogs would certainly love a run. It's probably cooler down by the water too."

Pulling the door of *Hedd* closed behind her, she walked towards him, stopping only a few inches away. The air between them fizzed as if primed with an energy that had not been there before.

"Which direction shall we take," she said. "Cable Bay, or Rhosneigr?"

"You choose, Jude," Owain replied.

She turned to him and smiled. "Cable Bay it is, or *Porth Trecastell*, as you call it."

They set off along the coastal path together, feeling the afternoon sun warm their shoulders like a gentle hug. A noisy gaggle of oystercatchers were busy in the rock pools, where they knew the water would be full of food for them. A single, lazy seal lounged on one of the rocks below, enjoying each cool wave as it washed over its silk-smooth body.

"This place is so beautiful," Jude said, as they stood on top of the cliff and gazed out over a sea that glittered like a million silver pennies. "I never want to leave, but I guess I have to return to reality some time."

"What reality is better than this?" Owain replied. "Without your husband, or your house, is Oxford really where you'd rather be?"

She looked at him and knew with utter certainty that he did not want her to leave either, but that he would never, ever say it.

"I don't know, Owain," she replied softly. "But I'm trying to find out."

·   ·   ·

Owain finished the building work the following Tuesday, as he'd predicted. Jude returned from her Welsh revision class to find him, his dog, his tools, and his red van gone as if he had never been here at all. She looked for a note but found none, though he had left an almost-pristine motorbike cover for the Harley. He rang her that evening while she was shopping in Rhosneigr and had a signal, to tell her to get in touch if there were any problems with the roof, but their conversation was strange and stilted:

"*If I'm coming over there with Meg for a walk, I'll knock on your door,*" he said. "*Hope the bike cover does the job.*"

"Thanks for that. It would be nice to see you." A long pause. "And to give you your first edition back, of course."

"Yup. Will do. OK. *Hwyl rwan*/Bye now," he said, and hung up.

Jude felt as if she'd been punched in the belly. Whatever had been between them, if anything, was well and truly over, he was clearly telling her. When she messaged Menna to tell her that Owain had left, and that she thought something weird had happened between their lovely walk and their frosty parting, her friend's reply was cryptic:

> Owain's wife will be glad to have him back
> under her thumb. It's best to leave him there.

Reluctantly, and very sadly, Jude decided to do just that.

NINETEEN

The following week brought unsettled weather and drab, grey skies that sucked the life out of the landscape and made Jude worry that the summer on Anglesey had been and gone already. Although he'd only been coming to the cottage for just over two weeks, she opened her front door each morning expecting to see Owain, tools in hand, and couldn't suppress a nudge of disappointment when he wasn't there. Whose house was he arriving at today? Did he have a "*panad*/cuppa" with them and give his sandwich crusts to their dog too? Perhaps he even tried the "poetry trick" with all single women, she thought, in her sourest moments?

But mostly, she kept telling herself that she was silly to miss a man she still knew next to nothing about. It had been nice to have some company, and yes, they had got on very well, but he'd just been doing his job and being professional. To Owain, she was probably just another punter, and an English one at that; that was all there was to it, poetry or no poetry. As she tried to push him out of her mind, she sought out the most secluded swimming spots, away from the influx of tourists, so that she could swim alone, naked, and strong. She had to get on with her life, push herself to accept being alone, but she was starting to find this harder and harder each day. A creeping tiredness inched over her entire body, and she began to long for nothing but sleep.

She had other worries too. With only her Welsh class to look forward to each week, and that soon to end over the summer, she began to feel the tightening grip of loneliness once more. Stella had suggested she get a part-time job in the care home with her, but Jude felt that she still needed too much care herself to offer it to others and her heart was heavy at the thought of spending time with old age, illness, and despair. Cleaning the cottage after weeks of building work, dust, and grime would be constructive, but she couldn't be bothered to do it. But when a text from Paula, newly delivered of a baby boy, arrived one afternoon, all choice evaporated.

> I have to get away from here. This baby cries ALL DAY and Georgio's f**king mother is here 24/7. I am going absolutely mad. PLEASE can I bring him and come and stay with you? I will commit a serious offence if you say no. P x

The thought of her luxury-loving friend and a tiny baby staying in her filthy cottage made Jude panic. The bedroom was a tip, the floor covered with boxes she'd brought from Oxford and never even unpacked. Every surface was covered with a thick layer of gritty dust after the building work and the tiny bathroom was a health hazard. Paula would have a fit. But she was her friend, and she needed her, which at least made her feel of use. The sofa bed would be absolutely fine for her for a few nights and here was a really good deed just waiting to be done. She replied:

> Dear P, really sorry to hear that things are so awful. Just let me know when you are arriving, so that I can book some industrial cleaners. Can't wait to meet little Christos! J X

Within a few minutes, an answer appeared:

> We will arrive tomorrow. Thanks a million. P X

When Jude immediately rang Jo to find out what had been going on, the news left her reeling. Paula had not been allowed out of the house since the baby's birth two weeks earlier, as Georgio's mother had insisted that she stay at home and "rest". Her friends had seen her and the baby once, for a few minutes, and all their phone calls and texts had gone unanswered. They had gone to Georgio's office in Summertown, but he had been evasive, saying that Paula was "finding it tough", but that his mother was "taking care of everything". Jo warned Jude to brace herself; she had done some online research and talked of "post-natal depression" and "puerperal psychosis" with a casual air that made Jude want to run for the hills. How could coming here possibly help someone who was that ill, that despairing? And yet, in her heart, she knew it could.

Looking out to the horizon, the sea glittered as if the finest of silver nets had been cast over it. A single, red-sailed yacht broke up the wideness of water and sky, tugging a small dinghy in its wake. Finally, a part of her old life was going to coincide with her new one, and it felt like the right time for that to happen. But beneath worries about what Paula would make of the cottage lurked a far darker dread. How would she feel when she saw her friend's new baby boy? Fear gnawed at Jude's guts.

She drove to the best-stocked supermarket on the island in Menai Bridge and bought courgettes, beef tomatoes, and velvety purple aubergines for ratatouille, pulses for a hearty soup and an organic free range chicken. The prices made her wince, but Paula needed to eat good, wholesome food now to regain her strength. Jude realised that she would have to brush up on her long dormant cooking skills, too, which filled her with alarm, as her diet has been very basic of late. She resisted the temptation to buy nappies, creams, and wipes as well, but she did succumb to a sweet, blue baby sunhat in a local craft shop, just in case her friend forgot to pack one. The breezes could be keen on Anglesey, even in summer, and the sun deceptively strong.

The next morning, she was up 6am, overjoyed that it was a beautiful day because it meant that her friend would see the island at its best. Armed with gels, sprays, and cloths, with all the windows wide open, she cleaned her cottage from top to bottom and made up the bed with sheets that had blown on her washing line for an hour or two and smelt of salt and sea. Finally, she put a tiny jug of sea pinks on the bedside table.

"Cath Kidston eat your heart out," she said, snapping the dusters clean in her garden with great vigour, as she had seen her mother do.

She cooked a big batch of soup, a pot of ratatouille and roasted the chicken, and enjoyed it immensely. With food ready to heat up quickly when they needed it, she could now focus on helping Paula over the next few days. Menna laughed out loud (a rare and precious sound) when she called for their lunchtime walk to find her friend splay-legged in her deckchair, wearing a bikini with an apron that read "*Wild women swim*" over the top of it.

"You look *wedi blino'n lân*/completely knackered," she said.

"I am, but in a good way," Jude said.

"Brought you a *bara brith* (currant loaf) from the shop, like you asked me to, a treat for her. Mind you, looks as if *you* need a boost before your friend and her baby arrive!"

"*Diolch*/Thanks, my friend. I don't know what's the matter

with me. I have zero energy, and everything just feels a bit weird," Jude replied.

Menna looked at her more directly now. "Let me know if it gets worse, and you need something," she said, a look of concern flashing across her normally matter-of-fact face. "You don't look yourself at all, but there's a lot of bugs going round at the moment. Do you want me to take Pip, until Paula settles in? Might be easier for everyone, and sometimes dogs get jealous of babies."

"That would be great, Menna. It may be for a few days, though. Is that OK?"

Menna nodded, and calmly led a very happy Pip back up the beach towards her home.

At half past twelve, Jude heard a powerful car roar past, stop, and then reverse back and onto the grass outside the cottage. Its engine tick-tick-ticked once it was turned off, emanating heat.

When Paula got out of the car, Jude hardly recognised her. Her hair was obviously dirty, lumped into a grubby-looking scrunchie, and her eyes were ringed with dark hollows. Jude walked towards her, arms outstretched and a huge lump in her throat. Could this possibly be her gorgeous, glamorous friend?

"Welcome. It's good to see you," she whispered into Paula's smelly hair.

Paula said nothing, but hung limply in her arms, barely returning her hug. Jude felt she might crack one of her ribs if she squeezed her any more, so she pulled back and looked at her old friend's face. One of her mother's phrases, "dishcloth grey", seemed remarkably accurate, as Paula's skin had exactly that ghastly pallor. Georgio got out of the car and came, shyly, towards them. He, too, looked awful and there was no sign of his usual Greek-Cypriot exuberance.

"It's good of you, Jude, to let them stay. I think she will be happier here," he said. "It's very beautiful."

"And it's peaceful. No pain in the arse of a mother-in-law here, thank God," Paula muttered.

Georgio sighed, then pulled a huge all-terrain buggy, a Moses basket, a packet of nappies, two big suitcases, a changing bag, and a plastic mat out of the boot and carried them silently into Jude's tiny bedroom. She resisted the temptation to make a joke about how long they both envisaged staying.

"So, where is he, then? Your gorgeous boy?" she said instead. Paula was checking her mobile for a signal and tutting to find it had none.

"The baby? He's in the back seat. He howled almost all the way here." She pressed her open palms to her forehead. "My head is pounding."

Jude looked into the back of the car, gradually making out a soft shape through the tinted windows, deep within the black leathery gloom. The little boy was asleep, his eyelids like pale pink sugar-icing. He was even more beautiful than she'd feared.

As Paula went inside and sat down, Georgio undid Christos' car seat and carried him into the kitchen. Then, to Jude's astonishment, he said that he was leaving to drive straight back to Oxford for a "meeting with clients". He promised to "be in touch", but failed to say when he might be returning to fetch his family. Skimming Paula's head with a light kiss, he waved self-consciously at his little son, got into the car, and drove off, leaving only a wisp of tinny bouzouki music amidst the blast of vapour from his exhaust.

Neither woman seemed sure of what to do, or what to say, next. After a few moments, Paula sighed, dragged a chair outside into the garden, sat down heavily, and shut her eyes. Her baby was still parked on the kitchen table in his car seat, blinking in the dazzling light. When Jude turned the tap on to fill the kettle, he fanned out his tiny fingers like the most deli-cate of anemones at the noise, before drifting back off sleep.

As she made a pot of tea and slathered butter onto a thick slice of *bara brith* for Paula, Jude looked over at the tiny person in her cottage, and felt a familiar, dull pain deep in her gut.

"How on earth am I going to stop myself from loving you, you beautiful boy?" she murmured.

TWENTY

Once she had drunk three cups of sweet tea and eaten three slices of buttered *bara brith*, Paula did not move for over two hours that afternoon. She sat in the garden, her face tilted up to the sun and her eyes closed as if paralysed. Jude gave her the baby when he cried, took him from her when he had been fed, winded him, made her friend hot drinks, cold drinks, a ham and salad sandwich and even gently smoothed sun cream onto her arms and face for her. When Christos stank, and clearly needed his nappy changing, she spread the changing mat out on the grass and got on with it. By 5pm, after several hours of trying to predict, interpret and respond to everyone else's needs, Jude was shattered.

"Look, Paula, this baby needs you – you're his mum."

Paula opened her eyes, her face completely expressionless.

"But I don't love him, Jude. I can't."

"Paula! Don't say things like that."

"But, Jude, I don't. I'm too tired to wipe his bloody bum all day. I'm too tired to wipe my *own* bum. I only just managed to stop Georgio's mother doing that for me too, for God's sake."

Both women laughed then, but Paula's eyes were brimming with tears.

"He's so *new*, remember. He needs time to, well, settle into himself," Jude said, hoping she had hidden her flicker of panic. Puerperal psychosis could end in the mother murdering the baby, or herself, Jo had told her. She pushed both possibilities away. Paula was just exhausted.

"It's you he needs and wants most of all," she said. "You need some good food, some sleep, and some fabulous Welsh air, and that's all on tap here for as long as you need it."

Paula smiled and the hollows under her eyes folded into dark almond-shapes. Jude wrapped her arms around her friend and held her tightly as she sobbed uncontrollably into her shoulder.

"My whole body feels as if it has been run over by a truck, and it even hurts to sit down. *He* wakes me up every two hours, and when he finally does sleep, I can't," she said, jabbing a finger towards the baby. "He poos, pukes, and chews my poor nipples till they look like sausage meat, and I never even *wanted* him, Jude. He is mainly the result of too much wine one Friday evening."

Jude quickly revisited memories of her and Alex desperately "trying" whenever she was ovulating but shut the thought down immediately. No, it helped nobody to remember that now, least of all her. But something had to be done to turn this situation around, and she was the only one here to do it. The advice she was one hundred per cent certain Gloria would give if she was here popped into her head: bottles.

"Has he ever taken a bottle, Paula?" she asked.

"Ha! Georgio's mother wouldn't let me even *try* a bottle. It feels as if I just pushed this baby out, but he's really hers – the only thing she can't do is breastfeed him. But neither can I!" More sobbing. "I know breast is best – but who for? Not for me!

I'm just no good at this mum-stuff, with all this blood, shit and stink. *You* should have had this baby, Jude, not me."

Jude stared hard at her mug of tea. What the hell could she say to that? She had lost two tiny, longed-for babies and now, would never have one.

"Well, I didn't, because I couldn't, remember?" she said.

Paula stopped crying abruptly. "I'm so sorry. Oh my God, how utterly..."

"It's OK, I understand, but I never want to hear you say a thing like that again," Jude said, cutting across her. "Just remember that Christos is yours, and you are so, so lucky to have him."

Paula hung her head, defeated.

"Go and have a shower, get into your nightie, get into bed, and go to sleep. I'll get him to take a bottle somehow, and I'll take care of him for today, but he is your baby, and he is perfect. Agreed?"

Paula nodded meekly, before mouthing "Thank you", going into the bathroom and closing the door.

And then Jude was on her own, with a baby. It felt terrifyingly wonderful.

She reckoned that she had about an hour before Christos woke up, hungry again. Quickly, she made a list of what she needed. Menna's shop stocked the basics, and Menna had had babies so would know what to do, when to do it and how it needed to be done. Everything else would just have to wait. She wrapped the tiny baby in one of his beautiful designer baby blankets, strapped him into his pristine all-terrain buggy and began walking along the beach towards Llanfaelog. She reached the shop without Christos even fluttering his perfectly curled black eyelashes. As soon as she bumped the door of the shop open with her bum, Menna rushed over to them.

"*O sbia del*/Oh look, sweet."

"And so hungry, so soon. Right, action stations. I need clean bottles, teats, and formula milk. Can you make me up a big bottle right now? No clue what type of milk he needs, but you'll know," Jude barked, knowing that Menna wouldn't mind a bit, and would just get on with what needed doing. Which she did.

Within a few minutes, a few older women slunk from behind shelves or freezers in the shop and began clucking and sighing over the buggy as Menna ripped the packaging off two baby bottles and boiled water in the kitchenette behind the shop to sterilise them. Ten minutes later, first bottle made up and cooling, Jude sat on the chair by the counter and prepared herself to give it to Christos... but absolutely nothing happened. He slept, for half an hour, unmoving. She was just about to pinch one of his gorgeous toes to wake him up, when one woman said,

"Oooh no, doll. Never wake a sleeping baby. Wait 'til they want it."

"Too true, Esyllt," Menna muttered.

Jude looked around at her audience, all of whom were nodding their agreement. Two cups of tea and a KitKat each later, they were still waiting. With each sweet-scented outbreath, Jude scoured Christos' face for signs of stirring, but he pressed his fat little lips together and slept on. The women talked in whispers, sharing gossip and local news and casting the baby a fond smile every so often so that he knew they were still there. Nobody seemed in a hurry to go anywhere, and Jude never forgot that perfect, precious capsule of time with these Welsh women, one that she knew would never come again.

"I might get you all to do my stock-take for me as you've all got so much time to spare, *pawb*/everyone!" Menna quipped, but Jude knew she was enjoying every minute of being, effectively, in charge of operations.

An hour and a half after he'd arrived in the shop, Christos

opened his eyes, screwed up his tiny face and began to cry. The whole team swung into action. One of the women folded back his blankets, Menna boiled the kettle to heat up the bottle, Jude lifted the squirming baby out of his buggy, her heart pounding. If she got this wrong, and he wouldn't take the bottle, she would have to race back to *Hedd* and wake Paula up to breastfeed him. One woman gently rolled Jude's sleeve up to make sure it didn't get in the way as she braced herself to feed him.

"*Diolch*/Thanks. Team effort, ladies. Right, here goes," she murmured.

Slowly, she brought the warmed teat to Christos' lips. Nobody breathed. He wrinkled his nose, paused as a drip of milk coated his lips, then clamped his mouth around the teat and sucked with such force that all the women cheered in unison.

"I told you. Got to wait until they're hungry, see," Esyllt said, beaming. "And this one is obviously *very* hungry."

With each huge, rhythmic gulp, Jude felt herself sink into this little body more and more, blending where she ended and he began. The warmth from his wet nappy spread across her stomach, and her arms ached with longing to hold him tighter, closer. Strangely, she felt her nipples tingle as he sucked as if *she* was suckling him herself, which she put down to cruelly wishful thinking. Bottle drained, the women cheered again when Christos produced an enormous burp on Jude's shoulder and then relaxed into a milky doze.

"I think I'd better take that open tin of formula milk, and another two bottles, please," she said, handing over her bank card.

Menna looked at Jude, her brown eyes kind, but searching:

"Don't let yourself get too fond of him, will you, *cariad*/love?"

"I'll try not to," Jude answered. "But I think it's already too late."

TWENTY-ONE

Over the following few days, Paula slept for hours and hours. Her face seemed to rehydrate as her body recovered, and within thirty-six hours, Jude began to see her old friend reappear, replacing the anguished wraith who had arrived on the island at the beginning of the week. Now that Christos was taking a bottle, and not as hungry, he was a little kinder to Paula's battered nipples, and breastfeeding became easier too.

The women soon established a failsafe feeding routine. If the baby woke wanting milk when his mother was asleep, Jude quickly picked him up, took him out into the garden and gave him a bottle. She was always faintly disgruntled if Paula woke and breastfed him before she could get there to do so. By the time her guests had been with her a week, Jude could not imagine her washing line being empty of tiny babygros and poppered cotton vests, or her freezer free of bags of frozen breast milk. It was as if he was meant to be there, the baby boy she'd never had.

When Paula felt ready to go out during the day, the two friends walked slowly from one end of the beach to the other and talked more openly than they had in all the years they had known each other. Amongst many other things, including death and bereavement, the pain of childbirth and how utterly useless the expensive hypnobirthing course she'd done had proved, Paula confessed to Jude how claustrophobic she found being part of a Greek-Cypriot family, how she had never intended to have a baby at all until she was at least forty, and then, preferably by surrogate. In return, Jude found that she needed to tell her a little about Owain, and whatever it was that they had shared. He still featured in her dreams, if not in her life, and she needed to tell someone to help "exorcise" him for good.

"I'll probably never see him again anyway," she said with what she hoped sounded like conviction.

"Well, on an island this size, I would have thought that extremely unlikely," Paula answered. "But he is married, Jude, and he sounds complicated, and *very* Welsh. I would steer well clear, if I were you. You'd be on a hiding to nowhere with that one. The locals would have your guts for garters if you tempted him astray."

"Too true, and I don't want to do that," Jude answered. "He didn't seem too sad to say goodbye to me anyway."

"Then it's probably for the best that you don't give him another thought," Paula said. "Promise me you won't."

Jude promised, but she had her fingers crossed behind her back. How could she promise to censor her dreams?

There was one topic of conversation that could not be broached, however. Jude knew that she should tell Paula about Tom, and the night they had spent together, but she could not bring herself to do so. He had sent a few messages since she'd rejected him, but after a while he seemed less heartbroken than disappointed that his plan for their future together hadn't panned out as he had hoped. Looking back, she felt nothing but shame that she'd allowed herself to sleep with her dead husband's best friend. Paula, she was certain, would be both

shocked and disappointed in her and that, she could really do
without.

Jude went to visit Menna and Pip each evening, while Paula
bathed Christos in the kitchen sink in the cottage and got him
ready for bed. This brief time away from each other gave both
of them some respite. Paula began to fall in love with her baby,
but Jude realised how much she'd grown to love him too – the
snuffling sounds of him sleeping and the alarmed "X" shape he
made with his little arms and legs when Pip barked made her
heart melt. Most evenings, she wept openly as she walked along
the beach to Menna's, as sadness and joy washed over her in
equal force. She assumed her heightened emotions were
because, with Alex's death, her hopes of ever having a child had
died, and having a baby around made her realise once more how
huge a loss that was. Whatever the reason, it helped to release
these feelings where only the sea and the sky would witness but
never judge them.

When Georgio came to fetch Paula and Christos ten days later,
Jude felt a confusing mixture of grief and relief. It would be
good to have some peace again, she told herself, to dampen her
dread of the quiet that lay ahead of her every day, and every
evening. But as soon as the luggage was all crammed into the
boot, she felt her heart sink as Georgio wrapped her in a huge
hug, his voice shaking as he thanked her.

"I will never forget this," he said. "It was all so bad, I
thought... well, I don't know what I thought. Now, all is good."

"Glad to help," she replied. "Perhaps you need a little time
together now – just the three of you." The look Georgio gave
her told her that he understood completely.

Standing outside *Hedd*, she waved as the car roared off

down the road, sending a scurry of rabbits darting into their burrows in the dunes. As she started clearing up, emptying the nappy bin caused such a wave of nausea to rise up in her belly that she bent double, holding herself with both arms. She had been sick so often in the early days after Alex's death that she knew her body could react this way to strong feelings, and to great loss. Clearly, saying goodbye to Christos so soon after realising that she may never see Owain again had cut her to the quick.

As she stripped the bed, a tiny blue sock fell out and onto the floor. Picking it up, she held it to her face for a few moments to inhale that heavenly baby smell once more, before tucking it into one of her drawers, amongst her softest sweaters.

TWENTY-TWO

The day after Paula left, Jude realised that it had felt good to care for someone, and that it had comforted her as much as it had helped her friend. She decided to get in touch with Stella about the part-time job in the care home she'd suggested to her a few weeks earlier. However hard it would undoubtably be, it could not be as hard as spending more endless days alone with her thoughts, and her regrets.

> I have to do something positive, especially now that I'm on my own here again.

Stella responded within the hour.

> OK. I've put in a good word for you with the manager. The rest is up to you, but let's meet up for a Welsh revision session very soon. Exam terrors kicking in here!

They both only had two weeks left before their Welsh exam at the end of June, and Jude knew she needed a lot more practice. She'd been lurking in the shop waiting for any opportunity to use her Welsh, but Menna had bluntly asked her to stop, as it was "a bit weird". Part of the assessment was to record a brief conversation with a Welsh-speaker, and Jude knew that Owain Pritchard would be the ideal partner. His Welsh was beautiful, and he'd been supportive of her learning the language, but weeks had now passed without a word from him. He was busy, doing a different job and had a life she knew nothing about, but she missed him more than she dared admit, however hard she tried not to. She told herself a) that this was purely business, b) he was a married man, so unavailable, and c) he would want to help her pass the exam. She kept her message simple:

> Could we meet for some Welsh practice plse?
> Exam soon! Jude F.

She had an answer within an hour:

> 6 heno/6 tonight. Hedd. Prepare to be very grilled.

"I think your English is as ropey as my Welsh, Owain!" she said, laughing.

The only way Owain would agree to be recorded having a conversation with her was if she were to present it to him as a *fait accompli*. Before he was due to arrive, she set up her phone so that she'd only need to surreptitiously press one button to record their conversation. For this part of the exam, the main proviso was that she should ask the questions, and the Welsh-speaker should not monopolise things.

"I'd better not get him onto R.S. Thomas, or he'll never shut up," Jude said to herself.

By 5.45pm, she was sitting stiffly in a deckchair outside her cottage, another chair directly opposite her, two glasses of water on the table between them and her phone primed and ready. Her eyes flicked quickly between her Welsh book and the road, and her stomach fizzed with nerves, which she chose to put down to the upcoming exam. She had got Owain's first edition of poetry ready to return, too, just in case this was the last time they met. She dared not admit to herself just how much she hoped it wasn't...

Swallows were skimming just above the surface of the sea, making shrill, mid-air squeaks as they looped and dived in their glorious summer evening dance. At 5.59pm precisely, Owain's red van appeared on the horizon. Jude put her book down, stood up, and waved far more enthusiastically than she had intended to. When he walked towards her, she could see that he had showered and shaved, that his clothes were unusually smart, and that his hair was still wet, perfect coils of chestnut brown. She tried to ignore how he made her feel; this was a business meeting only, a practical arrangement.

"Thanks for popping in. I hope it isn't too inconvenient. It's just that my exam is in two weeks, and I really have to pass it," she said.

"*Rhaid i ni siarad yn Gymraeg*/We must speak Welsh," Owain cut in, pointing a finger at her in mock strictness. His teeth were so bright against his face, which was tanned after weeks outside in the sun, that Jude wondered for a few seconds if he had actually had them whitened. She decided not.

"Haha, w*rth gwrs*/of course," Jude said with a laugh she hoped was light.

"*Reit 'ta; am be fyddwn ni cael sgwrs?*/Right then; what are we going to talk about?" Owain said, sitting in the deckchair Jude had put out for him and taking a nervous slurp of water. "*Hufen iâ, fel arfer*/Ice cream, as usual?"

She explained, in Welsh, that she just needed to ask him a few questions. She introduced him as a "local businessman" and made sure she used the polite "*chi*" form throughout. Owain pretended to look very alarmed when she deftly pressed the "record" button, which made them both laugh out loud, but they both soon fell into an easy to-and-fro. Jude watched his lips move as he spoke, forming shapes they never did when he spoke

English. Distracted, she glanced at her sheet of questions, though she knew them off by heart:

- Had he been born on Anglesey?
- Did he enjoy his job?
- What were his hobbies?
- Did he speak Welsh at home?
- Where did he like to go on holiday?
- What was his favourite kind of food?

She was only too aware that her questions did not venture into his family life, but that had been deliberate, for both their sakes. He had told her enough for her to guess that it was probably an unhappy one. She did learn more about him, however, as he began to venture "off piste" in his responses when he warmed up. He told her that he still, secretly, hoped to fulfil his long-held dream of designing buildings that both reflected the beauty of the island and invited it inside even if he could never formally resume his architecture studies.

He'd brought along a plan to show her, an intricate design of a stunning home he had designed with an outer wall of tempered glass facing the sea. His face, as he described it in Welsh for her, was a picture of bliss. Jude felt deeply honoured that he had trusted her enough to show her something so close to his real, hidden self, and responded warmly, but she was frustrated that her Welsh was not good enough to tell him how much she could feel his longing to fulfil this long-suppressed dream and hoped that he could, one day. He made her feel as Alex had done – heard, respected, and valued, and she knew that she cared about him, and his happiness, far more than was good for her.

Their conversation flowed seamlessly, and the only hiccups were when Jude forgot a word, or a pattern. When that happened, Owain theatrically mimed it to her, so that it would not be heard on the recording. (It was harder not to make their subsequent giggling audible, whenever this happened.) Once the allotted exam time-limit had passed, she switched off her phone and they both "phewed" in relief. As she was clearing up her notebook and peeling off the shoal of Post-its she'd stuck to the table, Owain drained the glass of water in front of him and asked:

"*Gawn ni fynd am dro, Jude, cyn i mi fynd? Mae'n dda iawn dy weld di*/Shall we go for a walk, Jude, before I go? It's so good to see you."

Jude felt the fact that he was now using the more familiar form "*ti*" in their conversation spread through her body like a gulp of good wine. Their relationship was now established, in friendship, closeness and familiarity, Owain seemed to be telling her. Much of her still wished it could be something more, but she knew that could never happen. Resisting a terribly strong urge to take his hand, she replied:

"*Wrth gwrs... ond gawn ni siarad yn Saesneg rwan, plîs?*/Of course – but can we please speak English now?" she said, laughing. "Exam over!"

PART 4

THE TIDE TURNS

TWENTY-THREE

High summer on the island came with a strange stillness, when it eventually came. Even the seabirds seemed to quieten during the hottest days of early July as if squawking and flying was just too much effort. The blue sky was raked with thick, white vapour trails as scores of sunshine-bound planes crawled silently overhead and the waves rolled up and down the shore with unaffected nonchalance. To Jude, they seemed to be endlessly whispering, "Stay here, enjoy, stay here, enjoy…"

As soon as the term ended, the Welsh exam was done, and the subsequent celebrations had finished, Jude got a call from Lisa, the care home manager, asking her to pop in for an informal chat. It lasted less than ten minutes.

"Well, you're good enough for me, once I've done all the usual CRBs and stuff," Lisa said. "And Stella says all sorts of nice things about you."

Jude blushed. "Oh, goodness. Does she?"

"Yes. She thinks you'll be a real asset to us," Lisa continued. "Do you think you could be, Jude?"

"Well, I'm quite organised. I can speak a fair bit of Welsh now, and perhaps do some crafty things as well," Jude replied.

"Yes, Stella told me about your artistic talent. That kind of thing works wonders here, honestly. Really cheers the clients up."

Jude smiled, feeling guilty again that she had yet to put paintbrush to canvas. "And of course I have lots of time right now."

"Time is key in our job. The job's only twelve hours a week at first, and it's mainly admin, but if you speak Welsh, you can get to know some of our clients a bit. They love a bit of a *sgwrs*/chat. Could you commit to that?"

"Ah, OK, I'll try,' Jude said. "But it's mainly an admin role, right?"

"We'll see what's needed most, when the time comes," Lisa said, standing up. The meeting was now over.

As the weather got hotter, gaggles of young mums arrived at the beach, dragging buggies through the sand and building sandcastles with their toddlers. After school, the older children joined them, and Jude smiled as she saw them threading through the dunes in their hot uniforms before peeling them off, yanking on bathing costumes and running into the waves with piercing shrieks. The tinny clankle of the ice-cream van as it left the beach marked the end of her day, whatever she was doing, and she grew to love this easy, summer routine. Although she had come a long way since the hands of the kitchen clock crawled through the hours in Howard Street, her evenings were still almost always spent alone, strolling along the beach with Pip, collecting shells and bits of driftwood. She started creating collages with her finds, trying to capture, to encapsulate the pared-back beauty she found here, and let it shine for all to see. This, rather than paint, now seemed to be her medium of choice, and she loved the combining of shape and texture that using just pure colour had never offered her.

The Sunday before she was due to begin work at the care home, she made herself a cooked breakfast and tried to read a newspaper online, in an effort to reconnect to the 'real world', but she could not settle. The blue sky was riven with banks of cauliflower-shaped clouds, and a chill breeze rippled across the sea as if the weather could not decide what to be today. Jude stood, washing up at her tiny sink when she suddenly felt a dull ache inside her.

"Probably my period on the way," she murmured, though those had always been frustratingly sporadic. "I really don't need that right now."

She felt restless, as if something, somehow, had to change, but what it was eluded her until, hanging out the washing to dry that day, she suddenly knew. She had to do something that would be both difficult, and painful – go back to Ynys Llanddwyn, the place she and Alex had loved most of all when they had visited it on their honeymoon. Before she started her new job, and the next phase of her future, she had to go back into the past, and leave it a little further behind her.

The drive down the coast of the island was stunning, and Jude tried to relive the thrill of their exhilarating motorbike ride by winding all four windows down and letting the wind rip through her car. The road dipped past Malltraeth with its wide, sandy estuary, where wild ponies grazed and huge flocks of birds gathered on the mudbanks around the water's edge. Some of them whirled up into the sky like a fine, white cloud as Jude drove past, her old Fiat's exhaust in full roar. Alex had crouched in one of the estuary's smelly bird-hides for hours before returning to their woodland lodge bursting with excitement at seeing snow-white egrets or blue herons fishing at the water's edge. She could picture his beloved face clearly now, so full of joy and hope. For a few moments, she stopped on the grass verge and watched the herons lift their spindly legs up and out of the water with breathtaking grace and precision, just as he would have done. In the distance, a group of curlews pricked at the mud with their scimitared beaks before their eerie cries pierced the air and they flew off. Whether people watched them or not, these beautiful birds went about their daily lives, and Alex had been right to admire that. These small things were worth noticing and valuing.

She paid at the entrance to the winding road that led down through the pine forest to the beach. They had parked the Harley here last time, and walked down to the shore, she remembered, because Alex knew a secret route through the forest and hadn't wanted to pay for parking.

"Typical!" she murmured. "But I think I'll pay to get to the sea faster today, my love, if that's OK with you."

Even though it was a glorious day, Jude pulled on the blue and white woollen hat Alex had worn the last time they had come to this place together. She'd promised him that she would come back, and that she would wear his hat, and she kept her promises. Emerging through the forest and out onto the huge expanse of sand, she was amazed that anywhere could be so utterly wild, and yet so perfect. The sheer strength of the wind that cannoned off the sea hit her in the chest, and huge waves thundered onto the shore. It seemed incredible to Jude that the sea had swollen and crashed on this beach, without stopping, every single day that Alex had been ill, during every single hour she had spent by his bed and even at that most terrible of moments, when his life had ended, at 3pm, on that gloomy February day. The waves had not paused, despite his suffering, and her grief; they went on, and on, and on. Today, this gave Jude enormous hope.

She looked to her right, and saw the island and the light-house, just as she had seen it back then, with her husband by her side. A few tiny figures were walking along the spine of the rocky outcrop it was built on, a good half an hour's walk from where she was standing. To the left of the furthermost rocks, a scattering of terns climbed to the perfect height before folding up their wings and legs and diving, bullet-fast, into the water to spear a fish. Closing her eyes for a moment, she let herself breathe in the strength of this place; it was still here, that freedom of spirit she and Alex had sensed that day, and so – despite everything that had happened since – was she.

TWENTY-FOUR

Jude was full of trepidation as she got dressed for her first day at the care home. She fretted that the elderly people would find her lacking if she was asked to chat to them in Welsh. Would they judge her English accent, her comparative "poshness" (something she had become painfully aware of since moving here)? Above all, she dreaded being surrounded by the imminence of death again. She spent so long picking suitable, sensible clothes and asking Menna to walk Pip at lunchtime, telling her how much tea to give him, that it took her friend saying, very sternly...

"Get in that car now or you are going to be late."

... to actually get her into the car.

Plas Hyfryd was a huge, redbrick house on the Bangor side of the Menai Straits, built as the luxurious home of a wealthy nineteenth century industrialist. Now, it was a care home specialising in the care of people with dementia and Alzheimer's, and it had an excellent local reputation (or so Stella assured her). Nevertheless, Jude braced herself for the smell of wee and the sound of distant wailing, which were her most vivid memories of going to see her grandmother Doris in a nursing home in Wells as a teenager. That had always prompted Gloria's dire warning "never put me in a place like that" whenever they'd visited her mother there. Jude hoped, however she felt about Gloria, that she would never be forced to do so.

Luckily, her first day began well. The admin work Lisa needed doing was straightforward enough: updating some records, calling medical suppliers and typing up the weekly menus. Her mouth watered as she read them: jam roly-poly, roast beef and Yorkshire pudding, lobscouse (a rich beef stew) and seasonal vegetables. In contrast, she remembered Gloria trying to spoon green mush into her mother's mouth, her lips pursed as it dribbled down the old woman's chin and into her plastic baby bib. Here, she could hear jazz music and low, animated chatter in the distance.

"Ready to meet the troops?" Lisa said, popping her head around the corner at about noon.

Trying to hide her slight reluctance, Jude followed her along the corridor and into what was called the "Unit". Lisa greeted several elderly people as she breezed past them. Some were walking unaided, others with wheeled frames, but most registered some degree of recognition when they saw her.

"Waiting for the bus are you, Gwen?" she asked a tiny old lady who was indeed sitting on a bench under a sign which read "Bus stop".

"It'll be here soon. It's never late, you know, the number 42."

Once they were out of earshot, Lisa said, "Things like that can really help them remember details from their lives. We've got a sweet shop, just in case you fancy a gobstopper or a packet of sherbet pips!"

The corridor walls were covered with posters and adverts for Bisto, Lea and Perrins sauce and Bourneville chocolate, and outside each of the bedrooms leading off the corridor Jude noticed a glass-fronted frame filled with photos and other bits of memorabilia – tiny snippets from each person's long, rich life. When Lisa stopped outside one room, she felt her mouth go dry. So, this was *her* client. Now she was going to have to somehow talk to a crotchety old person in Welsh, for goodness' sake. She silently vowed to kill Stella at the end of her shift.

"Before I take you in to meet Rhiannon, I'll fill you in a bit. Look, you can see what she looked like in her prime. Pretty, eh? Her daughter, Hâf, still lives on the island and comes to see her regularly. She brings in fantastic cakes that she bakes and decorates herself, but her mother won't eat them, and gives them to the staff instead. She won't say exactly why, but she is more and more confused these days. Her son moved away, though. Rhodri, his name is – apple of his mother's eye. Lives in London. He hardly ever visits but sends her a *lot* of chocolates."

Jude looked at the grainy black and white photo of a fresh-faced young woman with finely shaped lips and thick, dark hair. She had a toddler on one knee and a baby in a huge carriage pram next to her. Behind them all stood a young man in uniform with a toothbrush moustache, his shoulders held so far back he looked faintly ridiculous.

"That's her husband, Guto – died at the D-Day landings. Only nineteen," Lisa said. "He could have got away without going, as he had a bad leg, Rhiannon says, but he went anyway. She's still very proud of him."

"And she never married again?" Jude asked, intrigued by the story of this pretty young war widow, left to raise two children alone.

"Never. Nobody else was 'good enough', according to her. They ran away and got married at fifteen, pretending to be sixteen, and her family were furious at the disgrace of it. She talks about them sometimes, her mam and dad, but I have to tell you that when she talks about a 'Mari', we have no idea who she might have been, and Rhiannon won't tell us. The only family photo she has is from when she was about twelve or thirteen, and there's just her brother and her parents in that. If she mentions this mysterious Mari to you today, it's best to steer her away from it, in case she gets upset. She probably made her up, we think, as they sometimes do. Just ask her about her *own* family. She loves to talk about them!"

"OK, I will. In Welsh?" Jude said. Her face said it all.

Lisa smiled. "Well, she refuses to put up with my basic Welsh, so I usually speak English to her. She's easy with either and pretty clever with both. Don't worry. Just be yourself, Jude." She knocked and opened the door. "Morning, Rhiannon. It's Lisa. How are you today? I've brought someone to meet you. Jude, this is Mrs Rhiannon Jones."

The bedroom was warm and smelt very strongly of cinnamon. The curtains were drawn, and Jude was immediately reminded of her mother's house, where the curtains were always tight shut, whatever the weather. As her eyes gradually became used to the darkness, she could make out the silhouette of a tiny, white-haired woman sitting in the far corner of the room. She was wearing a string of beautiful, creamy pearls over a knitted pale lavender bed jacket and looked about as fragile as a dandelion clock. One puff, and she would be gone.

"What did you say? Who is it, Lisa?" Rhiannon said. Her voice sounded as if she was uncertain about these words, and their combination of nouns and consonants. They were so unlike those of her mother tongue, Jude realised; Owain and Menna had the same problem sometimes.

"It's someone new to meet, Rhiannon," Lisa said. "Mrs Fitzgerald, but she likes to be called Jude."

The old woman wrinkled her nose and screwed her eyes up tight, like a vole sensing threat. Only when Lisa sat down and began gently stroking Rhiannon's hand did Jude realise that the old woman was almost completely blind.

"Come a bit closer, love. She can see you then," Lisa said.

"I can see more than you think, you know," the old woman said. Her voice was so low it was almost a growl, and remarkably strong.

"Jude's come for a bit of a *sgwrs*/chat," Lisa went on. "Is that all right?"

"What'll we chat about?" the old woman replied, her near-sightless eyes twinkling, nonetheless. "Holiday plans?"

Jude and Lisa laughed, and Rhiannon smiled to hear it.

"*Dach chi'n siarad Cymraeg*/Do you speak Welsh?" the old woman said next, when they'd stopped chuckling. "You look English."

Jude braced herself and tried to let the words float out of her mouth as she had done in so many lessons, and in her exam.

"*Dw'in dysgu*/I'm learning. *Ond mae'n well gen i siarad yn Saesneg, dweud y gwir*/But I'd prefer to speak in English, to be honest."

Rhiannon nodded. "*Na'ni*/There we go. Good girl, having a go. It's not easy. We'll use a bit of both then, shall we? But I'm going to call you Judith, *cariad*/love, the name I assume your mother gave you."

Jude pushed down the irritation this awoke in her and sat down nervously on the other side of Rhiannon's chair. Lisa slipped out of the room a few minutes later completely unnoticed, because the old woman had now reached out for *Jude's* hand.

Lisa was right, Rhiannon loved to talk about her own family, and she did so without pause for almost an hour. She began with her children and her five grandchildren, telling Jude their names, ages, birthdays, and favourite foods. Smiling broadly, she lingered over every detail of her son Rhodri's life: his "beautiful home", the "friendly village" he lived in and the important job he had recently retired from. Her daughter lived in Llangefni, she said, and was "always busy doing I don't know what". She did not mention anyone called Mari, but at times, a cloud of sadness crossed her face, and she said nothing at all for several minutes.

"Will you be coming again, Judith?" Rhiannon asked, when she got up to leave. "I can tell you about my Guto then."

"I'll be here again on Wednesday."

"*Dw'in edrych ymlaen yn barod, cariad*/I'm looking forward to it already, love."

"*Fi hefyd*/Me too," Jude answered, folding both Rhiannon's small, thin hands in her own. "It's been really lovely to chat to you."

As she drove home that afternoon, her impressions of this strong but gentle old woman filled her thoughts. What a privilege it was to be able to get to know Rhiannon Jones, to hear her thoughts and ideas as she neared the end of her life. She, too, had experienced great joy and great sadness, and it struck Jude that this was the way of things for most people, not just her. Yes, this job would be good for her, she decided; it might help her to stop focusing on what she'd lost, or couldn't have, and be grateful for all that she still had.

TWENTY-FIVE

When the schools broke up, Anglesey became far too busy for Jude's liking. On sunny days, "her" beach was invaded with rowdy families carrying huge amounts of stuff, and often leaving a scree of litter, fag ends, disposable barbecues and punctured inflatables behind them. On rainy days, these families crammed into people carriers and clogged the roads, desperately seeking some fun before returning to their damp tent, lodge, cottage, or caravan.

Rhosneigr itself attracted a different kind of tourist than anywhere else on the island, but Jude liked them even less. Many of the cottages, and a swathe of the family houses in the little town, were Airbnbs or second homes. From Whitsun onwards, these ghost-homes were used for a few short weeks, their windows and doors then flung wide, their gardens littered with paddleboards, wetsuits, towels, and bathing costumes. Big groups of entitled-seeming visitors colonised the cafés and bars, greeted each other noisily across the street, made everyone step off the pavement as they processed to the beach en masse and lurched loudly home in the small hours. They reminded Jude of some of the wealthy, arrogant people she'd met in Oxford, at Helena's gallery. She kept her distance.

The drowsiness that summer brought affected her very deeply. Her period had still not arrived, which was nothing new, but she felt horribly lethargic, which was. On some days, she slept late into the morning, staying up until the early hours as a result. She put this down to her body finally, totally relaxing, and decided that overall, it was a good thing. Her two shifts a week *in Plas Hyfryd* were not enough to keep her from brooding, however much she now looked forward to talking to Rhiannon. She met Stella fairly regularly, but her friend had begun a relationship with a retired GP called Eifion, a widower she'd met in the Bangor community choir, and Jude did not want to seem needy by accepting their many invitations to meet up. She also did not tell Stella that she had briefly considered joining the choir herself, but decided against it in case she cramped her friend's style. Life ebbed and flowed, and the days passed, but Jude constantly yearned for something surer, and stronger, to anchor herself to. More than anything, she yearned to be loved.

One glorious afternoon in July, Owain Pritchard texted her out of the blue.

> Will you meet me for a walk at Llanelian
> tomorrow evening? I can't bear not seeing
> you. O

Jude hesitated. Why was this man playing with her feelings? She had not heard a word from him since her exam and their lovely walk together, but this sounded as if he wanted their friendship to resume – and perhaps something more to begin. Uneasy about what he wanted, what he might be expecting from such a meeting, she rang Paula.

"Don't go there, Jude," her friend said immediately. "Close friendships with married men are very rarely a good idea."

"But I need something to *happen*, Paula. How can things change for me if I don't take any risks?" she bleated. "We got on so well..."

"There's a difference between a risk and a sure-fire disaster. You really don't need to have your heart broken, Jude."

After five minutes of discussing Christos' progress ("He's a boy genius"), Paula's sex life ("Fab! Georgio actually *likes* my baby belly!") and how much she now loved being a mother, Jude said she had to go and do something, and hung up. In reality, she had made a decision, her own decision, and the one that seemed best for her. If there was even a chance of loving this man, and him loving her, it was worth taking a risk. She texted Owain back:

> That would be lovely. See you at the slipway at 5pm?

Gwych/Excellent

Porth Eilian is a tiny, shingled cove, surrounded by looming cliffs and watched over through all weathers by a crenelated white lighthouse called Point Lynas. The lack of sand on the beach made it less popular with tourists, as did the hordes of jellyfish that usually floated into the cove once summer temperatures rose. A few scraggy wild ponies grazed on the gorse-edged land above the sea, oblivious to the risks they were taking to lean over and nibble the most succulent buds. It was a wild spot, and the grassy slopes beneath the lighthouse were the best place on the island to watch porpoises play without fear of a careless jet-ski either alarming or wounding them. Jude and Alex had also come here on the Harley during their honeymoon and sat to watch them leap and dive in silent awe. It was good for her to come back here, and revisit another chapter of her past before closing it, she decided, as she drove the forty minutes over the island. But she knew full well that it meant even more to be meeting Owain Pritchard again. They would be alone together, somewhere remote and beautiful, and Paula had strongly warned her not to do this.

Jude saw him before he saw her. He was gazing out to the horizon, where a band of air above the surface of the sea shimmered with heat haze. There was nobody on the beach at all. The sun fell behind the cove as the afternoon drew on, so it became a shady, rather gloomy spot. Jude guessed that Owain's plan was for them to walk along the clifftop to Lynas, as it stayed sunny up there long into these summer evenings.

"Hi," she said, putting a hand on his shoulder as casually as she could.

As he turned around, she saw stress etched on his face, the wrinkles around his eyes forming a spidery web as he tried to smile. He had a large purpling bruise above one cheekbone. "Good God! Are you OK?"

"Let's walk. I'll find it easier to talk if I don't have to look you in the face," he said. "You'd see straight through me."

They set off, both dogs running excitedly ahead as this was a place of both new and vintage sniffs. For a few minutes, neither Owain nor Jude said anything; being alongside each other in this stunning place was enough for now. The only question that needed an answer was, what had happened to Owain's face? Eventually, Jude asked it:

"Owain, you look terrible. Tell me what's going on," she said.

He looked at her shyly, out of the corner of his good eye. "I've missed our walks, Jude. Missed talking to you, desperately missed being with you," he said. "Look at me! I got so desperate I walked into a wall!"

She did not laugh at his weedy joke, however. She would wait for him to say what he needed to say. Sharing deeply personal things was acutely difficult for him, she knew. Menna had told her how this man hid his feelings behind his wit and Jude had seen that. He would tell her the truth, in his own time.

"You really want to know what's been going on, do you?"

Jude nodded.

"OK, but I'll have to build up to it, so bear with me," he said, clearing his throat. He paused for a second or two, before beginning. "Right, here goes. Non, my wife, hates walks, you see. She says they're a waste of time. She says poetry's a waste of time as well. I've still not dared tell her how much I paid for that first edition, but she's guessed it was a lot."

"It's in my car. I brought it this evening, to return it to you," Jude said. She waited for a response, but none came. "I'm sure you share other things, other... interests, don't you?" she went on.

"Well, she's fond of the dog, I suppose," he said eventually.

"Well, Meg is a lovely dog."

Silence again, as they walked on towards the cliff edge, past a sign saying "Private land. Keep out" which alarmed Jude slightly.

"Where exactly are we going?" she asked. The palpable tension in the air was unnerving, and she felt a sudden flicker of fear. Menna had also warned her about this man several times, and said he was complex, wounded.

"There's a swimming spot down here that used to be The Place for skinny-dipping in the sixties and seventies, apparently." He paused, saw her face, and laughed. "Don't worry, I just wanted to show you it!"

"It does say it's private land back there..." she said.

"*Paid a phoeni*/Don't worry. Connections, that's all that matters around here. My brother Idwal takes care of this part of the coastline. He lives there," Owain answered, pointing to a large house on the hillside.

"Oh, I see. Is he your only brother?" she asked tentatively.

He had mentioned a brother with sadness once, she recalled, but she knew she must resist the urge to ask him too much, too soon.

Owain hesitated. "He is now, yes. I had two brothers, but one died. Motorbike accident. He was only eighteen."

"Oh, how sad. I'm so sorry, Owain," Jude said, shocked. "So the bike cover you gave me…?"

"Yes, it was his. I know he'd be happy that it's now protecting that beautiful Harley." He paused, and rubbed his eyes roughly. "My mother never really got over it. I don't know if you ever do – get over things like that, I mean."

"I don't think you do, no. Why should you be expected to?" Jude replied. "Losing a child, however old that child is, is agony, forever."

Owain looked at her intently but said nothing. He'd ground to a halt, and Jude knew she had to nudge him on. She blurted:

"So what does Non do – as a job, I mean? You didn't tell me."

"She's a teacher at Llangristiolus Primary. She hates it, which is ironic as I had to take any job I could to support us while she trained. Still do, to pay for all the stuff she buys online to 'cheer herself up', as she puts it." He sighed. "I'd wanted to become an architect, as I think I did tell you. I even did two years of a degree at Bangor, but that was scuppered when we had to get married."

"That's a shame," Jude said, as she frantically tried to put two and two together. Why had they *had* to get married? It was usually for one reason only. "So, any kids?"

Owain cleared his throat again. "No. We tried for years, but I've given up now. Non says the problem's mine, not hers – she insisted we had tests, see. I never saw the results – I didn't want to, but she told me that they showed I've got, low, er… a low count."

"Yes, yes, I understand," Jude said quickly, to spare him

embarrassment. "It could still happen for you both, though. 'Low' doesn't mean 'none'."

"If it was meant to happen, it would have done, I say, but she's like a woman possessed," he replied, his face clouding with anger. "I don't matter at all to her any more. It's all about getting a baby and the shame of not having one yet, like it's some kind of trophy."

Jude felt the myriad pieces of a mosaic slot into a pattern she recognised. This would be all he and Non thought about, all they talked about, all they argued about. Those four words, "trying for a baby", contained such suffering, so many disappointments and recriminations.

"I understand, Owain. I really do."

"So you and your husband...?"

"No, we couldn't have a baby either, despite all the tests, screening, and procedures under the sun. I lost two, boys, very early on. Our genes were 'incompatible', they said. It wasn't meant to be for us, as you say."

Owain rubbed his stubbly chin and murmured: "*Bechod*/Shame. I'm sorry."

"Thanks. Are you just going to keep going, keep hoping?"

"No. She thought she was pregnant when we got engaged, so we got married fast, but she wasn't. False alarm," he said mournfully. "Now she's started talking about 'donors', but it doesn't feel right to me. Not now anyway, not the way things are between us." He paused and looked at Jude. "Did you ever think about going down that route?"

"We didn't get that far, Owain. Alex died before we could."

"Of course. Jude, I'm so sorry." He covered his face with his hands, completely mortified.

She stopped, and stood in front of him, so that he had no choice but to walk into her. As she wrapped her arms around him, he lowered his head onto her shoulder and rested it there.

The rich brown tones in his hair reminded her of the conkers she'd prised out of their prickly green cases as a child.

"I understand, Owain," she said. "I know how this baby thing takes over your life and makes you say and do things you'd never believe you could or would. It's brilliant at souring relationships that were once good too."

They stood on the clifftop and held each other as the seagulls crowed and the wind raged around them. Neither wanted to break away.

"I haven't talked to anyone about all this, about Non, and the baby thing. Nobody, ever," he whispered into her hair. "But with you, I forget about the whole, ghastly embarrassment, the exhausting relentlessness of the whole business because I can tell you how it *feels*."

Jude nodded. "It's a truly terrible thing, to be told your body won't do the thing you most want it to. I feel that every single day."

He gulped, and words spilt out in a tumbled rush, as they had once before, when he had first asked her to walk with him:

"I'm not living at home at the moment, Jude. We've separated, and it feels wonderful. I had to leave her, to get out of that terrible atmosphere of resentment and hate."

Jude held her breath. He had left her. As the words sank in, she felt herself relax into his body. So he was free now, free to love her?

He looked like a small boy – hurt, crestfallen. Circles of dark pink had formed on both his cheeks, like new bruises. "Everything came to a head, and I left. Someone told her they'd seen us walking together. I told her we were good friends, like I did the first time she found out I'd lent you the R.S. Thomas first edition. She gave me a roasting, stood next to me while I rang you that evening after your exam to make sure I didn't give you any hope of our ever meeting again."

Jude sighed. "I knew something wasn't right, in that phone call. You didn't sound like you at all."

"I'm sorry, Jude. I keep telling her that, you know, we *talk* about things. But when she found out that I'd helped you out with your exam, she hit me with a frying pan, and you can see the results." He pointed at his bruise shyly.

"Yes, I sure can," Jude replied.

"I know she doesn't love me anymore. In fact, I think there might even be someone else in the picture at her school, but she's so jealous. She hates the idea that I might find happiness with someone else, I guess." He touched the bruise on his face again and winced. "Nothing *happened*, I told her. We're friends."

"Nothing happened, no. We walked, and we talked, because we understand each other." Could she say the words she so wanted to say at last? She had to. Opening her mouth, they were suddenly said, never to be unsaid. "We're friends, yes... if that's what you want us to be, Owain."

"What does it matter what I want? We may have separated, but I'm still *married*, Jude! I made vows in church," he exclaimed, his face contorted in pain. "She's so unhappy and her family are *hollol creulon*/completely cruel, 'as hard as nails' as you would say."

"But do you still love her?" Jude said, her voice trembling. This mattered, so very much, to what happened next.

He did not answer for a long while, but looked out to sea as if the answer would be on the next incoming wave. Finally, he said:

"No, I don't. I think I loved her when I married her, and thought she was carrying my child, but now, we hate each other, but I still don't think she'll set me free without a fight, because it would 'shame her'. I believe in commitment, Jude, and in keeping your word, but there's no love left between us and no future for us as a couple, I know that much."

Jude touched his arm. She felt a tingle like electricity as her fingers met his warm skin. There was danger here. "Don't blame yourself for that."

"But I do," he answered. "And so does she. Perhaps she never really loved me, just used me, and I gave up on my dream to do the right thing by her. I can't bear to think about that too much, and I just don't know what to do anymore." Nestling into Jude's neck, seeking comfort, she instinctively held him so tightly that she could feel his steady heartbeat against her body.

On the cliffs around them, gulls perched above them on rocky ledges, and their soft cries were the only sounds, until Jude murmured:

"Owain, *I* love you, even if she doesn't. I love you with all my broken heart."

He looked at her face, and kissed her without hesitation or reserve. Her knees softened, and she felt whatever doubts and reservations had been tethering her, melt away.

"And I love you, Jude, with all of mine."

Within a minute, they were lying on the soft grass, limbs entwined, surrendering to something neither of them could deny, or control. Above them, a skylark spiralled into the air and sang, purely for the joy of singing.

TWENTY-SIX

When she awoke the following day, Jude felt no regret, but only sadness that the love she and Owain shared was caught in the complexities of his miserable marriage like a rabbit in a snare. She understood his reluctance to divorce Non, but she resented it. If they were separated, and his wife didn't actually love him, why could she not let him go and be with someone who did? There must be more to it than he had told her, unless Non just delighted in his suffering. Like a mouse on a wheel, these thoughts went round and round in her head with no possibility of resolution. It was exhausting.

When Menna and her cousin Siôn called in unexpectedly mid-morning, Jude was grateful for the distraction. Siôn ran a tiny sandwich shop in a side street of Rhosneigr, inherited from his parents who had now gone to live in Spain. He'd shattered his leg the previous week on a rock when his canoe had overturned, and he limped into *Hedd* on crutches. As soon as Jude saw him, she guessed that their visit was not purely a social one.

"I'm here to beg for help," he began, his hands in prayer position. "I am really, really stuck. I need you to help run the shop for me for a bit, Jude. You won't be on your own. There'll be Ffion with you, and she knows the ropes. Menna thought you might enjoy it, as you've got some spare time over the summer..."

Jude looked at Menna pointedly. "Did you now?"

"Well, you did say you felt a bit at a loose end now that Welsh has finished and Stella's got a new bloke. You could still do your days in the care home," her friend said. "I do think you might enjoy it. It'll be good for you, get you out into the community a bit more, you know."

Jude looked from one to the other, smiling at their good-natured hard sell. They only wanted her to be happy, and she could do with keeping as busy as possible right now. She also knew what Alex would have told her to do – to go for it. What did she have to lose but loneliness?

"OK, Siôn," she said. "Tell me what I need to do."

He then made a pretty good effort at hopping for joy.

Things did not start well. When Jude arrived at the sandwich shop at 8.30am on her first day, there was a big brown paper sack with about thirty baguettes sticking out of one end and no Ffion in sight. She let herself in and turned on the lights and filled the coffee machine. Having been told that opening hours were 9am-5pm, she was alarmed to see *"Bacon baps from 8.30am"* chalked on the board above the counter.

"Stuff that," she said, rubbing it off.

She swept the place through, turned on all the machines and chopped piles of salad stuff. By the time Ffion finally arrived at around 10am, her dyed-black hair hanging in ironed curtains on either side of her face, Jude was seething. Another arrogant, sullen teenager, just like the hordes that roamed down Oxford High Street, yelling into their phones, tossing their fragrant hair, wearing their rich kids' clothes and blocking the pavement.

"Aren't you supposed to be here at 8.30?" she snapped.

"I start at ten. Didn't Siôn tell you? It's not usually busy before then," the girl replied sweetly. "I'll make us a *panad*/cuppa. I'm Ffion, by the way." She filled the kettle, swung back her sheets of hair, and sauntered off.

"You work at *Plas Hyfryd*, don't you?" Ffion said, handing Jude a mug of the strong tea she obviously assumed Jude was in need of. "Menna told me. My *Nain*/grandmother died in there."

"Oh, I'm sorry to hear that," Jude replied guardedly. She was not at all sure what to make of this young girl.

"It's fine. They looked after her really well, when Mum couldn't cope anymore. Even came to the funeral, her key worker did."

Jude smiled at her sadly. "I'm not at all surprised to hear that. We get really fond of them, and it's hard, to see the people they once were gradually vanish."

"Yeah. I think it's brilliant that you work there. Jude's your name, isn't it?" Ffion said.

Jude blushed at her rudeness. She thought she had learnt not to follow the, often insincere, Oxford rules of behaviour here, as they often didn't apply. Up here, people were more straightforward. "Yes, I'm sorry. I didn't even tell you my name."

"Don't worry! I'll let you off," Ffion said with a cheeky grin. "Right, we'd better get ready. The Big Bacon Bap Rush will start soon."

"All hands on deck it is then," Jude replied, with a mock salute.

"Another weird Englishwoman" was written all over Ffion's face, but her grin was a thoroughly forgiving one.

By 2pm, Jude and Ffion had sliced, buttered, filled, wrapped, and sold scores of sandwiches, bacon baps, and filled baguettes, and were friends for life. As soon as Ffion saw that fillings were running low, she topped them up from the plastic boxes in the fridge. Jude took the orders and kept track of who needed drinks with a logic and efficiency that genuinely surprised her. She was also amazed at how much she enjoyed herself, chatting and laughing with customers as they waited for their food. At the end of the day, Siôn called her:

"So how did it go?" he said.

"Great," she replied. "I loved it, in fact."

"Thank goodness for that. Right, you're all mine for the rest of the summer, and I'll give you a bonus at the end of the season. I feel as if you've saved my life, Jude."

"The feeling's mutual," she replied. "But make it a big bonus, please."

Most of the customers in the little shop were families from Manchester or Liverpool who had visited the island regularly for years and knew where to find it, hidden behind the glitzier eateries on the main street. They dripped in straight off the beach in their wet swimming costumes, bodies striped with strategic areas of sunburn, hair stiff with salty water. Their children clamoured at the counter like chicks in a nest, quietening only when something was put into their wriggling fingers. During each busy day, Jude thought back to the gallery in Oxford, where Helena had always made her feel inept and slow; here, she was hot and busy, and her feet were killing her, but she was buzzing with adrenaline. She felt like a person with a purpose.

As they were beginning to pack things away to close the shop one lazy hot afternoon, a woman's face appeared at the doorway, holding a cigarette and puffing the smoke straight into the café. Ffion scowled.

"You're that English woman from the cottage on the beach,

aren't you?" the woman said. She had pale, pastry-coloured skin and wore a yellow jersey dress. Jude's first thought was that she looked like a large fried egg.

"Yes, I'm Jude Fitzgerald, I'm English and I live there. Sorry, do I know you?" she replied defensively, aware of every syllable of her crisp accent.

"Not me, no, but I've heard about you from my daughter Non. She's married to Owain Pritchard. You know *him*, don't you, Mrs Fitzgerald?" she said contemptuously.

"I... yes, I know him. He repaired the roof on my cottage."

"That's one way of putting it," the woman said with a snort. "You stay away from him, you hear? He's a married man, and up here, we respect that fact. Go back to your own kind, who obviously don't."

Grinding her cigarette butt on the pavement outside the shop, she walked off with a parting glare.

"I don't know what you've been doing, and it's none of my business, Jude, but that's Nesta Evans. You really, really don't want to cross her," Ffion said. "She went to school with my mam and was the biggest bully in the school. A seriously scary lady, that one."

"I got the message loud and clear, don't worry, but she's not going to bully me," Jude replied.

Her words were brave, but she was shaking. That had been a very clear warning to stay well away from Owain. Had his wife found out about their last meeting and told her mother, who was clearly a past master at terrorising others? Had Owain gone back to his wife, told her that they had slept together, and dubbed her the stereotypical "predatory widow" as Nesta had just implied? She could not believe that of him, but *something* bad had happened, it was clear.

Whatever was to come, Jude had a terrible feeling this was only the beginning of it.

TWENTY-SEVEN

"Don't we both look fabulous?"

Jude held her phone up in front of Rhiannon's face, hoping she could make out the two people in the photograph: them. She had taken it the last time she had been to visit, and their friendship, which had grown in only a few weeks, was so clear to see that it shone out of the screen.

"Well, I'm sure it's a lovely photo of *you, cariad*/love," Rhiannon said with a chuckle. "I can see that my pearls look good, though. Gift from my Guto they were, when we had Rhodri, you know." Her hand fluttered up towards them. "My beautiful boy."

Jude felt a lump rise in her throat. She loved her son so much, but he hardly even came to visit her, whereas she rarely mentioned her kind, caring daughter, who so often did. "I'll get it printed out and put it in a nice frame for you," she said, to hide her feelings.

Rhiannon started to cough, so Jude unwrapped a cough sweet and put it into the old woman's mouth. As she sucked it contemplatively for the next ten minutes, Jude noticed how hollow her cheeks were, and how little flesh or hair covered her head. She resembled a tiny sparrow.

"I made over forty bacon sandwiches yesterday, Rhiannon," Jude said, popping a toffee into her own mouth.

"Mari used to love a bacon sandwich," Rhiannon said sadly. "Crispy, she liked it. Almost burnt, in fact." A pause, a sigh. Jude held her breath, sensing that a deep memory had surfaced, which might need time to sink down beneath the waves again. She was right. A minute or so later, it had gone, and Rhiannon said, "So where is it you work again, Judith? You've told me, but I forget things."

"In a sandwich shop in Rhosneigr," Jude said, as she told her every single time she visited.

Rhiannon looked at her searchingly. "You shouldn't be in here, with me, because he died, you know. People die, but you need to go on living."

Jude almost choked on her toffee. "Sorry? What did you say?"

"You told me that you lost your husband, like me. Well, you should find a new one now, and a good one. Don't do what I did, wait for years for a dream that's gone. Find a new one and chase it."

Jude had to get up and crossed the room to look out of the window to regain some composure. She was shocked. "Chase the dream" were the exact words on Alex's Harley that now languished undercover in the lean-to behind her cottage. How could Rhiannon have known to hit such a painful nerve, so precisely? Tears in her eyes, Jude focused on a blue tit determinedly eating peanuts from a feeder on the glass. When she turned round, Rhiannon was staring at her, her milky eyes unmoving. She began rubbing her thin hands together so that they made a sound like the crinkly paper lining in a box of chocolates, and it was clear their previous conversation had

been forgotten as easily as a wave softly washes away marks left
on sand.

"Rhosneigr. Beautiful beach. Clearest water on the island.
Rhodri used to go crabbing there, in the rock pools. My Little
Man I used to call him. He didn't like it, but that's what he was,
after Guto died – a little man. He had to be, really." A pause.
"Did your father die, dear?"

"Yes, he did. He'd left us, me and my mum, years earlier,
and I hated him for years for that, but when I saw him, near the
end, I still loved him."

"Of course you did."

Neither woman spoke for a long while but watched the
birds squabbling over the peanuts at the window.

"Can you pop to the shop and get me some more cough
sweets, *cariad*/love? I've lost them. I don't know where I've put
the last lot, and I must have them, you know, for my chest,"
Rhiannon said eventually.

Jude had a fair idea where the packet of "lost" cough sweets
would be: up Rhiannon's sleeve, in her hankie, or in the basket
at the front of "Trevor the Zimmer's" walking frame, but she
said nothing and set off to walk to the "sweet shop" on the Unit.
She was glad of the chance to think about her father for a few
minutes, before Rhiannon initiated a completely different
conversation when she returned, as she was sure to do.

The last time she had seen Donald was almost a decade after
he'd left them. He'd been a haggard shape beneath the blankets
of a hospital bed in Inverness. She did not like to remember the
smell or the awful noises he had made, because she had wanted
to see the man who had worn soft, brushed cotton checked shirts
and put his tweed trilby on the hook when he came in from work
each evening. Her mother had refused to see him, or even go to
his funeral, in case she met Brenda, the woman who had loved
him for the last years of his life. They'd never married, which

had horrified Gloria even more. But where was Brenda now? Jude wondered. Was she as bitter as her mother was? Surely *nobody* could be as bitter as Gloria. She must be lonely though, as widows were the loneliest souls on earth in her experience.

When she returned, Rhiannon was fast asleep in front of *Cash in the Attic* clutching the lost packet of cough sweets.

Throughout August, Jude worked six days a week: four with Ffion in the sandwich shop, and two in the care home. She was always so tired that she began to wonder if she had picked up some kind of virus, but when looked at her schedule, it was obvious what was to blame: exhaustion, and disappointment. Nesta Evans did not pay her another visit, and she hadn't heard from Owain at all. What had happened between them had been wonderful, but could not happen again, she told herself so often that she began to believe it. And so, when he came into the shop just as she and Ffion were closing up one day, she was dumbstruck.

"Hello, Owain. We're closed."

Ffion laughed out loud. "*Iesu*/Jesus, Jude! A bit of politeness to our customers, please. *Helô*/Hello Mr Pritchard. *Ga'i helpu chi?*/Can I help you?"

"*Mae'n iawn*/That's fine," he answered, looking only at Jude. "You look well, Jude. Filled-out a bit in fact. Eating leftovers from this place, I'm guessing. It's good to see."

Jude winced. "No woman likes to be told she's 'filled-out', Owain," she snapped, feeling a nervous fluttering in her belly. How did this man always have such an effect on her, and how did he have the nerve to walk in and want to talk to her now, having not contacted her for ages? The fact that he had just pointed out her weight gain made it easier for her to do what needed to be done: tell him to get lost.

"Don't suppose you've got an hour free now, have you?" he asked.

"No, sorry. I'm busy at the moment," she said, smiling vapidly at some new customers waiting behind Owain. "Lots to do, as you can see."

Ffion exhaled loudly with relief. Nesta would be back within the hour if she found out that these two had met again, and things would get very messy indeed.

Owain looked at his boots, and then at Jude again. His eyes were misted with tears, and he looked utterly devastated. "I understand, and I'm sorry," he murmured. "Take care of yourself, Jude."

She nodded wordlessly. She knew without asking him that she'd been right, and that he had done the dutiful, respectable thing and gone back to his wife. Having met his mother-in-law, she could easily imagine the pressure he had been under to do so. Now, it was more important than ever for her to be strong, and stay strong, but resisting her instinct to run after him as he walked away was incredibly, almost impossibly, hard.

TWENTY-EIGHT

At the end of August, Jude took a few days' leave from both her jobs as she was absolutely shattered and wanted only to vegetate in her own home and be left in peace. It was now almost exactly a year since she had arrived on the island, and she did not recognise the tanned, glowing face that looked back at her from the new mirror in her bedroom. She had an even shorter haircut at Stella's suggestion and had bought some gorgeous clothes online as she had gone up a clothes size and was looking a lot less scrawny. What she saw, made her proud of how far she'd come.

"I think I look 'well', Owain, rather than just 'fat', thanks very much," she murmured, standing sidelong. She'd not looked this healthy since Alex's diagnosis. "You've brought me back to life, Anglesey. Thank you."

It was drizzling outside that day and a walk did not appeal either to her or to Pip, so she decided to pamper herself instead. She spread on a thick, green face-pack, slathered her hair with intensive, gloopy conditioner and smoothed a layer of Dead Sea mud onto her décolletage because the summer sun seemed to have made it a bit wrinkly. She was just sitting down to attack her horribly horny toenails when there was a knock on the door. She froze, but Pip's immediate bark gave away the fact that she was in.

"I'm not really open for visitors at the moment. Who is it?" she said, the skin around her lips already tautening as the face-pack hardened.

"Owain."

"Shit."

She opened the door, registered the flash of undisguised shock on Owain's face before miming "Wait here" and dashing into the bathroom, where she stripped off, got into the shower, and scrubbed her face, body, and hair furiously. Ten minutes later, when she emerged dressed in an old tracksuit, Owain was sitting on her sofa stroking Pip, whose eyes were closed with pleasure. He looked tired, and much older than when she had last seen him in the café a few weeks earlier.

"Can I get you a drink... er... a *panad*/cuppa, I mean?" she said awkwardly. What was he doing here? Had she not made her feelings clear enough, the last time they'd met? Inside her, chaos churned, but Jude was determined to maintain a dignified outside.

"No, I can't stay, but I needed to see you," he replied. He would not meet her eye, but picked at a thread on his sleeve, like a shy teenager. The tension in the room made the air feel slice-ably thick.

"We can't do this anymore, Owain," she said. "I have heard nothing at all from you after our... *time together*." Her cheeks flushed at a sudden memory of their passionate lovemaking on the headland. "You have made your choice, it's very clear, so you need to leave me alone now."

He nodded. "I know, and I have tried to tell myself that these past weeks. She begged me to move back in, said she needed me, and I told myself I owed it to our marriage to try again. But it was a mistake, Jude. Life at home is intolerable, and

I can tell that Non knows all I am thinking about is you. She barely speaks to me."

Jude glared at him. "Is your misery supposed to make me feel better? Well, it doesn't." She got up, walked towards the doorway and then suddenly doubled over in pain, holding her belly. "God that really hurts."

Owain leapt up and put his arms around her. "What's wrong, Jude? Where does it hurt?"

She lowered herself into a chair, breathing deeply. "Not sure, weird, but it's easing up now. I just got up too fast, I think," she said. "I'll be fine once I have a few days' rest. It's been so full-on, all summer in the café."

Owain stood behind her, his hands on her shoulders, which she knew would make it easier for him to say difficult things. "I'm worried about you," he said. "And worried about what will happen to us, Jude."

She sighed. Yes, she was worried too. Worried about having her heart broken, worried about playing second fiddle to his bullying, manipulative wife and her obnoxious family if he was suggesting they have an affair. Not being able to see his face made it easier for her to hide her feelings, but she was trembling, which he would be able to feel. It was time to be brave, very brave. She removed his hands, stood up, and turned round to face him.

"What are you here today to offer me, Owain?" she said. "You can't, or won't, leave your wife and I refuse to be a part-time partner that makes you feel good when you need a boost. We love each other, we know that, we said it, but you still feel bound to Non: there is no easy solution to that."

Owain flushed. "If you give me some time, I'll find a way out, and we can be together... but this is a small place, and I'll be hated," he bleated. "I know it sounds cowardly, but people's goodwill matters to me."

"It matters to me, too, actually!" Jude said sharply. "And

yes, it does sound cowardly. If you want to be with me, then you need to face the situation you're in and do something about it."

"Isn't loving you enough?" he replied, his brown eyes pleading. "I can't offer you more than that yet, but I will, I promise I will."

"So we'll meet furtively every week or so, will we? Go to remote spots and hope nobody sees us and reports back to your mother-in-law?" Jude said, her voice seething with indignation. This man had a bloody nerve! "She came into the café to harass me – did you know that? If Non is anything like, or anywhere near as scary, as Nesta, I can quite see why you feel you can't cross either of them!"

Stung, Owain staggered backwards, towards the door, breathing deeply. Despite his size, his strength, he looked powerless, and beaten.

"What will you do if I say I can't promise to leave you alone?" he murmured, his hands resting on either side of the doorframe as if his life depended on their support. "I can't live with you yet, but I can't live without you, Jude."

"You need to go, Owain. This is not what I need. I've suffered enough. Please don't come here again. Promise me you won't." Her heart was pounding, but she held her nerve.

"I can't promise that, Jude. I'm sorry, I just can't, but I will go now."

Closing the door behind him, he left, and Jude could finally weep.

TWENTY-NINE

In September, when the schools reopened, it was as if someone had pressed a "delete the tourists" button on the island, because the vast majority of them simply vanished. Glorious sunny days still came and went, but there was a light dew, and a chill in the air in the mornings and evenings by the middle of the month. The beach was almost deserted now, with only a few groups of local children colonising the rocks and racing into the waves after school. The sandwich shop and many other little shops closed for the winter and Jude watched as the island begin to hunker down, almost to wrap a warm blanket around itself, preparing for the long, cold months ahead. She, too, felt an imminence in the air as if something had shifted. As she marked her first anniversary on the island, she felt once again that it was time for something to change.

When Mair Roberts called at *Hedd* to remind her that her lease would expire in the middle of September, there was no offer of a further extension. The owners had accepted that they needed to spend money on the place, as Anglesey was "on the up". They planned to put in central heating, fit a new kitchen and redecorate before trying to sell the cottage at an inflated price in the spring. Jude was not as devastated as she thought she would be, which unsettled her; she was tired of having to make huge decisions on her own. Waiting until the spring to buy *Hedd* was a possibility, but her heart was not in it, and she felt an emptiness when she thought of having to find a temporary home until then. A huge pall of weariness seemed to descend on her each day, and she could not be bothered to cook, to walk or to do anything very much at all. Heartbreak was clearly exhausting.

When Menna got a job in Bangor, it meant no more lunchtime walks. Lisa at *Plas Hyfryd* could not guarantee her many hours beyond October either, as budgets were squeezed. Welsh lessons would start again soon, but Stella had not committed to them, as she spent all her free time with Eifion and Jude saw less and less of her. It felt as if her island life was being dismantled around her piece by piece, and she felt she needed to find a safe, warm nest to snuggle in to get through the winter. For the first time, she began to consider that it might not be on Anglesey.

When she confessed her doubts to The Fearsome Foursome, they leapt on them. Why was she even considering staying there, for another gruelling winter? She needed to come back *now*, and be with them, where she belonged. They meant well, Jude knew, but the thought of returning to Oxford and risking losing the stronger person she had become terrified her. Her only hope was that her wise old friend Rhiannon would tell her what to do when she next went to see her.

But that hope seemed in vain. Rhiannon's memory had deteriorated a great deal over the summer, and she now forgot huge tracts of her life. Whenever Jude tried to talk about her dilemma, the old woman didn't seem interested. Her silly problems meant nothing; they were swept away in the vivid glimpses of the old woman's past that sustained her through each day. Upset and frustrated, Jude tried to remember R.S. Thomas' words in a poem in Owain's book. Her role here was to *"lean kindly across the abyss/To hear words that were once wise"*. But it was getting harder every time she came, to watch her friend slowly disappear before her eyes.

One especially gloomy afternoon, however, Jude did get the answer she'd been hoping for, if not in the way she'd expected.

"He is such a good boy, my Rhodri," Rhiannon told her, for the fifth or sixth time that day.

Jude was tired and felt so irritated with her friend's adoration of her son and neglect of her daughter that she could not hide it.

"But Rhodri doesn't come and see you though, does he, like Hâf does?" she muttered under her breath.

The old woman's hearing was as sharp as it had ever been.

"And why don't you go and see *your* mother?" Rhiannon snapped. "I'm sure she misses you. Whatever she's done to you in the past, I'm sure she regrets it now."

Jude gulped. The old woman had hit a nerve. "I'm not sure she does, but I've got my reasons for not wanting to see her."

"Well, Rhodri has his reasons, and I have my reasons for the way I feel about Hâf, ones I can never share with anyone. We all have our reasons and our regrets, Jude, that's the way of it." The old woman shifted in her chair, wincing with pain. She was now so thin that her bones ground into the chair. "You need to see her and forgive her. Especially now, with a baby on the way."

"A... a baby?" Jude stammered. "But I, I mean..."

"Babies sometimes come along without you expecting them, *cariad*/love. Make yours welcome in this world. Go home, surround yourself with friends, and get ready for the greatest gift of all."

. . .

Whenever she looked back at that moment, Jude always remembered the sharp jolt of shock, followed within seconds with absolute and total understanding. How could she not have realised before? Her periods had always been far from regular, but the overwhelming tiredness, nausea, tender nipples – all the signs of early pregnancy that she had so adored in the past. And as for the little flutterings she'd felt in her belly, well, she had never reached that stage before. Did it mean that she must be past the point at which she had lost both her previous babies? A pregnancy test confirmed Rhiannon's instinct with the deepest of blue lines. Looking at her calendar, Jude calculated that this baby was more likely to be Tom's, as she had slept with him before Owain, but her dates were embarrassingly vague as she did not keep a diary anymore. Her periods were so unreliable that she might never be completely sure, but she had to feel as certain as she could about this, so she opted for Tom as the father. At least he wasn't married, so there would be no incandescent wife and potentially violent family for her to deal with. She would decide whether to tell him about her slight doubts if the need ever arose and dearly hope it didn't.

"God, what kind of woman have I become, Alex?" she murmured.

And yet she was not sorry, because a child was coming, a child she had longed for, a child that would be hers to love for the rest of her life. Rhiannon had been right, this baby was a gift, and she deserved it.

Mair Roberts was not surprised when Jude said she was leaving the island and going home. A quick glance at her slightly rounded tummy and pale, sickly face told her everything she needed to know, and understand.

"You came here to get better, and you *are* better. It's time," she said, hugging Jude warmly.

Jude invited Stella and Menna to *Hedd* for supper together, so that she could get her confession over with in one fell swoop. She fed them, and then told them, in as matter of fact a way as she could, that a) she was pregnant, having slept with Tom, b) she had fallen in love with Owain Pritchard, and that they had made love just once, but they knew it could never happen again, c) that she really wasn't as promiscuous as they might think she was, and d) that it was time for her to go back to Oxford, and the world she knew, to have this baby. Though her friends were such very different women, they both supported her immediately and unequivocally, without any hint of doubt or judgement.

"I'm gutted, but I can see why you have to leave," Menna said. "To be near someone you love, and not be able to be together, would be torture. Non doesn't love him, but she got her claws into him good and proper."

"It's just such a shame, if you love each other," Stella said, shaking her head sadly. "But you need to put yourself and your baby first now."

"I know, but I'll really miss you both," Jude said tearfully. "You've been my guiding lights, in so many ways."

"You'll be back, *heb amheuaeth*/without a doubt," Menna said with a wobble in her voice that Jude had never, ever heard before. "And you're always welcome in our home."

"And in mine. You'll be back. It gets under your skin, this place, remember?" Stella added with a wink that exposed some very vivid kingfisher-blue eyeshadow.

Over the next week, Jude slowly packed, putting the things she loved most about her year on the island into a box. She had always done this, for every phase of her life – a habit that Gloria despaired of, as some of these "memory maker" boxes were still taking up room in her house in Taunton. For her Anglesey box, Jude saved sea-smoothed shards of glass, black pebbles shot through with a dash of white, crisping mermaids' purses, and bleached twigs of driftwood that told a tale of their own. She added scores of whorled, ribbed, pearlescent, mottled or barnacled shells, determined to create more collages with these treasures so that she could *feel* this very special place, as well as see it in her mind's eye, when she was no longer here. The rest of the things she'd collected over these months she sowed back onto the beach, for others to reap.

On the day she left, a keen autumn wind was tormenting the sycamore sapling behind the cottage, and it thrashed back and forth helplessly. Jude shivered, the bitter cold of winter was coming to the island once more, and she was glad, at least, to be escaping its merciless teeth. It was time to leave, but she would never forget this island, or its wild beauty. It had healed her and brought her to this miraculous point in her life.

As she drove away, a heron was making unsteady progress across the sky – neck hunched, bony breast stiff, brittle legs neatly folded underneath its body. It looked so fragile, but its wide, grey wings beat strongly as it fought onwards, head down into the wind, towards home.

PART 5

HOMECOMING

THIRTY

OXFORD

Alex had always said that Oxford was at its best in the autumn. As the relentless heat of summer gradually faded, vivid blue skies formed the perfect foil for the honeycomb-coloured stone of the colleges, and the leaves on the city's trees blazed with red, ochre, and deep cinnamon. The college gardens were still bright, and perfectly pruned flowering shrubs in each herbaceous border vied for attention before the morning frosts began, and their glory days were done. For this brief period of each year the city belonged to those who lived in it, the massed armies of tourists and foreign students having left, but the new year's university students yet to arrive. It was an ideal time for Jude to return to the city after her year on Anglesey, and she felt her husband's presence keenly as she drove along its tree-lined roads towards the next phase of her life – motherhood.

Paula and Georgio had offered to put Jude, Pip, and Tuna up for a while. In return, they asked if she would mind looking after Christos while Paula went into the office for a day a week, the first time she had done so since his birth. It seemed like an irresistible deal, especially as Jude knew she would soon have to tell her friends about her own pregnancy, but when Paula burst out of her front door, her tanned arms windmilling, all she wanted to do was drive away again.

"Jude! It's so brilliant to see you!" she shrieked, sticking her head through the open car window to kiss her friend. "Everyone's here, loads of people you know and there's a bucket of Pimms inside with your name on it!"

Jude felt her smile falter. The last thing she felt like was a big, boozy gathering. She was pregnant, not drinking, and dog-tired.

"I'd better get the animals settled first, otherwise we'll have a riot," she said, unable at that moment to match her friend's enthusiasm. She saw Paula's face fall and felt a stab of guilt. Fumbling to release Pip's crate from the seat belt, she took a couple of deep breaths to steady herself before emerging with a cheery, "So how's that gorgeous boy then? I bet he's grown so much," and a huge smile that was warmly returned by her friend.

"Oh, he *has*! Mother-in-law has got him tonight, though. She has him once a week. It keeps her at bay, and it helps us. Hooray for bottles, Jude! He's on solids now too," Paula said, her eyes bright with pride.

"Amazing. Just give me a few minutes to sort these two out and I'll be there," Jude replied. "It's good to be home, Paula." And she meant it.

She let Pip run around in the front garden for a minute or two before guiltily shutting both her pets in the garage, where Paula had prepared two comfy beds, a bowl of water and a litter tray for them. Jude resisted the strong temptation to join them, and just go to sleep. Gales of laughter from the back garden pierced the muggy air, punctuated by the chink of glasses. She crept into the downstairs toilet to brace herself.

All the people in the garden were her friends, and they were at this party for one reason only: to see her. Their faces would register a flash of: "Gosh, she's aged" or "She's put on weight", however hard they tried not to show it, because it had been well over a year since some of them had last seen her. It was also a long time since she had really thought a great deal about how she looked. After Alex had died, she hadn't cared a damn, and on the island, it hadn't mattered. Ordering new clothes online was just for fun, not to impress anyone or follow a trend, and she had indulged her long-suppressed love of baggy sweaters and dungarees once more knowing that nobody on Anglesey would bat an eyelid at a "more mature" woman wearing them. Now, she was moving in circles where appearances counted, and were judged.

She looked hard at her face in the mirror above the sink and saw once more how much it had changed. Wetting her hands under the cold tap, she ran her fingers through her cropped, sun-bleached hair, trying to relax the muscles of her face. When she did so, lace-thin creases of white appeared at the corners of her eyes where the sun had not tanned into her wrinkles. Well, these tiny, feathery marks were scars from the lonely road she had travelled for the last year or so, she decided. She would wear her wounds with pride.

"No, I am not the same woman I was when I left here – I am better," she said to her reflection, before walking out into the garden, where she was engulfed in arms, kisses, and welcomes. Tom was amongst the first to greet her, and she thanked him for agreeing to have the Harley back in his shed until she knew where she would be living longer term. As he hugged her shyly, she felt a fizz of excitement about what lay ahead for them both: the birth of their baby. She would have to tell him about it pretty soon, she owed him that, and felt sure that he would want to support her in any way he could, but not yet, not tonight. She wanted to hold her precious secret close for a little while longer and hope her friends wouldn't look too closely at her midriff this evening.

Morag rumbled her immediately, however, with a simple

but effective ruse. She came and sat next to Jude, who was nursing a glass of tepid mineral water, her eyelids heavy with exhaustion.

"Can I get you a drink?" she said. "You look as if you need one."

"No thanks. I'll stick to water." Her hand went instinctively to her belly seconds before she realised her slip.

"When's it due?" Morag asked with an eye roll.

Jude gasped and put a finger to her lips. "PLEASE don't tell anyone, Morag. I'm not sure when it's due, and before you ask, I'm not very sure who the father is either," she whispered. "But I don't *care*! It's all going to be *fabulous!*"

"Oh, Jude," Morag said mournfully. "That's what I said, back in the day when Finn made his presence felt for the first time. Remember – I threw up in a waste paper bin at your and Alex's house?"

Jude nodded. "Yes, I remember, but this baby is much, *much* wanted, and I had no terrible trauma when its life began, as you did, though I do feel a bit ashamed of having two potential fathers. It will be loved and cared for, and that's all that matters in my book."

"How I envy you, for believing that to be the case," Morag said softly.

THIRTY-ONE

Paula loved her job in a prestigious marketing agency in North Oxford and the glamour that went with lunching with clients and popping up to London for meetings and expensive dinners after them. Her chatter was full of Christos now, but Jude could tell that she was missing what she called "L.B.M." (Life Before Mummyhood). She was looking forward to returning to that world, if only in a very gradual way, and Jude was happy to be helping her.

The afternoon after the party, Paula took the little boy to a babies' swimming session, hoping that it would dispel her hangover. The fridge was full of organic fruit and veg (delivered each week but rarely eaten), so Jude spent the afternoon peeling, chopping, and steaming apples, pears, sweet potatoes, courgettes, and carrots, before mixing and decanting the results into plastic pots. When Paula and Christos got home, there were at least a month's worth of freshly cooked baby meals in the fridge and the kitchen was a bomb site.

"Jeez, Jude. Are you in training for a world record baby mush-making attempt? Let's hope the poor boy eats it all before his 21st!" Paula said.

. . .

When she came downstairs ready for work the following day, Paula looked nothing like the frazzled mother of a young baby that had gone to bed the previous night. Her biscuit-coloured linen suit had sharp creases down the front of each leg, her hair was straightened into glossy sheets, and any hint of tiredness had been disguised with perfect make-up.

"The routine for today is pretty straightforward," she said, handing Jude a printed sheet, which she read in silence as Paula cooed at her baby.

- 8.30 – 9.15am: 6oz bottle. Nappy change. In bouncy chair with toys.
- 9.15 – 10.15am: morning nap.
- 10.15 – 11.45am: nappy change, walk in buggy. Plenty of interaction, small toys in buggy, describing things etc.
- 11.45 – 12.30pm: in bouncy chair with (different) toys. Nappy change.
- 12.30 – 1pm: 8oz bottle plus small meal (baby jars in cupboard, or your stuff if he'll have it!).
- 1pm – 1.30pm: play time on mat under baby gym. Nappy change.
- 1.30 – 2.30pm: walk in buggy/fresh air/nap.
- 2.30 – 3.30pm: play time on mat/in chair/in nest. Nappy change.
- 3.30 – 4.30pm: baby singing group (Summertown).
- 4.30 – 5pm: nap on way back. Wake him up when home!
- 5.00 – 5.30 pm: teatime bottle and small meal of solids. Nappy change.
- 5.30 – 6.45pm – Mum home. Bath, books, bottle, bed.

Jude really wanted to laugh when she reached the end, but resisted. She'd never had a baby, of course, but she suspected very few of them would live their little lives to a bonkers timetable like this. She waved her friend off and walked out into the garden. Christos would be hers, and hers only, until the early evening, and nobody would know what she did with him. As to sticking to the schedule, and going to the "singing group", well, that was a no-brainer. This was time for her to get some practice in being a mum, and for Christos to have some fun!

Georgio had recently paid landscape gardeners to completely redesign the garden at the back of the house, and every inch was paved, cobbled, or planted with red-leaved acers, elegant bamboos, and twisty-twigged shrubs. Jude took Christos to sit in one of the garden's three new "low maintenance" arbours and give him his bottle, watching him gulp it down and remembering his very first one, in Menna's shop on Anglesey. Then she carried his bouncy chair outside and put it under the willow tree on one side of the garden where he cooed happily for half an hour or so, and she cooed back at him. It was bliss.

When it was time for lunch, she swaddled him in a muslin cloth to protect his pristine clothes and dipped the spoon into one of her home-made purees before gently bringing it to his lips. His plump, pink tongue flicked over the smear of food, his face registered several different emotions in quick succession and then his mouth gaped like a baby bird in a nest. Jude loaded the spoon with more puree and popped it into his mouth. Within five minutes, the food was gone, and the baby winded and sound asleep in her arms, his head flopped like a rag doll. He smelt delicious – a sweet mixture of milk, washed baby-fuzz hair and fruit. Closing her eyes, Jude wrapped her arms around him as tightly as she dared and began walking around the garden, inhaling him with deep, rhythmic breaths. This was as near paradise as she had ever been, and soon it would be her life too; the realisation almost made her weep with happiness. The only fly in the ointment was the fact that she would soon have to *tell* everyone about her baby, and about the probability that Tom, her dead husband's closest friend, was its father. That part was not going to be easy at all.

When Christos woke up and began to grizzle and squirm, she carried him inside, laid him down on his playmat and positioned the baby gym carefully over him. His brown eyes widened, his arms flailed towards the dangling bits and his legs kicked in undiluted joy. She used this time to make herself a sandwich, before gently pushing Christos' little arms into the sleeves of his jacket, popping on his gorgeous "blueberry" hat and putting him and some small toys in his buggy to go for a walk.

"Look! I'm following your instructions, Paula," she murmured happily.

Even as she was living it, Jude knew that this day would be fixed in her memory with a gem-like clarity. Daring to imagine once again that this was the way *her* days were soon going to be, she passed other North Oxford mothers pushing buggies and smiled at them all with what she hoped was a smile of confidence and belonging. They smiled back, but they looked tired.

When Paula got home, she was frazzled, stressed at how little she'd remembered of her job, and how hard it had been to *think*. She was also furious that one of her colleagues had told her that she "looked better with a bit of baby weight on her". She gave Christos a quick, irritated cuddle, and then asked Jude if she could change and shower before taking over.

"Fine with me," she replied, adding, in a whisper, "Looks like I'm in charge of 'bath, books, bottle, bed', Christos."

THIRTY-TWO

Jude had not realised how much of her life in Oxford had been predicated on her having a partner, until she came back. She had met her friends for a drink, seen a film with them, and gone to weekly pottery classes at the College of Further Education, but had always gone back gratefully to the security of being Mrs Fitzgerald. Now she couldn't.

On Anglesey, many of the people she knew had partners and families, of course, but she rarely met them. She knew that Menna had two boys, Cai and Iolo, but she'd never seen them when she had been round for a quick supper. They had either been in bed, at Sea Scouts, or just out playing in the village. Stella saw her separately from Eifion, as she was sensitive to how her friend might feel about her singleness. On the island, Jude had been grateful for these boundaries, and for being accepted as an individual in her own right, but in Oxford, people seemed to socialise in herds of similar stock, and those herds were all too often subdivided into pairs. When Georgio told her that he'd organised another "small gathering" of friends at the weekend, Jude's heart sank at the prospect of feeling on the periphery of things once more. In addition, she would have to come clean about her pregnancy soon. Might it be easiest to tell them all the happy news at the party, she wondered, but when the idea made her shiver, she decided against it. It would probably feel more like lighting a fuse and waiting for the explosion.

"It's not for you this time. It's actually to announce our engagement," Paula reassured her when she expressed her doubts about having to meet and greet lots of people again. "It will do you good, Jude, to socialise more. You've become a bit of a recluse since your time as 'Robinson Crusoe'. You're even wearing baggy old sacks these days, like he did. I can lend you some clothes if you like..."

"I like baggy sacks, OK?" Jude said with a twinge of guilt at her now-practised deception.

But she was still dreading the party, having last seen some of the people Paula had invited at Alex's funeral. Then, they'd excused the way she had looked (terrible), the way she had behaved after it (drunk, and out of control) and some of the things she'd said (appallingly rude) as a grief reaction. Now those same people would be expecting to see the Jude they remembered from before Alex's illness, and she was not sure she could oblige. Paula had also invited Tom again, and Jude felt thick, deep dread at the thought of how he might react to the revelation that lay ahead for him. As hormones surged around her body, she'd started to worry that perhaps he wasn't ready for unexpected fatherhood, let alone with her as his unexpected baby's mother. A party was the last thing she needed.

Paula and Georgio asked people to come at 6pm, just as dusk was softening the bright heat of another airless autumn day in the city. The garden was decorated with tea-light lanterns, tasteful terracotta chimineas, tiny fairy lights and solar lights whose glow strengthened as darkness slowly fell; it looked simple but beautiful.

Once she had dabbed some eyeshadow onto her eyelids, added a flick of eyeliner, lashings of mascara, and some cherry-red lipstick, Jude felt better, and knew that she both looked and felt glowing, as many pregnant women do. Her dress was a suitably diaphanous green silk shift, and her hair, newly styled in an expensive salon in town, moved up from her jawline in sculpted waves. Her skin was moist, rejuvenated courtesy of the luxurious face cream Paula had bought her, saying:

"We don't do 'weather-beaten' in Oxford, and I don't think you should do it anymore either, dear."

When the party began, Jude stood on her own in the shadows as she recognised faces, one by one. She spotted Alex's secretary, Annette, who had protected him from the wrath of clients whose cases were delayed as his illness swiftly took hold. Then she saw Harry, who'd been the coxswain of the boat Alex had rowed in, and so kind when he had been forced to give up rowing, even inviting him to the Boat Club dinner when he was far too sick to eat anything. These people had cared about him, and they cared about her too. It was good to see them again.

"You look marvellous, Jude," Harry said, his face lighting up when he saw her. "Your time by the sea has done you the world of good."

"Thanks, Harry. That means a lot."

"Lovely to see you looking happy again, Jude," Annette whispered at her side. "You were so brave, and it was so awful."

"It was. Not sure I was brave, though. I think I was in denial until he actually took his last breath."

The two women hugged, as there was no more to be said.

Darkness fell on cue, and all the lights in the garden twinkled pleasingly, tiny pinpricks of white. Paula and Georgio stood together under an arch of clematis and jasmine, and asked for "hush".

"Paula and I are going to get married at my parents' village in Cyprus. Anyone who can come and join us is most welcome, but they can buy their own plane tickets! Keep your eyes peeled for more deets," Georgio announced with a broad smile.

As roars of approval rang out, Jude joined in with genuine enthusiasm.

After the toasts, she saw Tom standing a little apart, and went to join him. He was trying to spear a cherry tomato with a plastic fork as his paper plate buckled and bent. With his cream linen jacket, powder-blue shirt and red and white tie, he looked very handsome indeed.

"You look gorgeous," he said with a smile. "That colour really suits you."

"Thanks, Tom. So do you, and it's good to see you again," Jude replied. "I was really grateful for your support, you know, with the roof and all the building work."

"I enjoyed myself on Anglesey, and I'm glad to help you in any way I can going forward, with builders, bikes, and babies," he said. An awkward silence followed, in which they both recalled what else they'd done that weekend, and its possible consequences. When he stabbed at the tomato so hard that it ricocheted away onto the grass, they giggled, which broke the tension immediately. "Why don't we meet up for lunch, or dinner? I'd love to see you more often now that you're back. No strings attached, of course."

Jude met his gaze and held it. Could she tell him now, in the middle of this lovely party, that she was pregnant with his child? It seemed unkind to spring it on him in public, but he needed to know, and soon.

"How about lunch tomorrow?" she said, her heart pounding.

"Great, yes," he replied, clearly surprised. "Browns at 1pm suit you?"

"Perfect. And could you possibly get me a glass of cold water?" she asked, suddenly in desperate need of some time alone.

As he scurried off, she sat down and thought how strange it was that she was carrying Tom's child while his friend, her beloved Alex, was dead, his ashes boxed and buried in a church-yard on the other side of the city. That thought stayed with her as she tried to sleep that night, and the prospect of telling Tom what huge changes lay ahead for both of them weighed heavy.

In fact, the anticipation of their conversation was far worse than the event. Jude told him gently, kindly, and waited whilst he processed the news, his expression moving from shock, through glee and finally settling on what looked like "grateful accep-tance". She did not tell him that she could not be entirely sure the baby was his as she had had a "one-night stand" with another man only weeks later. That would be too much, and it served no purpose to plant seeds of doubt in his mind.

"I can't believe we did what we did, but these things happen, even when they shouldn't," she said, blushing coyly.

"I for one am glad it happened, Jude – and even more so if the result is a baby. I will help you in any way I can, of course. And I want you to know that, if you need somewhere to live, I have a lovely house, as you know, and plenty of room..."

"Thanks, Tom. I'll sort something out in good time, and let you know. I haven't told the others yet, as I felt you should be the first to know."

He took her hand. "Why won't you consider coming to live with me, so that we can bring up our baby together? Alex would have wanted it, I know he would."

Jude flinched and took her hand away. "Alex would have

wanted me to be *sure* before I commit to anything or anyone. I'm really sorry."

He sighed. "Then I'll wait, and hope you change your mind," he replied.

"I may, I may not. I don't know how to feel right now, Tom."

But by the time they parted later that evening, as she watched him chat and laugh with such warmth and ease, Jude did know. She realised that the main obstacle between them was the past, and the fact that, when she looked at Tom, she thought of Alex. Having been "offered" both men, and chosen Alex once – for his gangly, tactless but strangely-appealing *awkwardness* as much as anything else – it was incredibly difficult to choose suave, gentle Tom now, having rejected him in the past. Alex had been a little vulnerable, like a lonely boy in need of comfort, a man who hid his fears behind his wit, just as Owain did. But Jude could not dispel the feeling she had always had, that Tom was, simply, too good for her.

THIRTY-THREE

Jude had not seen her mother for well over a year. She knew she should let Gloria know that she would soon be a grandmother, however little she would probably care, but the prospect filled her with nothing but dread. When she dialled her mother's number, still unsure what she would *say* to her, Gloria picked up after three rings, as she always had and always would.

"Hello, Mum. It's Judith." Her full name felt strange in her mouth as if it was something bulky she could not swallow. She'd always hated having such a frumpy-sounding name and spent her schooldays yearning to change it.

"Hello. I wondered when I'd get more than a postcard from you. Hang on a sec, while I turn the television down." Jude heard rattles and bangs, and then her mother's voice again. "So you've rejoined the land of the living, have you?"

"I'm back in Oxford, yes, Mum. Actually, I thought I'd come and see you this weekend, if that's all right with you."

"Oh. Right. I'll have to do some shopping then. And I'll have to move my hair appointment."

Jude heard the sour tang of martyrdom. "I'll do the shopping, don't worry, and I don't mind if your hair's not immaculate, Mum."

"But *I* mind."

Jude sighed. *Plus ça change.* "I'll have to bring my dog. Is that all right?"

There was a silence where a reassuring answer should have been. The strange, creeping heaviness that always accompanied a conversation with Gloria began to inch up Jude's body from her feet; it always started in her toes.

"It will have to be, really, won't it, if you now have a dog?"

"Mum, I've got some news for you," Jude said quickly. Perhaps she could tell her now, on the phone, and not go and visit at all?

"Have you, dear? I wish I had some news. Nothing ever happens here." A pause, a sigh. "I hope you feel better after your spell at the seaside. I always used to, but I haven't been for years. Not since you and Alexander took me once. Can't get there without a car, you see."

Jude closed her eyes. She knew that she had to go and see her mother, but she knew that she had to end this call or explode. "We'll get to the sea this weekend, I promise, OK? Got to go. See you on Friday."

Her mother certainly didn't sound as if she'd missed her or had any interest in her news. This was probably because she had never heard Gloria sound as if she was "interested" in anything apart from herself.

Jude had spent most of her childhood in a small, dark house on the outskirts of Taunton. She and her mother had moved there from a comfortable semi with a beautifully tended garden in Wells after Donald had moved to Scotland with Brenda. It was a house Jude always associated with sadness. When she arrived there on Friday afternoon, she parked outside and sat in the car, trying to muster enough courage to go in. There was a huge crack in the glass panel in the front door, with a trail of yellowed Sellotape behind it, and weeds framed the path. All the curtains were tightly drawn, as they always were, their linings faded to mothwing-white. Pip whined in his crate, anxious to be out.

"You're not going to have much fun here, sorry," Jude said to him.

She'd decided that she would take her mother out to Minehead or Porlock, walk the dog and get some lunch in one of the pretty tea shops on the seafront. Gloria would have nothing to eat in the house (because she never did) and this had been Alex's tactic whenever they had visited her: blast her out of her relentless self-pity with a series of outings. And always bring your own food.

When she finally rang the doorbell, it didn't work. The television was blaring inside, so she knocked lightly on the living room window, and her mother tweaked a corner of the curtain, nodded, and vanished again. Jude heard her slowly undoing chains and Chubb locks before the opened door released a blast of stale heat.

"Hello, Mum. How are you?" she said, moving forward to hug her. Gloria patted Jude's back as she was hugged, keeping their bodies apart from the shoulders down, as she had always done. No closeness allowed.

"Goodness, what a colour you've got on you! And you've got more wrinkles than me! It's that wind by the sea, I expect. Biting," her mother said. "Come in, come in. Oh, and the dog as well." She shuffled back into the house like an eighty-year-old, though she was not yet seventy. Jude followed, her heart already heavy.

The living room was just as gloomy, and just as hot as Jude had remembered; the gas fire was on "full", despite the relative warmth of the October day. Gloria made no move to turn it down, or to turn the television off, before she sat down in the only comfortable armchair in the room. Jude immediately had a strong urge to turn tail and run.

"I'll just let Pip have a run in the garden, if that's OK. Would you like a cuppa, Mum?" she said. "I could certainly do with one."

"The 'Meals on Wheels' ladies gave me some juice with my lunch, so I'm not bothered," Gloria said.

"Since when did you have Meals on Wheels?" Jude asked. "And it's only half past eleven – a bit early to have had your lunch, isn't it?"

"I have to have it when they get here. I've had them coming for a while now. *They* look after me very well," Gloria answered.

Jude allowed this comment to wash over her. "I see. Can't you cook for yourself anymore, Mum?"

"I can, but Eileen next door told me to take advantage of it. It's cheap and it saves me having to do it, or you having to worry about what I'm eating. Not that you would, of course." Her eyes were on the television, but her barb was not lost on Jude. Gloria really did have martyrdom down to a fine art.

"I'll make myself a cup of tea then," Jude replied, glad to be able to leave the room.

The kitchen was as depressing as the living room, if a little cooler. The milk was off, and globules of white floated to the top of her tea. True to form, there was nothing in the fridge apart from a tub of margarine and a greasy half-jar of jam. Two empty foil containers lay on the worktop, remnants of today's "Meals on Wheels", probably left out deliberately to shame her even further, Jude decided.

"I was going to suggest we went out for lunch, to Porlock perhaps, but if you've already eaten..." she called out. She was very hungry after her long drive but knew better than to mention it.

"My hips are too painful for me to sit in a car for long now,"

Gloria sighed as Jude came back into the room. She was gazing dolefully at the BBC newsreader for sympathy.

"Oh dear." A pause. "Well, I brought you some treats from that shop in the Covered Market you used to love."

Gloria's eyes snapped from the television to take the box Jude was now holding in front of her. She took out the short-bread biscuits, jam, toffees, and nougat, one by one, smiling fondly at them as if they were alive. "Alexander used to take me to this shop, didn't he? Made such a fuss of me, he did. Such a shame, isn't it, that he's gone? I do miss him."

Jude gulped her hot, sour tea too fast and spluttered it all over herself.

"Oh, for goodness' sake, you stupid girl! Get a cloth and sponge that chair!"

And Jude felt once more the hopeless, helpless victim of her mother's terrible disappointment, as she had throughout her childhood.

The rest of that afternoon passed very slowly. Gloria dozed in front of the television, Jude took Pip out and bought a dry sand-wich from the garage down the road, which she ate perched on the edge of her damp chair. Her mother asked her "what Anglesey was like weather-wise" but did not seem interested in her life or the people she had met there. If she noticed Jude's gently rounded belly, she said nothing. She had been to Wales, she said, with Donald when they were first married. Jude realised that it must have been then that he had discovered R.S. Thomas, and his poetry about his dour, dramatic homeland. She would never know, as she could never ask him, and he would never meet her child, she realised, wanting to weep for the tragedy of it. And why, on top of that, had she been left to carry the burden of her miserable mother alone? It was not one she had ever asked for or wanted.

"Such faith, in their chapels, in Wales," her mother said in an advert break. "You could almost breathe it in, like something in the air. And the singing was so happy and full of life. I always meant to go back, as we both loved it, but after your father left, well... I felt I couldn't."

Jude wished she had been to a service in a Welsh chapel on Anglesey, if only to understand what her mother meant, and share it with her. Her memories of interminable Methodist chapel services as a child were being scared of making a noise, or a mistake, and holding her hymn book so tightly that all her knuckles went white. Her grandfather, her mother's father, had been a minister, and the strictest, nastiest, most joyless man Jude had ever known. Yes, Gloria had been well-trained in meanness.

By 2pm, Jude was pacing between rooms like a caged animal. She had come home to tell her mother about her pregnancy, but the fear of her inevitable disapproval at the circumstances surrounding it was so powerful she simply could not do so. She could not find the words.

"Mum, would you like to go for a drive – just a short one?" Jude asked.

"You go, if you want to. I don't." Her mother's mouth turned down in the upside-down "U" Jude remembered from childhood. How could she tell this woman that she had slept with her husband's best friend and was now (probably but not definitely, as there was another man in the mix) carrying his baby? It was completely and utterly unthinkable.

"OK. Well, I might just have a whizz round with the hoover and a duster then," she said. She had to do *something,* and the place was filthy.

An hour later, the kitchen was mopped, sink bleached, surfaces wiped, and the stairs hoovered. As she couldn't clean the living room, where Gloria was now watching something horribly medical, Jude went upstairs. The three-toned *creeeeeakk* of the third stair took her back to being in her bedroom listening to Radio 1 and praying that Gloria would not come up "for a talk", which almost always ended in Jude getting shouted at for not being "sympathetic enough". Her mother was miserable, she had known, but Jude, a shy, awkward teenager, did not have the right words to console her. Yes, that creaking stair had been her early warning system: time to look busy or pretend to be asleep.

She dusted the ornaments in the bathroom: three glass balls; the figurine of a shepherdess with assorted lambs; the painted pillbox. Sweat dripped off her as she cleaned what she could in her mother's hot, musty bedroom before going into hers. When she pulled back the threadbare curtains, four or five bluebottles and a butterfly lay crisped on the thickly glossed windowsill. Poor things. There would have been no way out for them; the one day in the year that Gloria had opened the window to "air the room", and they had fluttered in hopefully, had sealed their doom forever.

Jude could see herself so clearly, that sensitive, lonely girl without any brothers or sisters, lying on this balding pink candlewick bedspread, waiting for rescue. Yes, she had waited years for Alex.

She wiped the china animals she had bought on "The Holiday in Torbay Before Dad Left", as it was always called, during the time before Gloria had pulled up the drawbridge on the world for both of them. Opening the top drawer in the dressing table, she pulled out the shoe box she had put there, the day before she left home; an early "memory maker". Inside was her old school tie, the photo of her and Christina, her only school friend who had moved to Glasgow in the third year. Here was the postcard with her A-level grades, good enough to get her into Uni and away from this house, and its pall of misery. This had been her golden ticket. In a second box, was her Glastonbury pass for 2009, smeared with brown, muddy fingerprints and a gold earring, from when she had the top of her ear pierced in Exeter and been roundly castigated by Gloria when she got home for "looking like a gypsy". Most of her other boxes, ones that contained memories of her life with Alex, were in storage in Oxford. She decided to gather them all together when she returned, and to look through them. It would feel like looking back through all the different phases of her life before she began a brand-new one.

"I am always changing, just like the moon: gibbous, waning, crescent, waxing, full. Nothing stays the same," she murmured to herself. "And thank goodness."

Downstairs, she heard her mother change channels, and cough. She would summon her soon, to make a drink, or plump her cushions.

Jude closed both boxes and took them downstairs. They would come with her, wherever she went, because she knew she would not return to this house for a long time. Tomorrow, whatever Gloria said, she would take her out to the seaside. She would buy her lunch, listen to her complaints, and try not to feel responsible for her misery or react to her Oscar-winning display of martyrdom. Then she would leave and return to Oxford. Her mother need not know about the baby at all, a grandchild she would probably never meet, and would certainly never love, nor spoil. It was not in her nature to do either.

"This torture ends with me, Mum," she murmured.

She wished Rhiannon Jones could see that she really did "have her reasons" for keeping away from Gloria, and they were bloody good ones.

THIRTY-FOUR

October brought a sea-change to Oxford, as the students returned. Groups of childlike freshers monopolised the pavements, talking loudly to each other in the hope that someone was listening. Armies of bikes ploughed up and down St Giles, and queues for the city's pubs and cafés bulged onto the pavements. Each morning, Jude and Pip walked on Port Meadow, as it was the only place where the sky had even the faintest hint of the wide skies on Anglesey. She often phoned Menna as she walked, as her friend was usually sitting on the bus to Bangor at that time, and Jude loved hearing whether there were shafts of sunlight on the sea today, or whether the clouds were massed solidly, or softly feathered, like lace.

"And how's that baby doing?" Menna always asked, but the questions Jude couldn't ask in return swam around inside her head like goldfish in a bowl every time they spoke: had she seen, or been in touch with Owain Pritchard? Had he found out about the baby? Was he still with his wife? Jude knew that, despite her brusque exterior, Menna secretly hoped that *he* was the father of Jude's baby, so that he could finally have a good reason to leave Non and the three of them could sail off into the sunset and live happily ever after. The chances of that were slim, if not zero.

So Jude never mentioned him, to anyone, and tried very, very hard not to think about him, but she could not forget R.S. Thomas' phrase, *"the honeyed warmness of his smile"*, whenever an image of his face drifted across her mind. She had to get him out of her head, she decided, so she walked around Oxford for hours, as she had walked on the beaches and headlands of the island to try and forget Alex. She took random turns and investigated unseen cul-de-sacs, and just as she had "seen" Alex everywhere for months after his death, she now saw Owain, a tall, lonely figure in an unfamiliar place. Her heart ached for what they could have had.

The evenings grew darker and the leaves on the thousands of trees in the city began to brown, crisp, and fall. This gradual change seemed so civilised and understated compared with the sheeting rain and gales that had battered *Hedd* to announce the imminence of winter, a year earlier. Jude missed the freshness of the night air in Porth Nobla, and the treacly blackness of the night. Here, even the seasons seemed unsatisfyingly diluted, and amateur.

Her friends responded to her pregnancy with their customary kindness, when she eventually told them.

"Well, we were wondering," Jo and Katie said in unison. "It's unlike you to have a beer belly."

"I guessed ages ago, of course," Morag said drily.

"I think *my* having a baby helped *you* to have one," Paula said, clapping her hands happily. "You're welcome!"

But when Jude told them that she thought Tom was the father, but could not be entirely sure, they were less understanding.

"Jude, how could you be such a cliché and go to bed with your *builder*?" Katie said. "Did you feel anything for him?"

Jude smiled. "Yes, I really did, and he was separated from his wife at the time, but now he's back with her. She's like a Rottweiler and would probably hunt me down if she knew."

"Ooh, I think we'd better pretend it didn't happen then, OK?" Katie added. "Nobody needs to be pursued by marauding Welshwomen."

"Are you and Tom an item now? He's always held a candle for you, I know," Jo said. "It will be really hard doing it all on your own, Jude."

"Too bloody right it will," Morag muttered.

"No. We're not an item and I don't love him right now, however much he wants me to. But I think perhaps I probably *could,*" Jude replied, painfully aware of how non-committal this sounded.

"You could do worse," Morag said. She was met with stony silence, in which the words "you could also do better" lurked.

"I think I need to find a job, and then a home of my own," Jude said. "I need a purpose first of all, so I don't just sit around and watch myself get bigger and bigger."

"Well, if you're up to it, we need someone to help in "*Baguette*" for a couple of months. Nothing too strenuous, of course," Jo said.

"Great. I now have ample experience in the hospitality sector, as you know," Jude replied with mock pomposity. "When can I start?"

Working for Jo and Katie was fun, easy, and much more organised than working for Siôn, though she missed the easy-going relationship she had forged with Ffion. Jude was impressed with Jo and Katie's ambition, their business acumen, and their genuine skill with people, but she loved the days she looked after Christos most of all. Whenever she saw the little boy's astounding smiles, and heard his irresistible giggles, she knew she had made the right decision to return to Oxford and have her baby here. She hoped the more she told herself this, the more it would feel true.

Despite this, a listlessness still stole over her from time to time when she thought about what she'd left behind, and her dreams were filled with the sea and the wind. When this mood descended, she pulled out the things she had brought with her from the island, fingering the delicate shells and smoothed pebbles with loving care before laying them out as beautifully as she could on the little table in her room. Soon, she had created spirals of pebbles which looped around tiny yellow snail shells, and flowers petalled with shards of sea glass. Brittle bladder-wrack framed the whole arrangement perfectly, and what she had created seemed to live and breathe the sea. She left it there for days, admiring its perfect form.

"That's lovely, Jude. I really feel as if I'm on a beach, looking at that," Paula said one day. "Why don't you stick it onto some hardboard, and frame it – make it more permanent?"

And so she did, adding some of the other things she had kept from the island, too: a postcard, a tiny paper sandcastle flag; a ticket from the island's "Sea Zoo" that she had visited once with Stella, and a parchment-thin, pressed sea pink from the headland near her cottage. When it was finished, she was ecstatic. She knew that she had done far more than stick some seaside souvenirs onto a hardboard sheet. She had begun to capture the essence of a place.

As winter drew in, and her pregnancy progressed, Jude found trying to reassure her friends that she was "doing fine", more and more difficult. She was not at all sure that she *was* fine, and vivid doubts stalked her sleep, but this was happening, and there was nothing she could do to stop it even if she wanted to. She went for long walks with Pip, bringing home bagfuls of leaves, acorns, sprigs of rosehips, and tiny wildflowers, which she carefully pressed between sheets of paper in the book of R.S. Thomas' poems Owain had given her, and never taken back. The table and the floor in her room were now permanently covered with "works in progress", as she tried to conjure up what she loved about the countryside in the Cotswolds, or a riverside meadow in winter. She felt she had to "fix" these places somehow, like specimens are pinned in a museum, as everything around her was about to change forever.

Tom came to see her regularly, bringing flowers, chocolates, parenting books, and a succession of gorgeous tiny baby outfits, and Jude began to look forward to these treats and to enjoy his company more and more. He still begged her to move in with him, so that he could take care of her, and at times, she was tempted. Living with Paula's little family had been an ideal stop-gap, but where would her home be when she had a child of her own? The thought of putting down real roots in the city and buying another house appealed in some ways, but not in others. It felt far too permanent. She had now fully convinced herself that Tom was the father of her child, having decided that continuing to doubt it was probably stressful for both her and the baby. This meant that a future with him, as a family, began to cohere in her imagination, but she still wondered: did she belong back in this city again, or not?

One evening, Tom called with a beautiful bowl of fresh lychees (Jude's favourite pregnancy snack), and they were sitting in the garden together, eating them, when he said:

"I know this is a long shot, but I have a spare ticket to a concert in the Sheldonian tomorrow evening. I wondered if you'd like to come with me. It's a beautiful programme."

"That's really sweet of you, Tom, but I don't know much about classical music," she answered. "I went to Alex's concerts, of course, but that was mainly choral stuff and his musical taste was *unusual*, shall we say. Even worse than mine!"

"I remember! Well, we could just stay for the first half if you like. It might be good for the baby, to hear some lovely music." Tom was blushing, Jude noticed.

"Oh well, in *that* case, how can I refuse?" she said, laughing.

"I'll pick you up at about seven, if that suits," he replied. "I have a friend who has a house just off St Giles. We can park outside her house so you won't have to stagger too far."

He just managed to dodge the prickly lychee she aimed at him.

THIRTY-FIVE

Oxford was always just as grand in the evening as it was during the day, but the lighting was different. Whereas the gardens were locked away at night, many of the city's magnificent buildings were lit from below, piercing the sky with their astonishing beauty. The Sheldonian Theatre, surrounded by a row of huge, carved heads of philosophers and thinkers, had always been one of the few buildings in the city that Jude found rather grotesque, but that evening, as she and Tom strolled across its cobbled courtyard towards the open doors at the front, it looked spectacular.

It was chilly, so Tom pulled Jude's pashmina lightly up and around her shoulders whilst they waited in the queue. He looked even more suave than usual; his checked shirt and mustard corduroy jacket were a perfect balance of formal and casual and his honey-blonde hair shone with good health and expensive shampoo. The regular, light squeak of his handmade brogues made Jude feel that, if anything untoward occurred, he would know exactly what to do – which was strangely reassuring. Only her husband had ever made her feel this safe.

She had been to a concert in the Sheldonian once before,

when she had first come to Oxford and met Alex. They had sat high up on the wooden benches, in the cheapest seats, and her main memory of the evening was of a very numb bum. Tonight, they had expensive, comfortable seats down in the main part of the theatre. When Tom had to respond to an urgent work email on his phone, Jude surveyed the scene. Middle-class vowels and well-heeled couples were everywhere and the whole place exuded affluence. She chuckled to herself, thinking how deeply Owain would hate it.

She decided to make conversation with the elderly woman next to her, who looked a little nervy and ill at ease. Chatting to strangers was a skill Jude had perfected on Anglesey, as people there were usually not as reserved as they were here in the city. In fact, once she began to feel more settled on the island, talking to random people in shops and on buses had become a social experiment, and one that was, more often than not, very successful. She had met some really lovely strangers.

That evening, she began conservatively. "Hello. I'm Jude. What a wonderful building this is. Have you been to many concerts here?"

"Oh yes. We come at least once a month," the woman replied. Her teeth were so large that, when she had uttered this *bon mot*, she could hardly close her lips over them again. Jude pressed on.

"I've only been once. Years ago. We sat up there – my husband and I. Such uncomfortable seats." Jude pointed up at the benches.

"Oh, Anthony and I always sit here," the woman said. She pronounced "here" as "heeyah", which, with the teeth, made Jude think of a donkey.

Tom leant across and said, "Can't beat Sibelius, can you?"

"Ah. I see your husband is as much of a music lover as Anthony and I," the woman gushed.

"Oh, he's not my husband. My husband's dead," Jude said,

realising an instant later that, despite that terrible truth, she was obviously pregnant. "But Tom's a very lovely man."

The mouth closed over the teeth, Tom buried himself in his programme, and Jude very carefully folded her coat.

When the audience hushed and the first notes sounded, she finally began to relax. She felt the first notes of the Sibelius symphony low in her body, as a vibration almost akin to trembling. Holding her breath, she watched the violinists' arms glide smoothly to and fro, so close that she could see their eyes, intent on the conductor. As the music swelled and grew, she allowed herself only shallow breaths, lest she somehow interrupt the flow of sound; she sat quite still and let all her thoughts dance freely. The music allowed her to flit between memories, between experiences, between places, with perfect ease. Nobody would ever know what she was thinking, what she was feeling, as she sat here, motionless, through all four movements of the symphony. It would always be her secret. Inside her, the baby squirmed and wriggled for joy. When the music finally ended, she applauded so hard her hands hurt. She smiled at Tom but was completely unable to speak.

"You enjoyed that then?" he said, smiling back at her.

"Oh yes. And so did our baby," she said, gently moving his hand onto her belly.

The final piece, Vaughn Williams' 'The Lark Ascending', Jude recognised as one Alex had loved. As the violin made its endless, effortless climb to the apex of the melody, swooping only to rise again, she could hear the skylarks above the cliff at Llanelian, where she and Owain had made love. Closing her eyes, she saw them both so vividly, walking on the beach below the cottage, her cottage, with its fringes of blue-green grass and sea-blackened rocks. It was all still there, as she sat in this theatre with hundreds of strangers. It was the same beautiful music it had been when her husband had listened to it in their house in Howard Street. How miraculous was that? And how tragic.

When the applause stopped, Jude turned to Tom, her eyes full of tears.

"Thank you – for this, for bringing me here," she said.

He leant towards her and wrapped one of his hands around both of hers. Jude, thankful for the companionable comfort of his touch, decided that there was a lot to be said for comfort.

THIRTY-SIX

Tom was away for a week after the concert and Jude found she really missed him. Evenings were long and lonely, as Paula and Georgio went to bed very early, worn out with work and baby-dom. She spent these empty hours laying out a new collage with more of the things she had brought back from Anglesey, as one of Paula's wealthy friends had commissioned her to do her what she'd dubbed a "seashore *mèlange*" to hang in her massive Victorian house. Jude blended the objects and matched the woman's colour scheme perfectly, as she had been briefed to do. This felt horribly limiting, when her memories of the island were of freedom and openness, but the money was great.

When, at 7pm one evening, it was finished, Jude decided to go and visit Morag, who now very rarely socialised, as no babysitter could cope with Finn. Despite her protestations of doom about being a single mother, Jude felt that they would soon have a lot in common, so it would be good to be able to talk about things and support each other. On the way, she bought a bottle of red wine to appease her friend, whom she knew did not welcome spontaneous visitors (a response she justified by arguing that Finn was "guaranteed to play up" if anyone called in on the off-chance). He was pretty much guaranteed to play up anyway, everyone wryly told her.

Jude could hear a child crying as she opened the gate and walked up the path. Knocking on the door, she heard a series of banshee-like shrieks, which stopped, restarted, and were rounded off by a slamming door. She looked at her watch: 7.15pm – perhaps not the best of times to call unannounced at a house with a hyperactive three-year-old. After several minutes of rather eerie silence, Jude knocked again and waited. As she turned to walk away, Morag opened the door. She looked terrible – her eyes were puffy, her hair flat and lifeless and her face speckled with flecks of blue mascara; she had obviously been crying. A cigarette burnt in one hand and she held a smeary glass of wine in the other. Her face was far from welcoming.

"Morag. Hi. I was just passing, and thought... Hey, I thought you'd given that up when you were pregnant." Jude pointed at the fag.

"Give me a bloody break," Morag snapped, lifting the cigarette to her lips and inhaling deeply.

"Can I come in?" Jude showed her the bottle of wine she had brought. "A problem shared, and all that..."

"Sure. Why not. Excuse the mess," Morag said, backing unsteadily inside.

"Mess" was the biggest understatement Jude had ever heard. Nothing could have prepared her for the state of Morag's house. The front door opened straight into the living room, but there was no possibility of anyone living in it. The floor was covered with plastic construction blocks, pieces of train track, and scores of less easily identifiable "bits of toy". There were several bowls with the dried dregs of cereal or pasta in them on the sofa, and Jude could hardly see an inch of carpet as she picked her way across the room. Discarded clothes and washing, both clean and dirty, covered every surface. She tried to keep her expression neutral, however, and did not react to the wee-sodden trainer pants she spotted behind the TV.

"I'll get myself a glass of water, shall I? The wine's all for you, of course," she said. Morag had already sat down on a pile of folded, faded clothes.

"Let's go into the kitchen," Morag said. "A bit more room in there."

But the kitchen was even more disgusting: months-worth of crumbs and grime covered the lino and the sink was full of filthy pans and dishes, some of which had gone mouldy. In the corner by the bin, lurked about twenty empty wine bottles. It reminded Jude of a student house, or a squat. She was genuinely shocked that her friend was living here, with a child.

Moving some small, grubby trousers from one of the kitchen chairs, Jude sat down, motioning for her friend to do so too, terribly anxious not to appear to judge her in any way. Something very bad had happened to this funny, clever woman to bring her to this low point. Morag shoved whatever was on the other chair onto the floor and undid the screw-top wine bottle while Jude reached across to the sideboard where she knew Morag had kept glasses the last time she'd called in. The glasses were still in the same place, but they were all filmed with grease and dust. Nobody had come to have a drink with Morag for quite some time.

"What's been going on, Morag?" Jude said calmly. "Tell me."

Morag glugged her wine. "Do you mean, how have things got this awful?" She paused. "I dunno, Jude. I don't know how, or when, but it just happened. Just ignore it – I do. Let's have a drink! Oops, sorry. Forgot. 'Baby on board' and all that. You can't. Bummer."

"I'm fine thanks," Jude replied. She didn't even dare risk a glass of water in this house. "It's not like you to let it all get on top of you."

"To let *him* get on top of me, you mean – that bastard James Guthrie! One too many vinos after work, a swift shag that I don't even remember consenting to, and – hey presto – one everlasting baby." Morag took another swig of wine.

"But you wanted Finn, so you kept him, Morag, however you felt about how he was conceived." Her friend had given up a lot for this baby, including her Scottish Presbyterian family, who'd all but disowned her.

"And much good has it done both of us, Jude. I don't get the promotions, I don't get the interesting clients, I don't get flexible hours, I don't get any understanding if he's ill and can't go to childcare. And I *certainly* don't get the blokes. Don't say I didn't warn you, Jude, cos I bloody well DID!" she said.

"But, Morag, Finn will get easier...' Jude said without much conviction. The little boy had never seemed to get anything but harder.

"Will he HELL! He'll just get bigger, and I'll get older, more knackered and even less attractive, if that's *possible*! Do you realise that that night with James Guthrie was the last time I had sex?" she sniffed. "And that was only my second time."

At that point, Finn started wailing again upstairs. Morag drained her glass and plodded up the stairs. Jude could hear her talking to her son through the floorboards.

"It's time to go to sleep now, Finn. Mummy's really, really tired, and I want to talk to my friend. Curl up with Billy and Thomas and go sleepy-byes, please."

Finn's cries did not stop; they grew louder.

Jude heard what she assumed were toys thudding onto the floor, again and again. Night after night, month after month, for three years, this had been Morag's evening. She had wanted her baby, despite her parents' dour encouragements to "banish the evidence of sin," but she had paid such a high price.

"Just go to sleep, Finn!" Morag shouted. "Right NOW!" The wailing stopped abruptly, the bedroom door slammed, and she stomped down the stairs and into the kitchen with such fury that the ceiling shook.

"Don't look at me like that, Jude, as if you're *judging* me! I know you don't think I should shout at him, but it's not fair of you to come here and patronise me," she said, blinking.

Jude swallowed her shock and hurt. Morag was so stressed, she was not being herself. "I'm not patronising you. I can understand why you shout at him, Morag. I'm sure I would too."

"How could you ever understand my life, or how I feel, or what I want? You could have anyone, do anything. You've got plenty of money, and loads of talent. You could have it all."

"What?" Jude said, feeling anger bubble.

"God knows, I'd love to bugger off to Wales and have a nice quiet year, with no bloody responsibilities!" Morag hissed, her words skewed by wine and venom.

"Excuse me, but my life has hardly been a bed of roses, Morag. My husband *died,* don't forget!" Jude answered sharply.

There was complete silence for about a minute.

"Sorry," Morag squeaked.

More silence, then the snuffle of her weeping. Jude took her hand.

"It's OK. I can see how bad things are. What about your mum? Couldn't you ask her for some support now? I am sure she would want to help."

"She did send me a message," Morag said, hiccupping. "After he was born, saying sorry for the way she'd reacted to my getting up the duff, but I was still so angry with her. So hurt. I never replied, and I can't now."

Jude suddenly saw Rhiannon Jones, sitting alone in her chair, waiting, waiting for her beloved Rhodri to visit her. And she saw Gloria too, in her gloomy sauna of a house in Taunton, waiting for her only daughter to care about her. Who was she, to advise her friend on asking for help after so much bitterness, hurt, and regret? It was not an easy thing to do.

Morag blinked tearfully at her. "I'm sorry, Jude. I really am. You need someone special to care for you, because it's so bloody hard if you're on your own. That's all I really want, all I ever wanted. A family of my own."

"I had someone special, Morag, and I loved him, but he died. And then I met another special man, on Anglesey, but he's married, and he won't leave his horrible wife," Jude said. "I think all that's over for me."

"No, it's not. There's another man who desperately wants to be with you – you know who I'm talking about," Morag said. "Tom."

A pause. "He was my husband's best friend, and it feels, well, a bit *weird,* and I've explained how *this* came about." She pointed at her belly. "And what would Alex think?'

"He'd want you to be happy, Jude. Tom is unattached, a nice bloke and the *probable* father of your child: three big fat ticks on my list. Four, in fact, as he buys you nice stuff as well. I know the others have reservations about the two of you getting together, but they don't have to live my life. Take a punt, Jude, or you could end up like me. I really don't recommend it." She got up to fill the kettle and make them some tea.

Jude took her mug, trying to ignore the stains on the rim. "Actually, you're not the first friend to tell me to take a risk."

"Let yourself be *loved,* Jude, before it really is too late," Morag said. "You said you thought you could probably love Tom, and your baby deserves a Mum and a Dad…"

Jude nodded. "Perhaps you're right. It must be so very hard, doing all this alone."

"It is, Jude. It really, really is."

"Then promise me you'll make peace with your mother, and ask if she can help at all," Jude said, remembering Rhiannon's words to her only too vividly.

"OK. I'll try," Morag said, sighing. "She's a good person really, I know."

The two friends sipped their tea in peace. Upstairs, they could hear Finn gently humming to himself and the thunderous rain of toys had stopped.

PART 6

TWO PATHS

THIRTY-SEVEN

As a second Christmas without Alex approached, Jude's feelings for Tom vacillated enormously. She was not at all certain that a relationship would work out, however nice a man he was, but Morag had rattled her, and the prospect of lone parenting now seemed less of a challenge and more of a nightmare. She'd already been through so much, might it be easier to accept what Tom offered her, and face whatever the future held together? Her child would need a father – if not in babyhood, then later, and Jude knew exactly how it felt to grow up without one when she had most needed him in her life.

Everyone had very complicated Christmas plans this year. Menna had invited her to Anglesey, and part of her ached for the island, but she agonised that perhaps it was too soon to be going back. Gloria sulkily announced that she would go to her sister, a lay preacher in Clevedon, as there was no possibility of her coming to Oxford. Jude had no home to invite her to and Gloria knew nothing of her pregnancy, so she ignored the barrage of martyrish comments. Jo and Katie were off for "A gay Christmas to remember" in a hotel in Kendal, and Paula was taking Christos to Georgio's huge Cypriot family in North

London. Jude was facing the very real possibility of being on her own.

Morag had phoned her mother the morning after she and Jude had spoken and told her very frankly how much she was struggling. Agnes had come to Oxford immediately, complete with rubber gloves, a Dundee fruit cake and ample Scottish good-heartedness.

"She's not actually *said* 'sorry' for the way she behaved, but she's *shown* me she's sorry, and I told her I had behaved badly, too, when I wouldn't tell her how I felt about what had happened and *how* it happened, because I was too ashamed," Morag told Jude, who had rung her to check in. "She's like a miracle-worker, the way she gets Finn to do things I can never get him to do. Thank you for nudging me to contact her, it's made everything so much better." A pause, an intake of breath. "And please think seriously about Tom. You deserve some happiness too."

Oxford was blanketed in a thick hoar frost each morning in December, so Pip, who had never met frost on the beaches of Anglesey, lifted his paws from the hard ground with the precision of a ballerina. The ponies grazing on Port Meadow were wreathed in clouds of their warm breath, giving them a mysterious grandeur, and their low harrumphs softened many harsh, wintry walks. Eventually, news reached Tom that all Jude's gang were leaving town for Christmas, as she had known it would.

"The word is that you have no festive plans at all," he messaged her. "I'd really like to celebrate with you – the last one before you're on stocking-filler duty!"

"That's really sweet," she replied, both touched and tempted. "Let me think about it."

As she sat alone in Paula's warm house after everyone else

had left Oxford, Jude finally felt her reality settle around her like a mantle, offering both warmth and comfort. Whatever the new year held, it could never be the same as the last one. It could never include Alex, but it could include Tom, if she wanted it to – and she'd decided she was almost sure she did, despite some of her friends' reservations. But there was still something stopping her accepting his offer of spending this Christmas together: a tiny knot of doubt, a blur in the corner of her eye.

She knew in her heart that only one option truly appealed: returning to Anglesey, to spend this midwinter festival with Menna and her family, if they would have her. She needed to go back to that small, rocky island with its rich history, perplexing language and weather to end all weathers before her baby was born and her life changed forever. She would go back as herself, by herself, one last time. It would not be to see Owain, that could not be. It would be a farewell trip, a closing of that chapter of her life. She rang Tom to tell him on December 22nd.

"I'm really sorry, but my friend Menna has just invited me to go back to Anglesey for a few of days over Christmas and I'm going to go."

"Oh," Tom replied. "I'm sorry to hear that, but I get it."

Guilt kicked in, as he sounded so woebegone. "But why don't we do New Year together instead? Everyone else will be back by then, and we could have a party."

"Fine, great," Tom said. "That's better than nothing, I guess."

"Listen, I'm sorry about Christmas, but there'll be lots more chances for us to do things together," Jude said slowly, deliberately, as if tasting each word. She wanted to make herself clear. "We've got so much to look forward to together, Tom. Just a few days away, then I'll be back."

A silence followed in which she knew he had understood.

. . .

Jude was nervous as she dialled her friend's number: it was such short notice now, and she knew Menna would already have a houseful, but hadn't she said that Jude was "always welcome in her home", and sounded as if she meant it? She need not have worried: the party was already in full swing in Llanfaelog.

"*Bendegedig*/Excellent! It's going to be a bit crowded here, so why don't you stay at my Aunty Delyth's? It's only ten minutes' walk away from us. She's gone to her daughter's, in Stockport. If you look after her cat, you'll save me doing it. Result."

"Well, if you're sure. I'll have to bring Pip, but he won't hassle her cat," Jude said, having to shout to make herself heard over the racket in Menna's house, and the pop and hiss of beer cans. "A friend's feeding Tuna," she added, with a niggle of guilt at having asked Tom, but he had been very happy about doing it, as the cat seemed to have formed an immediate bond with him. Jude had a suspicion that he wanted to find any way to be close to her, and adoring her cat was one of them. Pip, he still had no such fondness for, as he sneezed violently every time he was near him. This was a problem Jude refused to think about yet but knew she would probably have to face before too long.

"It'll be a lot quieter there than it is here, I can tell you, so you'll be able to rest at Delyth's. Let me know when the train gets in. Gotta go now. See you soon! *Hwyl*/Bye."

Jude felt a prickle of excitement, picturing herself walking along the beach and breathing in fresh, clean air that she knew would recharge her. It would be a fantastic time to collect more driftwood and sea glass, too, after all the winter gales. Several people had messaged her asking for more information about her collages, as word was obviously spreading on the North Oxford "competitive rustic chic" circuit. To do any more, Jude knew she would need more raw materials, and there was only one place to get the best ones: Anglesey. She hummed cheerfully as she began to make a list of what to pack and even dared to look beyond Christmas, and think about making plans with Tom, and preparing for their baby.

It felt good to be certain of what to do next. She needed to go back to the island, and then she needed to come home. How could she not have seen it before?

THIRTY-EIGHT

Tom arrived early the next morning, to be given instructions about feeding Tuna and to take Jude to the station for the 8.10am train. As the cat wound herself round his legs, purring loudly, he looked very disconsolate when Jude put on her coat, and the atmosphere was tense. She had clearly hurt his feelings.

"So will you go to your parents for Christmas Day?" she asked.

"Yes, I guess so," he replied. "It's a bit like *Groundhog Day* – the same old routine, since I was a child, but my sister's busy with her own family these days, so I feel I have to be at home."

"I'm sure your being there makes your parents very happy," she said. "And they're about to get the surprise of their lives, remember!"

"Yes," he said with a broad smile. "I guess I can tell them now, can't I?"

This felt a little uncomfortably real, but she couldn't refuse. "Sure."

At the station, his lips met hers, but they did not linger. Kissing each other felt like such a strange thing for them to be doing without the loosening effect of alcohol. As the train pulled away, and a waving Tom grew smaller and smaller on the platform, Jude felt herself relax. She had made her decisions, and they were the right ones. A return to the island had to come before committing to this man. He wanted her very badly, she knew, but he could not have her yet.

Every single seat on the train from Birmingham to Holyhead was taken, and the corridors were crammed with bags and people. Many of the passengers were Irish, heading to the ferry home for Christmas. By the time they reached Crewe, the train tables were full of empty cans and bottles, and bursts of carols or traditional songs blasted from neighbouring carriages as the doors whooshed open and shut. Buffet-bound people tottered down the central aisles, bearing bacon rolls and plentiful supplies of good cheer.

Jude was soon drawn into chatting with the sea of Irish people surrounding her. Their warmth, openness, and irresistible accent meant that she was soon bosom-buddies with a black-haired, blue-eyed young woman called Nuala, originally from just outside Dublin but who now lived in Kilburn. She had thin plastic tubing leading from a wine box in her bag directly into her mouth.

"Saves me a fortune, this does," she said, when Jude noticed the tube and smiled. "When's your baby due?"

"Some time in the spring, but to be honest, I'm not actually sure," Jude replied, blushing. "I've never had very regular periods, unfortunately, which makes it hard to work out dates."

"You haven't missed much. The Curse is the best name for it, I'd say," Nuala replied. "My ma said the day they stopped, and she couldn't have any more kids, was the biggest blessing of her life."

"Did she have many kids, your 'ma'?" Jude asked.

"Seven. So you can understand why she felt that way!" Nuala replied, and both women laughed.

"Do you like living in London?" Jude asked.

"Well, I'd rather be at home, for sure, but there's more work in London," she said, offering Jude a "suck" of the wine before pulling the tube away, exclaiming, "Oh Lord, you can't drink, can you? That must be *so* boring."

Jude thought about this for a few seconds, and then decided that "yes, it bloody well WAS!"

By the time they reached Chester, Jude had told Nuala all about Tom, and what a nice man he was, and all about Owain, and how she knew she still loved him. Unburdening herself to a stranger like this gave her more relief than she would have believed possible. She needed reassurance, without any hint of judgement, and she got it.

"Yer man won't leave his wife, Jude. They never do," Nuala said, very seriously. "You're making the right choice I think, but you might need to see that Owain once more, to 'lay the ghost', as my granny would say."

When Nuala fell asleep for the last part of the journey, Jude looked out across the sea, watching the hump of land that was Anglesey gradually come alongside the mainland. Was this wise-seeming young woman right? Should she try to see Owain again, or would it only make him wonder if he was her baby's father, as she herself had wondered for a while? She longed to talk to him again, very much, but decided that it was best to leave well alone.

The moment Pip stepped down onto the platform at Bangor, the little dog raised his head and sniffed as if recognising the old scents and familiar air. Jude breathed deeply too. Despite the shreds of diesel fumes left by the departing train, the air here was like no other. It was clear, with a cold purity that startled your nostrils. It told of glacial lakes high up in the mountains, and of peaks thickly dusted with snow and brittled with ice through the long winter months. It smelt of Arctic winds blasting over icy grey waves. It was air worth breathing.

Menna was there to meet her. "You look well, *cariad*/love," she said. "Not as big as I thought you'd be by now, though."

"Glad to hear it," Jude replied. "I feel like a prize heifer already!"

By the time they drove past *Hedd*, it was almost dark. She could see that someone had lit the wood-burner, as a snake of smoke wound up from the chimney. The cottage had had a fresh coat of whitewash since she'd left and glowed with almost evanescent brightness against the blackening sky. The owners had obviously done the work they had talked about before putting it up for sale in the spring, and she was glad to see its undulating walls and tiny windows lovingly restored. It was a sanctuary, defiant against the wind and waves, and she would hold it close to her heart forever.

THIRTY-NINE

On Christmas Day, only the scrubbed-clean shimmer of the landscape betrayed the heavy rain that had fallen the previous night. The sky was bright and clear, the few clouds carved-up by wide stripes of pale blue. Jude woke very early. Sleeping was getting more difficult, as the baby pressed on her bladder and trips to the toilet were now pretty frequent. She showered and set off for a walk to dispel the headache the riotous sing-along party at Menna's house the previous evening had given her.

A few hardy windsurfers were already on the water, their faces puce and pinched in their tight wetsuit hoods. A pair of young lads were trying to get dressed on the beach, hopping from leg to leg like ungainly insects, but their fingers were so cold that they couldn't unzip their wetsuits. When one of them recognised Jude from Siôn's café, they coyly asked her to help them peel themselves free, and then wished her a "*Nadolig Llawen*/Happy Christmas" through chattering teeth. She strode off, anxious not to seem like she was waiting for them to pull their trunks down.

At Porth Nobla, several different kinds of birds were sifting through the banks of seaweed that the night's tide had washed up, looking for sandhoppers or bits of crab flesh in snapped-off claws. Jude crunched over the drifts of razor shells marking the tideline and began to collect driftwood, pebbles, mermaid's purses, and pretty shells to take home to Oxford. When she passed *Hedd,* the curtains of the cottage were still firmly closed. Christmas Day had yet to begin for whoever was staying there this week. No doubt they had already had all their pricey eatables delivered, having ordered them online in the other world they had come from.

Climbing steadily around the headland path and up onto the ancient burial site that overlooked Cable Bay, she stood on the very top of the rounded *twmp*/mound and looked around her slowly. She could not see another living soul; no other walkers were out yet, as there were stockings to empty and turkeys to baste. Not even a fishing boat was out on the water on this, the quietest of all the year's days. Every shop was shut, every shopworker having their own exhausted Christmas before Boxing Day saw all the spending begin again. Alex had always felt so sorry for them and refused to go to any January sales.

As she stood and surveyed the landscape laid out around her like the most stunning of ancient parchments, she thought of her friends, and what they were doing to celebrate this festival. She hoped Paula's overbearing mother-in-law was letting Christos enjoy his very first Christmas. She wished Stella and Eifion in Granada and Jo and Katie in the Lakes a very happy Christmas. She hoped Morag was being moderate with the Cabernet Sauvignon at her parents' house in Fife. Finally, she thought of her mother, and the sad, joyless Christmasses they had both endured in Taunton after Donald had left them. Hopefully she, too, was as happy as she was capable of being, with Aunt Sarah.

Jude had to close her eyes to picture Tom in the Cotswolds with his parents. He had texted her to wish her a Happy Christmas at midnight the previous evening, telling her how much he was looking forward to the new year and hoping she would like her present. Whatever it was, Jude knew that the vintage leather-bound *Driver's Atlas of Britain* she had bought him in an antiquarian bookshop on The Turl would not come close. When a text pinged into her inbox, and she saw it was from Owain, her heart leapt into her throat.

> I hear you are on the island. Hope this finds you well. Nadolig Llawen/Happy Christmas.
> Regards, Owain.

So he knew she was here, which was no surprise. News travelled fast here, so him knowing was fine. What hurt her was his formal tone, and the fond things he'd not said, even though in her heart, she knew that she had no right to expect more of him. She had dismissed him from her life and given him no hope of readmittance. What was past, was past, but her peace of mind was shaken as she began the long walk back to Rhosneigr.

Menna had been to the upmarket supermarket in Menai Bridge especially to buy the "fancy food" they thought Jude would like: olives, cheeses, and spicy chorizo, and she had also gift-wrapped several jars of pesto, as a joke. Jude opened them first, to knowing winks and roars of laughter. Gifts were exchanged, and everyone said they were happy with them even if they weren't. Jude duly raved about the fluffy purple gloves from the boys, and wore them while eating dinner, which had them in hysterics as her fingers slipped off her knife and fork. A necklace of Welsh slate entwined with silver wire from Menna reduced her to tears with its simple beauty. Tom had given her a pair of beautiful, pellucid pearl stud earrings, and she texted him immediately in case she forgot later.

> Thanks very much, Tom. Simple but gorgeous. You know me well. X

The family took care not to speak too much Welsh, but Menna's youngest son, five-year-old Iolo, promised to translate for her whenever they did. When this extended to his telling Jude that his father Jac had just called Menna's mother a "*boen yn y pennol*/pain in the backside", his services were immediately suspended.

By the evening, the mood was somnolent. Pip was flat out behind the sofa, emitting regular ghastly smells. Slumped in chairs, Menna's family relaxed in the blue glow of the TV and laughed at old films and comedy reruns. As she looked around the room, Jude could not help but remember Christmas Day evenings with Gloria. Her mother had always been "overemotional" by this point, sipping sweet sherry and tearfully revisiting the good times with her husband when they were first married, before he had "discovered sin" with Brenda. In *this* family, the mum passed around a huge tin of chocolates and threw cushions at her sons when they farted. Jude knew which she preferred.

At the end of the evening, she followed Menna into the kitchen. Despite all her avowals not to care about Owain, there were things she needed to ask. She may never come back again to ask them, after all, and his text had unsettled her. Why had he messaged her at all, if it was just to say that?

"How's Owain Pritchard doing?" she said, in what she hoped was a casual way. "He texted me earlier, and said he knew I was back."

Menna's eyebrows arched ferociously. "Yes, I told him the other day. He's all right, I think. He won a prize at the Eisteddfod for poetry recitation, but that's nothing new. He's been winning them since he was five." A pause. "Do you still think about him, then, Jude?"

"Not really, no. Well, I try not to anyway," Jude replied. "But we did get on well together. We were good friends, Menna. Kindred spirits, even."

"I'd say it's a tricky thing, to be a friend of Non Pritchard's husband, good or otherwise," Menna said softly. "He's back where she wants him now, at her beck and call."

"Yes. I know she keeps him on a close rein."

"Has done since they first got together at school, but not sure why he married her. Everyone thought he'd moved on, and they even split up for a while when he started at Uni in Bangor. He wanted to be an architect, you know; he's got the brains for it, certainly."

Jude noted that Non hadn't let the gossip-mongers know that she'd told Owain she was pregnant when they married. Had shame stopped her releasing him, when she realised she was not? The fear of public disgrace seemed to run through their marriage, like colour shot through silk.

"What's she really like, this Non? I hear nothing good about her, from anyone."

Menna sighed. "It's complicated, and so's she, to be honest with you. She grew up in a rough household. Her brother's doing time in Wrexham jail and her parents have always cared more about booze and scratch cards than they did about their kids. Her managing to become a teacher was a miracle, but she did it, with Owain's support. I think the fact that they still haven't got kids has soured her over the years, though. She used to be a pretty little thing, but now she's dumpy and bitter. And jealous. 'Handle with care' is all I'll say about Mrs Non Pritchard."

As Jude listened, she felt Menna's eyes on her, laser-sharp. "You did the right thing, Jude, in case you're wondering. But I need to ask, while you're here; I've not liked to on the phone. Could Owain be the baby's father?"

Instantly, Jude felt cornered. Turning away to put the tea towel down, she felt the blood rush to her cheeks. She had to shut this conversation down immediately, because admitting the possibility aloud to someone else might make it real again. "No.

The dates don't match. It's Tom's, and actually I've decided I'm going to give it a go with him. He'll look after me, I know."

"*Da iawn ti!*/Good for you! A lucky escape, I'd say. He's a kind, wonderful man, but I sometimes think bad luck hangs around Owain Pritchard, and you don't need any more of that," Menna said, putting an arm around Jude's shoulder. "Right, time to tell me more about Tom, this knight on a white charger who's going to whisk you away from all this!"

And then Menna sat, captivated, as Jude showed her photos of Tom, his pretty house by the river, his sports car, and told her of his seemingly limitless kindness.

"All good, but do you love him?" Menna asked.

"Not yet, no, or not enough, but I think I could," Jude replied softly.

"I guess that's a pretty good foundation to build on. I'm glad for you both, yes. A happy-ish ending. That'll do for me."

But as Jude settled down to sleep that night, it was not Tom's face that floated across her dreams: it was Owain Pritchard's.

FORTY

As soon as she got back to Oxford, Jude texted Tom to ask if they could invite only their closest friends to his house for their New Year's Eve party. She wanted to prevent him inviting all his fellow "Oxford Law graduate" friends, most of whom she had always found unbearably snobbish (and whom Alex had dubbed "The Look How Great I Am" gang).

"It seems like the ideal time to tell our real friends we're together," she wrote, surprised at how easy she found it to hint at his friends *not* being "real". Ground rules needed to be established early, she'd decided.

New Year's Eve had never featured much in her life with Alex. They had shunned all the parties and walled themselves up at about 7pm on 31st December with some good wine, something nice to eat, and a bottle of Moët in the fridge. Sometimes, they opened the champagne at 9.35pm, and sometimes, not at all, so little did midnight matter. Safe in their life together, such things were unimportant; they'd assumed things would carry on like this, as they always had. But they hadn't.

. . .

The party did not start well. Jude was sad, as she had rung the care home to find out how Rhiannon was and to wish her a "Happy New Year" only to hear that she was very ill with a chest infection. She had sent her old friend regular postcards, and tried to see her over Christmas, but been told she was too poorly for visitors and Jude wondered if she would ever see her again. Paula was desperately tired, as Christos was teething, and Jo and Katie had obviously quarrelled on their way over. As the evening progressed, Jude became increasingly aware that Tom was not included in the old stories about drunken pedalo rides or encounters with randy Greek waiters. He'd never been part of their holiday crowd, just "Alex's nice friend" whom everyone secretly thought a bit dull. She watched him smile and laugh at all these stories when he thought he ought to, but she could see he was uncomfortable.

When she crossed the room to sit next to him, he beamed at her gratefully and began stroking the back of her head. Jude could feel how nervous he was, so aware that they were being watched. She was nervous, too, but this was no time for cowardice. She had planned exactly what to say, and it was time to say it.

"People, listen up! We have something to tell you all," she began. "Tom and I... have decided to give it a go – together." She laughed, eyes darting around the room for approval, for reassurance. She needed both badly.

Morag cheered, but everyone else was silent for a few awkward moments before a chorus of "That's great!"; "Fantastic news!"; "Hooray!" rang out.

"A toast! Here's to Jude, Tom, and whichever kind of little person's coming to join them in the spring," Georgio said, and everyone drank and congratulated them fulsomely until the bubbly ran out.

· · ·

"Well, that wasn't as hard as you thought, was it?" Tom said later. "I was pretty nervous about it, I must say." He was relaxed now and wrapped his arm around her shoulders proprietorially.

"Everyone seemed happy for us, didn't they?" Jude said. "Thanks for waiting for me to be ready to, you know…"

"You're well worth waiting for," he replied, kissing her on the lips. "Here's to our future, my love."

Jude tried to disguise how unnatural this endearment sounded as he emptied his glass in one, a pink rosette forming in each cheek.

"Talking of the future, I've been mulling over a sort of business idea," she said briskly. "I've brought loads of things back from Anglesey to make more of my collages, and Paula thinks I might be able to sell them into some of the arty shops in Oxford. I could add textiles, graphics, expand into pictures that sum up specific occasions, like weddings or christenings. What do you think? Once the baby's born, I can work while it sleeps."

"If that works out, great," Tom said, refilling his glass. "I say do something you've always wanted to, but I've heard that babies don't tend to sleep when you need them to. Ask my sister. It's all she ever talks about."

Jude was a little hurt. Was that it? She had hoped for more support for her idea. "Yes, I know it won't be easy, but I want to do it if I can."

"Then go for it! Alex always said that you had hidden talents, Jude. He would be proud of you right now."

"I hope so, very much." Another flutter of unease. She was not so sure.

"So when will you move in?" Tom said, his face eager as if a wonderfully gung-ho adventure lay ahead.

Jude pushed down the surge of very real panic this bald question prompted. Yes, this was really happening, just as the baby she could feel kicking and wriggling inside her was really coming out in a few months' time. She looked around the room at her friends, and felt grateful for their support, their friendship, but this was her reality now, and there was only one way to face any doubts she still had – head-on.

"Tomorrow afternoon suits me, if it suits you. It's a holiday, so there's no need for you to worry about work."

"Great. Let's do something nice in the morning and make a day of it. Here's to us!" he drained his glass again, smiling from ear to ear.

That night was very cold, and Jude could see her breath in the bedroom as she pulled the duvet up around her face for her last night in Paula's house. As a child, she'd always sought solace in bed when things worried her, or there were things she could not understand, or put right. When her father had left, she'd stayed in bed for a day and a half. She'd regularly retreated to her bed to get away from Gloria. When Alex had died, she had stayed in bed for days on end, stinking and stiff-limbed, getting up only to waddle to the loo, or fetch something very basic to eat. That night, as her tired muscles begin to warm and relax and the baby stopped squirming, she felt her anxiety gently leave her. Drifting towards sleep, she tried as hard as she could to focus on the good things, the happy things, the positive things that lay ahead. Tom loved her, he had a lovely home, and he was a kind man; she deserved a bit of kindness now.

"It's all going to be all right," she repeated like a mantra, until finally, she slept.

FORTY-ONE

Tom rang at 9am the next morning, long before Jude felt ready to be awake.

"How about a run out to the White Horse at Uffington, and then a pub lunch before I help you move in? I've never been there."

"It's a bit early, and I should really pack…"

"OK, I'll pick you up at half ten. We'll pack together this afternoon."

"Fine," she said to him, adding, "Oh shit," once she had hung up.

As she soaped her swelling body in the shower, a memory stirred. White Horse Hill – yes, she'd been there before, but when, or with whom, she could not remember.

When Tom hooted his horn very loudly outside, Jude bit her tongue so hard that she tasted blood. If he woke Christos before he was ready to be woken, Paula and Georgio would be furious. She looked out of the window to "ssssh" him and saw that he'd gone for "The Aviator" look today. He had lowered the hood of his sports car (despite the fact that it was January 1st) and was wearing what looked like a vintage pilot's hat and a fur-trimmed leather flying jacket.

"Good morning, Captain Byers," she murmured.

Tom grimaced and pointed at his head, miming "terrible hangover".

"I'm not surprised!" Jude hissed. "Is the hat helping?"

'Haha. Very funny. Are you ready?"

Jude picked up her thickest coat and went outside, lifting Pip into the passenger seat to sit on her lap.

"Do we have to take the dog?" Tom said, wincing. "Sorry, but you remember that I'm allergic to their hair, don't you?"

She looked at Pip's brown eyes. It would be so cruel to leave him in the flat for hours on his own, and he really needed a walk.

"I know you are, but the car's going to be full of fresh air with the roof down and he'll love White Horse Hill," she said, to Tom's evident disappointment. "And I can't expect Paula to walk him today, after the party…"

"OK, we'll see how it goes, but if I start sneezing, you'll have to stuff him up your coat."

By the time they reached the A420 that led out towards Swindon, it was so cold and windy in the car that Jude's eyes were watering, and her hair was whipping around her face in wild tendrils. She was very glad when they reached the car park. The moment she got out and looked around her, she remembered exactly when she had been here before – with Alex, very early in their relationship, to get away from the all-consuming pressures of his finals. They'd borrowed a friend's ancient Triumph Dolomite and taken nearly two hours to putter their way here. They'd come with no picnic, and no blanket, so they'd spread Alex's coat out on the grass and watched inter-city trains snake their way across the wide plain below them. The memory brought sudden tears to her eyes.

She could tell immediately that Tom did not do much walk-

ing. She'd worn her walking boots, but he was wearing his usual
brogues and their leather soles slipped and slid on the damp
grass, forcing him to windmill his arms crazily to avoid falling
flat on his face. When, inevitably, he *did* fall, Jude laughed out
loud before stretching out a hand to pull him up, and he looked
decidedly hurt. Their first proper day out together was not
going well so far.

The "white horse" itself is a fluid, elongated shape, hacked into
the grass and crudely whitened with chalk. It was only from a
distance that the graceful widespread legs and curved neck of a
horse became clear. From the summit of the hill, it looks more
like a series of unconnected ditches than a powerful pagan
symbol that had been there for aeons.

"Think how long it's been there, silently casting its eye over
us all scrabbling about," Jude said, as moved by the clean purity
of the horse's shape as she had been all those years earlier.

Tom frowned. "Doesn't really look much like a horse,
does it?"

"I guess not from up here, but it's very lovely," she replied,
slightly irritated. She and Alex had loved this place, and the
horse. How could he be so *prosaic*?

"I have to say that I'm a bit disappointed, to be honest," Tom
said. "I had thought it would be much more, well, *impressive*.
Perhaps I'm just not as knowledgeable about art as you are."

She looked at him, saw his crestfallen expression and
decided not to say any more. They were very different, but
every couple had their differences, didn't they? It was going to
take *time* for them both to get used to this relationship; the least
she could do was give him a chance, she told herself...

. . .

They arrived back in Oxford at around 3pm, and then Tom ferried all her things across town while she waited in Paula's house with Pip and Tuna until he made one final trip to pick them up. When she arrived at his house, he insisted on cooking a celebratory dinner, and Jude was happy to let him do so whilst she soaked in his huge freestanding bath. The house was as beautiful as she remembered it, with huge windows all along one side, overlooking the riverbank at Iffley. In the enormous kitchen, gleaming black granite stretched from one side of the room to the other, but Jude was reluctantly reminded of the undertakers she had once visited, to see her grandmother laid-out. She shut that thought down straight away. Tom had already told her it had cost thousands.

"Do you think you can be happy here, Jude?" Tom asked, as he chopped and fried some shallots with impressive deftness. "Does it feel right?"

"I think so," she answered, hoping her slight hesitation went unnoticed. It did not, and the atmosphere in the room cooled slightly.

"Well, I think we're going to be very happy *indeed*," Tom said. "Look, even Tuna loves me! This is what you wanted, isn't it?"

Jude laughed, as Tuna did seem to adore Tom already, but she was already worried that there was still no bond being made with Pip, and Tom's increasing sneezes and sniffles warned of trouble ahead.

"Yes, I think it is," she replied eventually. He was asking for complete reassurance, but at that moment, she could not give it. "I think I probably just need to take things one step at a time."

As she got ready to go to bed, to his bed, after a rather strained dinner, she felt even more ill at ease. Perhaps it was still the fact that Tom had been her husband's best friend, the one she had rejected all those years ago, that was making things so *awkward* between them? She had to get past these doubts if this was to stand any chance of working, but as she shut a confused Pip in the kitchen for the night and went up to the bedroom to join him, she ignored the absolute certainty that she would have gone to bed with Owain Pritchard without a second thought if he'd asked her to.

FORTY-TWO

The dynamics of the friendship between Jude and the Fearsome Foursome had altered drastically during the year she had been away: Paula had become a parent, Jo and Katie had become closer, both as lovers and as business partners, and Morag had been allowed to lose herself in self-pity and despair. New Year's Eve had been the first time they'd seen each other properly for weeks, and it made them all realise how much they valued their long friendship. In the middle of January, Jude, already uncomfortable with being alone in Tom's immaculate house all day whilst he was at work, suggested that the five of them went away for a weekend before she entered the final phase of her pregnancy and was "too fat to go anywhere".

"Let's go to Totnes, in Devon. I went there with Alex once, and we loved it. Really quirky, just like us!"

"That's a pretty random choice, but yes please! I'd go anywhere right now," Morag said. Finn was still at her mother's in Scotland to give her a break, so she was free and loving it. "Decorating the spare room for a lodger can wait."

Jo and Katie were also enthusiastic, as *"Baguette"* was closed for some maintenance work, and Paula even promised to allow Georgio's mother to help him take care of Christos so that she could come as well. Jude left Tuna with Tom, but, as she had feared, he did not offer to have Pip. She understood why, but it worried her. Tom had begun to complain of an itchy nose, and sore, runny eyes every day, and the little dog was miserable too. Jude booked him into an expensive kennels for a few days, postponing facing the problem of Tom's allergy until her return from Devon, but she wept all the way back from dropping him off. The only real solution was a heartbreaking one.

On the motorway, the five friends sang songs they had all loved, blasting out Sister Sledge's 'We are family' and Christina Aguilera's 'Beautiful' at the tops of their voices. They shared old memories, including Jude's hen party in Brighton, which had ended in total group-gastroenteritis after a dodgy curry, and Morag's chaotic Burn's Night gathering during which her haggis had exploded, splattering her kitchen with a gruesome melee of grey meat and grains swollen like fat maggots.

"Overstuffed," they all chorused, echoing Morag's mother's exact words when she'd been told of this culinary disaster.

Totnes had not changed much. The long, steep main street was still crammed with unusual shops selling hand-made jewellery, expensive "artefacts" or alternative remedies for all kinds of ailments. The ironmongers, where Alex had once been so thrilled to find a gimble for a lampshade, was now an "artisan bakery". The cottage they had rented was tucked away in the network of lanes at the top of the town, called, appropriately, The Narrows. It was so old that the walls bulged with as many bumps and cracks as those in *Hedd*. Jude loved it straight away.

"Please don't start your strange wall-stroking thing again," Paula said with a look of fake alarm.

Few cars drove up The Narrows, so it was wonderfully quiet, and a background burble of people in the High Street was the only sound. At exactly 12.30pm, Jude heard the shouts of children in a nearby playground drift over the rooftops; at 1.20pm precisely, their joy ended, when their lunchbreak did.

"Wow. That will be my child in a few years' time, playing with their little friends," she murmured, feeling a shot of pure joy at the thought.

The women spent their first afternoon exploring the town. The weather was cold, but dry, so even Paula consented to walk quite a way along the reed-bordered banks of the River Dart in her designer trainers. Coots and moorhens darted between clumps of bullrushes, and Morag told them all she was sure she had seen the speckled shadow of a trout in the shallows. They went slowly, to accommodate Jude's pace, and talked as only walking *alongside* someone else enables. Gradually, secrets that had not had the chance to be told in the busyness of Oxford life, slunk out.

Morag told them that she had given up alcohol as her New Year's resolution. Having matched her Scottish uncles drink for drink over Christmas, she had recognised that she had a problem and said she was determined to deal with it, for Finn's sake and her own. Paula confessed to feeling torn by her love of her job, and guilt about not having seen Christos' first steps (Jude had been looking after him on the day he'd taken them). Jo talked of her longing for a child, and her hopes that she and Katie could adopt one day, but Katie strode ahead in angry silence, which told everyone that this was very unlikely.

"And what about you and Tom, Jude?" Jo said. "Is it all working out well? Must be a bit, well, *weird*."

"Look, I know you're not sure, Jo, but I like him."

"Bit like a pet poodle. I quite like those," Katie said bitterly.

Jude stopped and glowered at her friend.

"Give us a chance, will you? I can't be on my own anymore, don't you see? Morag, you understand that, don't you?"

"I most certainly do."

Jude took a deep breath, before saying, her voice shaking with feeling, "Look, Alex has gone, and that will never, ever change, no matter how much I wish it could. Time is running out for me. You were the ones telling me to 'move on', for God's sake! Well, I'm trying to move on – trying really hard." She was nearly crying now.

Katie took her arm. "I'm sorry, Jude. I understand you wanting to be with someone. I just think there could be other men for you, *better* men, than Tom, mainly because of your history. You didn't choose him back then, you chose Alex, and you told us all that you and Tom just weren't suited as a couple. We worry, that's all, after that.'

Jude wiped her eyes with the back of her hand. "Thanks for the explanation, at least. The truth is that I can't spend another ten years looking for a second Alex; there isn't one – well, not one that's available to me," she said. "The way I see it, I have one last chance at being some kind of family with Tom, and I think I have to grab it before it's too late."

A murmur of agreement.

"We'll all support you, whatever you do,' Jo added. "It's your life."

"Yes, it bloody well is! And Morag said he ticks at least four boxes, which has to be good. I mean, *four bloody boxes*!"

They laughed, and Jude felt the tension in the room disperse like a popped bubble.

"Well, he'd better tweak his dress code for nappy changing," Morag said, in her strongest Scottish accent. "Cream linen blazers? Forget it!"

FORTY-THREE

Despite the size of her belly, Tom wanted them to have sex. Jude sensed that this was another part of his need to feel she belonged to him and, as he was being so caring in every way, she had no reason to refuse, but she was reluctant, nonetheless. When it happened though, she was surprised at how much she had missed being touched. There was always a little fumbling, and Tom insisted on complete darkness, but Jude found this a relief, and it made the experience very different from sex with Alex. He'd always made a point of throwing the curtains wide or leaving a light on, often making cheeky references to their nosey neighbours "being in for a treat tonight!". Darkness meant that Jude did not have to see Tom's face, screwed tight in his efforts for sex not to hurt her, and he did not have to see *her* face, which was just as well, because it did.

As soon as it was over, Tom always fell asleep immediately, but Jude lay awake, as she had learnt to do with Alex, when she was always desperately willing his sperm to find their way to her eggs. Once they learnt that the two of them were doomed never to create a child, she was so traumatised that she had not let Alex come near her for months. Within a year, he was dead, and she was left to mourn all that they had lost, and brood on her regrets. That was all in the past now, she told herself as Tom began to snore. She had to leave it behind her. Turning over in the hope of relieving the weight of her belly, she felt his sperm trickle out from between her legs and eventually fell asleep in an uncomfortable dampness.

Very quickly, they settled into a pretty regular routine at home. They had sex (once they had found a comfortable position for Jude), he cooked them lovely meals and she had nothing much to do all day. Each morning, she lay in bed and listened as Tom hummed to himself in the shower. Then he gave her a quick kiss, dressed and left for work. It all felt so staid, so suburban, that Jude was always left with the feeling that they had shared a business transaction rather than made love the previous night and none of it made her feel any closer to Tom. Their life felt like a dull drama in which one of them needed to do something unexpected soon to move the plot forward. Jude tried to dismiss these childish thoughts as fast as she could. Tom had given her a baby, kindness, and a home, and that should be more than enough. And yet, somehow, it was not.

One Friday, Tom booked a table at The Randolph for 8 o'clock that evening. Jude was touched. A romantic dinner could be just what they needed. She replied:

Lovely. See you then. J X

As she was trying to find something smart to wear that still actually fitted her, Menna rang. This was rare, as Menna never rang to chat, but only when she had something particular to say. True to form, she had now:

"I'm pregnant, Jude. Baby's due in March. Bit of a surprise

– but a nice one. I was more than twenty weeks along before I even realised! Hardly any bump at all."

"That's brilliant, Menna!"

"*Bendegedig*/Fantastic, isn't it? Big question coming up next. Will you be the godmother?" Menna continued. "I'd love it if you would, and kill you if you won't."

"Of *course* I will! Honoured to be asked," Jude said, to a cheer from Menna. "Actually, though, talking of bumps, the midwives are a bit worried about mine. They say the baby seems 'small for dates', but as I'm not even sure about the dates, I don't know what to think."

A weighted pause. "I know exactly what you're thinking, Jude, but there's no point in fretting about it yet," Menna said. "This whole baby business always comes with pros and cons, however you do it."

"At least you're certain of the father of your baby, Menna," Jude said. "That's a big pro in my book."

"Well, there's not a single thing you can do about that right now. Everything that might need sorting can be sorted, I promise you, and your baby will always be loved, however things turn out," Menna said, and Jude was hugely thankful for her practical, sensible approach to life. "How are things with Tom, the 'probable-but-then-perhaps-not' father-to-be?"

"It's going OK, I think," she replied, trying to sound upbeat. Saying anything that might worry Menna now did not feel appropriate; she'd rung her with happy news. "Look, I'd better go. I'm in a rush. Tom's booked us a table for dinner."

"Ooh, lucky you. Could it be *proposal* time?" she said with emphasis.

Jude gasped and closed her eyes. She'd not even considered that possibility, not for a second, and when she did, it did not feel good. In her heart, she still felt firmly married to Alex.

"Doubt it. Take care of yourself, and congratulations again," she managed to say before hanging up.

Looking out of her window and up at the drab, grey sky, framed with buildings on all sides, she felt a familiar heaviness descend on her. Was this really to be her life now? A sluggish breeze had sprung up, and the television aerials were jerking on the rooftops. On Anglesey, the sea would probably be a glowering January green, reflecting the winter sky. She missed the wind that whipped the sea into such a fury that even the clouds went scudding for cover. She missed weather that made you feel *alive* rather than weather that formed the backdrop to each day.

Dressing quickly, she was putting on more make-up than usual when her mobile pinged again:

> See you later :). An old friend of mine will be
> joining us. She can't wait to meet you. T

Jude frowned. No romantic dinner, then, which was a shame as she really needed to feel closer to this man. At least there would be no proposal, though, which was a blessing. And she didn't have to dress up to the nines anymore, which was another.

She pulled on some boots she had bought in the sales and an old winter coat that she could still just about button up and set off to walk to the hotel instead of getting the bus she usually got into town. Today, she needed to feel the wind in her hair and on her face, and to let her irritation settle. Surely Tom wouldn't dare comment on it if she looked a little dishevelled when she arrived if she had to make conversation with a stranger all evening? She still considered "windswept and weather-beaten" to have been her best-ever look anyway, whatever Paula said.

By the time she arrived at the foyer of the Randolph, she regretted her rashness, however much she'd relished the walk. It had started to pour on her way down St Giles, and rain had played havoc with her attempt at glamorous make-up. She peeled off her dripping, dog-scented coat, and handed it to a young doorman, who seemed rather reluctant to take it. Smoothing her hair quickly, she walked into the dining room with her head held high; she was here, despite everything, and she was feeling good right now. In the restaurant, it was very warm, all candle-flicker, brocade, and gilt. It took her a few moments to spot Tom, who was sitting at a table in one corner of the room. She waved, glad to see him, and then noticed a fabulously dressed woman at his table.

"Goodness, Jude – it *must* be wild out there!" Tom said with a fleeting frown that he did his best to disguise. "Do you remember Sophie? She did Law with Alex and I, and came to all the Law Society dinners with us, but she moved to London last year for, er, personal reasons. She's back in town just for tonight, so I invited her along," adding, "She's a lovely person," in a whisper. Jude tried very hard indeed not to look doubtful about this fact, as Sophie was giving her a far from welcoming glower behind Tom's back.

Jude did not remember Sophie from tedious Law Society dinners with Alex and Tom, or much of the evening that followed, and she always looked back on both as thoroughly unpleasant. The food looked beautiful, but she couldn't eat it as stress was giving her terrible heartburn. Gorgeous Sophie worked somewhere Jude didn't care about, doing something legal she couldn't be bothered to explain, and she *very* much wanted to return to Oxford. The conversation centred around uproarious college memories, house prices and various points of law, so Jude quickly opted out of it. Sophie seemed totally uninterested in her anyway, probably as she had no useful contacts and looked an embarrassing mess in comparison to her. When Tom went to the toilet, they both sat in silence for about five minutes whilst she checked her phone. Had these two been together in the past? Jude wondered. If so, that would explain the positively glacial vibes now emanating from across the table.

"When's the baby due?" she asked dully, when Tom still had not returned.

"Probably in about six weeks, but I'm not really sure of my dates," Jude said. "It's Tom's, in case you were wondering."

"I wasn't. I assumed it," Sophie replied brutally.

Jude knew that Tom was not at all pleased with her once Sophie's taxi had driven away. This was such a new feeling that she responded with anger, rather than understanding when he tried to talk to her about it.

"Well, that didn't go too well, did it? I really wanted to... well... to *show you off* to Sophie and get you two to be friends."

"*Show me off*, what, like you're a stallion and I'm some mare you've impregnated, you mean?" Jude snapped. "I thought she was absolutely horrible."

Tom pressed his lips together, and Jude saw the little boy he must have been, the one who was never invited to join the best gang at school, go to the cool teenage parties, or included in the Oxford drinking marathons. He had wanted her to be nice to his friend, to impress her, which was perfectly normal in the strange, competitive world he inhabited. Instead, she'd turned up looking like a scarecrow and not played the game at all. She sighed and reached for his hand.

"I'm sorry if I let you down," she said. "I'm just not feeling like competing with a thoroughbred right now, I guess, to continue the equine theme."

Tom laughed unconvincingly. "OK. I get that. Sorry, let's forget about it and go home." Jude stood up and felt her tummy muscles clench and tighten.

"Are you all right?" Tom said, seeing her face. "Gosh, sit

down, and have some water." He fussed around her for a few minutes, until he could see that she felt better; it was a welcome tension-breaker for both of them.

"Look, love, I'd wondered about us both going to my parents in Burford next weekend. I've told them about the baby, and they're dying to meet the mother of my child."

Jude hesitated. "*The mother of my child?* Hmm, I'm still getting 'brood mare' vibes here, Tom..."

"They want to meet *you,* I mean," Tom added quickly. "I'm trying here, Jude. You're making things so difficult."

"OK. Point taken. Let's do it. I've heard a lot about your parents over the years, so it will be good to finally meet them. Alex met them several times, didn't he?"

As their taxi drove away, Jude tried as hard as she could to banish the hilarious memory of a, very drunk, Alex impersonating Tom's parents, Henry "Right-oh" Byers and his wife, "lovely" Lavinia. Her late husband's wit was always brilliantly, cruelly accurate.

FORTY-FOUR

Reluctantly, Jude dropped Pip off at the kennels again on the Thursday morning and then spent hours trying to decide what to pack for the weekend in Burford. Would Lavinia let her borrow an iron? She could not risk looking like a tramp again. Would they dress formally for dinner, or were they "come as you are" people? What was their stance on illegitimate grandchildren? After The Randolph Debacle (as all her friends now called it), Jude nursed a very real dread of letting Tom down again, and by the time they left Oxford, she could hardly speak, she was so anxious. She turned the radio on to give herself time to calm down. Half an hour later, when they turned onto the, smaller, road that led into Burford, Tom speed-dialled a number, leant back, and shouted at his hands-free phone above the music:

"Hi Mum. We're about ten mins from *Northwick*, so you can get the rice on now. You asked me to let you know."

At this exchange, Jude's nerves finally evaporated, and she stifled her laughter just in time.

. . .

Northwick House was in fact a modest mock-Tudor detached house at the end of a carefully manicured gravelled drive. As the car crunched over it, the ghostly undersides of several plump birds flashed in front of the car, before coming back to rest again on a white dovecote. Jude heaved herself out of the car and lurched towards the front door, which was already open for them.

"Mum, Dad, this is Jude," Tom said, after his "mwah mwahs" and/or handshakes with both his parents had been completed.

"*Lovely* to see you both!" a woman said, though Jude could not make out more than what looked like a huge halo, as the light was behind her.

"Hello," she said, completely mesmerised by Lavinia's hair, which was architecturally swept up into an amazing series of waves and wavelets and tinted a very pale violet. Henry shook Jude's hand repeatedly, and with a grip so firm that it made her wince. He was flushed and sweating, and she could tell even from the hallway that the central heating in the house was set at "tropical". Jude was strongly reminded of Gloria's idea of "cosy" in her childhood home, which was not at all helpful at that moment.

"Well, you look positively blooming, just as you should," Henry boomed.

"Thank you," was the only reply Jude could muster, as Tom's dad ushered her into the living room while he took their bags upstairs.

"Absolutely *lovely* news, about you two, and such a complete surprise," Lavinia cooed. "We thought Tom was very keenly pursuing Sophie, you see, er, *Jude*. But nobody can argue with a woman with a baby on the way, can they?" Her mouth smiled, but her eyes did not, and Jude heard this woman's distaste for her casually abbreviated name loud and clear. She felt herself flush from her toes to the roots of her hair as she found a seat and plopped down in it thankfully. So, Tom and Sophie *had* been an item before all this had happened. Questions ricocheted around inside her head once her suspicion was so baldly confirmed. How serious had he been about her? Why had he not told her the truth about their past relationship? Did he break it off before he came to Anglesey, or afterwards? How on earth did he think Sophie would react to meeting her last week if she was still in love with him? Did these people think that she had entrapped their son because of her pregnancy? Her head began to spin, and the room was so hot...

"Could I possibly have a glass of water?" she squeaked.

"Right-oh!" Henry replied.

After an excruciating "aperitif time", Lavinia led them all into the dining room, and lifted the lid from two dishes of exceedingly creamy-looking stroganoff and perfectly fluffed rice. Tom poured Jude a very small glass of white wine, and she had to stop herself from glugging it down in one. A rivulet of sweat ran down between her breasts.

"Very good to get to meet you at last. Heard about Alex from Tom, of course. Sad business. He came here quite a few times you know, during the boys' Oxford days," Henry said.

"Yes. A terrible shame," Lavinia said. "Such a *lovely* man."

"More wine, anyone?" Tom said with a quick glance at Jude, who was now looking very pale.

"A smidgen, please," Lavinia replied. She pecked at the glass as a bird does water, holding it in her mouth and then tilting her head back. Henry drank deeply, turned to Jude and sallied forth again.

"So what about you two lovebirds? Good things come from naughty things, I suppose?" Henry laughed, winking at Jude.

Jude half-smiled and focused on folding her napkin into a triangle.

"Oh, Alex and Tom were such good friends. But I feel, overall, it's... *lovely* that you two are together now."

Jude wondered if she was the only one who was really uncomfortable with all these references to how close her late husband and Tom had been. She felt rather like the dastardly villain in a fairy tale who had scuppered everyone's "happy ever after" in the pursuit of her own.

After dinner, Henry retired to what he called his "den" and Lavinia, refusing Jude's lukewarm offer of help, went to clear up in the kitchen. Tom led her into the living room and patted the cushion next to him on the sofa. She sat down with a sigh and, as he leafed through the newspaper, gradually relaxed a little and felt the rich stroganoff progress very slowly down towards her stomach.

"I'm not sure I'm what they expected – after Gorgeous Sophie, I mean," she said. "Why didn't you tell me you two had been together?"

Tom grimaced. "I'm sorry I didn't tell you. Yes, we had a thing, but it's always been you, Jude. You know that now. Mum and Dad cling onto the fantasy of me and Sophie, as they really liked her – or rather, they liked her extremely wealthy family," Tom replied. "They're terrible snobs, as you can probably tell, but they'll soon get to know and like you. It's all such a surprise for them, and they don't really do surprises."

"I can imagine," Jude replied.

Tom took her hand in his. "I think perhaps I'd always hoped it would happen between us, so I could never fully commit to Sophie for some reason. I don't know, and I haven't analysed it much and don't intend to. All I do know is that I had no idea we'd wind up where we are now, with a baby coming, but we have, so let's try and make it work. Seems best all round."

Squeezing her hand, he picked up the remote control and turned on the television before she could agree or disagree.

· · ·

Everyone trooped up to bed by half past ten, bearing mugs of Horlicks or hot chocolate. The spare room was so hot that Jude turned off the radiator as soon as Tom fell asleep. She also pulled back the thick, swagged curtains to let some air into the room and unplugged the sickeningly sweet vanilla air freshener beside the bed. Gloria would have loved this place.

Long into the night, Jude lay listening to this man breathing beside her: in, out, in, out. She had not entirely believed him about Sophie; they did seem such a well-matched couple in so many ways, as his parents had clearly felt too. Had he really held a candle for her throughout her marriage to Alex and waited for his opportunity to tell her so once she'd lost him? It all sounded pretty calculated, even naïve of him. Such "dot-to-dot" relationships rarely fared well in all the novels she had read. As she heard the church bells in the town strike three, Jude began to wonder what on earth was she doing, trying to love this man when the ones she truly loved were a) gone forever and b) miserably married on an island several hundred miles north of here. Like a mouse on a wheel, round and round she went, hour after hour, getting nowhere fast.

FORTY-FIVE

The following morning, Jude was alone when she woke up at 11am. She went downstairs to find an aproned Tom sitting at the kitchen table, chopping vegetables while his mother rolled out pastry.

"Sorry – I couldn't get to sleep for ages..." A frown from Lavinia stopped Jude dead. Gloria always told her it was very rude to tell your hostess that you hadn't slept well.

"Yes, you do look tired, Jude. I'll make you some lovely free range scrambled eggs. That should do the trick." Without making eye contact with Jude at all, Lavinia scrambled eggs and toasted toast.

"Mum's invited some old family friends over for lunch today," Tom said. "They all want to meet you."

"Oh, great," Jude answered, feeling her stomach lurch. "What time are they coming?"

"About 1.30, for a light lunch, so there's plenty of time for you to get yourself in order. Tom and I are getting everything ready," Lavinia said, putting a plate of vividly yellow eggs in front of her. "You just relax."

Jude tried to swallow, but each mouthful was sheer torture

as she thought of the day ahead of her. She had never been good at small talk and felt even less able to make it with "lovely" Lavinia's family friends.

"I think I'll get dressed quickly and go for a little walk before they come, if you don't need my help," she said, once she had eaten just over half the mountain of eggs. She needed to get outside in the fresh air, immediately, and prepare herself for what came next. This weekend was turning into one gruelling trial after another.

"Remember to take things easy, in your condition," Lavinia said, without feeling.

The countryside around Burford was exceptionally beautiful, and as Jude walked, she remembered Alex opening up the throttle of the Harley as they'd passed through this same valley, perhaps three summers ago. They had admired the tablecloth of hedge-checkered countryside laid out before them, spiked with lush trees and lonely church spires and decided, in the future, to think about moving out of the city to live.

She dipped down to the path that followed the River Windrush, which threads through Burford. The air was crisp, and a shimmering haze rose off the fields as the weak wintry sun warmed the ground a little. Most trees were still leafless, their twigs silvered against the sky, but down at the water's edge, willows hung, their lowest leaves dipping gracefully into the water. Jude heard shots, followed by the outrage of a pheasant.

The fields were stubbly and bare, the earth such a richer colour than the bleak winter fields in Anglesey. Here, she could almost feel the land still sleeping through the dark quiet of winter, waiting for a new round of growth, ripening and harvesting. This time last year, she had spent each day striding up and down the beach below her cottage on Anglesey, and there had been precious few signs of spring in evidence at all.

Whenever she began to feel rising panic about the future, and what to do about it as she walked, she focused on a particular object – a flag of red leaf still clinging to a tree, or a vivid clump of berries glowing in the winter drabness – because they were a small, bright spark of beauty in dark times. This technique had helped her during Alex's illness; the certainty that the kindly hospital auxiliary team would do the tea-round, or the WRVS volunteers would bring the trolley. She'd carefully chosen Alex's dinner menu on the day he had died, hoping that death would not take him from her that day if she did, but it had, nonetheless.

Jude heard the first guests arrive as she was still desperately trying to smooth the creases out of the smartest dress she had packed. It was clearly not a good moment to ask to borrow an iron, so Gloria's technique of "hand-ironing", which entailed smoothing your dampened hands over any creases repeatedly, would have to do. Luckily, her walk had made her look less peaky after her disturbed night, so she might "pass muster", as Henry would no doubt have put it.

The dining room was full of people when she came downstairs, and their chatter reminded her of the sounds from Menna's chicken coop as her hens waited to start another busy day's pecking. The talk stilled when she appeared in the doorway, and Lavinia said:

"Jude, come in and meet everyone. Tom, come over here and stand next to her. Henry, get Jude a drink."

"Right-oh!" Henry fired back.

As she was introduced to a succession of remarkably homogenous, grey or white-haired people, Jude concentrated on trying to remember their connection to Tom, even if she could not retain their names. After answering their opening questions, and thanking them for their congratulations on imminent parenthood, she began asking them about themselves. Alex had taught her this, something he had dubbed his PSGT (or

"Painful Social Gathering Technique"), and it never failed. Everybody loved talking about themselves, he'd always said. As always, he'd been absolutely right.

When the guests began chatting to each other instead of her, Jude sat down in a corner and took a surreptitious look around the room, taking in the faux-walnut drinks cabinet, crystal glasses and thick, swirled carpets; everything exuded middle-class aspiration. To live in this world with Tom and his parents would mean being cushioned and safe, but could she actually endure it? Luckily, they would be living in Oxford, amongst friends, she consoled herself, and she was not obliged to follow Lavinia's lead, manner, or taste in anything, but still, Jude felt unsure. This simply was not *her* at all.

Later, when everyone had left, Tom wrapped his arms around her from behind and nuzzled the back of her neck as she gazed out onto the garden.

"I hope that wasn't too awful. You did so well. Even Aunt Dorothy liked you!"

"Only because I was fascinated with her osteoporosis," she replied, turning to face him reluctantly.

"I was proud of you," he said. He kissed her, smelling of wine, pushing his tongue into her mouth and his obvious erection into her leg. Jude was very relieved when Lavinia came in and began clearing abandoned coffee cups.

FORTY-SIX

Pip became increasingly miserable at Tom's house, as he had to be confined almost exclusively to the kitchen, where the floor could be quickly and easily hoovered and mopped. When Jude found puddles on the floor most days, a macerated rug and scratched antique chair legs, she knew that the writing was on the wall for her dog if she did not do something, and fast.

Things came to a head one evening when Tom tried to shut the kitchen door on the little dog again as they went into the living room to watch TV. A desperate Pip growled at him with teeth bared and hackles up and he nudged the yelping dog back into the room with his slipper.

"Jude, this can't go on," he said, once Pip was safely secured. "Look, I'm sorry, but your dog really hates me, I'm mainlining antihistamine every day and I no longer feel comfortable in my own home."

"I know, and I'm sorry. I don't understand why he's like that with you," Jude said miserably. "He's so loving and sweet with everyone else."

"That doesn't make me feel much better! Look, his behaviour towards me is simply explained, as far as I can see.

He's jealous. And as for my allergy, either I go or he goes, and sorry, but this is my house…"

And Jude knew he was right. If she stayed here, as she needed to – now more than ever – she was going to have to give up the companion who had sustained her through so many lonely days and nights on the island. As Tom looked at her semi-apologetically, waiting for her decision, she could see no real alternative in the short term. They were all miserable, especially Pip, so she had to think clearly. For now, her baby needed a dad more than she needed a dog. What would happen in the long term, she would face in due course.

"I'll sort it," she murmured.

She rang everyone she could think of to see if they would adopt the little dog, but no one could, or would. A frustrated, jealous Jack Russell was nobody's ideal pet. Even Menna would not risk taking him, with her own baby due very soon.

"He had you all to himself from when he was a pup, so he can't share you," she said. "It happens, and I really don't care about the moulting, but I'm really sorry I can't have him here."

Eventually, Jude rang the kennels, to ask for advice.

"Basically, my dog hates my partner, and my partner hates my dog and is very allergic to him to boot."

"Ah. That's a thorny one," the manager said. "One of them will have to be rehomed, I'd say, and that's unlikely to be your partner. Sorry."

When she then gave her the name of a dog rescue centre in Evesham, Jude wept, sure that giving him up was something she would regret, but whenever she tried to think of quick, alternative solutions, there were none. Perhaps once the baby had arrived, there would be a way forward, but not now. As she drove out to the rescue centre, she remembered the day that Owain had brought her this runt of a puppy, and she sobbed uncontrollably at the memory, but she had to be sensible now, for all their sakes.

The centre was decorated in jolly yellows and greens, but its walls were studded with photos of dogs with liquid-brown eyes just like Pip's, begging visitors to love them, to rescue them. It reminded Jude of the deceptive welcome of the hospice ward where she had taken Alex when the pain had become too great to bear. They'd admitted him for the weekend at first, to "monitor" him. He had never come home.

Pip trotted into the reception room happily, but when he smelt things only he could smell, and heard sounds only he could hear, he flattened his ears against his head and flicked his tail up beneath his legs in abject misery. Handing him over to a gentle young woman called Maggie, Jude signed the papers authorising the centre to "act in the dog's best interest" and rehome him if a vetted, suitable home became available. The small print reassured her that the centre "never destroyed a healthy dog," but that was of little comfort today.

"I hope they *never* find you a suitable home, Pip. I'll be back for you, somehow, I promise," she said as she drove away alone.

As the third trimester of her pregnancy crawled past, and more and more doubts about a future with Tom began to colour her thoughts and dreams, Jude desperately needed distraction. She had to get safely to the end of this pregnancy before deciding what to do, and so for now, she needed other things to focus on. Setting up a workshop in the shed in Tom's garden, she began to think about her business plan for multi-media artworks, whether he thought it was the right time or not. Mondays with Christos were sacred, but on other days, she headed down the garden as soon as Tom left for the office. She ordered two dozen sheets of 30cm x 30cm hardboard, and slowly began organising all her materials into colours, moods, environments, and textures. It took many hours but was deeply satisfying. She often returned to the shed after dinner too; she had become so used to her own company on the island that sitting watching TV with Tom felt a totally unnatural thing to do.

From time to time, she paid Menna's boys a tenner to find her something that she particularly needed and post it to her – a handful of small pieces of clear, green sea glass, or a particular dune-growing wildflower. Pressed flowers, pots of glue, pebbles, shells, and sheaves of dried grasses soon covered Tom's expensive but unused "workbench" as she placed and re-placed each element of every picture, making sure that each one was as vibrant as the place it represented. She also began to add more paint, either as a subtle, washed background, a flash of colour, or a precisely drawn portrait of a bird, or plant. She let her memories and her senses guide her, and was amazed at how vividly she could recall even the tiniest of details. She realised that this was how Rhiannon Jones remembered things so clearly, from many years ago. She went right back inside her memories, and saw them again, in her mind's eye.

"Are you ever coming out of here?" Tom asked, as he brought her a cup of herbal tea across the garden late one night.

"I'm just finishing this one of Rhosneigr in the winter," she answered. "I've got to get at least three ready this week, as Paula's set up a meeting with the director of a chain of bougie shops, a woman called Olivia Grant. I really want to make an impression on her before the baby comes. I just hope she's *nothing* like Helena, because she certainly sounds it on the phone!"

"Guess artsy people are always a bit on the snooty side," Tom said. Jude did not respond as she wanted to but did sweep the sandy floor with a little more vigour.

"I think you brought most of that island back with you," Tom said, tutting as he crunched across towards the door.

"I wish," Jude muttered.

. . .

In the end, Olivia Grant sent her deputy, Anna, to meet Jude as she'd had to go to London, but she was not disappointed, and quickly warmed to a young woman she recognised as a version of herself a few years earlier – keen, talented, and decidedly put-upon. Within a week, Olivia had placed an order for no less than six collages, on different themes, in different sizes. The biggest one was to hang on the wall in a new "Soho farmhouse" conversion in a picture-perfect Oxfordshire village, and Jude had to bring the hardboard into Tom's dining room to create it (which he accepted with reluctant grace despite having to move his games console). The finished result needed more paint than Jude had ever used before, blending textures and colours to create a collage of the green and gold of summer in the Cotswolds, punctuated by lush, flower-dotted hedgerows and a Wedgwood-blue sky. It was astonishingly beautiful. This commission not only made Jude a sizeable amount of money, but filled her with secret hope that, with her savings and a steady source of income, perhaps she *could* afford to bring up her baby alone and pay for some childcare so she could work if things did not work out with Tom. She said nothing to him about her doubts, but he seemed more and more preoccupied these days anyway, and she found him emailing or messaging (ostensibly about "a tricky case at work") more and more. Each day dragged, as heavy and slow as her body, and instead of love growing, Jude sensed a growing distance, forming an insurmountable barrier between them as an incoming tide separates land from shore.

FORTY-SEVEN

Although she'd said she would not return to Anglesey after her Christmas visit, Jude could not refuse to go to Gwilym, Menna's new baby's, christening. He was born early, to the surprise of her friend, but it got Jude thinking about her own dates. Her due date had, originally, been before Menna's, but the midwife still wondered "if Jude could possibly have miscalculated" at every check-up. Her irregular periods made it impossible to be sure, and she'd no intention of confessing to having slept with two different men within the space of a few weeks, but the alarm bells were now very real, and very loud. Jude secretly allowed herself to consider that her baby could, in fact, be Owain's. If this was so, Tom's reaction would be hurt and shock, followed, probably, by anger. It would be truly awful for him, in many ways.

It would be very difficult for her, too, and she would feel ashamed of her apparent promiscuity, but she could not suppress a very slight feeling of relief at the possibility. If this baby was not Tom's, it would automatically set her free, perhaps free enough to return to Anglesey if she had to leave Oxford and bring up her child alone. Perhaps, she even dared to fanta-sise, Owain would leave Non for good and join them?

"Whoah! One step at a time, Jude," she told herself, when these thoughts ran away with her. "Let's get this baby safely here first."

As well as attending Gwilym's christening, she decided to visit Rhiannon when she was on Anglesey and take her a small collage she had made especially for her. The old woman had been very poorly for several weeks, and Jude could not suppress the feeling that this might be the last time she would ever see her friend. She also hoped to have a meal with Stella, finally meet the famous Eifion and hear all the latest gossip about the horrific "The Tented Coven", which always made her laugh.

Jude got a rare, direct train to Holyhead rather than drive, as her belly could hardly fit behind the wheel of her tiny Fiat now. She booked herself into a B&B right on the seafront in Rhos-neigr and on the day she arrived, sat in the window watching the windsurfers' boards zigzagging through the waves for a couple of carefree hours before letting anyone know she was here. A little further from the main beach, she saw kite-surfers being lifted up like small, trussed angels before returning to skim the water again. The sea and the wind had not changed here, and never would; they did as they pleased, when they pleased, and Jude envied them that enormously. As she sat, unmoving, a deep peace descended on her in those two hours, seeping through her tired body like the warmth of the first sunny day in late spring. She had not felt that peace for a long time.

"I promise I'll bring you here often, my darling," she murmured, hand on her belly. "And you'll love it as much as I do, I know."

The christening was to be held in a beautiful old church in Llanfaelog. It was a perfect March morning, sunny and bright, so at 11.30am, the small party marched out of Menna's house adrift on a babble of happy voices. Menna's husband Jac carried a smiling Gwilym in his arms with ineffable pride and care. The service was simple, and short; the chilly, holy water did not make the baby cry and even the harsh, open-throated yells of two gulls on the church roof throughout the hymns did not mar the sonorous notes of the organ. Menna's late father had been one of the parishioners who had helped maintain it, and she wept as its music hummed and reverberated in the old beams above their heads.

"It's as if Dad's here with us now," she said.

"I'm sure he is," Jude answered, taking her hand. "I think that the people we have loved are always with us. I hope so anyway."

Jude had told Menna that she was happy to try and make her promises to Gwilym in Welsh, but when the time came, she was so overwhelmed by the fervent looks of encouragement coming from everyone around her at the font that she completely forgot what to say. It was only when Menna's mother mouthed the correct responses at her, that she got through it.

By 4pm, the party in the village hall opposite the church was drawing to a close, and Jude had exhausted both her smiling muscles and her Welsh conversational skills. She'd done her best and chatted to so many of Menna's friends and family that her head was splitting: her Welsh was indeed very rusty, which made her sad.

"You've done well, Jude, today. *Da iawn hogan*/Very good, girl." Menna looked down at Jude's belly, and then into her eyes. "But tell me; do you have to go back tomorrow? Why not stay here for a few more days, and rest? You look, well, 'out of sorts', I think the English phrase is."

"I have time for a quick visit to Rhiannon tomorrow, and to see Stella and her partner for lunch, but then I have to go back," she replied. "This little one could decide to make an appearance at any time."

Menna's brow furrowed. "If you say so. *Dw'in poeni amdanat ti*/I'm worried about you."

"I think I'm a bit scared, about a lot of things," Jude said, and then a question popped out of her mouth before she had time to stop herself from letting it:

"How is Owain Pritchard, Menna? I keep dreaming about him, and I wish I could stop. Perhaps if I know he's forgotten me and moved on, it will. Have you seen him around at all?"

Menna sighed. "I knew you were going to ask that sooner or later. He usually sings in the choir in this church, actually, but was tactful enough not to join us today," she said. "He's well, but Non left him just before Christmas, and I heard he's living in a rundown place somewhere near Penmon with his dog. Non got the house, of course."

Jude gasped. "Goodness! She left *him*? Do you know why?"

"He won't talk about it, Jac says, but she's telling everyone who will listen that he couldn't father any children," Menna answered.

"Poor Owain. He was so loyal to her. I bet she'll have a new bloke on the go before long."

"I heard she has already, another teacher in her school, but please forget about Owain, Jude. He'll hide away, bury himself in his poetry, and talk to his dog into his old age. I know you think I'm an old romantic, and I am, but from where I'm sitting, as you would say, you've got a man with a lot more to offer you than Owain Pritchard will ever have."

Jude nodded silently. "I've never thought you were an old romantic, Menna, but perhaps a wannabe one," she said. "But I get your point, boss."

Menna laughed, but concern was still etched on her face.

FORTY-EIGHT

The next day, it was pouring with a relentlessness that Jude had only ever seen in North Wales. Rain hammered onto the roofs of Rhosneigr all morning, and she was soaked before she even got on the bus to Bangor, where she would visit Rhiannon first. She had FaceTimed her ever-cheerful daughter, Hâf, who warned that her mother had deteriorated a lot since Jude had left the island, but that she was looking forward to seeing "Judith, that nice English girl" very much. The hour-long bus ride was such a familiar one that Jude even recognised a few of the regulars on the route. They cheerily nodded at her and then all steamed in their seats in companionable silence all the way to Bangor.

Plas Hyfryd looked less than welcoming that day, darkened by the driving rain, and there was nobody at the reception desk: staff cuts had clearly hit hard. Jude signed the visitor's book and made her way along the corridor, smiling at the refreshed displays of old adverts, and an updated destination on a placard at the "bus stop": *"To the zoo"*. But before she got anywhere near Rhiannon's room, she heard the insistent beeping of something medical, and stiffened. In an instant, she was back in that pale green hospice cubicle, with Alex pinioned to the bed by an unforgiving web of wires and tubes. She approached the door to her friend's room with dread.

Rhiannon was attached to several buzzing, flashing machines, and fast asleep. The room still smelt very faintly of cinnamon, but there was a denser smell Jude recognised underlying it: the thick, sweet scent of mortality. She sat down and covered the old woman's hand with her own. It was cold, so she rubbed it gently, feeling the layer of thin skin slide over thin bones, slippery and smooth. Rhiannon opened her eyes slowly; her pupils were now completely grey.

"Hello, Rhiannon. It's me... Judith, come to see you after far too long," Jude said, holding back her tears. There seemed little point in asking the old woman "how she was", Jude could see that for herself.

"*Helô cariad*/hello love," she murmured. "Baby not here yet, then?"

"Not yet. Soon, hopefully," Jude replied. "Rhiannon, I brought you something."

She let Rhiannon's hand drop gently onto the bedcover and tugged the brown paper off the special collage she had made for her. Taking the old woman's bony hand, she placed it on a craggy oyster shell on one side of the collage. Very slowly, her fingers started to feel around, spidering from one thing to another, from the snail-coils to the crisp seaweed, the tiny, sea-smoothed pebbles and the wide strip of gritty sand that made a "sandbank" across the centre of the collage. As Rhiannon's fingers crept across the canvas again and again, she smiled.

"Seaweed, that is. My husband Guto cooked it fresh, you know. Disgusting it was," she whispered. "Stank."

"But can you *feel* the beach, Rhiannon?" Jude asked. "I do hope so."

"Oh, I can see it, *cariad*/love, as clear as when I was a girl, or with my Rhodri. He made sandcastles. Such a lovely boy."

Jude stopped herself asking if Rhodri had come to see his mother lately. The three, unopened, boxes of chocolates on the bedside cabinet told her that he hadn't.

Rhiannon fell into a doze soon afterwards, both her hands spread wide across her gift. Kissing her lightly, Jude left. She hoped that her friend's softly fluttering eyelids meant that she was dreaming of the sea, of the beaches she'd loved and of her beloved Guto, lost at war so long ago.

Stella looked like a different woman. Her luridly hennaed mane had gone, and her hair had been coloured a soft blonde and cut into a series of choppy sections that made it seem as if water was flowing through it. She was wearing a beautifully cut blue linen dress and driving a shiny red Golf when she picked Jude up outside the care home.

"Jude, dahling! You look amazing," she shouted, beaming at her.

"So do *you!*" Jude replied, laughing as she slowly eased herself into the passenger seat of the car. "Nice wheels!"

"Someone's got to raise the tone around here," Stella replied with a wink. "Colin finally coughed up!"

By the time they pulled up outside her cottage in Tregarth, the rain had eased, and Stella was bubbling with excitement about Jude finally meeting Eifion.

"I really thought I'd end up on my ownsome, seeing the boys if and when they deign to let me, but now I know I won't, I can bear not seeing them," Stella said. "I'm glad you're with Tom, Jude, even if he isn't quite the man of your dreams. We weren't meant to be on our own, you and I, and you need to remember that Alex was always going to be an impossible act for anyone to follow."

"I know that, but…" she stopped. There was no point in spoiling their meal by sharing her doubts about Tom yet, but she would need to talk to Stella about it later, or risk despair. She was the only friend she could fully share them with. The Fearsome Foursome would be full of "I told you so's" and Menna was neck-deep in baby care.

The two women linked arms as they strolled up the path to Stella's cottage, and Jude admired the swathes of spring bulbs just beginning to show themselves, and the newly planted herbaceous border. The transformation inside the cottage was even more impressive. The kitchen was now full of natural light from a pretty new window in the far wall and painted an eggshell blue. A jugful of bright forsythia obliterated any memory of the stale smoke and patchouli from that awful lunch with the horrific Tented Coven. As they went inside, a grey-haired man in a Fairisle sweater greeted them with the widest smile Jude had ever seen.

"You must be the wondrous Jude," adding, "Welcome, both of you!" pointing at her belly. "Congratulations too. Stella has been so excited to see you again."

Eifion had cooked fresh Anglesey sea bass and potatoes dug from the growbags in the greenhouse in the garden, which they slathered with butter from the farm shop in Llanberis. A goat's cheese and raspberry roulade for pudding, also made from island produce, meant that every mouthful was so evocative of Anglesey that it made Jude want to weep with her love for the place.

"Is this goat's cheese from Dominic's farm? It's superb."

"It is. He always asks after you, you know. He's got big plans for that place, as he always said he had. And he's MARRIED, to a local girl!"

"Aw, that's good to hear. So no chance of you matchmaking the two of us anymore then," Jude said with a grin. "Thank goodness for small mercies!"

They took their drinks and coffees into the into the new summerhouse, and sat under the huge copper beech tree, listening to droplets of water plip rhythmically around them from the earlier rain. Jude watched Stella and Eifion touch each other's arm or stroke each other's cheek as they related the tale of how they'd met, what they planned to do next in the house, or the garden. He laughed when she was happy and offered her some water when she began to get garrulous after her third glass of Prosecco. It was a joy to see.

And Jude knew with sudden certainty that nobody would ever look at her and Tom and see that easy, mutual happiness. There was still a strange formality between them, a space that, despite their being lovers, neither of them had been able to breach and, she was more and more sure, neither of them really wanted to. When Eifion went inside to clear up, Jude's doubts tumbled out.

"It feels as if he's following a manual, like a DIY 'relationship instruction booklet'. We follow it to the letter, do everything the right way, but he seems disappointed all the time as if there's a step missing. I thought I could love him, but now, I'm really not sure I ever can, and I think he's beginning to feel the same way."

"Look, he's been in your life for years, and he was your husband's best mate. He probably misses Alex just as much as you do and feels a bit awkward, especially with a baby on the way," Stella said. "Give yourselves some breathing space, at least until the baby's born. Then, you can decide what's best, for both of you. You can't now. Give it time, girl."

"That's what everyone says, 'give it time', but it doesn't feel right and life's short, Stella. I know that more than anyone," Jude replied.

"I know you do but remember that sometimes life throws us unexpected blessings as well landing terrible blows on us. What were the chances of me meeting someone as brilliant as Eifion? I'm still hoping that Tom will be one of those if you just give yourselves a chance. *Dim stress rwan cofia!*/No stress now, remember!"

But as Jude sat on the bus later, she was not as convinced as Stella seemed to be that time would sort things out. Tom wanted to care for her. He said he'd always loved her, but there was something very wrong about the way things were between them now, and she was not sure that any amount of time or breathing space could fix it.

PART 7

DECISIONS

FORTY-NINE

Back in Oxford, "Waiting For The Baby" became a stifling preoccupation for both Jude and Tom. Even the air in the house felt sluggish and heavy, as it does before a storm. Jude was constantly on edge, aware that, once her due date passed, Tom might begin to quiz her about why the medics were not rushing her into the John Radcliffe Hospital to be induced. She also began to wonder if she should tell her mother about the baby, after all. Not doing so felt unnatural, even slightly cruel, to her as the stressed, hyper-emotional and tired heavily pregnant woman she had now become.

"Bloody hormones have a lot to answer for," Jude muttered one morning, writing a list of "reasons to tell Mum" and "reasons to avoid telling her like the plague".

Gloria had been grumbling more than ever lately, which was both annoying and a little concerning. A persistent cough had led to the inevitable rounds of antibiotics, and then a chest X-ray, the results of which were due next week. Her mother had had so many tests, scans, consultant's appointments, and X-rays over the years that one of the receptionists at the hospital called her "Mrs Indestructible", a moniker that Gloria, oblivious to any kind of irony, had always revelled in, but this time it felt real.

Jude added "Mum might actually be seriously ill this time" to her "reasons to tell her" list.

When a padded envelope popped through the letter box one morning and Jude lumbered to pick it up, a very vivid memory of Rhiannon Jones suddenly flashed into her head. Opening, the envelope, she immediately knew why, as she was hit with such a strong whiff of cinnamon that it caught at the back of her throat. Inside was a tightly folded cotton handkerchief with an "R" embroidered in one corner, and the framed photograph of her and Rhiannon that she'd taken in the care home all those months ago. When she opened the handkerchief, a string of pearls slithered into her hand. There was a long letter from Hâf, too, written in the warm, chatty tone Jude remembered her having when she had spoken to her in the past:

Dear Jude (though I know Mam always called you 'Judith'!)

Mam passed away last week, peacefully, in her room at Plas Hyfryd. *She asked me to send these few things to you, so I hope they mean something. I'm afraid the pearls are fake, but we never told her, as they were a gift from Dad. Mam used to talk about you such a lot and said you were her friend when she needed one most, so diolch yn fawr/thank you.*

I want to tell you something, Jude. Both you and Lisa, the manager, said that Mam sometimes talked about a "Mari", but nobody knew who she was and you suggested I try to find out. Towards the end, Mam started calling me Mari, which upset me a bit, so when she died, I decided to take your advice and I started by looking at our family tree. Well, guess what? Mari was Mam's older sister, who died of diphtheria when she was about ten years old. When I found a picture of Mari in an old school photo from her primary school, I realised that I look so like her it's uncanny. In many ways I'm the spitting image of her beloved sister who died, and I must have reminded Mam of that loss every time I went to see her, so perhaps that's why she treated me the way she did when she became confused. Thank you for suggesting I look into it, and I'm telling you all this because I thought you deserved to know this final piece in the puzzle of the amazing woman who was my mother. They don't make many like her anymore.

I hope you don't mind, but I would like to keep the beautiful picture with the shells and seaside things you gave her. Mam loved touching it, even near the end. It was such a thoughtful gift, with her sight being so bad. I hope you are making them for other people too.

My brother Rhodri sends thanks too. I know you never met him, and that he didn't visit Mam much, but I want to explain that he was asked to bear too heavy a burden, too young, when Guto, our dad, died, but he loved her as much as I did, in his own way. He was also the spitting image of Dad, which probably explains why he was flavour of the month for Mam in her last years!

One more thing, Jude. Mam made me promise to tell you something a few days before she died. She was a great keeper of secrets, so wouldn't say why I have to do it, but I'm just keeping my promise. She said I had to tell you to "Forgive her". I hope you understand what she meant.

Mam said you are having a baby soon, so I send all the luck in the world to you and your family and hope we meet again one day.

Cofion cynnes/Warmest wishes,

Hâf Lloyd-Jones

Jude put the letter down and picked up the pearls. Fastening them behind her neck, she let her fingers linger on each one of them, as she had seen Rhiannon do so often. She saw, of course, what Hâf was telling her, that motherly love had shown itself as motherly *need* in Rhiannon's relationship with Rhodri, but that he had still loved her. Almost exactly the same had happened in her home; Gloria had needed her support when Donald left, and she had found it similarly overwhelming. Did she still love Gloria, after all the bitter words and lack of kindness, as Rhodri had still loved Rhiannon? She covered her belly with one hand and breathed in deeply. A new person was growing inside her, a grandson or granddaughter that deserved the chance to love her grandmother. Gloria would probably never change towards *her,* but she might, just might, be able to love her child. Perhaps the best, most healing way of spending these last days before her baby's birth would be to go and see her mother, and tell her the news in person. She called her before she changed her mind. After three rings, Gloria picked up.

"Mum, it's me. I'd like to come and see you this weekend, if that's OK."

A sniff, a cough, and then, "That would be very nice, Judith. I'm not too good at the moment, to be honest. I've got an appointment tomorrow with the consultant, and I, well I... would like it if you came with me."

Jude hesitated. This voice sounded subdued, even vulnerable. "I'll be there, Mum. But I do have some news for you. Are you sitting down because you might be a bit shocked."

"I'm always sitting down, dear," came the weary response.

Jude crossed her fingers. "I'm going to have a baby, Mum. Very, very soon. You're going to be a grandmother."

Silence, and then the unmistakeable sound of sobbing.

FIFTY

Jude was shocked at how ill her mother looked. She seemed to have folded in on herself as if someone had pulled the plug on an inflatable toy. Far from filling her armchair, she was cradled by it, like a wizened nut inside a big, padded shell. Every few minutes, her whole body shook with a rattling cough, after which she closed her eyes in exhaustion. The house was hotter than ever, but Gloria complained repeatedly of draughts and chills. They greeted each other more warmly than they had for many years, and when Jude felt her mother's arms close tightly around her in a fierce hug, she was fired with sudden hope.

"Look at you!" Gloria exclaimed. "Can I touch you, and feel the baby kick?" And when she did, and the baby did, her eyes filled with tears. "Oh, we need a celebration!" she said. "Let's go out to eat!"

Jude was astounded to see her mother start to comb her hair and try to put on some lipstick. As her cough made this well nigh impossible, she soon had several smears of red around her mouth.

"Oh gosh, Mum!" she cried, touched. "Let me help you."

Something had changed in Gloria – she could feel it. She

was smiling, and she seemed somehow softer as if all her years of bitterness had slowly begun to melt away. It was more than Jude had ever dared to hope for, but when she wondered *why* this was happening, anxiety re-gathered like a dark cloud.

The pub was quiet, and Jude found a table near the window, bathed in spring sunshine. Gloria was happy to be fussed over and smiled her most endearing smile when the waitress brought them their drinks. She spent ages choosing what to eat, her mouth working in obvious anticipation of something tasty. "Meals on Wheels" had begun to lose its lustre, Jude noted. They ordered, sipped their drinks and then Gloria suddenly asked:

"Can I ask who the father is? I won't judge you, I promise, but I would like to know."

Jude hesitated. She had to sound sure, even if she wasn't anymore.

"It's Tom, Mum. One of Alex's friends. We're trying to make a go of it together," she said, adding under her breath, "Well, we were."

As she watched this news sink in, Jude knew that the reaction, when it came, could either spoil or cement their newfound closeness.

"Well, if Alex liked him, he must be a good man," she said, cupping Jude's face between her hands. "And this is the best news I could ever have wished for, especially now."

"What do you mean, *now*?" Jude asked, though she already knew the answer.

Gloria looked directly at her. "I'm not well, Judith. I mean *really* not well. I may be daft, but I'm not stupid, dear."

"Mum, let's wait until the appointment tomorrow... the doctors will tell us about the X-ray then, and sort you out."

"I know what they are going to tell me. The cough, and I've got so thin. I have seen too many people go down this road, including your dad."

"You didn't see Dad when he was really ill, Mum," Jude whispered. "You said you wouldn't go."

"But I did. I went after you went. I had to say my goodbyes too," Gloria said.

Just as her steak and ale pie was put in front of her, Jude began to cry.

"I'm afraid it's cancer, Mrs Dumbarton. Right at the base of your left lung."

The doctor pointed at a cloudy area the shape of an apricot on an X-ray fretted with Gloria's ghostly ribs. Jude waited for the hysterics, but her mother sat as upright as she could manage, looking perfectly calm.

"I knew that before I came here. But what can you do about it?" she said.

"It's a relatively small tumour at the moment, but I'm afraid we can't remove it, because of where it is," the young doctor said. "We can use various treatments to alleviate the symptoms, and we'll make sure you're comfortable, of course." He smiled conclusively.

"So it's incurable?" Jude said. She remembered this word from Alex's illness, among others in the ghastly vocabulary of cancer: "inoperable"; "spread"; "secondary"; "discomfort". They never said "pain" or "death".

"I've asked Jayne, the specialist nurse, to talk to you both now. She'll tell you everything you need to know. You'll need time to think about how you want things to proceed, going forward." The consultant stood up, so Gloria and Jude did too.

"How long do you think I've got, doctor?" Gloria asked.

He hesitated. Jude knew how doctors hated being asked this question. "I think you'll get to meet your grandchild, Mrs Dumbarton," he replied.

Hands were shaken, doors opened and closed, and a silence followed.

"I saw what chemotherapy did to that woman in the post office," Gloria hissed as if the doctor was still listening outside the door. "No hair, her face all yellow. She looked like a corpse *before* she died. I don't fancy it."

"It has to be your decision, Mum, but first of all I think we both need a cup of tea."

Jude swung into action when they got home to Taunton; she had done all this before. She organised care, a food delivery of the "basics" and hospital transport for the course of radio-therapy the doctor had suggested Gloria should begin next week. Until then, she made sure her mother's pain relief was always topped up by managing the morphine driver she had been given. Both women were very tired, for different reasons, so they spent a great deal of each day dozing, watching period dramas on TV, and taking turns to make each other a drink. Neither was very interested in food. Gloria was not hungry, and Jude could eat only small portions of anything because she felt so full, all the time. By the end of the week, they could almost read each other's minds and knew exactly when a cuppa was due or a plain biscuit might go down well.

Tom put no pressure on Jude to return, and sounded stressed and distant whenever she called him. Sophie had moved back to Oxford to work, he said, but had not yet found a suitable house to buy. Jude was astounded to learn that she already owned a townhouse off St Giles, bought for her as a student by her parents, but she had rented that out when she'd moved to London and felt she couldn't ask her tenants to leave early. When Tom also told her that she was staying in their spare room "for the moment", Jude was surprised at how little she cared.

"You stay there as long as you need to. I'm heads-down with work here," he said. "Family comes first, but I think you need to be back here next week in case the baby decides to arrive. Does it feel imminent yet?"

"Not sure, really," Jude said, glad that he could not see her blushes. As each day passed, she became more and more sure that this baby had not been conceived when Tom thought it had, and so could not be his.

When she was given an antenatal appointment she could not miss, Jude had to return to Oxford. As she kissed Gloria goodbye and the taxi drove away, she was flooded with memories of the thousands of times she'd done this exact same thing in the past. She had left this grotty-looking little house as a shy teenager, going off to a party she would not enjoy; as a carefree student, leaving to return to Exeter with a bagful of resentfully washed clothes; as a young, married woman, hating the fact that she had to visit her complete pain of a mother at all. This had been home, and her mother had been Mum, throughout all these versions of Jude and all the sad things that had happened to her. That constancy was not something granted to everyone; she had had that, at least.

Rhiannon had been right, and Jude thanked her for it. Gloria probably "had her reasons" for the way she had behaved for so long, which she might or might not choose to share with her daughter one day. Whatever else she may be, she was a person who should be respected, and forgiven, before she died; she deserved that, even if to love her was still too much to ask.

FIFTY-ONE

When she got back to Oxford, everything felt different. Jude saw very little of Tom, as he was out of the house by 8am, and often had commitments most evenings, as "the practice was expanding" he told her. Sophie was living with them, and she and Tom were sharing several important cases and "sang from the same hymn sheet", Tom said, but the reality was that Sophie was always at home when he was, and out when he was not. Jude sometimes found them sharing a drink together, melodramatically hiding the bottle when they saw her, and she noted that Sophie waited for her to leave the room before resuming the conversation they'd been having when she'd entered. It all made things very uncomfortable.

"Tom, can I ask when Sophie might be moving out?" Jude asked Tom in bed one night, after another evening spent listening to them talk about work. "She has other friends she could stay with for a while, surely?"

Tom frowned. "I know it's a bit awkward, but she's an old friend, a very valued colleague and needs to find her way in the practice, after almost a year in the legal wilderness."

"In Kensington you mean?" Jude said.

He cleared his throat. "Look, Jude, there's nothing going on between us again, if you're worried about that."

Jude said that she wasn't, but as he drifted off to sleep beside her, she sensed that Tom wished something *was* going on again very strongly indeed.

Jude saw her friends, and Tom saw his, during these strange days, but neither of them tried to merge their lives or introduce their friends to each other anymore; the two circles remained politely concentric. Jude enjoyed buying a few baby things, buying a cot and a changing unit, but there was no joy in the house. Sophie never referred to the imminent baby at all, so Tom took his cue from her and only did so when he and Jude were alone.

"On some days, we have almost nothing to do with each other," Jude complained to Stella on the phone. "It's as if the fairy-tale crush he's had on me all these years has just evaporated, and he sees me just for what I am – vulnerable, damaged, weirdly arty and very fat INDEED!"

"Hmm, doesn't sound good, but all you can do is focus on getting this baby safely born right now. The rest can always be sorted later," Stella said.

"That's *exactly* what Menna told me," Jude said, laughing. "Sound advice."

"Well, if you pick such astonishingly wise women as your friends, that's exactly what you're going to get!" Stella replied.

Gloria was finding daily radiotherapy very tiring, and her vivid descriptions of being "tattooed" and "laid out on a butcher's slab" Jude found distressing. She still refused to consider chemotherapy.

"What good would I be to you, or to anyone, being sick and

bald as an egg?" she said. "I want to meet your baby with some hair on my head!"

The doctors accepted her decision, telling her they would keep chemo as "something up our sleeve", but nobody was pushing for a more aggressive treatment regimen, and nobody mentioned a prognosis. Jude had learnt during Alex's final months exactly how to read between the lines when dealing with oncologists. Their manner towards her mother meant that the end would be sooner rather than later, so she decided that each of these days were to be savoured, like the ripest of fruit, as it might be the last ones in which Gloria felt relatively well.

They spoke every day, as Jude's baby was definitely now overdue according to her, very rough, dates and Gloria was on tenterhooks. Within the anonymity of a phone call, and the imminence of death, they talked about anything and everything, which Jude found both very uplifting and incredibly sad. How many years had they wasted, not being this loving or simply *honest* with each other? One day, Gloria said:

"It wasn't all your dad's fault, you know. I wasn't easy to be around, or easy to get close to. But there are reasons for that, ones I've never told you. I want to tell you them now." She stopped, her voice breaking as Jude had not heard it do for years. "The first reason was my father, Grandad Cecil as you knew him."

Jude's memory of him was as a tall, black-suited man, with a shock of white hair and a very angular, stern face. He had died when she was about eight or nine, but she could not recall him ever hugging her or showing her, his only grandchild, any affection at all. She also remembered, for the first time, that she had never seen him show any affection to his daughter Gloria either.

"He was a minister, as you know, and he was the harshest, dourest man I have ever known. For him, there was nothing and nobody of value in this world, as he was completely focused on the next." She paused to steady herself. "He instilled such fear of giving in to mortal weakness in me that it took your dad years to persuade me to love him and marry him. My father had forbidden love in our house. We weren't even allowed to open the windows in case we let sinfulness in."

There was a silence. This was awful to say, but more awful to hear.

"I see," Jude said. "But Dad did love you, and you had me. Were you able to be happy then, Mum?" She could never remember her mother being 'happy', but she asked, hoping that she had been wrong.

"I tried, so hard, Judith. Donald was a wonderful, kind man, but I couldn't love anyone with my whole heart, because my heart hadn't been allowed to breathe and grow and learn to love in my youth. And then something terrible happened that made me feel I had done wrong, sinned, in being with a man at all. We had a son, Judith – just over a year after you were born, and he died."

Jude held her breath. "Oh, Mum. I had no idea. What was his name?"

Gloria sighed. "Ronald. Your father insisted on it, after R.S. Thomas, that Welsh poet he loved. I always hated the name, and his miserable poems, so he was always 'Ronnie' to me."

"Oh, I love his poems, and I remember that Dad did. A friend introduced me to them recently, and yes, they are rather sad. Beautiful, but sad." A pause. "Mum, can I ask what happened? How did Ronnie die?"

"He caught a chill outside in the pram, then pneumonia, and then he died. He was six months old, and I never forgave myself, or your father for telling me 'babies should always be out in the fresh air', as he had been up in the Highlands. We always quarrelled about things like that, his way and my way, and even though we still had you, and you were a beautiful, carefree little thing, I never allowed myself to love anyone else in case they died too, and I was punished again. After years of it, Donald left us."

Jude sighed, as everything about her mother made sudden, heartbreaking sense.

"I wish Ronnie could have been my little brother," she murmured.

"Me too. I know I'm not easy, and my behaviour towards you and your father are not something I'm proud of, but losing Ronnie hardened me, you see. I put my heart inside an iron cage then and threw away the key. But I have always loved you, Judith, in my own way. Always."

Jude swallowed hard, and gripped her phone hard. These were words she had waited years to hear, and yet they sounded so small, almost inconsequential now. "But why did you make me feel Dad was wicked for abandoning us?"

"What else *could* I say, Judith? You were stuck with me, the person who had driven him away. I couldn't very well tell you I thought you'd drawn the short straw, could I? I had to be strong – or seem strong," Gloria said with a long sigh. "If I told you it was my fault he'd left, how would that have gone down?"

"I understand, sort of, but you took it a bit far, Mum," Jude said with a mirthless laugh. "It broke my heart when he left us."

"It broke mine too, for the second time." Gloria said. "I blamed myself, but I couldn't bear you to do so, as well. That would have destroyed what was left of me completely."

"I *don't* blame you, Mum. Not anymore, not now I understand." Jude stopped, and then she said the words Rhiannon had told her to: "And I forgive you; you know that, don't you?"

A pause. "Bless you, Judith. I don't deserve your forgiveness, but now you understand more about how things were, I hope it's easier for you to give it to me," Gloria said. "I'm sure you'll do a much, much better job of being a mother than I ever did."

"I can only do my best, Mum, just as you did," Jude replied.

FIFTY-TWO

Every day at the end of her pregnancy, Jude woke up drenched with sweat, and every night she was shaken awake by night-mares of the people she loved, leaving her. Her life was about to change forever, but she did not feel ready, or even willing for it to happen, not like this.

Most nights, she had to get out of bed to dispel these fears. Searching for a way to centre herself in the small hours, she went out to the shed and laid out some of the little things she had collected in her "memory maker" boxes, or been given over all the different phases of her life. It brought her comfort that Alex's Harley was now there in Tom's shed with her too, still swathed in the thick cover Owain had given her to keep it rust-free and gleaming. There were the gifts from Rhiannon: the handkerchief, the photo, and the pearls. She found Alex's striped hat, his watch, his walking map, the snap of them both on Ynys Llanddwyn, now fading fast. The small souvenirs of her lonely childhood she lingered over for longest – her Brownie Sixer badge, the photo of her lost schoolfriend – as she prepared herself to begin another child's childhood. These things had been glimmers of light in the darkness of much of those years and she would pass them on. Only when she had done this, could she go back to bed and sleep.

In the past, whenever she'd talked to Gloria about her keeping all this "silly memorabilia", they had quarrelled, so it was a shock when a box arrived in the post and Jude opened it to find some of her father's small treasures: his favourite silver tie-pin, his old Kodak camera, a photograph of their wedding and his tweed trilby, its lining rimmed with yellowed hair oil.

"You should have these now, Judith," a note inside the box read. "I have looked at them, and they have fuelled my regrets, for long enough."

Unable to do much except rest, and think, during the day, Jude began to plan how she would use these precious things. Each of them brought flashes of the past, like the slow ripple a pebble makes when thrown into water, but they could only be an outline, a skeleton. What she wanted more than anything was to somehow convey the true worth of the people who mattered to her, as her collages had managed to recreate a beach, a meadow or a forest. How could she capture the very *essence* of them, and show why she had loved them? The closest she felt she could come to them was in photographs, where a moment was frozen, and immutable, but she had too few of those. Her mind whirred with ideas and possibilities, but she knew that time was against her now. Her opportunity to make that dream of making a living out of her creativity could lie months, if not years ahead.

As she waited, she knew that, despite her fears and doubts, she would not be alone: she would be a mother.

FIFTY-THREE

The tension in Tom's house finally came to a terrible head one evening, as a storm breaks when the black, roiling clouds can do nothing but crash and create thunder and lightning, splitting the sky. It was the first time Jude and Tom had been able to have dinner without Sophie for several weeks as she had finally started house hunting, but the atmosphere was far from relaxed.

"It makes sense that she finds her own place as soon as possible. I guess she won't want to be here when the baby comes, and nobody can get much sleep."

"We need to talk about that, actually," Tom said. "I need sleep to work, to function in court, Jude. I'm a bit worried about it."

Jude wondered what she was expected to say. Babies cried, and sleep was not plentiful for new parents, end of. Surely Tom had always known this was part of the deal? She said nothing, concentrating on trying to eat some of the very hot curry he had made as he'd read it could encourage the onset of labour. To Jude, it felt as if this baby was more and more her responsibility, and all promises of sharing the nitty-gritty had not been repeated for a good long while. Yes, everything had changed, she decided, there was no pretending anymore. He had with-drawn more and more in the last month or so, stopped wanting to be close to her in any way, stopped listening to her complaints sympathetically, stopped asking how she was feel-ing, full-stop. She had googled "prospective father's jitters" and read a few confessional outpourings from nervous dads-to-be, but there was something almost clinically detached about Tom's behaviour, as if even being near her made him panic. What could have altered so quickly and so radically?

"Are you frightened about becoming a father?" she asked him as he was washing the, many, curry pans in the sink.

There was a pause in the clattering of dishes. He turned around, his rubber gloves dripping onto the tiled floor.

"I just mentioned the sleep thing. I really don't want to have a heavy discussion this evening. I'm tired."

"I need you to answer my question. Are you frightened about becoming a father?" she repeated, feeling her pulse quicken. "Please answer me." Something very bad was coming, very bad indeed.

"It seems that I am already a *father*, in that I have created a child with you. I'm more frightened of not being able to be a *dad*."

"What on earth does *that* mean?" she said angrily. "All I see is that you're never here these days, you won't help me prepare for the baby and you really don't want to know much about it. It's as if you think it will all go away if you ignore it, but it won't! You said you wanted this, remember. You said you wanted *me*."

He was very pale now, and shaking. "Yes, Jude, I did. I have wanted you for years and years. But once I had you, I… don't know, I…"

"You *what*, Tom? You owe it to me to be honest," Jude said. Her heart was thumping in her chest, and her tummy tightening alarmingly.

"When Sophie came back into my life, I didn't feel I

wanted to be with you anymore," he said quietly. "I don't know exactly why, but that's how it was. It just happened, a little more each day, and I couldn't stop it. I knew that I wanted to be with her again, that we were good together."

"Right," Jude said. "So you fell back in love with her and out of love with me, basically? Is that about right?"

Tom moved his feet slightly further apart as if trying to steady himself on the deck of a pitching boat. He was breathing rapidly, his lips white, and slightly open as if he was struggling to get enough oxygen.

As she held his gaze, she could almost feel their relationship recalibrating in front of her eyes, like the fine mechanism of a watch. He turned around to face the sink again and so Jude heaved herself out of the chair and marched towards him.

"I need the truth. Whatever it is, say it now, while there's still only the two of us here to fuck up."

"OK, I will. I'll say some things I should have said a while ago but felt I couldn't." He slowly peeled off the rubber gloves, turned and looked at her, face to face. "I just don't think I realised what it meant. I don't think I fully understood the level of commitment it all entailed, the complete life-change a baby will necessitate..."

"Oh, spare me the jargon!" Jude yelled, and the baby jerked inside her. She laid her open palms over her belly to calm it.

"Look, firstly, I've really tried to make this work, and I care about you enormously, but... I..." He tailed off and cleared his throat. "Secondly..." He stopped.

"*What*, secondly? Why did you pursue me, invite me to come and live here with you? Tell me that!"

A pause, a sliver of silence. "Because I thought I loved you, but – I'm so sorry Jude – I don't. Not really, not enough anyway," Tom said. "And I can't pretend anymore, I just can't! You can never truly love me, and I belong with Sophie – all three of us know it."

Jude scraped her fingers through her hair and closed her eyes, trying to breathe deep, as the NCT group leader had told her to do – to relax, to lighten the burden of the baby pressing down on her pubic bone. So nearly here, at last, this little person who would change her life forever.

Tom was weeping now. He stretched out a hand, but Jude turned away, shaking her head in the hope that this would keep her spinning thoughts from cohering into this ghastly, new reality. She was going to have to do this as a single mum, without a partner, just as Gloria and Morag had had to. The prospect filled her with a mixture of dread, panic, and acute relief.

"I'm sorry, Jude, but you know I'm right," Tom said. "We just don't work together as you and Alex did, and we never will. You chose the right man, back then."

"Yes, I did, and I have always known I did," Jude murmured.

Tom looked relieved as if a massive weight had been lifted off him.

"Listen, Jude, it will all be fine. I will organise somewhere for you both to live after the baby's born and I will support you, in whatever you both need. It will all be much better, in fact. We'll be friends again, as we haven't been of late, which has made me sad," he said. He was calm now as if having released his pent-up feelings had left him at peace. Jude watched as he picked up his car keys and put on his coat. "I'm going out to meet Sophie now, we'll book a room in a hotel for tonight. That seems best, don't you think?" He waited for her agreement, which did not come. "Why don't you get some sleep and remember that whatever happens, this baby will be loved just as much as it was wanted. I'll see you in the morning."

"Yes, this baby was very much wanted," Jude whispered, as she heard him drive away, "but I really, really hope it's Owain's, and not yours."

FIFTY-FOUR

Jude slept very badly that night and her body groaned with fatigue the next morning when she woke up in Tom's bed, alone. She went downstairs and made two cups of tea, as always.

"Back to drinking both cups of tea myself then," she said aloud. "Nothing changes."

As she ran a bath, she wondered what she was doing in this house, in this city, that she now knew for certain could never be her home again.

She couldn't face the shock and sympathy that would follow her ringing her friends with this news, not again. When Gloria rang her, as she did every morning, she did not pick up. There would be time for telling her the developments later. Instead, she drove out to Woodstock, and to Blenheim Palace. However tired she was, however swollen her belly and her ankles, she needed to walk, and to cry, on her own.

The first glimpse of the Palace always made Jude's skin tingle with admiration for the creative mind behind it. Today, the rich, caramel stone glowed in the sun, and she marvelled once more at the breadth of vision that could unite a building so beautifully with its setting. On the lake, a few swans cruised, the peace only broken occasionally by the raucous "*qqquaaackkk*" of a duck. Trees that had been saplings when these grounds were laid out now soared around the lake's edges, and in the many groves and copses all over the estate. How many centuries had they seen come and go as they made their own, silent journey through each season, and each year? How could she ever call herself a creative, when someone had achieved *this*? And what did her troubles today matter, compared to the long sweep of history this place had witnessed and survived?

The walk she chose took her along the least arduous route around the edge of the lake, past the pretty groundsman's cottage she and Alex had always coveted, before looping up to join the wide drive over the bridge. She waddled slowly, tilting from side to side, stopping to breathe and rest when she needed to. Her tummy was as tight as a drum.

Blenheim was one of the few stately homes Alex had liked, because, he said, despite its mathematically designed landscape, it still retained a sense of space, of wildness and vast, natural grandeur that no architect or landscape gardeners could ever quite contain.

"Even John Vanbrugh couldn't tame the sky," he'd once said, and Jude now knew exactly what he had meant, which gave her comfort. She needed a wide, untameable sky and to feel small, today.

By the time she reached the café, she was desperate to sit down. She chose a corner table, and glanced around, wondering who else had the time to walk around Blenheim on a Thursday morning. Most of the customers were pensioners, but Jude's interest was caught by a young couple and their toddler, perched in a highchair. Both parents looked very tired, the mother had darkened grooves like tram lines under her eyes.

Sipping her tea, Jude watched, transfixed, as the little girl

picked single raisins out of a tiny box and offered them to each
of her parents, one at a time. Each offering took ages, as her
fingers were so small that getting a grip on a raisin was a feat of
co-ordination; she screwed up her plump face with the effort of
it. If the dad tried to drink his tea, or shook his head, as if to
refuse a raisin, she offered it again and again until he had no
choice but to open his mouth. If she offered one to her mother,
she had to open her mouth very wide, like a starving fledgling,
and only then would her baby pop a raisin in. As each parent
was "fed", the other cheered, which made the child chortle with
glee. When all the raisins were gone, the baby clapped her
chipolata-pink fingers, and her parents chorused "All gone",
before quickly drinking their tea in grateful silence.

As the little family got up, zipped the toddler into her warm
suit, mittens, bootees and, finally, slotting her into her buggy,
Jude finally felt her envy bite. Tom had been right, they would
never have worked together as a couple and she could not
imagine them and their child here, or playing any game, ever,
anywhere. When she tried to picture family birthdays, outings,
or Christmases, or a grainy cinefilm of loving moments, she
simply could not do so, and the images remained unfocused.

No, she and Tom did not have love as a lodestar to guide
them through life together as that young couple did. Theirs had
been a relationship of convenience, of trial and error, however
hard they'd tried to make it otherwise. Tom was right; he might
yet prove to be her child's father, but they both knew that they
could never truly be a family.

Jude could not stay in Tom's house any longer. That evening,
she packed the things she and the baby would need for the first
few weeks into her car and waited for Tom to get home. Her
estimated due date had long gone, but the midwife had said that
the baby was still a little small for dates, the placenta was func-

tioning well, and its head was not engaged, so they would not consider inducing her for at least a fortnight as long as she checked in regularly. Jude, knowing she now had some leeway, decided to drive to Gloria's and have her baby in Somerset once she had completed one last task: picking up Pip, who she knew had not been rehomed, having secretly rung the sanctuary every single day to find out.

"I'm coming, Pip. I'm keeping my promise," she said aloud.

Tom was horrified at both decisions. "Jude, please reconsider, at least until the baby's here. Pip was jealous and nasty, and with a tiny baby..."

"He was never nasty to me. We'll be fine," she said resolutely.

"OK, but stay here in the house, I beg you. We can work something out, and Sophie can move out..." He looked guilty, and ashamed.

"No, but thanks for your offer. I grew up in the toxic atmosphere of a loveless home. I am not having my baby being born into one. I'll go to my mother's in the morning, and then take things from there."

"But your mother is so ill, Jude, and she was the *cause* of that toxicity! Your friends will want to help. *I* want to help. You need support at the moment, in every way."

"My mother needs to be needed, now more than ever; she's dying, Tom, and I want to be with her. I know it won't be forever, or probably even for very long, but it will work out. It's the right thing for me to do, honestly. Alex would agree, I know."

"Jude, I..."

"Sssssssh! I don't want my friends fussing, so I haven't even told them why I'm going. I will explain it all before I leave, so don't worry that you'll have to face the music unprepared," Jude said with a wry smile. "They'll probably think it's as mad as when I moved to Anglesey, but they know I'm as stubborn as hell."

"I will make sure you have money," Tom said weakly. "And anything else you need, of course."

"I won't say no to that. I'll repay you when I'm sorted and have time to talk to a financial manager about what to do for the best. Same with all my stuff here, and in the storage container, and the Harley, of course – I'll let you know what to do with all that as soon as I can. As for Tuna, I think she'd be delighted to stay here with you, if you'll have her. I can't take her to Mum's and she's too old to move again."

Tom nodded meekly. "I will have her, of course." He looked exhausted. "Thank you for being so honest with me."

"We should have been more honest with each other long ago, but it's good that we were in the end," Jude said, feeling strength of purpose surge through her body, and her baby. "And what better example can we set for a child than that?"

FIFTY-FIVE

When Jude rang each of her friends to tell them her news, their response was a slightly indigestible mix of anger, bafflement, and sympathy. Morag was now deliriously happy, seeing a young curate called Derek who had rented her spare room, and Finn was a transformed boy, with Granny, Gramps and a possible Dad-in-waiting to keep him in check. But more than anyone, Morag was especially wracked with guilt as she had pushed Tom's suit so hard.

"It IS incredibly tough with a baby on your own, as I said," she said, "but, in a way, if you know the cavalry is never going to arrive, you stop waiting for it and just do what has to be done. I think you're much stronger than me, Jude, and you *can* do it on your own. And as long as the midwife says it's OK to transfer your care at this late stage, it should all be fine."

"Well, the midwife wasn't keen, but she really feels this baby isn't ready to appear any time soon, so she agreed in the end."

Jo and Katie were worried about her, but quite sure she was doing the right thing in extricating herself from a relationship with Tom. Paula was the saddest of all of them, as she felt so invested in Jude's happiness after their precious time together on Anglesey.

"I guess I wanted you to be looked after, but I feel such an idiot now, and blame myself for not saying that I had a niggling feeling he wasn't right for you."

"Paula, I don't blame anyone, and I feel sorry for him, actually. He did a good job of convincing himself that he could love me until the long-term reality hit him, and I told myself that I could love him so often that I eventually believed it. If anyone was foolish, it was me. And you *did* warn me, all of you, in Totnes – remember? I just chose not to listen."

"Are you sure about going to your mum's? Will she be able to cope with a newborn in the house?" Paula's doubts had the authority of experience.

"Who knows? I have to hope so, for all our sakes, but guess what her words were, when I told her last night? She said, 'It all starts here, my second chance.' How wonderful was that?"

"Sounds great, but how will you manage when she begins to go downhill? You do know that will come, don't you?"

"I've been there before. I know what to do around death, remember?" Jude replied with a sad smile that precluded the need for anything else to be said.

It was raining when she drove out to the dog rescue centre in Evesham early the next morning to fetch Pip. Jackie, the manager, came out to greet her personally, but Jude was so excited about seeing Pip that she could hardly speak to her, her eyes darting around hopefully whenever a door opened into the reception area.

"Guess you don't have happy endings like this very often?" Jude said.

"No, we don't. He never stopped missing you, you know," Jackie said as they walked towards the kennels. "We did try him in one nice home, but he didn't settle. I have to say we always hoped he could come back to you, Mrs Fitzgerald. Sometimes, a dog can only love one person."

"I just hope he remembers me, and forgives me," Jude said. "It was the hardest decision, and probably the biggest mistake of my life, to give him up for a man."

"Dogs are for life, unlike many men," Jackie said with a wink.

Jude need not have worried. The little Jack Russell danced on his hind legs, quivering with bliss at the bars of his kennel the moment he saw her; it was quite clear that there was nobody else he would rather be with for the rest of his life.

"You need to be prepared for him to be a bit jealous, when the baby arrives," Jackie said. "It can happen, but may not."

"Oh, my mother is already setting up dog-barricades, but I think we'll be fine. There's plenty of love from me to go round. Perhaps he wasn't really jealous of my ex-partner at all, with all that growling. Perhaps he was *warning* me that he was the wrong one for me, just being a good mate, as all the best dogs are."

Jackie turned to her, and grinned. "Dogs know stuff, you know."

Georgio insisted on driving Jude and Pip down to Taunton in her old Fiat Punto and then getting a train back, for which she was hugely grateful. He even found a suitably vintage roof rack so she could bring at least *most* of the things she'd said were "absolutely essential". The deal was that she had to promise not to go into labour on the M5, because the little car was packed to the gunnels and Georgio said he "absolutely *could not cope* with any more crises".

"Consider us quits on the favour front, Jude," Georgio said, when they finally arrived. "That is the most terrible car I have ever driven."

"Well, I love her. I feel like a snail, carrying my home on my back, when we go places together. I'll have lots more stuff once all that baby clobber I ordered online arrives! I'll have to hire a van. I suppose I need to get Alex's Harley from Tom's shed too, when I know where I'm going to settle. Goodness knows what I'll do with it."

"I will always drive you, your stuff and your little one wherever you wish to go, *agapi mou*/my love," Georgio answered, raising her hand to his lips and adding, softly, "Any thoughts about where that might be?"

"I keep thinking about the island," she said. "I can't imagine anywhere more wonderful to bring up a child, but it's such a long way from all of you, I know."

"You need to put your family first now. You, your baby... and your mother, while you still have her," Georgio said. "Nothing is more important than them – you taught me that, when Christos came, for which no thanks can ever be enough."

As his taxi to the railway station drove away, and she went inside to sit with Gloria, Jude could feel the warmth of Georgio's words spreading through her like a slug of good whisky. One word in particular made her smile with joy: he had used the word "family".

FIFTY-SIX

For the rest of her life, whenever Jude could feel sunshine on her face, she remembered the last week of her pregnancy. It was mid-April, and the days were warm, so she lay on her side in the garden on Gloria's faded sun lounger, with Pip pressed against her back like a small, furry bolster. Soon she looked so sun-kissed that the neighbours asked her whether she had been living abroad. Nobody asked about the baby's father; Gloria had shut down any gossip with one of her most ferocious glares.

As Jude rested and relaxed, her mother weakened day by day. The consultant had called a halt to radiotherapy and told them that her cancer was growing rapidly now, and they both knew that they were waiting as much for death, as they were for birth, but they did not discuss it. Each would happen, in its own time.

On the morning of 21st of May, as Jude was hoisting the pole to raise her mother's washing line, her waters broke. She waddled inside, stuffed a towel between her legs and rang an ambulance. Within an hour, she was in the birthing pool, and contractions were ripping through her body. Gloria knelt beside her – still in her coat and hat – rubbing her back and offering

her sips of water between her own gut-wrenching coughs.
Neither woman wanted to be anywhere else.

Nothing could have prepared Jude for the pain of childbirth, for the sounds she made, or for the desperation with
which her eyes begged Gloria for comfort and relief. As each
contraction gripped her body, she focused on her mother's face,
smiling, encouraging, and believing she could do this. When the
baby arrived, slipping into the bloodied water with a silent,
rippling whoosh, she knew, even as the experience ended, that
nothing else in her life would ever come close to it.

"This is the best day of my life," Gloria said, tears rolling
down her cheeks. "I have nothing to be sad about, nothing to
regret, when my last days will be spent with this little angel, my
very own grandson."

As her little son nestled close, mouthing for her nipple, and
as he sucked, Jude twirled his chestnut brown curls between her
fingers and knew without a doubt that this baby's father was
Owain Pritchard and that he had been conceived in love on a
grassy clifftop on Anglesey. She called him "Jonathan", Alex's
second name, despite Gloria putting in a pretty serious bid for
"Ronnie".

Gloria died five weeks later. Day by day, cancer had clawed her
a little further into its maw, but she did not struggle, or protest.
She told Jude that she said she was ready, that she had been
blessed, and that this was what God had meant for her. Riding
the waves of pain, she wrapped her bony arms around her baby
grandson and held him tightly, her thin face aglow with happiness. Later, she watched him sleep as she drifted in and out of
the lonely dreams of morphine. For the last days, Jude breastfed
her son next to her mother's bed, with the curtains and windows
thrown wide to let in the May sunshine. She slept on a mattress
on the floor, with Jonathan next to her. At night, their calm,

regular breaths mingled with the sighing of the machines around Gloria's bed, and the sound was like the breezes that Jude remembered in *Hedd* on summer mornings, when she had opened the front door wide and let them in.

Tom came to visit the baby briefly after he was born, not wanting to intrude as Gloria was so ill, but Jude had had to tell him what he already knew the moment he looked at the child.

"I'm sorry, Tom. He isn't yours. I... I... went with another man on the island not long after you'd left, and he's his." She hated the Hardyesque phrase she had just used, but it felt like the softest, kindest option.

Tom paled, but his words took Jude by surprise. "You mean I don't need to feel guilty for the rest of my life?" he said, slowly letting a shy smile spread across his face as the news sank in. "Oh, thank goodness for that."

"No guilt necessary, and you are now absolved from all and every responsibility towards us," Jude said. "I am really grateful for your kindness, Tom, for trying to make things work, but both of us knew it wasn't right. I'm only sorry Lavinia won't be able to sign Jonathan up for that posh prep school next week, after all, but perhaps you and Sophie will..."

"Er, one step at a time," Tom said quickly, as the colour returned to his face. "I think I'm probably over babies for a while, but I'll explain it all to Mum and Dad. Wish me luck!"

And she did, though she knew he wouldn't really need it. His parents would be absolutely delighted: they wanted him to marry someone with status, style and money, and Sophie had plenty of all three. Yes, Jude knew that Tom was too good for her, as she'd always suspected. He needed someone with drive, grit, and an almost selfish determination to make life *work*, as he was such a kind and sensitive soul. Sophie fitted the bill almost as perfectly as she had not.

FIFTY-SEVEN

"Where will you go now?" Morag asked Jude, as they sat in Gloria's tiny garden later that week. They had stayed on for a few days after the funeral, and it was good to spend that time together. They were both ignoring Finn, who was torturing woodlice with a magnifying glass. "I guess you can afford to go anywhere you want to, really."

"I suppose so," Jude replied. Gently, she pulled Jonathan off her nipple, and he lay back, his milky lips fat with contentment.

Ironically, she was comfortably off now, with the money Tom had invested from Howard Street and the money to come from the sale of Gloria's house, but this excited her solely because setting up her business could now become real.

"I know you're going to curse me," she said, running a finger over her baby's forehead. "But I think I'm going to go back to Anglesey."

"To be with that Welshman you loved? You never told me his name. Didn't you say his wife's left him now?"

"His name is Owain, Owain Pritchard. And yes, she has, but I can't assume he'll want to have anything to do with me, Morag, and I don't know whether I want him to know about the baby if he's not in the right place to hear it. I'm financially independent, and I think Jonathan will be fine with just me," she said, pausing in the hope that she had managed to hide her residual doubts about that fact. "Owain's probably got a new partner by now. He is *very* handsome, you know!"

Morag hesitated. "I don't know what to wish for you on that score, but I can see how that island helped you heal when we couldn't. Whatever happens next, I hope you're going to carry on with your art. You've wasted too many years, being too scared to trust your talent, Jude."

"Oh, I will... when I have a nanosecond!" she replied with a laugh.

"Paula said she had never seen you looking better than you did on Anglesey, so I think you are meant to go back there now, sad as we'll be to see you go," Morag said. "You'd better prepare for lots of visitors, though, so get yourself a bigger place than that teeny-weeny cottage you rented last time, please!"

Clearing her childhood home took one long, emotional day, which did not seem much after so many years of life spent in those few drab rooms. Jude did not cry over her mother's threadbare towels, flannelette sheets, and frosted crystal vases. Her clothes were harder to sort, as she could still see Gloria wearing the lavender Viyella suit at her Sunday school concert, or the brown Danimac coat at her school prize-giving, and she wept as she folded them and put them into black bin bags. She left them all outside the Cancer Research shop late one night while she was driving around to get Jonathan to sleep, and hoped with all her heart that they would make another few elderly ladies very happy indeed.

But it was only when she opened the reproduction mahogany bureau her parents had been so proud of that she fully understood her mother would not be coming back. In every one of the little drawers in the bureau, she found something small but significant that Gloria had saved from their life together. She had obviously made sure these things were safe after she had been diagnosed, and that Jude would eventually find them, as part of her careful preparation for death.

Among these treasures was a clumsy wooden serviette ring she had painted in primary school, and a photo of her with a tiny monkey, snapped on the pier in Llandudno when a hawker had thrust the little animal into her arms and then dared to ask her mother to pay for it. To Jude's enormous surprise, she'd done so – and here the monkey was, proof of an incredibly rare but impulsive loving gesture that she had not even seen as one, at the time.

"Thank you, Mum," she murmured.

A clutch of gymkhana rosettes filled another drawer, and an impressive collection of swimming medals another. Jude's school reports, certificates for piano exams, cycling proficiency test, and winning first prize in a painting competition were all neatly organised and tied in ribbons in another drawer. Her mother had also included things from her own life for Jude to find: her Mother's Union badge, from the year she was the proud secretary of the local branch; the cameo brooch from her own mother Doris, who had died when she was only twelve, still in its musty jeweller's box; a thank-you card from the Sunday school class she had taught for years, and a beautiful picture of her and Donald's wedding day, their faces radiating a love Jude had no doubt they had once felt. Finally, she found a christening photograph, yellowed with age, of Ronnie, her dead baby brother, wearing a traditional long white gown. His smile was so very like her own that Jude's eyes brimmed, and it almost broke her heart to think of the long and happy life he had never been granted, whereas she had.

Last of all, she found a large envelope. Her hands trembled as she pulled out the folded note inside it. She knew it was significant, as it was written on smooth, pricey Basildon Bond notepaper – stationery Gloria always kept only for formal messages of sympathy and letters to the vicar. Reaching inside, she found the starched embroidered christening gown that had been in her mother's family for generations, and in the photograph. It was a truly beautiful thing, that both she and Ronnie had worn – sewn many years earlier with one mother's love for her baby and imbued with that of many more. She opened her mother's note and read her spidery writing:

Dearest Judith,

I am sorry not to be able to see Jonathan wear this gown, but I feel blessed to have got to see him at all. You wore it, and Ronnie wore it, as did many family babies before that, so it's only right that your boy does too. I hope you enjoy finding the things in these drawers as much as I enjoyed looking at them again. Such precious times we had.
You were one of the best things in my life, Judith, and your father was another. When you face troubles, as we all do, remember these words from Ecclesiastes:

'For everything there is a season, and a time for every matter under heaven.'

All will be well. Until we meet again, as I know we will, may God bless you and Jonathan through all the years of your lives.
All my love, always,
Mum

Laying the letter down gently, Jude wept for the mother she had grown to love.

PART 8

NOTHING VENTURED, NOTHING GAINED

FIFTY-EIGHT

The house in Taunton was sold to a young couple who were expecting their first baby, who had great plans for knocking down walls, doing the loft and extending the kitchen. Jude relished their excitement and, delighted to be able to accept their relatively modest offer, rented the top floor of a large and airy house in Oxford for herself, Pip, and Jonathan until she could find somewhere suitable to live on Anglesey. Time passed, autumn came again, but no house she saw felt right enough to make the trek to view it, let alone put in an offer online. This might have been because the fixed image in her mind was of *Hedd*, with its softly undulating walls, cornflower-blue door and the wide, clear sea glistening below it. It was a place she could never forget.

For the first time since Alex had died, Jude felt settled for a while and enjoyed the build-up to Christmas. Jonathan's smiles lit up each day, meals were made, shared and eaten and friends came and went. Mother and son established a routine that suited both of them. Jude tried to paint or sketch as much as she could while her baby slept (which was more often than Tom had led her to believe he might!), or bounced in his fabric chair, guarded by a protective but loving Pip, and as the weeks passed, she felt vague ideas beginning to cohere into more definite, achievable, pieces, as they had never done before. The future looked bright, which was so long-forgotten a feeling that it filled Jude with gratitude for all that had happened, both good, bad and sad. She was meant be here, now, but not for much longer, as she could almost feel the sea calling her to return to it.

Christmas Day was spent with Paula, Georgio, and Christos. Paula said that she felt far too tired to go to London as she was halfway through her second pregnancy, so Christos opened his stocking at home for the very first time. Their wedding in Cyprus had been postponed until Paula "had her figure back", at her own insistence. So, Jo, Katie, Morag, Finn, Jude, and Jonathan arrived at their friends' house at 2pm, and everyone helped Georgio serve up a delicious Greek-Cypriot-style Christmas meal. Succulent charcoal-cooked "*souvla*" were a definite improvement on dry turkey, soggy sprouts and gooey stuffing that stuck to the roof of your mouth, everyone wholeheartedly agreed.

"Are you sure you want to leave us again?" Katie said, as they all sat, bloated, in Paula's new conservatory, after the meal. "We love having you back."

"I have to go," Jude answered. "I can't live in this inland city again, and I really want my little boy to grow up on the island, by the sea."

"But won't you be lonely, like you were before? Miss us all?" Jo added.

"I will miss you, but Stella and Menna are there, so I won't be starting from scratch this time. And my friend Dominic is still there, the goat farmer, don't forget about him, folks! You must all come and visit us and see what I keep harping on about. It's such a beautiful place."

"It is somewhere special, that's for sure," Paula said. "But Jeez, Jude, promise me that you'll let me buy you a few beauty treatments before you go! We do *not* want the return of The Wild Woman of Anglesey."

Georgio poured everyone (except Paula) a huge Metaxa, and they drank a toast "to the new year, whatever it may bring us all".

"What about those rugby-loving Welshmen, Jude?" Jo asked quietly as they all prepared to leave. She was cradling a sleepy Jonathan in her arms, where he had spent most of the day, and she was clearly reluctant to surrender him. "Have you gone off them for good?"

"Men aren't at the top of my list, no," Jude replied, kissing her son on the forehead, "present company excepted."

But when she got back to the silence of her flat, Jude knew that she had been lying to her friend, and to herself. There was a man who had started appearing again in the dream-clouded moments between sleep and wakefulness, striding towards her across a strip of sandy shingle. She had heard nothing from him, though she knew that Menna had told him about her singleness, and the baby. As she had told Morag, Jude doubted that they could ever be together. If he was finally free of Non, he would want to forge his own future, and his own family. Too much water had gone under the bridge for them both, and she knew how much he hated any whiff of scandal. If that was the situation she found when she got back to the island, perhaps he need never know that Jonathan was his, as that too might be shameful.

And yet she hoped that wasn't what lay ahead very, very much.

By January, Jude felt very low indeed; the short days and long, dark nights took their toll on her mood, as they did every year.

Life felt like she was treading water, rather than moving forward. She decided to take a risk and gave notice on her Summertown flat with nothing definite on Anglesey to go to. Trembling, she dialled the familiar number for Môn Cottages. The moment she heard the lilt of Mair Roberts' voice, she felt her spirits lift.

"It's Jude, Mrs Roberts. Mrs Fitzgerald. I lived in *Hedd* for a year, and then had to leave to have a baby." A pause. "You probably don't remember me, you see so many people but, well, I'm coming back – with my baby boy!"

"*LLongyfarchiadau*/Congratulations!"   Mrs   Roberts exclaimed. "Of *course* I remember you. I was waiting for you to tell me about your baby first, though I have to be honest with you, I had already heard he was safely here and about you intending to come back, from Menna in the shop in Llanfaelog."

Jude grinned. News still travelled fast on Anglesey. "I thought you might have done, Mair." A pause, in which Jude could almost hear her heart pounding as she asked the most pressing question on her mind:

"I don't suppose *Hedd* is available, is it? I'm hoping to buy a house on the island, but I need to rent somewhere while I find the right one."

"I'm so sorry, *cariad*/love, but no, it went last week. A... er... local chap rented it only last week, as it was priced far too high to sell. It was too basic for the tourists, even with all the work the owners had done. They all expect hot tubs now, for goodness' sake."

"I see. Is there anything similar available? I keep looking, but they all seem to be inland, don't want dogs or aren't for long-term rent," Jude asked, trying to keep the wobble out of her voice. "Might the new tenant be willing to reconsider?"

A pause, and Mair cleared her throat. "No, I think not. He was delighted to get it, to be honest. He's always loved the place."

Jude blushed to the roots of her hair. How rude of her, to assume that somebody would just move out because she wanted that cottage so badly! What a spoilt brat she'd been, to even ask it.

"I'm sorry, Mair. It's just such a special place for me," she said.

"I know, and there aren't many properties like it, but let me think. It's for you and your baby – and your animals, of course?"

"It's just my dog Pip, now. My cat fell in love with someone else," Jude answered.

"Typical!" Mrs Roberts answered, laughing. "Ungrateful, cats are, like men. Walk over your dead body to get to a plate of food."

Jude laughed and understood why she rarely heard mention of a Mr Roberts. "I don't know what to do now," she said. "I've given in my notice in here as I really need to come back. I'm hoping to buy somewhere, but until then, I need somewhere to rent…"

"*Paid a phoeni*/Don't worry. Give me your email address and I'll send you some possibilities by the end of the day," Mari replied briskly, and hung up.

On January 31st, Jude packed Pip into his travelling crate, strapped Jonathan into his car seat and stood in the hallway waiting for Georgio to pick them up. Her friend had loaded everything he could fit into his enormous 4x4 whilst still leaving room for people. The rest of her possessions would stay in storage with all the other things from her past life until she had a permanent new home and her old Fiat Punto, Georgio would sell for scrap, he happily promised. Menna had offered to put them up until Mrs Roberts could find them somewhere accept-able to live, and she was "desperate" for Jonathan to meet Gwilym, her new baby. They were sure to grow up to be the best of friends, she said, a thought that made Jude almost glow with joy. Her son might not have a dad, but he would have so many wonderful friends.

It was almost dark by the time they pulled up outside Menna's house. The moment she opened the car door and smelt saltiness and seaweed, Jude wanted to drink the air down in huge gulps. Looking left, towards the sea, she could see the wind stirring the waves, sending skips of foam across the surface and onto the shore. Was a storm blowing in? There was an eerie charge in the air that usually meant as much. The house was completely dark and completely silent, which worried Jude a little. Had she told Menna the wrong day? Had something awful happened?

While Georgio texted Paula to tell her they had arrived safely, Jude knocked on Menna's door. Still silence. Disconsolate, she wondered where they could go to wait for her friend to return; it was chilly, and Jonathan needed a nappy change. But as she was walking back towards the car, she heard the front door open and a huge gale of *"Hwre!*/Hooray!" shattered the quiet of the night. As arms were flung around her and an unseen child wrapped small arms around her knees, Jude realised that Menna, Jac, her boys, her mother and her *Nain*/grandmother had all been waiting to surprise them. Georgio was similarly engulfed.

"You mean gits!" Jude said. "I really thought you weren't home!"

"As if. You're so gullible, *cariad*/love," said Menna, putting her arm through her friend's. "Now bring everything inside and let me see your lovely baby."

"We didn't know you had *this* car. Me and Dad found you a new car," said a small voice from Jude's waist. It was Menna's son, Iolo, the self-appointed family translator who had always made sure she was included in every conversation, however ribald.

"Oh, this car isn't mine – it's his." She pointed at Georgio, who beamed at the little boy proudly. "And I *will* be needing a new car. I'm sure you've found me a good one, haven't you, Iolo?"

"What Dad actually said – in Welsh, was – 'at least it works, which your old one bloody well didn't,'" Iolo replied, with a gappy smile.

FIFTY-NINE

The next morning, Jude woke just as Jonathan began rustling in his cot. She had a headache and a bitter, salty taste in her mouth – the result of the two Tequila slammers Menna's *Nain*/grandmother had insisted she drank to celebrate her return the previous evening. She was even more horrified to discover that she had got into bed with all her clothes on, something she had last done with Alex after a spectacular evening in a pub in Connemara.

"I'm not a very responsible mother, am I?" she cooed to her son, as he thrashed his arms and legs in glee at seeing her face for the first time that day. She gave him a bottle in the cosy kitchen, looking out onto the grey waves as the headache tablets Menna had left out for her kicked in. Georgio's car was gone, but he had left a bottle of vintage Metaxa for the family as a gift.

"Hmm. Think we'll wait to sample that," Jude muttered.

The house was quiet. Everyone had gone to work and school. Rain streamed down the windows, but Jude dismissed it as "light drizzle". When it "rained heavily" here, you knew about it. She drank a cup of tea, ate two slices of thick, white-bread buttery toast, wrapped herself and Jonathan up warmly, and set off for a walk on the beach. When they reached the dunes, she deliberately turned right, rather than left, towards *Hedd*, deeply counterintuitive as it felt to do so.

Mrs Roberts had sent Jude a list of four cottages to look at. None of them were as near Rhosneigr as she would have wished, but Jac had assured her that none of them were far away. She knew that nowhere was "far away", in Jac's world, mind you, it was just "a bit further".

As this rental was only until she found a place to buy, Jude's needs were simple. Her temporary home needed to be four things: dog-friendly, to have a washing machine and tumble drier, to be above freezing in winter and have views of the sea. The last one presented most problems for Mair Roberts. "Sea views are at such a premium, see," she said ominously.

The first place Mair took them to was in Pentraeth, a village halfway across the island, which was fine on the first three points, but had views of a septic tank. The second, on the edge of Menai Bridge, had been prettified so much that it was almost a parody of itself. Jude could tell that Mair thought she would love it, as the décor was decidedly "English country cottage", but it had bowls of dusty potpourri in every room and smelt of air-freshener, which was *far* too redolent of Tom's parents' house in Burford. Jude turned on her heel and left.

"If you just want something like *Hedd*, I can't help you, *cariad*/love," Mair said, exasperation writ large on her face.

Jude was disappointed but felt a little guilty too. "Sorry. I know I'm being a pain. I'm sure the next one will be fine." She patted her friend's arm. "Where next? Moelfre, or Marianglas?"

"Moelfre. But this cottage has been having some work done on it. It's due to be finished next week."

Jude signed. She knew how "flexible" builders' schedules

tended to be up here, but unless the place was a dump, she would have to take it.

The road to Moelfre from Menai Bridge was almost as beautiful as the one that wound its way to *Hedd*. The huge expanse of rippled sand to the right told Jude that the tide was out in Red Wharf Bay, and she could see a few fishermen digging for lugworms far out on the flats. When they dropped down into the fishing village of Moelfre itself, Jude suddenly remembered having come for a walk here with her husband. It had been a warm, summer's evening and they'd sat on the cliffs eating fish and chips, watching the seabirds loop and whirl for hours before choosing their roost for the night in the pitted cliffs. The birds were still here, riding the thermals and diving for fish, but Alex was not, and never would be again. The sheer devastation of that simple, terrible fact never lessened.

The cottage Mair was about to show her was one of a row of one-storeyed fishermen's cottages that faced out to sea, and Jude could tell which one she would be viewing straight away: it had scaffolding around it, and a tarpaulin over its roof. It looked tiny, but the setting was breathtakingly beautiful, made more so by the evening sun which made the glass in the cottage windows blaze like sheets of copper. Mrs Roberts parked at the end of a track, which was as near the cottages as anyone could reach by car. She looked a little on edge and was picking the bobbles off her wool-mix coat.

"Everything all right?" Jude asked. "This one looks fab, or will be, once the scaffolding's gone."

"I have to tell you that Owain Pritchard's doing the work here, Jude: roof, painting, everything. I know you two... *knew* each other, when you lived here." She cleared her throat. "But he should be finished next week, as I said, and I don't think he'll be here now. He doesn't know you're coming to look at the cottage today, but I just wanted to keep you 'in the loop'."

Jude smiled at Mair's deliberate use of this very English idiom. Somehow, the prospect of bumping into Owain did not alarm her as much as she'd thought it would. Perhaps it would be a good thing, to get it out of the way. He was living his life, and she was living hers. He knew her circumstances, and she, his. They were bound to come across each other, as the island was small, and the community close. They just had to be adult about it, she told herself.

"Don't worry. I am absolutely cool about Owain Pritchard, in every way. Just to clarify, though, if I want to take it, how long will I have to wait to move in?"

"Owain usually finishes a job on time, but it would mean you would be waiting another week. Let's see if you like it first."

Despite the dust, the tarpaulin and the very basic facilities, the cottage felt right. Its tiny living room windows looked out onto a grassy headland and, beyond, to the sea. Just offshore was an island about the size of a football pitch that seemed to be home for more birds than Jude had ever seen in one place. As Mrs Roberts opened kitchen cupboards and tested taps, she listened to the gulls screech and watched the kittiwakes taunt the waves with playful swoops as the sun set.

"It's great, Mair. We'll take it. I'll pay the rent for six months, but we'll move out as soon as I find the right place to buy."

First, there was the sound of an engine, an engine she recognised. Owain's red van pulled up on the track. Pip strained at her lead, whimpering with excitement. Then Meg shot in through the open cottage door and wreathed herself around Jude's legs, wagging her whole body in greeting and licking Pip from nose to tail. Finally, Owain Pritchard appeared in the cottage doorframe. He was so tall, Jude only now remembered, that he had to stoop to avoid his head hitting it.

"Hello, Owain," Jude said.

"*Croeso yn ôl*/Welcome back," he answered, with a smile that lit up his whole face and tested her poise to its limits. "And congratulations, too, on your new arrival. *Ga i ddweud helô*/Can I say hello?"

Jude nodded. Owain looked at Jonathan for several long seconds. It felt like there was an almost audible hum in the air, like low static.

"*Wrth gwrs*/Of course. This is Jonathan," she said.

Owain nodded and rubbed his calloused hands together as if to soften them before going near the child. When he squatted down, Jude was shocked to see that his rich brown curls were now lightly threaded with grey. When he touched the tips of the little boy's tiny fingers with one of his own, so gently, Jonathan gurgled and kicked his legs in glee.

"He is very beautiful, Jude," he said. "*Hollol berffaith*/Completely perfect." When he looked up at her, she saw that his eyes were filled with tears and his face was suffused in wonder. She was quite certain, at that moment, that he knew this baby was theirs... but he said nothing.

After a few moments, Mair said, "Well, if you're sure about the cottage, Jude, perhaps we'd better get out of Mr Pritchard's way."

The two women picked their way beneath the scaffolding and started walking towards Mrs Roberts' car. Owain offered to carry the baby seat, and Jude searched for the right words to say to him – something to let him know that she knew about his divorce, that it was OK about the baby, that she would be fine on her own if he had begun a new life. Best, like him, to be direct, she decided, as they walked together.

"I was sorry to hear about you and Non," she blurted.

"It was for the best, and we are both much happier now," he answered, adding, "I'm sorry that things didn't work out with, er, Jonathan's father."

Their eyes met, but again, nothing was said. So many words needed to be set free between them, and yet none felt appropriate. There were no wisecracks or jokes from him today. Owain's whole demeanour was very serious, his expression grave and his face shadowed with greying stubble, Jude saw. He looked as if he had not slept well for a very long time.

"Oh, Tom you mean? That was all… a bit of a misunderstanding, really. But he was a kind man."

"I'm very glad to hear that," Owain said stiffly. "We all need kindness, and it's completely free to both giver and taker."

"Good to see you again, Owain," she called after him as he walked away briskly. "I still read the poems, you know, in the book you gave me. I'll return it to you, I promise, but they help me *understand* life a bit better, and accept when it's not fair."

"Keep it, Jude. R.S. Thomas answered most questions about life, in one way or another, and he finds light in the darkest of times."

Watching his broad frame heading towards his van, Jude realised how little she still knew about this man: he loved poetry, beautiful architecture, the sea and the mountains, and he had a remarkable way with words. And yet despite this, she felt she knew him better than anyone she had ever known.

SIXTY

The following week was one of the most difficult of Jude's life, fraught with a succession of incredibly powerful emotions that left her struggling to manage them. Because she had a baby now, she could no longer retreat to bed and wait for it to pass, but it was hard, very hard, and she hardly slept at all. It took her back to her despair at Alex's diagnosis, her euphoria at the hope of treatment and then the utter desolation of his death, all of which had been utterly exhausting. She knew why she was so upset, and why sleep was now impossible: she had to tell Owain the truth about their baby before he finished the job at the cottage and vanished from her life again. Their secret had to be out in the open, and their baby's parentage acknowledged, by them, if nobody else. If he chose to be with her and Jonathan, it would then be a fully informed choice and if not, she would accept his decision. She knew that without complete honesty, she could not begin her new life here, be it with him, or without him.

It was a leaden-skied February morning, with no definable horizon between sea and sky, when Jude set off for Moelfre in

her new car, a two-year-old shiny green Vauxhall Corsa (nick-
named "The Flying Bean" by Menna's boys). She had decided
she would talk to Owain at the cottage, where they would be
able to speak in private. She could almost feel the weight of
countless Welsh winters pressing down on the scrubby land
around her and there was precious little colour, anywhere, as
she drove. Small groups of miserable sheep huddled in the lee of
the scrubby hedgerows, looking as if they could not wait for
spring to arrive. Jude knew exactly how they felt. She remembered one of R.S. Thomas' apt descriptions of North Wales:

A place huddled down between grey walls
Of cloud for at least half the year.

She had left Jonathan with Menna's *Nain*/grandmother,
telling her that she had to go to the cottage to "sort out paying
the deposit".

"*Paid a siarad lol*/Don't talk rubbish! But don't do anything
I wouldn't do," the old woman said, seeing straight through her
flimsy fib.

When she approached the row of cottages and saw that Owain's
van was not parked outside, Jude was devastated. Owain had
gone, he'd finished ahead of schedule, of course. The scaffolding
had vanished, and the tiny garden at the front of the cottage had
been tidied up, the stone path swept clean. An oblong of vivid
yellow grass where the skip had been was the only sign that
building work had gone on here at all. A few courageous bulbs
were pushing up through the hard ground; how typical that
Owain had not disturbed them, these frail harbingers of spring.

She stood, feeling foolish, on the thick, tussock grass in
front of the row of cottages, clapping her gloved hands to
warm them. It was bitingly cold, with a wind off the sea that

penetrated any clothing. Despite the grim weather, the little cottage she would soon be living in looked much more appealing now; she noticed how perfectly the new slates over-lapped, and how Owain had ensured that those of a similar grey-green were next to each other on the roof. The gutters had been cleared and cleaned, and the front door of the little cottage was painted a beautiful purply-blue – almost the exact same colour as the wild scabious flowers that covered the island's cliffs in the summer, and she loved so much. Had she told him that? She was sure she had, and he had remembered it, of course.

Out at sea, terns scoured the water for unwary fish, diving with a white flash when they sighted prey. In one small way, Jude was relieved that Owain was not here today, so that she could take in all this unexpected beauty on her own. This would be her and Jonathan's home for a while, and they would be happy in it. As real relief began to seep into her about the tricky conversation they were *not* going to have that day, she concluded that it was probably a good thing. Now, she had more time to think things through and decide exactly what to say when she ran into him, and how to say it. Owain was not a man for spontaneity, so this was for the best. And yet, these things needed to be said soon, for her new life here to begin.

As she had organised childcare until noon, she decided to go for a walk. The sky had lightened a little, and there were breaks in the clouds. Whenever the sunlight streamed through them and hit the sea and the headland, the landscape was trans-formed, suddenly illuminated as Jude had only ever seen happen on Anglesey. She took the coastal path, which ran parallel to the sea for several miles towards the glorious sandy beach at Lligwy. Pip raced off in search of rabbits, and Jude had to call him away from their burrows as she had heard of Jack Russells that had vanished down such holes and never come out again.

"Don't even think about it," she warned him. "Stay close to me, please."

As she walked, she filled the bag she took with her everywhere with shells, pebbles, sprigs of dried heather, and some rare, greeny-blue sea holly she found nestling in a sheltered inlet. Looking out over the water, she glimpsed two small fishing boats across the bay, ploughing through the white-tipped waves into the strong headwind, followed by a ribbon of hopeful gulls. This unending rhythm of wind and wave would continue, day in, day out, for the rest of her life, and her son's life, whatever he chose to do with it. The thought gave her as much solace as it ever had. Yes, she had done the right thing, to come back.

Jude walked for almost an hour, until she reached Lligwy. The last time she had been here, it had been teeming with people, the sea full of bathers and surfers and the beach patchworked with blankets, towels, and windbreakers. Today, there was nobody. She shared the beach with only half a dozen chilly-looking redshanks. Sitting on a rock, she tried to visualise herself living the rest of her life on this island, growing old here. Once Jonathan was older, and could go to nursery, she could really expand the art business she had started in Oxford, rent a light, warm space to paint and work in, set up a website, perhaps sell her work in bigger and better shops, or even galleries. All this she could imagine and believe as she watched the relentless rhythm of the waves.

She saw Jonathan as a winsome toddler, as a boy playing cricket on the beach, as an awkward, spotty teenager, at ease in both Welsh and English, and a long-limbed young man who loved the wildness of this place as much as she and his father did. But her image of herself in the years ahead was less clear, and seemed almost unfinished. Something was missing when she looked ahead, a gap that still yawned wide at the centre of it all. How often had she encountered this frustration in her work, this inability to find the true heart and soul of something, or someone, leaving a sense of absence? She tried to pinpoint what it was, this blank space in her vision of her future self, but she could not, though she knew it was no longer the absence of Alex. No, what was missing now always slipped away from her, vanishing into the shadows just beyond her reach.

SIXTY-ONE

The cheering hopefulness of spring was a long time coming that year. February days were so short that, by the time Jude had got Jonathan up, fed, dressed, and ready to go out for a walk, it was time to come back for lunch, and by the time she had dealt with that, daylight was fading. The cottage was constantly festooned with damp baby clothes as she had strung up a network of washing lines between the exposed rafters. She'd very soon abandoned the fabric nappies she had brought from Oxford, where a laundering service had conveniently delivered and dealt with them. Stella and Eifion came over most weekends, and she visited Menna and her family regularly, but as hard as she tried, creative ideas did not flow, and she could not work. Something was wrong, and it felt as if her imagination was dammed, blocked by something that she could not identify. Each week she didn't even catch a glimpse of Owain, her determination to tell him the truth ebbed a little more, and she began to wonder if this was what was paralysing her, somehow. What if he wanted nothing to do with either her or Jonathan once he'd realised that the baby was his son? If so, formally telling him could go very wrong indeed. It was best to try, once again, to forget him forever, she told herself, but he floated into her dreams almost every night, nonetheless.

Increasingly restless, Jude found she did not want to be inside, trying to come up with ideas and berating herself when she couldn't. She needed to be outside, in all the raging, still-wintry elements, hoping that the wild winds and driving rain might dispel whatever it was that was stifling her happiness as they had somehow purged her grief for Alex. She walked for miles with a sleeping Jonathan wrapped up snugly and crammed into a baby carrier on her back, but still, her unease would not lift. Again and again, she pulled out the collections of things she had garnered from her past, before returning them to their respective boxes and slotting them back onto the shelf. What should she do with them? What did they represent to her, as the woman she now was? They seemed like clues to a mystery, and Jude felt as if they were trying to tell her something, but she simply could not hear them clearly, so she could never solve it.

She looked at a few houses to buy, but all of them were either too dark, too damp, too small, too big, or just too unlike *Hedd* for her to consider. As despair and the familiar chill of loneliness began to settle around her more than was comfortable, March arrived, the weather suddenly improved, and with it, her mood. She had got through it, she had endured another Welsh winter and emerged, blinking, into the warm sunshine of early spring! That was no mean feat, she told herself proudly.

The sky almost cracked with blueness in the first week of that spring, and she ordered an expensive digital camera so she could take photos of the gradual renewal of life on the island. She photographed the newest, whitest lambs; the daily, soft greening of the trees and the blazes of daffodils that appeared, almost overnight, on so many banks and verges. The zoom on the camera enabled her to capture the delicate markings on a robin's eggshell and the beautiful opalescence of a beached

"Moon" jellyfish that had ventured into the freezing waters off the island. Soon, the walls of the cottage were almost covered with hundreds of pictures of the landscape, interspersed with ones of Jonathan, who was now eating all the mushy mixes Jude had once so lovingly made for Christos. She took photographs of Rhiannon's pearls, Gloria's last letter, and even more everyday things, such as Jonathan's tiny hairbrush or the whorl of soft chestnut brown hair on his head. She did not want to contact Owain, he did not contact her, and she felt that she had almost succeeded in erasing him from her new life when she glimpsed him in the distance one day, walking with Meg near *Hedd,* and then again, on the beach below her old cottage. Jude felt long-suppressed feelings revive almost immediately, like a wound she thought had healed but still hurt once she pressed it. He was still here, then, but did not want to see her again. Agonisingly curious, she decided to risk asking Menna about him the next time she visited her.

"Menna, I need to ask you some tricky questions, and I need straight answers, OK?" she said. "You would expect the same from me."

"I'm nervous now. You look so *fierce*," Menna replied.

"I *feel* fierce, because this really matters to me. Look, I keep seeing Owain over this side of the island. He always seems to walk in the same places, near my old home. Where is he living, do you know?"

A slight hesitation. "Somewhere around here, I think. He has lots of time on his hands, to walk, these days," Menna said. "The last time I saw him, he said that he hadn't got much work. The second-home owners are using their own people more and more, so he's struggling."

Jude made an appropriately sympathetic noise, but she could tell her friend was not being entirely open with her.

"So he's alone, living near you, with no work," she pressed.

"I hope you're not thinking of rekindling things with him,

Jude," Menna said darkly. "Still waters run deep, remember, and Owain Pritchard is very still and very deep indeed. And recently divorced."

Jude immediately decided not to tell Menna that she had recently found tiny posies of wildflowers left in chinks of the stone wall around her garden, and, once, a beautiful, hand-carved wooden toy for Jonathan. If Owain had left them, as she felt certain he had, there was a flicker of possibility for them, but "proceed with extreme caution" was probably sound advice. Once more, she tried to douse her hopes.

One Wednesday morning, Dominic from her Welsh class called her. She had seen him a couple of times at Stella's house but was surprised to hear from him. He was in Bangor "to see the bank manager" he said, and asked her to come and meet him and Stella for lunch at 1pm.

"It's of great import," he said, so she agreed, providing Menna's *Nain*/grandmother would have Jonathan. She, of course, jumped at the chance, despite the fact that she was also now Gwilym's childminder.

"With babies, the more the merrier," she told Jude. "That's what I told my husband anyway, which is why we had five of 'em!"

Jude set off for Bangor unsure of why she was going there, which felt a little unnerving. When Dominic had told her of his past career in the City, Jude had not been able to imagine him wearing anything other than the smelly donkey jacket and old army trousers he'd always worn to Welsh lessons. Today, however, that same Dominic was wearing a very well-cut three-piece suit and an exceptionally natty tie. He whooped when he saw Jude walking up the High Street towards him.

"Jude! How wonderful to see you again! But where's your little baby? I've been desperate to meet him!" He then hugged her with such vigour, she could hardly breathe. She could feel excitement buzzing in his body and he smelt surprisingly clean.

"He's with a friend's grandmother. I wasn't sure what we were meeting for, or for how long, you see…"

"Of course, sorry, short notice I know, but so grateful you came! The man from bank said 'Yes!' Well, 'Probably' anyway," he gabbled, hugging her again.

"That's great, Dom – but what did he say 'yes' to?" Jude said, rubbing her sore, just-squeezed breasts. She checked her top for milky leaks.

"Let's go and meet Stella, and then I'll tell you all," he said, dancing rather than walking down the street, whirling around the lampposts like Fred Astaire. "She knows all about it and thinks it's a *syniad da*/great idea!"

When Stella joined them in the little café near the cathedral, and they all ordered coffees, Jude could no longer contain her curiosity.

"What is this all about, people? I'm totally intrigued," she said.

"It's about our future, Jude – *all* our futures! Ceri – my wife – and I have been talking about it for months, while you were away, and Stella's ex-husband Colin even came up trumps and helped us put the business plan together. He proved a good egg in the end, eh, Stella?"

"Yes, but not good enough for me to go back to him," Stella said with a grin. "Get on with it, Dom, and tell Jude. I'm stoked for her to know!"

Dom took a deep breath and sat back in his seat. "Picture the scene, Jude: a beautiful, working farm up in the glorious Carneddau Mountains with views to die for. That's where I live, by the way, in case you didn't know that," he added, winking conspiratorially. "Now, wait for it, what do you think about my setting up reasonably priced family-friendly breaks in this beautiful working farm?"

He looked at Jude, his eyes wide with expectation. "Er, it sounds really good, Dom," she replied, sipping her coffee nervously.

"Doesn't it just? Well, with this bank loan, we're going to do up the house and the derelict shepherd's cottages on our land, which we will rent only to families, who will be as close to nature as we are up there – a bit too close for some, perhaps, if we install the compost loos Ceri favours!" Dominic guffawed so loudly that everyone turned and stared.

"Calm down, Dom," Stella whispered, putting a finger on her lips.

"Sorry, sorry, sorry," he whispered. "So the kids can help milk the goats, feed the chickens, help us cultivate the veg patch and pick fruit from our fruit trees, collect the eggs, and go on guided nature trails in the hills. We'll get a few sheep, too, and perhaps a couple of cows." Spraying the two women with flecks of saliva in his enthusiasm, Dom told them all his plans for the next twenty minutes. "We could even teach basic Welsh, conversational stuff 'to help you on your holiday'. It makes such a difference when people *try* and use it, as we do, doesn't it?"

"And dare I ask who's going to teach that, if you're thinking of me and Stella?" Jude asked, smiling at him. "We were hardly fluent back then, Dom, and we'll be even worse now."

"We'll sort that out later. *Dim stress*/No stress. Everything's here, we just need to get the right team together: someone to help me with their livestock expertise – mine's a bit limited to, well, goats. Someone to do the renovations of the house, see the potential in the old place, someone who can turn his hand to lots of different things, and respect the traditional materials and ways of working and using the space. We also need a little café, and Stella's up for running that if we can source some great locally made cakes. And last but by no means least, we need someone to help us run art sessions for both kids and adults and set up a gallery for local artists. There are *loads* of them up here!"

Dom finally put his first mouthful of food into his mouth at this point.

"That all sounds fantastic, Dom. But where exactly do I fit into all this?" Jude said.

Dominic swallowed. "You're going to do all the art stuff, of course," he said. "You understand North Wales, Jude – you love it and you '*get it*'. And we all know how focused you can be when you want something badly enough. Who else would have come up here after losing their life partner, and forged their own path, as you did? And who better to take photos, run workshop sessions, do the artwork in the brochure, and write the copy? Stella's shown me some of your collages, Jude, they are absolutely brilliant."

This project was as eccentric, vivid, and daring as her friends were, and Jude loved the idea of it. Her heart was now beating about twice as fast as usual, or it felt that way. She popped a sugar cube into her mouth and sucked furiously; this had always been Rhiannon's failsafe remedy for anything challenging, and as she had no cough sweets to hand, neat sugar it was.

"But I don't know whether I could do any of those things professionally, Dom," she whispered.

He smiled, strands of cress between his teeth. "Yes, you could. You know you could."

"Of course you could, you daft woman," Stella said. "Let's get rid of that bloody bushel you've been hiding your light under for far too long."

And Jude knew they were right. "OK. Count me in," she said.

"Right, that's decided. Let's get down to brass tacks," he said, moving their cups aside, gratefully loosening his tie and getting some documents out of his briefcase. "For once, we have to pretend we're grown-ups, girls."

The three friends spent the next hour poring over the costings approved by the bank manager and discussing the business plan Stella's ex-husband Colin had put together, which even included a figure for Jude's starting salary. She was so astonished at this thoughtful detail that she could hardly speak.

"I think finding a livestock expert should be relatively easy around here. We should get some grant funding as we're restoring an old building, but probably not much. We'll need some legal advice, too, to make sure everything is absolutely covered and insured..." Dom said.

"Tom would help us with that, I'm sure. He's a lawyer, and I know he'll want to offer his expertise," Jude said.

"Great. The biggest fly in the ointment that I can foresee is getting a reliable, versatile builder to do the renovation works for a less-than-enormous fee," Dominic said, frowning. "Reliability can be a problem up here, let's be honest. We can all speak some Welsh, but we're incomers, and always will be. We need someone who has real vision, works fast but does things well, uses traditional methods and materials, and for a sensible price. A very tall order indeed. Any ideas, my friends?"

Jude's thoughts whirred. Owain would be perfect for the job, and he needed work, but she needed to be absolutely sure she wanted him to be involved and that she was potentially happy to be bumping into him on a daily basis. Perhaps the others knew people who would do as good a job, without any possibility of awkwardness? That would be better, all in all, so she said nothing.

But she wondered if this might be what happened next in her life, what she had felt was missing in it – not love, with Owain or any other man? She needed creative fulfilment, and this amazing project would offer it. The more she thought about

Dominic's idea, the more she saw how successful it could be, and excitement started to bubble up inside her.

Within days, the plan began to take shape. Jude rang the Fearsome Foursome to tell them the news, and they were genuinely overjoyed that something so wonderful had come up and told her to "go for it". They all offered their time and expertise in any way they could, and Jude was once more amazed at their limitless capacity for kindness.

"We'll all come up as a working party – and then *have* a party!" Morag said. Her sobriety and her recent engagement to Derek the curate had in no way dampened her zest for life, Jude was delighted to see.

Tom was more than willing to help with the legal aspect of the project, and even offered Sophie's input as well, as she had relevant property law experience from her time in London. He also told Jude that they were expecting their first baby around Christmas, and that Lavinia was "very happy" about that, but "absolutely furious" that they saw no need to get married, as she had hoped to book them The Orangerie at Blenheim for a huge wedding reception. Jude could only imagine how elaborately her halo of pale purple hair would have been styled on that day!

Menna and Jac suggested a farmer called Alun Hughes as the farming and livestock adviser, as his reputation was unmatched on the island. Menna's *Nain*/grandmother offered to have Jonathan whenever Jude needed some uninterrupted time to work, as he adored both her and Gwilym, in equal measure. Surrounded by such good will, Jude did not mention Owain to Dom and Stella until it had become patently clear that the only thing still missing from this amazing project was a sound craftsman with an eye for bold architecture and a love of conservation. He needed the work, and he and Non were divorced now, so Jude felt she had no right to let their feelings for each other, whatever they were, or had been, get in the way of this opportunity. It could be life-changing for him.

Hesitantly, she texted him:

> Hi. I wondered if we could have a chat about a
> business proposition. J

Half an hour later, his reply appeared on her phone:

> Meet me in the car park at Niwbwrch, 8am on
> Saturday. Bring Jonathan. O

He had chosen not to take up her suggestion of discussing this on the phone, and his message was hardly warm, but he had been through a terrible time, so perhaps it was hardly surprising that his dry wit was still not much in evidence these days, but Jude hoped it would return, once he'd heard her proposition. He really deserved some hope, and she missed hearing him fill her heart with laughter.

SIXTY-TWO

The weather was blustery, but dry, when Jude arrived at *Niwbwrch*/Newborough to meet Owain that morning. She fastened Jonathan into his baby carrier and hoisted him up onto her back. Tugging on Alex's old striped hat, she felt her fingers go through the wool and make yet another hole for her to mend. She would keep wearing it until it was absolutely beyond repair, but that might not be too far ahead, looking at it now. What would she do, and how would she feel then? she wondered. Could anything possibly replace either the hat, or the husband it reminded her of so strongly every single time she wore it? She had to hope so.

"You're getting so heavy, young man," she said to Jonathan, who was thrashing his feet on her back. He was excited too. "Stop growing, please!"

Pip heard Owain's van arriving before she did and raced off towards it. The car park was relatively empty, as it was so early, so he let Meg cannon out to greet her and the two dogs vanished into the dunes, as happy to be reunited as the fondest of old friends.

Owain walked over to her, his eyes fixed on something above her head.

"He's giving me the most wonderful smile from up there, you know," he said.

"Ah – he's good at those," Jude answered. On the tip of her tongue were the words "like his father", but she did not say them. She was waiting for the right time to tell him, as she knew for certain she must if they might be working together soon.

A few brave kite-surfers were enjoying exhilarating rides above the waves, but walking was hard work. The beach, very exposed, was often strafed with powerful inshore winds at this time of year. Within a few minutes, Jude was struggling to walk with Jonathan on her back. How was she going to talk to Owain about Dominic's plan, if she could hardly breathe?

"Can I carry him for you? Once we are the other side of those rocks, the wind will drop," Owain said, his mouth right next to her ear so she stood a chance of hearing him.

Goosebumps rippled across her skin. She nodded, and they transferred the baby carrier to Owain's broad shoulders, Jonathan squealing happily at how high he now was.

"*Reit*/Right. Now you can tell me about this business proposition you have in mind," Owain said. "I could really do with some good news."

They walked, and talked, the whole length of the beach, and the one beyond it. Owain asked a barrage of questions about Dominic's idea – many of which Jude did not know the answers to – but she could tell that he was impressed. He agreed to meet Dominic, and visit the house and the derelict cottages, before making up his mind, but she felt enthusiasm pulsing under his measured words. When they talked about her work, and how she had ground to a halt of late, he was concerned, which made her feel both heard, and valued. How different from Tom's lukewarm reaction to her plans, she realised, and how differently that made her feel.

"So why have you stopped making things?" he asked. "There are few enough ways of making living up here, but being creative is one of the best of them. We have plenty of driftwood and shells to inspire you!"

"It just wasn't working anymore. I even tried painting instead of using the things I found, but it wasn't right. Then I felt I wanted to concentrate on people rather than places, but I couldn't find the right way to make them come alive on canvas either. Oh, I just know I need a different way of putting the things together, but I can't see what it is," she told him, in her frustration. "How do you pin a person down, immortalise them?"

"I see the problem," Owain said, and then paused thoughtfully. "How about combining objects, paint, and words with photos of these people? You've got a good camera. That might work."

Jude thought for a moment. "But photos only capture a second, the blink of an eye – they can't sum someone for any more than that moment in time. I need to capture a person and everything about them."

"Why? All you can hope to do is hint at all the many things that made them who they were. That's what a poem does, with words – or a good poem anyway. You can't bring the people you've lost back, however much you want to," he said quietly, meeting her gaze.

Jude longed to reach for his hand but held back. "Yes, I know. I just felt I needed to try, and I don't know what else to do," she replied.

"Anyway, what's to be gained by trying to fix a memory of somebody, like a fly in amber?" Owain added, his brow furrowed with the effort of finding the most appropriate words and phrases in English. "Memories change as time passes, as people do."

"Perhaps that's what I'm so scared of," Jude replied.

Owain stopped walking and looked straight at her again. "Don't be scared anymore. You will never forget the people you have loved and lost, as I will never forget my brother. Never."

She stopped as well, directly in front of him. The wind had lulled a little now, and the air was calmer. "Thank you. I know I'm very lucky, to have enough money, to have friends, to have Jonathan, after everything that's happened to me. And to be able to come back here on a whim, just because I can."

"Some would say *he's* lucky, to have you," Owain answered, touching the little boy's hand as his fingers, tiny pink tentacles, fluttered above his head. "*I* would say that, certainly."

When Jude heard his words, she knew that now was the right time, the time Gloria had told her to wait for, when everything has its reason and its purpose. "He's yours. Jonathan is. You know that, don't you?" she whispered, looking up at his face.

Owain did not answer, but stood looking out to sea, where the wind had whipped the sea around the rocks into a quivering bed of creamy foam. Jude could not read his expression, as it was such a turbulent mix of emotions. As his silence lengthened, she wished the wind could take her words and dash them onto the rocks, and let her replace them with other, blander, ones. Had she said too much, too soon? She held her breath until he eventually replied, his voice so rich with solemnity and resonance that it cut through the howling wind around them.

"Yes. I knew that the second I saw him, but I felt I had to wait for you to tell me yourself, before thinking I had any right to share him, my love," Owain said, taking her hand. "And for the record, I think you came back because you both belong here, with me – not for any 'whim'." When he leant forward and kissed her lips, she leant into him, both body and soul.

"Come to my house, Jude. We can talk about what happened before, and how it's going to be now," Owain said, a few blissful minutes later.

"OK. But where do you live? I don't even know that."

"Well, funnily enough, I live in *Hedd*, he said with a broad smile bordering on the mischievous.

She gasped. "What?! But... I... Mair and Menna... did they know?"

"Yes, they knew, but I asked them not to tell you," he said. "I wanted to live there when I heard it was free, but I didn't want you to think I snatched it from you out of spite or to be angry with me about it. Bad timing, really; you were only a week too late to get it yourself."

"And Mair Roberts wouldn't hear of asking you to give it up for me, which I can quite understand. Well, at least I know the truth now," Jude gasped. "That's incredible! And I'm so glad."

"As I am glad you have come back to me," he said, enfolding her in his arms. "Now we can bring our boy up together."

They kissed again, as Jonathan tugged at their ears in an effort to pull them apart. A plump little finger up Jude's nostril did the trick, and they laughed, and walked on along the beach.

"I remember how R.S. Thomas put how I feel right now, Owain, as if I've been waiting '*as at the end of a hard winter for one flower to open on the mind's tree of thorns*'."

Owain nodded in recognition. "Not bad, but at risk of being accused of quotational one-upmanship, how about '*We met under a shower of bird notes*'?'

"Ooh that's lovely, and it's true!" Jude said. "You win."

"Thank you, *cariad*/love, for saving me," he murmured.

"Ditto," she replied.

SIXTY-THREE

The decision to have Jonathan christened at the same time as they got married caused a bit of a stir locally, but when Jude gently told people that doing so was becoming "more and more popular" (and Menna told some of them a little more firmly), the mutterings stopped. Gloria had left the beautiful family christening gown for Jonathan, a gift Jude had to honour, and she had dispelled her memories of dour childhood church services enough to agree for him to be christened at all, but she was still determined to make the day as riotous and happy as it could possibly be.

"A wedding and a christening, both on the same day? Well, that's a two-for-one offer we can't afford to miss," Owain joked one evening, as they started to draw up simple plans.

"Are you happy with it, though?" Jude asked. "Say if you're not."

"I am. I think it's great to do both things at once, especially as so many much-loved babies are born 'out of wedlock' these days for various reasons, like ours was." Owain had drunk several glasses of his lethal home-brew, and so was being particularly free with his views. "And for us all to become a real family on the same day is brilliant. *Hic!*"

Jude didn't disagree, but she did hide his glass.

The day they chose was a clear September day, almost exactly two years after Jude had first come to Anglesey, and only the smallest of clouds punctuated the blue sky. Guests were coming from all over the island, as well as from Oxford, Taunton, and Brenda had even made the trek from Scotland, genuinely thrilled when Jude had contacted her, and even more thrilled when asked to be "honorary step-grandmother".

"Brenda was kind to my dad, when my Mum couldn't be," Jude said, when anyone quizzed her about it, which shut down their nosiness straight away.

Owain lumbered around on the morning of the celebration, fumbling with his cufflinks and swearing in Welsh as he tried to remember the short speech he'd spent hours writing, because he knew it had to be mainly in English. His sheer size made it difficult for them all to manoeuvre round the room in *Hedd*, which they had bought that summer, and he had plans to beautifully extend with a glass-fronted wraparound conservatory that faced the sea on all sides. He had based the plans on those he had shown Jude in her Welsh exam, many months earlier. She had wanted to keep the cottage as her studio, and buy them a bigger house, but Owain talked only of *Hedd* being full of "*the litter of children's voices*", as his beloved R.S. Thomas had put it. He would have to be very sure it was right for his little family to leave it, he said, and it was not right yet.

As Jude wrestled Jonathan into the stiffly starched christening gown, the postman delivered two large boxes: the first proofs for the publicity material for Dominic's project and some freshly printed flyers for her new business (bespoke montages of treasured times in peoples' lives that mingled pictures of people and objects with sweeps of colour and light). She called herself "The Memory Maker" and she had already garnered great reviews from customers and had some prestigious commissions to fulfil. There was talk of an exhibition both in Oxford (courtesy of a suddenly-very-helpful Helena) and in the stunning gallery Owain had helped design for Dominic's new venture. If she made enough money after they had extended *Hedd*, Jude was determined that Owain would finish his architecture degree.

"I really haven't got time for any of this stuff now," she said, opening a cupboard and throwing the boxes into it before ramming the door shut. "Today, we get married. Tomorrow, we conquer the world."

"You must find a studio to conquer it from, though, *cariad*/love. We can't swing a cat in here, even if we had one that we wanted to swing."

Jude laughed at his use of language, as she laughed at nobody else's. They tried to mix English and Welsh at home, so that Jonathan would learn both languages, but there were still plenty of gaps where the right words and meanings got lost down the cracks.

"Why don't you go outside, Owain, and pick a sprig of honeysuckle for your buttonhole. Mmmm, I can smell it from here."

At 11am, they set off for the twenty-minute walk through the dunes behind the beach and then along the little road to the church. Pip and Meg were tied to Jonathan's buggy with ribbons, and their procession was such a heart-warming sight that it stopped the traffic. When they arrived at the church gate and Jude looked around her, she saw all the people she loved, and remembered those she had lost, waiting around the stone doorway and wreathed in smiles.

"How lucky am I?" she murmured, as she walked towards them.

"We really wanted to see you arrive!" Stella said. "You look wonderful, all three of you – but especially *you*, Jude." Stella had spent ages helping her friend choose a dress, and they had, eventually, found a gorgeous long, shot-silk one in a shop hidden in the backstreets of Bangor. The colours of the sea, sand, and the sky mingled as one in the fabric, and it rippled softly as Jude walked, just as the grasses on the island's beaches moved in the warm breezes of spring and summer. The effect was stunning.

Jude glimpsed Paula and Georgio, with Christos and their tiny new baby, Antigone. They were all dressed in co-ordinating pinks and purples, setting the grey stone and slate roof of the church alight with colour. Morag and her new husband Derek, now a parish priest, were next to them. Finn was reluctantly standing still for Jo to take a photo of them while Katie zealously guarded his iPad. A little apart, she saw Tom on his own, as Sophie was having a tricky pregnancy and could not travel. He had come up on Alex's beloved motorbike, and Jude was delighted to see it there, gleaming in the sunshine on this most special of days. She had decided that he should keep it, a gift she felt was appropriate for such a good friend both to her, and to Alex. He would love that bike as her husband had, and she hoped that he, too, would "chase his dream" whenever he rode her, whatever that dream turned out to be.

Menna, Jac, and their three boys cheered as Owain and Jude hugged them each in turn, and both the *Nains*/grandmothers dabbed their eyes in unison. Stella's fiancé Eifion, a skilful amateur photographer, had agreed to take photos of the day and was already snapping away freely. Rhiannon's daughter Hâf had made a traditional iced fruit cake based on her mother's recipe that ticked both "wedding" and "christening" boxes. She had also agreed to supply the café at Dominic's with cakes and was relishing "being my own boss" after years in a humdrum admin job in the council. It made Jude smile to see her there, looking more and more like her glorious mother every time she saw her.

Owain gently lifted his little son out of the buggy, and carried him into the church, his long gown fluttering behind them all like a wisp of fine, white cloud. Above them, the sky was filled with the joyful chattering of the swallows who had returned to skim the same waves they had left last autumn to seek a warmer winter. They were always welcomed back.

"Oh, I do love it here, Owain," Jude said, squeezing his arm. "When it's not raining, that is."

"*Mae'n berffaith*/It's perfect, Jude, even when it *is*."

As the priest began the service, Jude heard words she remembered from her own childhood, when her mother had taken her to so many baptisms and weddings in the gloomy Methodist chapel in Taunton. Today, the words filled her with happiness, not dread, and she felt Gloria's presence more strongly than ever, set free from her regrets and her sad, loveless childhood at last, and steeped in joy.

As the Welsh and English words and responses rang out, they seemed to dance in a seamless fabric of rhythm and sound, imbuing all that were there with certainty that this day was a very good one indeed. When Owain and Jude made their vows, they chose to do so in their own languages, but they knew that in their family home, both would always be as closely inter-woven as their lives.

EPILOGUE

On the evening of her wedding day, Jude sat outside *Hedd* and watched the sun hang above the sea for almost an hour like a thin, gold disc. When its edges were almost touching the horizon, a glittering strip began to unroll across the water as if beckoning her to step onto it. Within minutes, that invitation vanished, and the sun had set.

She breathed in the thick scent of the honeysuckle that scrambled over her garden wall: its sweetness distilled so many memories of the two years she had known and loved this place. In the growing darkness, the waves hit the shore with a soft pulse on the beach below, as they would do throughout the night, while she, her husband, and their baby slept.

Down on the rocks, she could still hear the peeping cries of the oystercatchers. She hoped that they, like her, would sleep peacefully.

LETTER FROM THE AUTHOR

Thank you for reading *Secrets at the Cottage by the Sea*. I hope that you enjoyed reading Jude's story, and seeing how Anglesey, an island I love, helped her heal from her terrible bereavement. Nature has a way of showing us that life goes on after such things, as it shows Jude. If you'd like to join readers in hearing all about my new releases and some bonus content too, you can sign up for my newsletter.

www.stormpublishing.co/caroline-young

If you enjoyed this book enough to take the time to leave a review, that would be very helpful to other readers, and much appreciated by me. Even a short review can make all the difference in encouraging a reader to discover my stories for the first time...

Thank you for coming on this journey with me, and do stay in touch. I have lots more stories to tell, and plenty more beautiful places and strong women to celebrate!

 facebook.com/caroline.young.9250

ACKNOWLEDGEMENTS

Although this is my second published novel (as *The Forgotten Farmhouse by the Sea* came out before it) it is actually the first one I ever wrote. A diagnosis of breast cancer over ten years ago finally gave me the impetus I needed to start writing the stories I had wanted to tell for years, instead of just talking about them. Out of something bad, came something good, as is often the way in life. This novel lurked on my computer, unpublished, through another brush with breast cancer and many other life events, both sad and happy, until now, it's time to come into the world. I believe that many things happen as and when they are meant to, and, as Gloria, one of the characters in this novel, quotes from Ecclesiastes:

"*For everything there is a season, and a time under heaven.*"

I have lots of people to thank for helping *Secrets at the Cottage by the Sea* get to this point. Firstly, I need to thank Geoff, my husband, for allowing me to uproot our family and move to Anglesey over twenty years ago, fulfilling a dream I had held for a very long time. The island has given me the inspiration I knew it would, and is at the heart of almost everything I want to write about. I also want to thank Richard and Gwenno Brown for letting me spend a lovely week alone in their home in Hope Cove, Devon, where I wrote the first draft of this book.

Many friends have cheered me on through years of frustration, self-doubt and disappointment, from every phase of my life thus far, but I think they all know who they are by now. None of them have read this novel in its early stages, so I hope they approve! Special thanks to Idris once more for checking my Welsh, which is indeed as "ropey" as Owain's English at times. Diolch, Idris. As ever, many thanks to Kate Smith, my wonderful editor, for believing in me.

Finally, thank you to my three glorious daughters, Bethan, Rhiannon, and Mari, who have heard more about "Mum's books" than perhaps they needed to at times, but who understood how much telling these stories meant to me. This island was in my heart when I gave you your beautiful Welsh names, as it now remains in yours, and I hope will always do so.